Mr. Darcy's Magpie

by

KARA LOUISE

© 2018 by Kara Louise

ISBN-13: 978-1726299442

ISBN-10: 1726299449

Cover images by Cheryl Wallace
Cover design by Kara Louise

Printed in the United States of America

Library of Congress Cataloging-in-Publication Data

Kara Louise
Mr. Darcy's Magpie

Published by Heartworks Publication

A Note to My Readers

It is always a joy to publish a new book, accompanied with great hope that my readers will find its contents a delight to read. This story evolved quite a bit once I began writing it, and before I knew it, I had given Mr. Darcy quite an unusual diversion. I shall let you discover that on your own.

I wish to thank Mary Anne Hines and Gayle Mills for their excellent editing skills. They have such a way with words, and I appreciate all their suggestions, corrections, and changes.

I also must thank Miss Austen for her great inspiration and coming up with the characters in the first place. They are loved by so many people, and it is out of that love that I continue to write their stories. I hope you will enjoy *Mr. Darcy's Magpie*.

.

Chapter 1

Elizabeth Bennet made a futile attempt to calm the feeling of trepidation coursing through her as the carriage in which she and her Aunt and Uncle Gardiner were riding drew closer to Pemberley. She feigned an air of composure as her aunt spoke about the manor owned by Mr. Fitzwilliam Darcy, recollecting how esteemed the family had been when she was growing up in nearby Lambton, how beautiful the home was, and how much she looked forward to seeing it again. Elizabeth, however, would not be able to view it as a mere tourist. Her chest tightened as she struggled to draw an unhindered breath, and that discomfort, together with her thunderously beating heart, were constant reminders that the very same Mr. Darcy had asked for her hand in marriage but three months earlier, and she had refused him.

As they traversed the woods leading to Pemberley, she was grateful for the shade of the tall trees lining the road, for it cooled them on this particularly warm summer day. She shivered, however, wondering whether it was because it had actually become cooler or if it was the unease she felt, knowing she would soon be walking through the home and grounds that might have been hers.

Her aunt continued to share her memories of Pemberley and the family, but despite Elizabeth's curiosity, she could barely attend to her words. They had been assured Mr. Darcy was from home, but she knew there would be nothing worse than encountering him, should he be here.

They made an unexpected sharp turn to the right, causing the three passengers to lean to the left, laughing as they did. But as the vehicle and the riders straightened, Pemberley – being more majestic than Elizabeth ever imagined – suddenly appeared before them.

Her breath caught in her throat, and she could not stifle her gasp when she saw the magnificent structure before her. She understood it was a grand home, but she was not prepared for what she saw.

5

"It is beautiful, is it not, Lizzy?" her aunt inquired.

Elizabeth nodded mutely, at a loss to know how to ascertain her true feelings, considering how she had come to view the man, how lightly she had taken his offer of marriage, and how uncivil she had been in refusing him. She had not spoken of it to her aunt and uncle, for they would never understand how she could have refused such a man. She glanced at them and wondered what they would think if they knew.

They were only aware that, by his words and actions, he had offended their niece and almost everyone else in their country neighbourhood. As the carriage drew closer, Elizabeth's senses were flooded with all the beauty this place offered. It was an idyllic setting with a small lake in front, in which the manor, perched upon a low hill, was reflected. A small stream led into it, and a grassy ridge rose up from behind. Elizabeth could not but delight in the beautiful stately trees scattered about, the variety of colours in the flowers lining the walkway to the front, and the overall beauty of the grounds.

She drew in a slow breath, hoping it would calm her. She clasped her hands tightly and slowly let out the breath, but it did nothing to calm her rapidly beating heart.

When they came to a stop in front of the manor, Elizabeth reached over and took her aunt's hand. "I know you think me foolish and needlessly worrying, but I truly do not want Mr. Darcy to know I was here. If any introductions are made, please only call me Elizabeth or, if pressed, Miss Gardiner."

Mrs. Gardiner patted her niece's hand. "If you wish, Lizzy, but I am certain Mr. Darcy would not mind that you are here to see his home. After all, tourists go through all the time."

She shook her head. "With our... slight acquaintance, I would feel awkward encountering him."

"I think I understand," Mr. Gardiner stated. "The poor man probably has women coming to tour his home all the time in the hopes they will meet him. I would imagine there are many young ladies who would give anything to become Mistress of Pemberley."

"Now, Lizzy, I know you disliked him, but I would imagine he was not even aware of it. We shall do as you bid, however, and introduce you as our niece, Miss Elizabeth Gardiner." She patted Elizabeth's hand. "No one need know."

Elizabeth smiled. "I thank you, Aunt."

At length, they were admitted into the manor, and the housekeeper, Mrs. Reynolds, cheerfully took them on a tour. Once inside, Elizabeth found herself captivated by the beauty of the home's interior.

She could not find fault with the relaxed, yet elegant style of the rooms and décor. It was a home one would be proud to live in, graceful and comfortable, stylish yet practical, but with an appreciation for its history. She found herself absently stroking the cushion of a chair, wondering whether Mr. Darcy ever sat in it. She looked out the various windows and pondered whether he gazed out and enjoyed the view as she was doing now, or if he was immune to the beauty because he had seen it all his life. There was a delightful prospect from every room.

She could not order the variety of feelings she felt as she was delighted with each room, prospect, piece of furniture, and window covering. It was altogether agreeable to her sensibilities.

Despite admiring the home, Elizabeth could not rest easy, dreading that the information given to them might have been incorrect and Mr. Darcy was not from home. But when Mr. Gardiner inquired of Mrs. Reynolds about the Master of Pemberley, she confirmed that he was away, however he was to return on the morrow.

Elizabeth let out a sigh of relief, yet she was also struck with how fortunate they had been in deciding to come to Pemberley this day and not putting it off a day later. She could now enjoy seeing the house in a more composed state.

They stepped into the music room and viewed the instrument that had just arrived for Mr. Darcy's sister, Georgiana. It was a beautiful pianoforte, and Elizabeth thought it would be a delight to hear it played. She recollected Miss Bingley's praise of Miss Darcy's accomplished playing, and Mrs. Reynolds commented similarly. The housekeeper also could not speak well enough of the excellent brother Mr. Darcy was to his sister.

Elizabeth was grateful for her scheme to go by a different name when Mrs. Reynolds discovered she was acquainted with her master. Mrs. Gardiner had inquired of her niece whether a small portrait they saw of Mr. Darcy was a good likeness. The housekeeper was delighted that her master was known by her, so Elizabeth did all she could to make light of their acquaintance.

Knowing now that he was to return on the morrow, she said, "It could hardly be considered an acquaintance; it was so trifling." She laughed nervously and then added, "I doubt he would even know who I am." Her aunt gave her a teasing raised brow but said nothing.

She shuddered when she saw the small portrait of Mr. Wickham, likely kept as one of the late Mr. Darcy's favourite possessions. When Mrs. Reynolds spoke of his wild ways, Elizabeth could not help regretting how she had been deceived by him and felt a great deal of self-loathing for it.

With this confirmation by the housekeeper concerning his behaviour, Elizabeth was grateful she had been able to talk her father out of allowing Lydia to go with Colonel Forster's wife when the regiment left for Brighton. She shook her head as she pondered the trouble Lydia could have gotten into there. Knowing now what she did about Wickham, she doubted he would have had any interest in a young girl with a pittance of a dowry, but she felt that Lydia's behaviour would have been even more unchecked and the possibilities for disaster would have been endless.

After viewing several more rooms, the small group began their stroll down the picture gallery. Elizabeth's aunt and uncle listened with great interest to Mrs. Reynolds as she gave a fascinating account of the Darcy family, going back two hundred years, but Elizabeth heard not a single word spoken by the housekeeper as she searched the portraits ahead for one in particular.

At length, she espied a full-length portrait of the man who had been occupying her thoughts almost since their first meeting in Hertfordshire nine months earlier. Initially, those thoughts had been of a more critical nature – how he had insulted her, offended the neighbourhood, shown himself to be arrogant, and finally, the ultimate offence of interfering in Jane's relationship with Mr. Bingley by persuading his friend that her feelings had not been as strong as his were.

In the past few months, however, Elizabeth had begun to

wonder how much of what she initially thought about him was incorrect. The fact that he had confessed his ardent love for her had played only a minor role in her change of heart, but it had affected her deeply.

She could no longer recollect the words she had thrown at him in rejecting his offer of marriage, as her anger directed at him had been so very violent. The very next day he had presented her with a lengthy letter addressing some of the misconceptions she held concerning him and his actions. She was forced to re-examine her estimation of his character and the accusations made against him by Mr. Wickham.

Since then, she had realized that in much she had erred. She still strongly felt, however, that Mr. Darcy could not be absolved in meddling with Jane's happiness, no matter how deeply he felt justified in doing so.

That mere thought produced a stifled huff as they walked the long hallway, past men posed with rifles, hunting dogs, and occasionally with their wife and children. Mrs. Reynolds stopped at a family portrait of a gentleman, lady, and a young boy. Elizabeth knew at once that it was a picture of a young Fitzwilliam Darcy and his parents. It was not so much the features of the boy, but those of his father. He looked very much like his grown son did now.

She was captivated with the portrait, curious about what his parents had been like. It was an indoor setting; she thought she recognized the fireplace from the front parlour. Mrs. Darcy had a kind, gentle countenance and held her son's hand in one of hers. His father, while appearing stern and strong, wore a soft smile and had a hand on his son's shoulder. The other arm rested on the mantel of the fireplace; much like the pose she had often seen his son display. A fire blazed behind them, adding warmth to both the family and the scene.

Mrs. Reynolds moved along, and at last they stopped in front of the portrait Elizabeth had been eager to see. It was not life size, but its likeness to Mr. Darcy was exceptional. He was standing in the woods; Elizabeth was certain it was somewhere on the grounds of Pemberley.

She gazed up at the portrait and unwittingly shivered. As she looked up into his eyes – painted so strikingly realistic – she almost felt as though he were looking back at her. She silently chided herself at the foolish thought.

"Is this portrait not a finer likeness than the smaller one we saw earlier?" Mrs. Reynolds asked.

"Yes, I believe it is very much like him," Elizabeth replied.

Mrs. Reynolds smiled and looked back at the painting. "I think it captures him well. It was painted while his father was still alive." She shook her head. "He lost his mother at a young age, and a few months after this portrait was completed, his father died. The responsibility of Pemberley and his sister was placed squarely upon his shoulders. He has always displayed such strength of character, and one could not meet a more honourable gentleman. The love and care he has for his sister is beyond measure."

With the housekeeper's profuse and often repeated praise of her master, Elizabeth could not help considering this as she gazed up at the portrait. One striking feature was his smile, such a one that she had rarely seen. He seemed content and relaxed, almost amiable, and she wondered whether her initial opinion of him would have been any different had he been more willing to display such a countenance to her friends and family in Hertfordshire upon his arrival. While musing over this, however, she also considered that the heavy burdens placed on him in the past five years – after this portrait had been painted – had surely taken a heavy toll on him.

In the portrait, he stood erect, holding his gloves in one hand and a walking stick in the other. It was a finely carved walking stick with something at the top, but she was unable to see what it was. This portrait was different than the other paintings in that most of the other men in outdoor settings carried a rifle.

Mrs. Reynolds continued to lavish praise on her master and then let out a long drawn-out sigh. "While it has been difficult for him in recent years, I have to admit he has done an admirable job."

"He seems like a fine gentleman," Mr. Gardiner said, catching his niece's eye and winking.

Elizabeth was fairly certain her uncle suspected the housekeeper was being overly generous in her praise of Mr. Darcy.

She, however, felt the woman was expressing a deep, heart-felt conviction, which continued to undermine everything she had once thought about him.

"There is truly none finer," Mrs. Reynolds said, content to keep her gaze fixed on the portrait.

They reached the end of the hall, and the housekeeper informed the party that the tour of the home was complete. The gardens, however, would be open to them if they wished. She offered to arrange a tour with the gardener, and they readily agreed. Mrs. Gardiner explained to the housekeeper that she had visited several times as a young girl and recollected the grounds being lovely.

Elizabeth watched the others walk towards the grand staircase as she battled a mixture of emotions. She certainly felt a more gentle sensation towards Mr. Darcy than she had in the height of their acquaintance. She no longer considered him as despicable and insufferable as she once had, although there were some elements about him that certainly still provoked her.

She slowed as the others began to make their way down the stairs. She took in a deep breath and let out a barely audible sigh. Had she truly been this wrong in sketching his character? She shook her head and turned back one last time to gaze upon the portrait.

Even though she no longer stood in front of the painting, from where she stood, it seemed his eyes had continued to follow her and were still upon her. She trembled and turned quickly to take the stairs down.

But too quickly!

Mr. Gardiner had paused at the top of the stairs, and her rapid movement caused him to propel forward. He grasped at the railing in an attempt to prevent himself from falling, but he stumbled down several stairs. Both Elizabeth and her aunt cried out as he landed on his side.

"My goodness!" exclaimed Mrs. Reynolds as she looked back at him. "Is the gentleman hurt?"

Mr. Gardiner waved them off as they gathered around him.

"It is nothing, I am certain." As he attempted to move, however, he let out a groan.

"I am so sorry, Uncle. I was… I was not watching where I was going." She winced as she saw the pain in her uncle's face.

"Do you think you can stand up, dear?" her aunt asked him.

"Yes, I think…" Mr. Gardiner started to get to his feet, but he quickly closed his eyes. "I think… my back… it is in a great deal of pain!"

"Oh, heavens!" Mrs. Reynolds clasped her hands together.

"Dear, sit still for a moment," Mrs. Gardiner said. "Hopefully the pain will pass, and then you can try to stand up again."

Elizabeth shook her head, angry with herself for her folly. "Perhaps he should not attempt to move." She began to wring her hands. "We cannot be certain if he seriously injured himself."

"I think it would be best if I rest a bit. I am feeling a little unsteady."

"Edmund!" Mrs. Gardiner said. "You are not well; your face is so pale!"

Mr. Gardiner opened his mouth to speak but said nothing. He slowly shook his head.

Mrs. Reynolds looked at Mr. Gardiner. "We have an infirmary room in which we can let you rest. I will call the doctor, but I first must ensure the room is prepared, and then I will summon a servant to carry you down to it."

Mr. Gardiner waved a hand through the air. "If you give me a moment, I might be able to do it on my own."

He sat for a time, turning his body slightly in one direction and then another, but he let out a moan with each move.

"I think I will be able to walk, but if you would call a servant – a fairly large servant – I would certainly appreciate any assistance he might give."

"Yes, sir." Mrs. Reynolds turned and quickly took the remaining steps down.

When the housekeeper disappeared, Elizabeth leaned down next to her uncle and took his hand. "I am so sorry, Uncle." Tears began to spill down her cheeks. "I cannot believe how careless I was."

Mr. Gardiner squeezed her hand and smiled. "Do not berate yourself, Lizzy. It could have happened to anyone."

"How *did* it happen?" Mrs. Gardiner said.

Elizabeth dropped her head, shaking it. "I had turned back to look... I was so foolish! So foolish!"

"Now, now," Mr. Gardiner said. "It is as much my fault, for I paused, and you had not expected me to." When he turned his head to look at his wife, he stiffened and groaned.

"Try not to move, dear," Mrs. Gardiner said as she sat down on the step next to him. "You might make things worse." She paused and then asked, "Does it feel as though anything is broken?"

Mr. Gardiner shook his head. "No, I do not think so. At least, I hope not." He drew in a sharp breath. "But it certainly hurts."

"Oh, Uncle!" Elizabeth cried out as she wrung her hands. "Please take care! I am so sorry!"

A moment later a brawny manservant appeared and took the stairs up to them. "I am at your service, sir. What would you like me to do?"

"If you would be so kind as to help me up and then support me as we take the stairs down. I do not think I need to be carried."

Elizabeth and her aunt watched silently, wishing to do something to assist their loved one – or at least alleviate his pain – but were unable to help at all. Once up and supported by the manservant, he took slow and careful steps down. When they reached the bottom, they paused to allow Mr. Gardiner to take a few breaths of relief.

"Edmund, how do you feel? Is it worse?"

He shook his head in answer and gave a slight wave of his hand.

"If it would help, sir, I can certainly carry you," the manservant suggested.

Mr. Gardiner tried to protest, but his voice was weak as the pain overtook him.

"Thank you, sir," Mrs. Gardiner said. "While he may not wish it, I feel it would be better. Please be careful, however, as we do not know the extent of his injuries."

The manservant carefully lifted him up, making certain he did not jostle him or aggravate his injuries in any way.

As they walked, Elizabeth turned to her aunt and grasped her arm. "Oh, Aunt! I feel so responsible! How could I have done such a thing?"

Mrs. Gardiner cupped Elizabeth's cheek with her other hand. "Please do not fret, Lizzy. I am certain it is not as serious as it could be. He is in pain, to be sure, but that is to be expected."

"Do you suppose the doctor will allow us to return to the inn? I would not want to move him if it is not safe, but…"

"That remains to be seen. I wonder if we should have moved him at all."

"Yes," she said softly, a sharp wave of unease passing through her.

"Lizzy, I know you do not wish to be here when Mr. Darcy returns, but I would not worry. You know the families who live in these fine houses are used to having people tour them."

Elizabeth closed her eyes briefly, merely nodding her head in response to her aunt's supposition. The nods turned to slow shakes of her head as she could not help but silently disagree with her aunt. *But most women who have turned down an offer of marriage would not do such a thing. If you only knew the truth of what happened between us, Aunt. If you only knew.*

Chapter 2

Elizabeth's frustration and annoyance with herself increased as they made their way to the infirmary room. *Why did I have to look back at that portrait? Why was I so moved by it, as well as by Mrs. Reynolds' words of approbation about him – about Mr. Darcy, of all men?*

She dreaded what might happen if they could not return to the Lambton Inn and were still in Mr. Darcy's home when he returned on the morrow. She shook her head and admonished herself to think of what was best for her uncle and not her unease.

Mrs. Reynolds joined them again as they continued towards the room. "We have sent for the doctor. Your driver has been apprised of the situation, and he will wait until we give him a report. I have asked the kitchen to prepare some food for you as I am certain you would like some refreshment at this hour."

"Thank you, so much, Mrs. Reynolds," Mrs. Gardiner said. "That is very kind of you. Perhaps you can dismiss the driver so he can return to the Lambton Inn. We can always summon him when we have need."

Mrs. Reynolds nodded. "I shall send him back, but when you are ready to return to the inn, Pemberley's carriage and driver will convey you there."

"Thank you," Mrs. Gardiner said appreciatively.

After walking down a long hallway, Mrs. Reynolds stepped into one of the rooms and pulled back the coverlet of the bed. She stepped aside so Mr. Gardiner could be set down. Upon doing so, he let out another groan.

Mrs. Gardiner immediately went to his side. "Just rest, dear. Now that you are in bed, try not to move until the doctor comes and determines what injuries you sustained and what can be done."

"I do not think I am going anywhere for a while, as much as I would have enjoyed touring the grounds," Mr. Gardiner said with a soft chuckle. "But I truly do not think anything is broken."

Mrs. Gardiner went to the end of the bed and removed his shoes. "Only the doctor will be able to tell us that for a certainty, dear."

Mrs. Reynolds extended her hand towards the west wall of the room. "I have readied the adjacent room for you and your niece if you wish to rest or if you are required to stay…"

"I am certain we shall be able to return to the inn," Elizabeth interjected.

Mrs. Gardiner walked over to Elizabeth and took her hand. She then looked at the housekeeper. "Thank you, Mrs. Reynolds. I will let you know if we will have need of it."

Mrs. Reynolds looked back at the door when a maid appeared. "Ah, here is Harriet with your food. I shall return shortly to see if there is anything else you need."

"Thank you, Mrs. Reynolds. We appreciate everything you have done." Mrs. Gardiner glanced at her husband who had closed his eyes and appeared to be resting.

The young maid, whose small round face was framed in beautiful copper curls, smiled nervously as she placed the tray on a table.

"Thank you," Mrs. Gardiner said.

The young girl curtseyed and quickly backed out of the room.

Once she had stepped out, Elizabeth turned to her aunt. "I cannot believe what happened – that I did such a thing!" She looked at her in desperation. "What are we to do?"

"We are not going to do anything until the doctor sees Edmund," her aunt replied. "I would not have you feeling uneasy about either the condition of your uncle or the possibility of encountering Mr. Darcy. I am certain that if he knew you were here, his thoughts would be on your uncle's recovery more than any surprise or misgivings at finding you here." She paused and then added with a smile, "Let us hold off our worrying until the doctor comes and tells us what is wrong and what is to be done for his recovery."

"Pray, forgive me for my foolishness, Aunt. I truly am more worried about my uncle than encountering Mr. Darcy." She only wished she could convince herself of that.

"And Lizzy, if we are required to stay, consider how much

better care Edmund will receive here than if we were at the inn." She let out a soft laugh. "Of my few friends still in Lambton, I doubt any of them would be able to provide the care we will receive here."

"I am certain he will. I can readily see from what Mrs. Reynolds has said and done so far that she will do everything possible to aid in his recovery." She did not add the lingering and distressing thought that the housekeeper would also certainly inform Mr. Darcy of the matter once he arrived!

"Why do you not go to the room next door and lie down, Lizzy. You look tired."

"No, I am feeling well. What about you? If you are tired, I can certainly remain with my uncle while we wait for the doctor."

"No, no. I plan to remain in the room with him. Even through the night I shall remain by his side."

Elizabeth looked around. "But Aunt, the only other place to sleep in here is in the chair."

Mrs. Gardiner chuckled. "Do not fret, my dearest. I have spent many a night in a chair when one of our children was ill. I shall sleep soundly – as long as he does."

Elizabeth shook her head and looked down at her uncle's sleeping face. "I am so sorry. I was not paying attention to where I was going back there."

A knowing smile lit her aunt's face. "If I am not mistaken, my dear, you seemed captivated by the portrait of Mr. Darcy."

Elizabeth let out a forced laugh. "Hardly. He…" She drew in a rather shaky breath. "I was merely comparing the portrait to the man with whom I had become acquainted in Hertfordshire."

"And what is your conclusion? Do you still find him insufferable?"

Elizabeth pursed her lips together as she considered her response. "He is… he is a complicated man, and I hardly know what to make of him anymore, especially after the housekeeper's endless praise of him."

"Mrs. Reynolds certainly gave us a very different report of him than I expected. Were you as surprised as I was?" Mrs. Gardiner chuckled. "Or do you suppose she feels that she always has to speak respectfully of him? I imagine he would likely be displeased if he heard she had spoken ill of him."

Elizabeth thought for a moment. "I believe there was truth in what she said, as she knows him better than any of us in Hertfordshire did." She smiled weakly. "But I am also certain she is completely loyal to him and would not wish to sketch him in a bad light."

"That is indeed possible." Her aunt paused and looked about her. "But tell me, Lizzy, do you not think it is a beautiful home? Every room we saw today was beautifully, yet tastefully, done. Perhaps living in such a place endears one to even the most disagreeable master."

Elizabeth laughed softly. "Perhaps, but only because in living in such an immense home there would be a high probability of seldom encountering that disagreeable master in the course of the day."

Mrs. Gardiner tilted her head at her niece and smiled.

The two ladies quietly ate some of the food that had been brought to them, but after a few bites, Elizabeth shook her head. "I fear I have no appetite. While everything is delicious, I am just not hungry." She placed a small biscuit back on her plate and picked up her tea, bringing it with her to the window to look out. "The grounds are beautiful. I wish we could have seen them."

"Perhaps we will still get the opportunity to do so."

As Elizabeth continued to gaze out, Mrs. Reynolds returned and inquired how they were faring and whether they had need of anything else.

"We are doing well," Mrs. Gardiner said. "Everything was delicious. Thank you."

"Shall we remove the tray?" she asked.

"No, my husband has been asleep this whole time. He might like something to eat when he wakens."

"Of course. I shall return once the doctor has come." Mrs. Reynolds turned to leave, but Elizabeth stopped her.

"Mrs. Reynolds, would it be possible for me to take a turn about the grounds?" Looking to her aunt, she asked, "Aunt, would you mind? There is nothing I can do here." She knew if they were to remain and Mr. Darcy returned on the morrow, she would not feel free to stroll about the grounds. This might prove to be her only opportunity to do it without a sense of trepidation.

"Oh, by all means!" Mrs. Reynolds waved for her to follow her. "Come. I shall show you the most direct way out through the courtyard."

"I thank you." Elizabeth turned to her aunt. "You do not mind, do you?"

"Not at all, Lizzy, You go on and enjoy yourself."

Elizabeth picked up her bonnet and put it on as she followed Mrs. Reynolds down the hall and along a small passage, leading to a door.

"This door leads out to the courtyard. Walk out towards the right, and you will see the lake before you. There are some small gardens in front of the manor, and there is a rose garden beyond those. But in the other direction, you will see a path that follows the stream leading into the woods. I would not stray too far, for it is easy to become lost if you are unfamiliar with the grounds."

"Thank you. I shall take care." Elizabeth stepped out and took in a deep breath of the fresh air as she looked about. She wished she could become more familiar with the place – both the house and the grounds, but that could never be. That would mean becoming more familiar with the Master of Pemberley, and she had great doubts that would ever happen.

She walked out of the courtyard and saw the pristine blue lake ahead, just as Mrs. Reynolds had said. When she had first seen it from the road, the majesty of Pemberley – both the manor itself and the towering trees – had been reflected in its waters. That had been all she had been able to see. Now, however, she noticed the sparkling colours of turquoise, blue, and silver rippling across the surface, stirred by a gentle breeze. It looked very inviting on this warm summer day, and she hurried down to it.

A bench was situated directly in front of her at the lake's edge, and she briefly considered sitting down to enjoy the view when she spied the path that Mrs. Reynolds had mentioned. A small bench was on the other side of the stream, which Elizabeth realized would give a lovely view of the house and grounds.

The stream was not wide and did not look very deep, but Elizabeth determined it would be best not to attempt to cross it. While there were several rocks that she could use to hop across, the last thing she needed was to fall in.

As she debated what to do, she looked down the stream and saw a small stone bridge that arched across it. "That looks like a less treacherous way to get to the other side," she said with a laugh.

She set off for the bridge and when she reached it, she quickly walked to its centre, stopping to look down from either side of the bridge into the stream. The bridge was shaded by mature oak trees, and a mild cooling breeze ruffled both the leaves on the trees and the ribbon ties beneath her chin.

She reached up to untie and remove her bonnet, holding onto it as she braced her hands on the wall of the bridge. She took in a deep breath and looked about her. It was beautiful.

"It is too bad its owner would never approve of my being here!" She let out a nervous laugh but felt a surprising sense of regret.

An unexpectedly strong gust of wind almost snatched the bonnet from her hand, and she quickly reached out to secure it, catching it on the edge of her fingers. As she did, however, the sight of movement drew her attention, and she looked up to see a gentleman cross the stream as he jumped from rock to rock, the very same thing she had earlier pondered doing.

She stiffened and gasped when she realized it was Mr. Darcy! The only thing she could think to do was to duck behind the wall of the bridge, but as she did, the wind pulled the bonnet out from her fingers. She felt around the rocky crevices for it, but to no avail. It was gone!

She slowly lifted her head to cautiously peer over. She watched Mr. Darcy agilely continue across the stream, as if it was something he had done all his life. Fortunately he was facing away from her, obviously headed towards his home.

But just as that reassuring thought crossed her mind, he turned to brush something off the bottom of his boots. Her eyes widened in shock when she saw her bonnet floating in the current of the stream towards him, and just as suddenly, he hopped back across two rocks to pick it up. When he lifted his head and looked in her direction, she ducked beneath the wall again.

Elizabeth felt a surge of anxiety course through her, even down to the tips of her fingers. She held her breath and closed her eyes, much as a child would, thinking it would prevent her from being seen if he approached. Her heart pounded as she feared he would seek out the source of the errant bonnet; it was possible he had already seen her. As she waited, crouched in hiding, she wondered how long she ought to remain out of sight and contemplated how she was going to return to the house without his seeing her.

She gave her head a shake, her loose curls tickling her face. Now that he had returned a day earlier, the odds of his seeing her were much greater. She sat with her back against the stone wall and brought up her hand and began to nervously twist a curl around her finger. If only she could summon up the nerve to face him, yet she could not even imagine what she would say to him now.

She slowly rose and looked for him. She breathed a sigh of relief when she saw he had set out towards the front of the manor. Having lost her bonnet and the ability to shield her face, she began to walk quickly with her head bowed. She was grateful when he was finally out of sight, and even more so when she entered the protecting walls of the courtyard. She would not rest easily, however, until she was secluded in the room.

"Or back safely ensconced at the Lambton Inn!" she whispered in a trembling voice.

Once inside, she went directly to her uncle's room. She stepped in, dishevelled, out of breath, and her pulse racing.

"You have returned," her uncle said.

"And you have awakened," she said as she leaned over and kissed him. "How do you feel?"

"I have certainly felt better," he said with a small smile.

"I am so sorry," she said.

He waved his hand weakly. "I am certain a large part is due to my getting older." He shook his head with a smile. "There is no denying it."

"You are not old, Uncle." Elizabeth drew in a breath, wiping her brow with the back of her hand.

"Lizzy, it appears as though you did not have a restful walk."

"No, Aunt, I did not. The most dreadful thing…"

"What is it?" Mrs. Gardiner's eyes widened, and she abruptly stood up.

"Mr. Darcy has returned! He has arrived a day earlier than expected!"

"So you have seen him? Was he understanding? I am certain he was, and now you know you had no reason to worry about his seeing you."

Elizabeth shook her head. "He did not see me." She walked to the chair on the far side of her uncle's bed, sat down, and briefly told them what had happened.

When she had finished reciting the events, they again reassured her that she had no need to worry about what he would think if he found her at Pemberley.

Elizabeth gave them both a forced smile and eagerly changed the subject. "Has the doctor arrived?"

"Not yet," Mrs. Gardiner replied. "I expect he will be here soon." She clasped her hands and smiled weakly. "At least I hope so. Despite your uncle's levity, his pain is unrelenting."

Mr. Gardiner let out a moan of protest, and Elizabeth reached for his hand. She leaned over to kiss her uncle's cheek, and when they heard the sound of footsteps drawing near, Elizabeth looked up at her aunt with a smile. She was about to express her gratitude for the prompt arrival of the doctor, when she heard a voice more clearly.

"Mrs. Reynolds, can you tell me how it happened?"

Elizabeth's eyes widened, and she sent her aunt a helpless glance. "Oh, no! This is dreadful!"

"What is it, Lizzy?"

"It is Mr. Darcy!" she exclaimed in a hushed tone.

"Mr. Darcy?" Mrs. Gardiner whispered back. "Are you certain?"

"Yes!" she answered softly.

Mrs. Gardiner turned towards the door, and when she looked back, her niece was no longer there.

Without thinking, Elizabeth dropped to the floor on the other side of the bed. She could see just enough under the bed to have a view of the floor by the doorway. Her heart beat thunderously as she saw the small shoes of Mrs. Reynolds appear, followed by a pair of gentleman's boots. She closed her eyes to say a prayer that she would not be discovered.

"He is in here, Mr. Darcy," Mrs. Reynolds said softly.

Elizabeth's every muscle tensed as she watched and listened.

"Mr. and Mrs. Gardiner, do you mind if we come in? Mr. Darcy arrived a day early, and when I told him what had happened, he wished to come immediately to be introduced and see how you were doing."

"Certainly," Mrs. Gardiner replied. "Please, do come in." Her voice wavered a little. "My husband has been resting."

Mrs. Reynolds performed the obligatory introductions.

Mrs. Gardiner curtseyed while her husband gave a nod of his head. He added with a smile, "Pray forgive me for not bowing, sir, but I fear I would not be able to bring myself back up if I did."

"I certainly understand. It is a pleasure to make your acquaintances, although..." Darcy paused. "I regret the circumstances. I am very sorry about the accident today."

"An unfortunate tumble, but I hope my husband will improve soon," Mrs. Gardiner replied.

"Mr. Darcy, it is a pleasure to meet you, as well." Mr. Gardiner's tone was very sincere, and Elizabeth surmised he was making every attempt not to display the pain he was experiencing. "We thought you were not to arrive until the morrow."

"I had planned to arrive tomorrow, but I received word of a rather urgent matter that brought me home a day early."

"I see," he said. "We are sorry for any inconvenience we have been to the staff, sir, but they have been most attentive and helpful."

"Trust me, it is no inconvenience."

Mrs. Gardiner smiled. "Mr. Darcy, I grew up in Lambton and heard much praise for your parents when I was younger. We appreciate everything Mrs. Reynolds and your staff have done." She smiled. "We have now experienced first-hand that same goodness that I had often heard spoken about."

"I am glad to hear that. We will do all we can for your husband. If there is anything you require, please feel free to ask."

"Thank you, sir."

"I understand your niece is also here. Does Miss Gardiner have need of anything?" Darcy asked.

There was a slight pause, and Elizabeth drew in a breath and held it as she waited for her aunt's response, fearing her aunt would wish to correct him.

"Hm? Oh, my niece. She is…" Mrs. Gardiner abruptly stopped. "Thank you, sir, for your generosity, but I believe we have everything we need for the moment."

"Good. I can assure you my housekeeper will continue to look after you. I can recollect times when I was ill as a boy that Mrs. Reynolds did everything in her power to care for me. There is none like her."

"I only try to do what is necessary and what will help," Mrs. Reynolds said warmly. "Back then, it also helped that he was such a good patient. He never complained and was always cooperative and very appreciative."

Everyone laughed, except Elizabeth. She had her eyes fixed on their feet. Mr. Darcy appeared to step forward slightly, and she hugged herself to the floor and closer to the bed, hoping he could not see her. She felt rather silly and could not imagine the further mortification she would feel if he found her hiding from him on the floor.

"Just ring for one of the servants if you have need of anything, and someone will come directly." Mrs. Reynolds nodded her head towards the door. "Harriet will be available to be at your beck and call."

"Thank you," Mrs. Gardiner said.

"I shall leave you now. I have guests arriving on the morrow and need to meet with my steward." He turned to Mr. Gardiner. "I hope you get a good report from the doctor and have a swift recovery."

"Thank you, sir."

Elizabeth waited until she was certain Mr. Darcy and his housekeeper were gone, and she slowly peeked over the side of the bed. "Oh, Aunt! This is dreadful! How will I rest knowing he is here? I have almost encountered him two times in less than an hour. How shall I ever keep him from seeing me here?"

Mrs. Gardiner walked over and took her niece's hand, helping her up. "Lizzy, I doubt that he will feel a need to pay another visit to the sick room, especially as he is readying for his guests. He has left your uncle in the capable hands of Mrs. Reynolds, and he fully trusts her good judgement. There is no need to fret."

Elizabeth drew in a breath and let it out through her teeth. "Thank you for not revealing my real name."

"Oh, I almost did, did I not?" Mrs. Gardiner chuckled. "I could have sworn I heard you gasp, and it brought me to my senses."

"Hopefully he did not hear me or see me!" She sat in the chair and shook her head. "What a predicament I have caused."

Mr. Gardiner watched the interaction between his wife and his niece, and at length he said with a laugh, "If I had been thinking more clearly, I might have given the man who insulted my niece a piece of my mind!" He looked at her and smiled. "What did he say? You were not handsome enough to tempt him?"

Elizabeth felt her face warm. "Something to that effect."

"Would you not have taken great delight in watching me give him what he is due regarding that slight?"

"I would take no delight in such a thing, Uncle, and you had better not say anything of the sort to him!"

Her uncle laughed, and then stiffened with pain. "You are serious about this, are you not, Lizzy?"

"Yes, I am," she said softly as she watched her aunt and uncle eye each other. "And while we are here, do not forget that my name is Miss Gardiner."

"As you wish, Miss Gardiner," her uncle said with a smile.

Chapter 3

Elizabeth took refuge in the room next door as her aunt and uncle waited for the doctor. She knew she would have to leave when the doctor came to examine her uncle, so she decided to go directly, in case Mr. Darcy unexpectedly came by again. She needed time alone to gather her thoughts – and her wits. Her heart had not ceased racing since first seeing Mr. Darcy. His unexpected visit to the room had only exacerbated the unsettled gnawing deep within her.

The room was simply furnished, but was decorated charmingly, with sheer window coverings dotted with small roses. Two pictures of painted florals hung on the wall, and a simple wood-carved bird was perched on a doily on the small table.

She walked to the window and stared out, not really seeing anything, and drew in a long breath, closing her eyes. Behind her lids was the man who presently had her so confused that she did not feel like herself or know who she was.

She tried to sort out her thoughts. "Why am I so apprehensive to encounter him, when I had no qualms about disagreeing with him at every opportunity mere months ago?" She dropped into a chair, stretched out her legs, and leaned her head back.

She had just begun to feel calm when there was a knock on the door. Mrs. Gardiner stepped in to report that the doctor, Mr. Holmes, had arrived and was examining her husband.

"Did he give any indication of how serious he thinks the injury is?"

Mrs. Gardiner shook her head. "No, but when Edmund extended his arm to shake his hand, he was gripped with pain." She let out a long sigh. "It was not that the doctor had an unusually strong grip. Unfortunately, your uncle did not anticipate the pain he would experience in doing something as simple as shaking a hand."

Elizabeth hung her head, slowly shaking it.

"Oh, now, Lizzy, I did not say that to make you feel guilty. I am certain it is nothing too serious."

"I hope not," Elizabeth said, a look of regret consuming her features.

At length, the two ladies were summoned into the room to hear the doctor's report.

He welcomed them in and addressed them both. "I do not believe anything is broken, but it is possible your husband has cracked a rib or two, possibly a small fracture, which can actually be extremely painful. I have assured Mr. Gardiner that he should recover completely in due time, but I have put a tight wrap about his chest to restrain movement." He smiled. "I doubt he will be able to move very much since he is still in a great deal of pain. That pain ought to be enough inducement for him to remain sedentary. Whatever the extent of the fracture, we do not want it to worsen." He rubbed his hands together. "I have admonished him to remain still for the next twenty-four to forty-eight hours. After that, I shall allow only short walks within the confines of the room, as much as he can handle." He folded his arms across his chest and smiled. "You shall have to remain at Pemberley a few more days."

Upon hearing the doctor's diagnosis, Elizabeth felt a great sense of relief concerning her uncle, even as a tremor of dread passed through her. She shook her head as she resigned herself to having to stay longer at Pemberley.

"We are so grateful for the kindness that Mrs. Reynolds and the staff have shown to us, but we all feel the inconvenience this must be to them," Mrs. Gardiner said.

The doctor shook his head. "You have no need to worry about that. I can assure you that the Pemberley household and staff will not be at all inconvenienced by your presence, and you will receive the best care while you are here. They will give you everything you need." He gave a small bow. "Until tomorrow, then."

"Thank you, Mr. Holmes," they all said as he took his leave.

When he stepped out of the room, Elizabeth gave a slight shrug and looked at her aunt, who smiled back at her.

"So we are to stay at Pemberley," Mr. Gardiner said. "Who would have imagined when we set out today that we would be spending the night here?"

"Not I," Elizabeth said. "Not in a thousand years would I have imagined it, and I would never have wished it in a million years."

Elizabeth made a futile attempt at a smile as she considered that a few months ago she had been offered the chance to live at Pemberley not merely as a guest, but as its Mistress. She had entertained no idea the magnificence of the home when he had asked for her hand, although it would likely not have made a bit of difference to her, considering how she felt towards him.

Mrs. Gardiner looked at her niece. "I know you had concerns about coming here, Lizzy, but I doubt Mr. Darcy will come by again. He came by once to check on us, and that is all that is required of him, especially as he must be a busy man and has guests coming."

"I certainly hope so," Elizabeth said. "I would rest much easier if I knew for a certainty he would not come anywhere near this wing of his home!"

Mrs. Gardiner sent her a pointed look. Elizabeth was aware her aunt knew her well enough to suspect there was more to what she said than the words she used.

~~*

Once Mr. Gardiner was resting comfortably and had fallen back asleep, Mrs. Gardiner suggested to Elizabeth that perhaps they ought to return to the inn to bring back their belongings.

"Perhaps I can ask Mrs. Reynolds if we might have the service of a maid and manservant to give us assistance. We cannot wear the same clothes for the entirety of our stay here, and we shall likely need other items. We might as well get everything packed up and brought here."

"You are right, Aunt. Unfortunately, we need to do that." Elizabeth gave her aunt a slight smile. She considered that stepping out of their room and possibly into Mr. Darcy's sight was not something she wanted to do at all, but retrieving their belongings was something they needed to do.

They rang for Mrs. Reynolds to inquire about the possibility of servants accompanying them, and as they waited for her to arrange that, Elizabeth quickly penned a letter to her family at Longbourn, acquainting them with all that had happened.

She took care to ensure them that her uncle was being well taken care of and there was no need for them to worry. She knew how easily her mother could make any situation a dire calamity. She would believe, despite all assurances otherwise, that her brother would likely die from his injuries.

A manservant and maid were sent to accompany them to Lambton, and Harriet came to stay by Mr. Gardiner's side in case he wakened and needed assistance. Elizabeth addressed her letter and decided to post it from the inn at Lambton to ensure that Mr. Darcy would not see it.

"Lizzy, where is your bonnet?" Mrs. Gardiner asked as they walked out into the courtyard where the carriage was waiting.

Elizabeth tugged at some of her loose strands of hair. "I lost it when I went out earlier. The wind caught it, and it ended up floating down the stream."

"At least you have others at the inn. Be sure to put one on before we return."

"Believe me, Aunt, I shall!"

The driver of Pemberley's carriage expressed great regret over Mr. Gardiner's injuries as he handed them up, and once settled in, they set off for Lambton.

~~*

Darcy paced about the study as he listened to Rowland, his steward, give a report of the state of Pemberley, the grounds, tenants, and their homes.

He was always interested in the report his steward had to give, but this report was a long one, as he had been gone many months. He could not regulate his thoughts, concerned as he was about the urgent matter Rowland had just detailed to him, the situation that had necessitated his return a day early.

Mrs. Wickham's health was failing, and she had asked to see both him *and* her son. It was undeniably the worst time for it to have happened, with both Georgiana and his guests coming to Pemberley, although one had no control over such things. In addition, he was unsettled because of the accident that had occurred in his home. He was grateful the gentleman was not more seriously injured.

He walked to the window, pressing his fingers to the back of his waist and arching his back in a much needed stretch as the report continued. As he glanced out, he noticed Mrs. Gardiner and a young lady walking towards a waiting carriage. He started.

"That is odd," he said.

His steward looked up. "Which part, sir? The losses or the gains?"

Darcy waved his hand through the air. "None of that, Rowland. For some reason I pictured the niece of the injured gentleman as a young girl. She is…" He shook his head and narrowed his eyes. For a moment, seeing the niece from the back, the colour of her hair and her manner of walking, he was reminded of Elizabeth Bennet. "She is instead a young lady." He watched them as they quickly stepped up into the carriage. As he watched the carriage pull out of the courtyard, he instructed his steward, "Continue."

Once he and his steward completed their business, Rowland stood up. "Let me know when you wish to visit Mrs. Wickham. I shall await word."

"Thank you, Rowland. I have a few things I must tend to, and then I shall depart directly."

"Yes, sir."

When Rowland stepped out, Darcy walked back over to the window and looked out, drawing in a deep breath. There was so much pressing on him. He was deeply grieved to hear about Mrs. Wickham's declining health as well as Mr. Gardiner's injury, but in addition to those things, there was something else bothering him. First there was the bonnet he had found floating in the stream. He had not seen where it came from, but as it was not completely wet, he had assumed it had recently fallen into the water. The young lady he just spotted entering the carriage wore no bonnet. This might answer as to its owner, but he wondered where she had been when she lost it and why he had not seen her.

In addition, as he and Mrs. Reynolds had approached the infirmary room earlier, he could have sworn he heard what sounded like two different ladies speaking in low voices. When he stepped in, only Mrs. Gardiner was there with her husband. Then there was the slight sound that seemed to come from the other side of the bed, where he thought he saw some lavender fabric. It was because of that he had reasoned that perhaps the niece was a young girl who was terribly shy. This young lady stepping into the carriage was wearing a lavender dress.

Apparently, the Gardiners' niece was not a young girl, but a young lady.

As he contemplated this, Mrs. Reynolds tapped at the open door. Darcy turned and bid her enter.

"I just returned from sending Mrs. Gardiner and her niece to Lambton to retrieve their belongings. They are to remain here another few days, as the doctor has advised Mr. Gardiner not to travel or even move. He thinks it is merely a small fracture and will check on him daily."

"Thank you, Mrs. Reynolds." He drew in a breath. "I trust they will be well taken care of."

She nodded. "Certainly."

"Mrs. Reynolds, what can you tell me about the Gardiners?"

"The Gardiners sought permission to view the house earlier today. As you heard, Mrs. Gardiner grew up in Lambton. They had been touring Derbyshire and had been staying at the inn there."

"I see." He rubbed his chin and asked, "And what can you tell me about their niece?"

"She is a delightful young lady, about twenty." She paused and then added. "She claims a prior acquaintance with you."

Darcy looked up, surprised. "Miss Gardiner? I do not recall anyone…"

Mrs. Reynolds waved her hand through the air. "She said it was a trifling acquaintance, and it was unlikely you would remember her."

Darcy nodded. "I see. Thank you."

He was surprised at that revelation, not even being able to guess from where he might know a Miss Gardiner. Unfortunately, many young ladies would claim an acquaintance with him when they had made only a minimal impression on himself. And most of those impressions would not be highly favourable. She was probably correct. He doubted he would remember ever having met her.

He shook his head. It was not important. Mr. Gardiner was being well taken care of, and for that he was grateful.

He sat down at his desk and pulled out some pieces of mail his steward had deemed important for him to read. He would quickly look through them and then set out to see Mrs. Wickham. He shook his head and closed his eyes, hoping her son had not yet arrived. He wondered if the man would even make an attempt to see his mother before she was lost to him forever.

Whether or not Wickham would come to see her, he would go to her. He put the last piece of mail down, stood up, and set out to pay her a call.

~~*

The next morning Darcy went to the library, where he could listen and watch for the first sign of the carriage conveying Georgiana and her companion, Mrs. Annesley, when they pulled into the courtyard. Bingley and his family were to arrive shortly, as well. His other guests would come later that afternoon.

He checked with Mrs. Reynolds and was pleased to hear Mr. Gardiner had slept well. The doctor was expected to return later in the day.

As he waited, he thought back to his visit the previous day with Mrs. Wickham, who had been living with her daughter, Alice, and her family in Lambton for many years. She was thin, pale, and exceptionally weak. He found it odd, therefore, that her twisted fingers had reached out and taken hold of his hand in a tight grip. He could tell she was happy to see him, but it was an effort for her to speak.

His visit with her was much shorter than he had anticipated. Visiting a mere ten minutes had worn out the frail woman.

Fortunately for Darcy, he did not have to face Wickham. The man had not yet arrived, for which he was grateful, but another day not seeing her son had deeply grieved his mother. She fretted that he might not arrive until after she "departs this life for another." She pleaded with Darcy in her slow and slurred speech to do something to facilitate his coming to see her. That was her last request to him before she drifted off to sleep.

He distractedly tapped his fingers on the desk. It had been many years since George had come to Lambton to see his mother and sister, but because of what had occurred the year before between Georgiana and him, Darcy was grateful. He had forbidden him to come near Pemberley. Grimacing, he considered the lies the man had spread in Meryton about him. He leaned his head back and closed his eyes as he shuddered, realizing he had no idea what the man might do once he was back in the vicinity. Was it too much to ask that the man come and go without causing any kind of distress to himself, his sister, and… his guests? He doubted the man would be so obliging.

As much as he was loath to do it, he picked up a piece of stationary and penned a note to Colonel Forster in Brighton, where he had learned the militia was encamped. He offered whatever pecuniary help he could give to enable Wickham to visit his mother if he had not already departed. It left a sour taste in his mouth, but he would honour what was possibly a dying mother's last request.

It was later that morning when Darcy heard the clip-clop of horses entering the courtyard. He glanced out the window and, seeing the Pemberley carriage pulling up, he gave his waistcoat a quick tug and hurried downstairs.

Darcy walked out into the courtyard and up to the equipage, waiting eagerly while the door was opened. When Georgiana stepped out, she ran into his outstretched arms. He picked her up and spun her around.

"Do you not think I am too old for that?" she said with a laugh.

Darcy set her down and pressed her fingers under her chin, lifting it up to him. "As long as I am almost twelve years your senior, you will never be too old for that!" He leaned over and kissed the tip of her nose.

"It is so good to be back at Pemberley!" she said. She pulled away and looked around. "I have missed it."

"And it has missed you, I dare say!" He gave a loose strand of her hair a tug. "But I have missed you more."

"Fitzwilliam, we saw each other not four days ago!"

"But not at Pemberley. I have missed you at Pemberley."

Darcy greeted Mrs. Annesley as she joined them. "I hope it was a good journey."

"It was, sir," the woman replied. "It was frightfully quiet and boring, as it ought to have been."

"I am glad to hear that," Darcy said.

Mrs. Annesley informed them that she would go to her chambers to freshen up before she set off to visit her family for a few weeks.

After expressing their thanks to her and saying their goodbyes, Georgiana leaned in. With a mischievous smile she said, "Would you think me ill-mannered if I told you I am grateful that the Bingleys decided against coming? Here is a letter Mr. Bingley asked us to deliver to you explaining their absence." Georgiana handed him the letter, and then said with a soft laugh. "I do not speak so much of Mr. Bingley, but I own that I rather enjoyed the quiet and solitude, which I would not have been able to do had Miss Bingley been riding with us, which I am sure she would have insisted upon."

"So what prompted their decision not to come?" he asked as he broke the seal on the missive and opened it. Shaking his head, he said, "Oh, Bingley, if only you would learn to write a legible letter!"

"Mrs. Annesley and I have our opinions on why they did not come, but I shall hold my thoughts until you have read the letter."

As Darcy read – or at least attempted to read – his friend's letter, he began to shake his head with his lips turning down in a frown.

When he finished, he folded the letter and placed it in his pocket. He glanced down at his sister. "So, Georgiana, what are your thoughts as to why they did not come?"

"We know that they became aware of the fact that you had also invited the Westerfields to Pemberley. Miss Bingley inquired of me before we left town if it was true. She also casually inquired whether the rumours circulating amongst the ton were correct that you are to settle your affections on Miss Westerfield. Of course, I denied knowing any of my brother's intentions, but it was later that day that Mr. Bingley came by and offered his apologies that they would not be joining us and asked that we bring his letter of regret to you." She smiled up at her brother. "I would assume Miss Bingley did not wish to witness Miss Westerfield securing your affections, would she?"

Darcy pursed his lips. "If I can decipher his letter correctly, Bingley does allude to something to that effect." He lowered his brows. "But I wonder if that is all there is to it."

Georgiana tucked her hand into her brother's arm as they began walking towards the house. "I confess, Brother, that I am sorry Mr. Bingley chose not to come. He is always so friendly. On the other hand, his sister…" She paused and said no more.

Darcy let out a sympathetic sigh. "I know."

Georgiana smiled sweetly and glanced up at her brother. "So is it true?" she asked.

"Is what true? That there are rumours circulating about Miss Westerfield and me?"

Georgiana shook her head with a laugh. "Oh, I have no doubt there are rumours circulating. You have been the subject of a great many rumours over the years."

"Have I? And how would you know?"

Georgiana gave him a teasing smile. "Fitzwilliam, I have acquaintances in town who are not averse to asking me if this or that is true about you. Most have older sisters who harbour hopes that they might become the object of your affections."

Darcy frowned. "I see. I regret that you are put in that position."

"It matters not. But I would like to know if you are planning to settle your affections on Miss Westerfield."

Darcy rubbed his jaw for a moment. "I wrote to you that there was someone I would like for you to get to know better."

"Indeed, you did. But…" Georgiana paused.

Darcy looked at her and nodded his head for her to continue.

"It is just… I was a little surprised when you told me you had invited the family to Pemberley, and then I heard those rumours concerning her. I had no notion at all that your affections were already so strongly attached… to another." She gave him a questioning glance. "Are they truly?"

Darcy pressed his lips tightly and rubbed his jaw as he pondered how to answer his sister. "I have invited her and her family to Pemberley allowing for both of us to get to know each other and our families better. Miss Westerfield and I spent a great deal of time together when we were young as our families were close acquaintances. She is a highly accomplished young lady, and…" Darcy swallowed, his throat suddenly dry. "I do, after all, need to begin seriously considering taking a wife."

Georgiana's face grew sombre as she studied his face. "I see. When do they arrive?"

"Later today. Not likely for several hours."

Georgiana drew in a breath. "I know I have met her before, but I cannot recall… Shall I like her, do you think?"

"I hope so," he replied, as he stopped and drew her into a tight hug.

They continued on and stepped into the house, and Georgiana smiled. "It is good to be home." She looked up at him. "How do you find Pemberley? Is all well with her?"

Darcy stopped again. "Georgiana, there was a slight accident yesterday in the house…" He was not yet prepared to discuss Mrs. Wickham, but she certainly needed to hear about the gentleman's injuries.

"Oh, my!" Her hands flew to her cheeks, and her mouth widened. "Is it serious? What has happened? Who is it?"

He placed his hand on her shoulder. "It is not serious… not terribly serious, and it is no one you know. A party was touring the house, and the gentleman fell down a few of the stairs."

"How dreadful! I am so sorry to hear that!"

"He is presently in one of our infirmary rooms. The doctor believes it is a small fracture of a rib, so he does not want him to move or be moved for several days. His wife and niece are also staying here while he recovers."

"Should I go see them?"

Darcy smiled. "Would you like to go see them?"

Georgiana winced. "I believe I ought to. What are their names?"

"Gardiner." He took her hand. "If you are at all discomfited with the thought of paying a call on strangers, you do not have to. Mrs. Reynolds is doing a superb job caring for our guests. I have already visited them, and they are doing well under the circumstances."

Georgiana smiled. "No, I would like to go." She tucked her hand inside her brother's arm as they stepped into the parlour.

"Are you certain? I know you find it difficult to speak with strangers."

Georgiana laughed. "As does someone else with whom I am very close." She looked up at him with a mischievous grin. "No, I must do this. I might not know the proper thing to say in this matter, but I shall make every attempt to make them feel welcomed and to be assured we will do everything possible to make their stay a pleasant one."

Darcy smiled. "I am certain you shall!"

"I do hope Mr. Gardiner will be all right."

"As do I, Georgiana." Darcy shook his head. "I would hate to think someone was injured inside my own home and suffered due to neglect or poor care."

"I shall go freshen up and then pay them a visit."

"You do that," Darcy said as he leaned over and kissed the top of her head.

As they were about to part ways, Darcy told Georgiana he would be away for a time as he and his steward needed to see a few of his tenants on the property. He would also visit Mrs. Wickham again, although he did not mention that.

"How long will you be from home?"

"Possibly an hour or two." It was difficult to predict, as visits could end up being longer than he anticipated or sometimes shorter. "I doubt that the Westerfields will arrive before I return, but if they do, Mrs. Reynolds will see to their comfort. I want to be with you when you first meet them."

"Thank you, Fitzwilliam. I appreciate that."

Darcy left his sister and set out to meet with his steward. He now felt even more unsettled after what Georgiana had said and that Bingley had hinted as much in his letter. He had hoped he could entertain the Westerfields without the force of the rumour mill propelling them towards a rushed engagement. He rubbed his jaw, suddenly realizing it was tightly clenched. At least he could be grateful the Bingleys had decided not to come. It was one less thing he would have to worry about.

He pulled out his friend's letter and shook his head. Bingley had taken great delight in teasing him both about this rumoured admiration he supposedly had, as well as the sour expression his sister had been wearing since first hearing it.

Darcy shook his head. His friend knew nothing about the ardent admiration he once had for another lady, and he wanted so much to put *her* out of his thoughts, mind, and heart. He hoped Miss Westerfield would be the one to do just that!

~~*

That morning, Elizabeth had awakened and eaten a small breakfast with her aunt and uncle in his room. She had been pleased to hear he had slept well, waking only a few times due to the pain. After their meal, she had returned to her room to read while they awaited the arrival of the doctor.

At length, the sound of horses coming into the courtyard below drew her attention. She walked over to the window and looked out. Her heart skipped a beat when she saw Mr. Darcy walk to the carriage and then wait for the doors to be opened.

She watched as a young lady stepped out and hurried over to him. She was soon in his arms, and he swung her about. Elizabeth smiled as she determined it had to be his sister, and she watched with curiosity as he displayed a great deal of brotherly affection towards her.

Once Mr. Darcy and his sister had walked back towards the manor and disappeared out of her view, she decided it would be safe to join her aunt and uncle as they waited for the doctor to arrive. She assumed – and greatly hoped – that with the arrival of Mr. Darcy's sister, he would not be paying a visit to the infirmary room again any time soon.

Chapter 4

Later that day, Elizabeth was conversing with her aunt and uncle in his room when she was startled by a tap at the door. She turned, half expecting – and fully dreading – to see Mr. Darcy; instead, a young lady, the one she had seen arrive in the carriage earlier that morning, stood next to Mrs. Reynolds.

"Pardon me," Mrs. Reynolds said softly. "There is someone who wishes to make your acquaintance. Is this a convenient time?"

Mrs. Gardiner smiled. "Certainly, please come in."

Mrs. Reynolds made the introductions.

"We are delighted to make your acquaintance," Mrs. Gardiner said.

"Thank you. It is a pleasure to meet you, as well." Georgiana clasped her hands tightly together and looked at the housekeeper. "Thank you, Mrs. Reynolds." She turned back to the others as the woman nodded and stepped from the room. "My brother informed me of the unfortunate accident yesterday." Turning to Mr. Gardiner, she said, "I was so grieved to hear about it. Mrs. Reynolds told me the doctor has not yet been to see you today."

"Not yet. He said yesterday, however, that it looked as though it is a slight fracture in at least one of my ribs."

Mrs. Gardiner smiled. "It is likely more painful than serious. We are grateful that it was not a broken rib, as a slight fracture will allow for a speedier recovery as long as he is careful not to cause more damage to it."

"I am glad to hear that."

Elizabeth stood up and gestured towards her seat. "Please, come take my chair."

"Oh, thank you, no. I cannot stay long, and besides, I have been sitting in a carriage for most of the morning." She smiled hesitantly and then asked, "May I inquire as to how the accident happened?"

"We had just been through the portrait gallery and had begun descending the stairs after seeing the fine portrait of your brother," Mrs. Gardiner said. "Somehow, Elizabeth and Edmund collided, and he fell down a few stairs."

Elizabeth shook her head. "It was solely my fault, as I was not paying attention. When I had turned and moved forward, I had wrongly assumed he was further ahead of me than he was."

"Now, Lizzy, we have an equal share in the fault." He looked at Georgiana. "It could have happened to anyone."

Georgiana shook her head. "I am so glad it was not worse."

Mrs. Gardiner smiled. "Indeed, we all are."

"Miss Darcy," Elizabeth said. "Pemberley is lovely – the manor and grounds are beautiful."

"Thank you," she replied. "It is good to be home."

Have you been away long?" Elizabeth found the young girl sweet and shy, just a little uneasy, but not at all prideful as Mr. Wickham had described her.

"Far too long. I have been in London since the autumn."

Elizabeth smiled at her. "Do you prefer the hustle and bustle of London or the quiet and beauty at Pemberley?"

Georgiana's eyes lit up. "I am delighted to be back at Pemberley, particularly as my brother is here."

"Mrs. Reynolds was certainly effusive in her admiration of your brother and how good he is to you," Mrs. Gardiner said. "You are very fortunate to have such a caring brother looking after you."

Georgiana nodded her head. "Indeed, I am very fortunate. I could not ask for a finer brother." She looked about her, as if searching for something more to say.

"We understand you have guests coming. Have they arrived?" Mrs. Gardiner asked.

"No, not yet."

They visited a while longer, and then Georgiana said, "My brother is gone from the home for a few hours to pay some calls on several of our tenants, so if you have need of anything, feel free to ask Mrs. Reynolds or myself."

"Thank you for coming by," Mrs. Gardiner said. "We appreciate it. Everyone here has been so kind and helpful."

"It is my pleasure."

When she was gone, Elizabeth turned to her aunt. "She is nothing like what I expected!"

"I cannot say that I had any particular expectations about her, but I found her pleasant, if only a little shy."

Elizabeth nodded, picked up a book she had brought back from the inn, and began to read. She did not find it particularly engaging, and after a while, she put it down. She was beginning to feel restless and trapped. "I wish I had something else to read. This book is a drudgery to get through."

Mrs. Gardiner tilted her head at her niece. "According to Miss Darcy, Mr. Darcy is from home for a few hours. Why do you not inquire whether you might visit his library?"

"Oh, Aunt, I could not! Besides, that was some time ago, and the doctor is about to come."

Reaching out and taking her niece's hand, she said, "I know you want to see it, and there is no need for you to be here when the doctor arrives." She patted Elizabeth's hand. "Mrs. Reynolds told us how grand it was, but we only have her word. Are you not just a little curious as to whether it meets up to her lavish description?"

Elizabeth thought back to Caroline Bingley's assessment of Pemberley's library when Jane was ill at Netherfield. From the moment she had praised it, Elizabeth had to confess it was a library she wished to see. She had actually been disappointed it was not included on the tour.

Despite Elizabeth's protests, Mrs. Gardiner grabbed the bell pull. "All you can do is ask."

A short while later, Mrs. Reynolds stepped in. "What can I do for you?"

Mrs. Gardiner looked at Elizabeth and then turned back to the housekeeper. "Elizabeth was wondering if she might be able to visit the library and find a book to read."

Elizabeth shook her head. "I would not want to intrude..."

"Certainly! You will find everything you could possibly want... and even more! Come! I will show you the way. It is almost directly above us, as a matter of fact."

Elizabeth could not argue with such an enthusiastic response, and with eager, albeit nervous anticipation, she followed Mrs. Reynolds.

As they walked the halls of Pemberley and traversed the stairs, Elizabeth argued with herself the whole way that this was the most foolish thing she had ever agreed to do. At the sound of every footstep, door opening, or voice speaking, she faltered, certain that it was Mr. Darcy returning. If it were not for the continuous stream of praise from the housekeeper in her description of the library, she would have turned back. She decided she would argue with herself later for allowing her curiosity to overrule her common sense.

When the two ladies stepped into the library, Elizabeth came to an abrupt stop. She could never have imagined anything more beautiful. She opened her mouth to speak, but no words came forth.

Mrs. Reynolds clasped her hands. "Is it not magnificent?" The housekeeper looked about her, as if she were looking at it for the first time.

"Yes... yes!" Elizabeth replied. "It is unlike any library I have ever seen."

"I have not seen one finer." Mrs. Reynolds turned to Elizabeth. "I am certain you will readily find something to your liking."

"Thank you."

"And I trust you will be able to find your way back to the infirmary room."

When Mrs. Reynolds stepped out, Elizabeth pressed her hand over her heart, her fingers creeping up to her throat. She found it difficult to do anything but gaze about her. She finally willed her feet to move and slowly began to walk about as her fingertips reached out and gently ran across the leather book spines. She drew in the deep musty scent of old books and polished wood, and oddly enough, she noticed a slight floral fragrance.

She walked over to the heavy dark wood desk where several books were stacked in a pile. A small wood-carved owl on a perch stood next to the books. Elizabeth carefully picked it up and ran her fingers over the intricately carved creature. While not particularly large, it was beautifully crafted. She gingerly replaced it and picked up the books from the table, looking at the titles. Upon seeing one that sounded like it would be something she would enjoy reading, she set the others back down, keeping that book in her hand.

She began to walk to the bookshelves but was stopped when

she noticed an unfinished carved bird sitting on the corner of the desk upon some papers. She picked it up and examined it. It looked like it was to be a medium-sized bird with a long tail. She thought it odd that a wood-carved bird – an *unfinished* wood-carved bird – would be sitting on Mr. Darcy's desk. As she looked at it more closely, she smiled as she thought it looked like it might be a magpie.

"That would be interesting if I am correct," she said softly to herself.

She replaced the carving and walked slowly through the library, wishing she had more time to examine every title on the shelves. She tilted her head to aid in reading the titles that were written down along the spine. She occasionally picked one up and carefully turned the pages, trying to decide if that book would be of more interest to her than the one she already held.

A tall free-standing wall of shelves stood in the middle of the library, adding to the beauty and grandness of the room. It was filled on both sides with books.

She walked along the front, and then stepped behind it as she continued to glance at the titles. There were many classics she had only heard about yet never read, and other titles she had not heard of at all. There seemed to be every type of book: fiction, biographies, politics, and war strategies. Amazingly, it appeared that every one of Shakespeare's works were present in the collection. Many books looked to be intriguing, and she debated whether to keep just the book she had earlier selected or look for another.

Oh, to have access to this many books would be…

Elizabeth paused as a thought came to her. *This could have all been mine.* "No!" Elizabeth admonished herself with a light stamp of her foot. She would not allow herself to feel any regret over what had happened in the past.

She did not know how long she had been in the library, for all time had ceased, and her thoughts and cares vanished. She pulled out another book and began perusing it. She was still standing behind the middle shelf of books and had just decided to take that one instead of the one she had picked up from the table when she heard the familiar voice of Mr. Darcy approaching!

"I have a few surprises for you, Georgiana. The first one is in here."

Elizabeth gasped lightly as Mr. Darcy and his sister stepped into the library.

Elizabeth's heart pounded, and she stood rigid behind the shelves. She was just barely able to see him over the tops of some of the books on the shelf. She hoped he could not see her; fortunately, he was not looking her way.

She watched him step over to the small table and pick up the stack of books she had earlier picked up. She began to feel a swelling of dread within her. She unwittingly shook her head as she looked down at the book in her hands.

"This is odd," he said. "I put the book right here for you."

"What was it?" Georgiana asked.

"It was a book I acquired for you. On the way out of town I stopped at a bookstore and bought several books; I thought you would particularly enjoy one of them." He shook his head and looked around. "I hope no one shelved it. I do not understand. It was here earlier."

He began to walk towards the shelf where Elizabeth was hiding, and she stiffened. An array of scenarios played out in her mind as to what he might do if he were to discover her cowering behind the book shelf. She had been feeling such turmoil over the possibility of his discovering her in his home that she actually considered stepping out to finally end her concealment and bring her presence here to light.

"We can come back later and look for it, Fitzwilliam. I am eager to see what else you have for me."

Elizabeth relaxed slightly at hearing Georgiana's words. She closed her eyes and prayed he would agree.

"I just do not understand." He shook his head. "There have been a few times lately when I felt as though I have been imagining things." He laughed. "Perhaps I only imagined I bought it for you."

"Well, if you only imagined it, I will hold no grudge, as you spoil me with your generosity, and I have told you that you have no need to do so. You are such a good brother, that if you were to give me nothing, I would still love you as much as I do now."

"And you are too generous in your praise, but if I gave you nothing, then our cousin would not be pleased. He continually admonishes me to provide you with such things as would make you happy."

"And I have told you that there is nothing I lack as long as I still have your love… and respect."

Elizabeth heard the young girl's voice crack.

"Georgiana, that is all in the past." Darcy put his arm around her shoulder. "You are dearer to me than anyone, and I want you to know it not only here," he said pointing to his head. "But in here." He then pointed to his heart.

Georgiana mutely nodded.

"Come. Let us go to the music room. Your other surprise is in there."

Elizabeth felt a great relief wash over her when she heard they were about to leave, but she moved slightly, causing the floor beneath her to squeak. She froze, lifting only her eyes to see Mr. Darcy pause and look back.

At that moment, however, another voice called out. "Mr. Darcy! How good it is to see you again!"

Elizabeth looked to the door as Mr. Darcy and Georgiana did the same.

"Miss Westerfield!" Darcy said, suddenly clearing his throat. "Mrs. Reynolds informed me that you and your parents had arrived, but I was made to believe you were all resting in your chambers. Otherwise I would have greeted you properly. Pray, forgive me."

The young lady, with blond hair pulled atop her head and tight ringlets framing each side of her face, smiled, revealing two dimples. "Think nothing of it. Mrs. Reynolds has been most attentive to us. We arrived earlier than we anticipated, so we fully understand. We were shown to our rooms – they are beautiful – but I wanted to walk about, as I had been sitting idle most of the day." She drew in a breath. "Pemberley is everything I remembered it to be, although I appreciate it so much more now. It is amazing how differently one sees things through the mature eyes of an adult instead of the simple eyes of a child."

"Thank you," Darcy said with a quick bow. "I am delighted you are pleased with it."

Elizabeth watched through pinched brows as the young woman turned to Georgiana. "This must be your sister. You have grown so much since we last saw each other."

"Yes, this is Georgiana. Pray, forgive my manners. Georgiana, do you remember Miss Angeline Westerfield?"

Elizabeth saw Georgiana smile sweetly and curtsey. "Yes, but I was young."

"You were! It is a delight to see you again, Miss Darcy."

"Thank you, Miss Westerfield. It is a pleasure to see you, as well."

"Oh, please call me Angeline, as you used to when we were younger."

Elizabeth held her breath as Miss Westerfield stepped into the centre of the library and looked about. "So many books!" She tilted her head at Mr. Darcy. "Have you read them all?"

Darcy shook his head with a soft chuckle. "No, and I highly doubt that I ever will. I have read many, but as more and more books are written every year, more will be added to the library. I can only read so fast, so unfortunately, some books shall likely go unread."

"Yet so many books add to the elegance of the library. There is nothing more unpleasant than a library with empty shelves."

"On the other hand," Georgiana began, "my brother often says there is nothing more unacceptable than a library filled with books that are never read."

"And I would hope," Darcy said, "that one would not say either about Pemberley's library."

"It is beautiful," Miss Westerfield said as she began to walk aimlessly about.

Elizabeth began to dread that she might venture further in the library and discover her. She breathed a sigh of relief when she returned to Miss Darcy's side.

Darcy turned to the young lady. "If you do not mind, I must beg to have a few more minutes alone with my sister. Feel free to look around the library and take any book you find to your liking. I shall meet you and your parents in the sitting room at... say, four o'clock?"

"Certainly," the young lady replied with a wide smile.

Elizabeth watched as Darcy stepped out with his sister and saw a quick look of disappointment cross Miss Westerfield's face. The young lady walked over to a side wall of shelves, looked at a few of the books, pulled one out, and then immediately returned it to its place.

"This library is nicer than I remembered," she said softly. "It shall be looked upon with great admiration by all my guests who come to visit us here."

Elizabeth remained still until Miss Westerfield stepped out. She let out a long, pent-up breath. *"Does she anticipate becoming Mistress of Pemberley one day?"* she asked herself. She placed her fingers over her mouth as her breath caught. *"Why does that thought distress me so?"* She pinched her brows as she considered she ought to be delighted Mr. Darcy had turned his affections elsewhere.

Elizabeth waited several minutes after the young lady walked away before stepping out cautiously from behind the wall of shelves. She still held the two books in her hand, and as much as she would have liked to read the first one she picked up, she placed it back on the table, knowing Mr. Darcy would not only wonder how it had disappeared, but would now also wonder when and how it reappeared. She would not worry about that now. She was only eager to get back to the refuge of the infirmary with her aunt and uncle.

~~*

Darcy escorted his sister to the music room, feeling rather unsettled that Miss Westerfield had shown up when he had wanted some time alone with Georgiana. At least his guest had not insisted on accompanying them. He did not want anyone else there, even the woman he might one day marry. His brows lowered at the thought.

Despite Georgiana's protests that he need not bestow gifts upon her as he so often did, she was delighted – as he expected – with the new pianoforte.

"Oh, Fitzwilliam, it is beautiful! I cannot wait to play it!"

"I was hoping you would play something for me now."

"Truly?" She ran her fingers over the polished wood. "Are you certain you do not need to see to Miss Westerfield?"

"Whilst I certainly could – and I assure you I will – I want this time with you." He shook his head. "There shall be time enough to spend with her and her parents in the next few weeks. I doubt they will be leaving any time soon."

"No, I would imagine not." Georgiana sat down on the bench and her fingers moved across the keys as she played a simple melody, gazing up at him with a smile. As the piece grew more complex, she turned her attention back to her fingering.

Darcy rested his elbows on the instrument and waited for her to finish before saying, "That was beautiful, Georgie. You have greatly improved over this past year."

"I have been applying myself more diligently. You have greatly improved over this past year."

"I have been applying myself more," she said gravely.

Darcy moved behind her and placed his hands gently on her shoulders. "I know it has been a difficult year for you, but you have done well. I am proud of you." He gave her shoulders a soft squeeze and then paused for a moment. He drew in a deep breath. "Georgiana, there is something I must tell you. It is the reason I came home a day early."

Georgiana stopped playing and turned to look at her brother. Her expression of concern mirrored her brother's. "What is it?"

Darcy swallowed. "Mrs. Wickham is failing. I have visited her twice and am certain she has no more than a few days left."

"I see," Georgiana said softly. She cast her eyes down and then back up. "Shall I go visit her?"

Darcy adamantly shook his head. "No! Her son may return at any time. I will not have you encounter him. My visits are enough. She is not even aware you are home."

The young girl nodded mutely.

"Georgiana, you seem troubled. I hope telling you this has not grieved you."

"Oh, no! It is not that, although I feel sorry for Mrs. Wickham and her daughter."

"Then what is it?"

She turned back to face the piano and began playing again. Her fingers continued to move nimbly across the keys as she gazed back up, a sad look in her eyes. "Miss Westerfield... is she... do you love her?"

Darcy closed his hands into fists and began rubbing his thumbs and index fingers together. "Georgie, do we... does anyone really know what love is?"

Georgiana stopped playing, resting her hands in her lap. "I would imagine it is different for everyone." She rose. "But I believe you knew what it was to love... once." She stood up on her toes and kissed his cheek. "I shall be in my room readying myself to meet Miss Westerfield's family." She turned and left the room.

Darcy drew in a hitched breath as he watched her disappear out the door. "*Why did I ever tell her about Elizabeth?*" He shook his head as he silently pondered what he might have said to her. It had only been in letters he had written about her. He could recollect mentioning her in at least one letter from Hertfordshire and then again when he and Elizabeth had seen each other again in Kent. He could not recall everything he had said, but he knew he told her he was going to offer for her and assured Georgiana she would welcome her as a delightful sister.

After Elizabeth had refused his offer of marriage, his sister had seen what it had done to him. She had readily recognized the depth of love – and pain – he had suffered. She had asked little, and he had offered even less information regarding what had transpired between them.

He clasped his hands and looked down, shaking his head. He had hoped coming to Pemberley would be everything he needed to rid himself of the crushing pain of Elizabeth's refusal. He had so looked forward to spending more time with Georgiana in the home he loved. It had been a spontaneous decision to invite the Westerfields and Bingleys. Miss Westerfield had always been polite, kind, and considered a beauty. He hoped to turn what had been a lifelong friendship with her into something more – and put Elizabeth behind him.

He had not anticipated, however, having to deal with Mrs. Wickham's fading health and her asking for his help in bringing her son back to her before she died. The last thing he needed was

Wickham in the vicinity, especially with Georgiana here.

He drew himself erect and dropped his head forward. When he had earlier gone to see her, she appeared even more pale and weak than she had been the day before. He wondered if Wickham would get there in time – if he even chose to come at all.

~~*

Elizabeth hurried back to the infirmary, grateful to enter the somewhat secure sanctuary of the room.

"There is my niece!" Mr. Gardiner said. "The doctor has already come and gone."

"He has? What did he have to say? Anything new?"

"He is still concerned with the amount of pain I am in and wants me to remain sedentary for at least another day or two. I am sorry, Lizzy. We will not be leaving."

Elizabeth took his hand in hers. "Trust me, Uncle, as long as you get well, I am content to remain here."

"Did you find a book, dear?" Mrs. Gardiner asked.

Elizabeth rolled her eyes. "I did, but at the expense of nearly being discovered by Mr. Darcy!"

"What happened?" They both asked at once.

Elizabeth explained her ordeal. "I think it would be best if I remain secluded in my room for the remainder of our stay here. I think that is the only place I will be safe from him." She almost laughed as she thought how true that statement was, for oddly enough she felt that she was in very great danger of developing a regard for him, a very strong regard.

She sat down in the chair, feeling as though her heart had finally returned to beating at its normal pace. She continued. "While they were in the library, Mr. Darcy told his sister he had a surprise for her in the music room. I imagine he was showing her the pianoforte he just bought her."

"That is right!" Mrs. Gardiner said. "Mrs. Reynolds told us it had just arrived, as he had bought it as a present for her."

"She is fortunate to have such a devoted brother," Mr. Gardiner said.

Elizabeth could not agree more, although she really did not

50

wish to. It would have been much easier to continue to dislike him if she had witnessed him being a demanding, or even indifferent, brother. It would have given her additional justification for her former feelings and refusing his offer of marriage. The longer she stayed here, despite not actually being in his presence, the more likely it was that she would admit to the realization that she had made the biggest mistake of her life.

Chapter 5

Darcy readied himself with the aid of his valet to go down to meet the Westerfields. He felt a great deal of agitation because he had hoped Georgiana would be delighted with the prospect of gaining Miss Westerfield as a sister, but for some reason, she did not appear eager at all. He knew she would support any decision he made regarding his taking a wife. At least he hoped she would.

When he finally came to the sitting room, he found it empty. He was glad. This time he would be there to greet the Westerfields when they came in. He paced about the room, clasped his hands behind his back, and took several deep breaths to calm himself. He was not nervous about welcoming Miss Westerfield or her parents to Pemberley; something else pressed upon him that he dared not contemplate.

Georgiana joined him a few minutes later, and it was another fifteen minutes before the Westerfields arrived. He greeted Mr. Westerfield with a hearty handshake.

"It is good to see you, again, sir. Pray forgive me for not being available to welcome you when you first arrived."

Mr. Westerfield waved his hand through the air. "Think nothing of it, sir. We arrived much earlier than we had anticipated." His gaze turned to his daughter. "Some of us were eager to arrive." He let out a hearty laugh. "I am well aware that there are many things you must see to when you are in residence, particularly when you have been from home a long time."

Darcy nodded a thank you to him and then introduced Georgiana to Mr. and Mrs. Westerfield, since it had been several years since they had seen her. After inviting them to sit down, Georgiana took the chair next to Mrs. Westerfield and her daughter, while Darcy sat with Mr. Westerfield. The two men conversed, and as hard as he tried to attend to the conversation, his attention was drawn to his sister and how she was faring with the two ladies.

"You have preserved the elegance of Pemberley, Darcy," Mr.

Westerfield said. "You have much to be proud of."

"Thank you, sir."

"The grounds are well-maintained, and the rooms are a delightful balance of modern and antique furnishings." He laughed. "We all agreed your good parents would be well pleased."

Darcy nodded appreciatively.

"Mr. Darcy, your sister is absolutely delightful!" Mrs. Westerfield said, glancing his way. "She told us of the gift you presented to her earlier. Despite her reserve, which is both charming and sweet, both my daughter and I can see how delighted she is with it... and with you! What a generous brother you are!"

"She is certainly fortunate." Miss Westerfield turned to her mother. "Can you imagine James ever bestowing such a gift on me?"

Both ladies laughed and shook their heads. Mrs. Westerfield looked at Georgiana. "James is Angeline's elder brother, Miss Darcy, and only concerns himself with his sister when absolutely necessary."

"Perhaps Darcy is more like a father figure than a brother to Miss Darcy." Mr. Westerfield turned to Darcy. "Would that not be true?"

"I... I cannot speak for Georgiana as to whether she sees me more as a brother or a father or both, but I highly doubt I could ever replace my father." Darcy began tapping his fingers on the arm of the chair. "And I would not wish to."

"That is perfectly understandable," Mrs. Westerfield said with a pleased nod.

"What do you think of the matter, Miss Darcy?" Miss Westerfield asked. "Do you look upon your brother as such or more like a father?"

All eyes turned to Georgiana. "I... I regret that my brother has had to take on the role of father to me, to have the burden of responsibilities thrust upon him at such a young age."

Darcy's chest tightened, and his jaw clenched when he heard his sister's sentiments.

"I am certain you have never been a burden to him." Miss Westerfield looked at Mr. Darcy. "I doubt you have had to employ your time worrying about her. Am I correct?"

Darcy glanced at Georgiana when she cast her face down, and he then turned back to Miss Westerfield. "While it is true she gives me no reason to worry, I still care for her deeply and intentionally make her my concern."

Miss Westerfield reached over to Georgiana, placing her hand on hers. "You are so fortunate, my dear. One could not ask for a finer brother."

They were soon called in for the meal. While it was a pleasant conversation, Darcy could not help but feel his sister's eyes upon him. She spoke little, and he attributed it to her getting used to the idea that he might soon be married. He unwittingly looked at Miss Westerfield, whose eyes were on him. He smiled, a more nervous than encouraging one. She returned the smile then quickly looked away.

Miss Angeline Westerfield was beautiful, kind, generous, and attentive. She was intelligent and accomplished. What was there not to like about her? A pair of fine, dark eyes suddenly flashed before him. He shook his head, and his fork clattered down onto his plate. That was in the past, and he needed to now consider Miss Westerfield as his future.

~~*

After eating another delicious meal in the privacy of her uncle's room, Elizabeth bade her aunt and uncle goodnight and said she would retire to the adjoining room to read.

"I shall likely join you there tonight, Lizzy. I think Edmund is feeling well enough that he can survive the night without me at his side."

"Uncle, do you truly think you can sleep well knowing she is not at your beck and call?" Elizabeth asked teasingly.

"I am the one who suggested it," her uncle replied.

"No, you did not suggest it," Mrs. Gardiner said. "You demanded it!" She looked back up at Elizabeth. "Since we are just next door, I told him if he has need of anything to rap loudly on the wall."

Elizabeth laughed, kissed her aunt and uncle, and then stepped from the room.

~~*

"No! Please, no! Please do not make me!"

"Elizabeth?" Mrs. Gardiner called out. "Is something wrong? Are you awake?"

"No! I cannot marry you!" Elizabeth cried out. "I must get away before I change my mind!"

"Elizabeth, dear, everything is all right."

Elizabeth heard her aunt's voice and felt her gently shaking her. She opened her eyes, struggling to wake up enough to make sense of what was happening.

Mrs. Gardiner took her niece's hand. "Lizzy, you were having a nightmare. Wake up, dear."

Elizabeth sat up, a little more cognizant of her surroundings. She had no idea what she might have cried aloud, but she certainly knew what had been happening in her dream. Mr. Darcy had discovered her at Pemberley and insisted they marry. But he was not the kind, caring man she had witnessed here and heard so much about, but a demanding and cruel one.

"I am all right, Aunt. I know I was having a dream, but it is odd, as I rarely have nightmares." She laughed slightly. "I suppose it is due to my fear of encountering Mr. Darcy here."

Mrs. Gardiner sat down on the bed next to her and began to pat her hand. "I suppose, but was he the one you were insisting you could not marry?" Now it was her turn to chuckle. "If it was indeed him, I find that interesting. Imagine, you marrying Mr. Darcy!"

Elizabeth groaned and drew her legs up, wrapping her arms about them. She rested her chin on her knees. "Oh, Aunt, I really did not want to tell you this, but now I feel I must." She bit her lip and drew in a breath. "I suppose it will help you understand why I have such a dread of encountering him."

Elizabeth lifted her head. She could barely see her aunt's face lit by the subdued moonlight shining through the window coverings. That was probably best so she would not see her aunt's expression when she told her what had happened in Kent.

55

She stretched out her legs and reached over to grasp her aunt's hand. "I know you and my uncle have felt that my uneasiness about being discovered here by Mr. Darcy has been foolish, unreasonable, and perhaps a little immature."

"We merely felt he would think nothing of it. You seem to think that by having had a slight acquaintance with him he would consider it wrong or improper for you to be here."

Elizabeth looked down and shook her head. "Oh, Aunt, if only we had been mere acquaintances."

"Lizzy? What are you saying? What happened?" Her voice reflected her concern.

"He..." She looked up and drew in a deep breath. "Oh, Aunt, he apparently had developed rather strong feelings of admiration for me. He...he came to me one day at the parsonage in Kent and declared that he was... that he was ardently in love with me." Elizabeth lifted her eyes and despite the darkness of the room could readily see the stunned look on her aunt's face. She chuckled. "I can see that you do not believe it, either. I was just as astonished as you now are when he made me an offer of marriage."

Her aunt's eyes narrowed. Very softly she said, "I see. Go on."

Elizabeth shrugged. "It was the last thing I would have ever expected from him and..." She pursed her lips together tightly.

When she did not continue, her aunt asked, "How did you answer him, Lizzy?" She suddenly let out a gasp. "You did not refuse him, did you?"

Elizabeth mutely nodded. She was surprised when a surge of regret passed through her. "Yes, I had to."

"Oh, dear!" Mrs. Gardiner abruptly stood up and crossed her arms about her. "I think I need to walk."

Elizabeth watched her aunt pace about the room, knowing there was so much more she had to say.

Finally, she said, "Aunt, there is something else."

Mrs. Gardiner stopped walking. "Yes?"

"Not only did I refuse him, I was..." She drew in a breath. "I was rather indignant to him in my refusal."

Mrs. Gardiner came back to the edge of the bed. "I think I need to sit down."

Elizabeth took her aunt's hand. "Are you all right, Aunt?"

Her aunt nodded quickly several times but no words came forth.

"I cannot make any rational excuse now, but in addition to those things that had prompted my initial dislike of him, there were some things that I had just come to learn about him that had angered me greatly."

"What kind of things?" her aunt asked softly.

"Well, in addition to his treatment of Mr. Wickham, which I told you about, I had just been informed by his cousin that Mr. Darcy had been proud of the fact that he had been a great influence in separating Mr. Bingley from Jane."

Mrs. Gardiner opened her mouth with a look of surprise. "It was *his* doing?"

Elizabeth nodded. "His and Miss Bingley's doing."

"So, you let him know how you felt about that?"

Elizabeth nodded. "How could I not?" Elizabeth began to pull a strand of her hair through her fingers. "There was also the manner in which he proposed. Although he declared his love and admiration for me, he told me that despite all of his efforts, it had been impossible for him to conquer his attachment to me, someone he had considered to be greatly inferior to him." Elizabeth paused and winced. "While he had spoken warmly to me, as if that might somehow soften any offense I might feel, I was unable to think reasonably on the matter. I lashed out at him in anger, refused him, and…"

"And what?"

Elizabeth frowned. "I told him he had acted in a most ungentlemanly manner and that he was the last man I could ever be prevailed upon to marry."

Mrs. Gardiner's eyes widened. "I see. Well, this explains why you have not wanted to encounter him. I imagine he was angered by your answer."

"Indeed."

"I imagine he was not expecting you to refuse him, was he not?" She said it as more of a statement rather than a question.

Elizabeth paused to consider this. "No, I imagine not; yet, while he was not expecting a refusal, I had not been expecting a proposal." She shook her head. "I had no idea of his strong regard."

Mrs. Gardiner smiled. "I suppose the man had never found himself in love before and was not certain of the right way to go about letting his feelings be known."

"Or the right way to propose to a woman." Elizabeth sighed. "If only he had given me some indication of his feelings…"

"But would you have welcomed them?"

Elizabeth looked down and shook her head. "Certainly not. But if he had, I could have politely discouraged him instead of ruining his hopes and dreams as I did when he…" Her voice trailed off.

"But Lizzy, I sense you feel some regret now. Have your feelings towards him changed?"

Elizabeth lifted her eyes. "The next morning I encountered him while out walking. He had purposely come in the hopes of seeing me and presented me with a letter explaining some of the things of which I had accused him."

"Lizzy! Mr. Darcy gave you a letter! If anyone had seen it…"

"No one did, Aunt. We were a good distance from anyone and anything." She took in a raspy breath as tears filled her eyes. "In reading it, I realized how wrong I had been about him in so many ways. I regretted… I deeply regretted the manner in which I refused him."

"How were your assumptions wrong?"

Elizabeth also explained that one of Mr. Darcy's reasons for separating Mr. Bingley from her sister was because he had not observed any outward signs that Jane loved him as strongly as Bingley did her. "For that I could almost forgive him," she said with a chuckle.

She then told her that she had not been aware of the truth about Mr. Wickham when he proposed.

Mrs. Gardiner drew in a breath. "Well, my dear. This does explain a few things." She took Elizabeth's hands. "Lizzy, I know you must have had your reasons, but why did you not feel as though you could tell your uncle and me of this? Especially when we suggested coming here."

"The only person I told was Jane. I think if you had not held such a favourable opinion of the Darcy family I may have, but how could I tell you he asked for my hand in marriage and I refused him?"

Mrs. Gardiner gave her a compassionate nod. "We would have understood, Lizzy."

Elizabeth let out a long sigh. "And yet to this day, I do not." She looked up at her aunt. "I do feel a great deal of regret over what I said and did." She began to shake her head. "Not that I feel I should have accepted him, but that perhaps I ought to have made an attempt to understand him better before responding as I did."

Mrs. Gardiner took Elizabeth's hand. "Well, Lizzy, what is done is done. We cannot change the past." She squeezed her hand. "We can only hope that you have learned something from what happened." She smiled. "Perhaps he did, as well."

~~*

That morning, when Mrs. Gardiner had dressed and left to check on her husband, Elizabeth remained in her room, knowing that her aunt was going to tell him what she had been told the night before. When she felt enough time had passed for her aunt to furnish him with the details, she carefully opened the door, looked out to see if anyone – particularly Mr. Darcy – was in the vicinity, and walked to her uncle's room.

Her uncle greeted her when she walked in. "Well, hello, Lizzy. Your aunt has been telling me an extraordinary tale that I find rather hard to believe. Did she imagine all of this or is it true? Could it have possibly been just a dream?" He let out a hearty chuckle, but then leaned his head back in pain. "I have to remember that it hurts when I laugh."

Elizabeth gave her uncle a weak smile. "Please take care, Uncle. And yes, it is all true. I could never have made up a story like that."

"And neither could I!" declared her aunt.

Elizabeth looked apologetically at her uncle and waited for him to say something. He seemed to be contemplating his next words.

"I am not going to admonish you for refusing him, Lizzy, for everything you knew – or thought you knew – about him was what you had witnessed. His behaviour and his actions all combined to make up the man you believed him to be."

Elizabeth silently nodded.

"I wonder what you think of the man now, though. In seeing his home and in hearing the praises of his housekeeper, has your estimation of him at all changed?"

Elizabeth drew in a long breath. "I own that from the moment we saw the house from the carriage, I was gripped with a realization – almost as strong as a jolt of physical pain – that this could have been my home." She slowly shook her head and cast her eyes down. "But still at that moment, I felt no regret in refusing him."

"And since then?"

She walked to the window and gazed out. Her heart skipped as she saw Mr. Darcy step out into the courtyard. It was apparent he was going out walking or riding, something he had done with frequency in the mornings while at Netherfield and in Kent. When she saw him stop and turn, offering his arm, she waited, hoping to see Miss Darcy. Instead, she saw Miss Westerfield, who seemed delighted to take it.

She shook her head and looked at her uncle. "Pray, forgive me. What did you ask?"

"Since coming here, have your feelings changed?"

"Oh, I do not know!" she cried out. "I have heard him spoken of with words so full of praise and admiration and even witnessed some of that myself that I do not know what I think anymore." She glanced out the window again and sighed. "As beautiful as Pemberley is, however, if he were truly as disagreeable as I had believed him to be, I could not regret my refusing him." She shrugged. "Besides, I am certain he must still despise me for all I said to him… that day."

Mrs. Gardiner walked over to her and placed her hands on her niece's shoulders. "Perhaps not, my dear." Looking out, she asked, "Is that Mr. Darcy, and who is with him?"

Elizabeth drew in a shaky breath and let it out slowly. "That is Miss Westerfield, and I believe she is here because Mr. Darcy intends to make her his wife."

"I see." She nodded her head towards another woman who had

stepped out. "And I assume that woman is their chaperone." She returned to her husband's side. "Well, Lizzy, we likely have only a few more days here. Once the doctor gives his approval for Edmund to travel, we shall be gone."

"Yes," Elizabeth said softly. "We shall be gone."

~~*

Later that afternoon, the doctor came by to check on Mr. Gardiner. He was not pleased with the pain level the gentleman was still experiencing.

"It is possible the injury was more than just a small fracture. Just as a precaution I am going to recommend bed rest for another day just to make sure. If you move even a little, it could worsen."

Elizabeth was disappointed. She was not only tired of staying out of one gentleman's sight, she was restless and wished she could go out for a walk. But she did not dare.

Miss Darcy arrived soon after the doctor departed.

"May I come in?" she said when she came to the door.

"Please do!" Mrs. Gardiner replied.

"What did the doctor say?" she asked. "I noticed he did not stay long. I hope Mr. Gardiner received good news."

"He wants him to continue to remain inactive for another day," Mrs. Gardiner said. "We shall have to impose on your gracious hospitality a little longer."

Georgiana clasped her hands. "Oh, please, it is no imposition at all! Do not think anything of it!"

Elizabeth smiled. "You are too kind, Miss Darcy."

Georgiana smiled and pursed her lips, seemingly at a loss to know what to say next.

"Tell me, Miss Darcy. What do you do to occupy yourself when you are here at Pemberley?" Elizabeth watched her eyes light up when she asked the question.

"Oh, I love to play the pianoforte, and just yesterday my brother presented me with a surprise for my birthday. A new instrument!"

"It is lovely!" Elizabeth said. "Your housekeeper showed it to us as we toured the home."

"I could not believe it. I was not expecting it at all. Sometimes he does the most unexpected things!" Her face brightened with a smile. "The pianoforte that I had been playing had been here since before my father was born, I believe." She laughed softly. "It was getting more and more difficult to keep it tuned for any length of time."

"You must have been delighted with it," Mrs. Gardiner said.

"Yes, I was. He is so very generous."

Elizabeth readily noticed the look of admiration on the young lady's face.

"I spent all morning playing. Did you not hear me?"

"No, unfortunately we did not," Elizabeth said. "I would love to hear you play sometime."

"Would you like to come up and hear me play now?" Miss Darcy turned to Elizabeth. "I am not used to performing before many people, but I need the practice. A smaller audience is easier for me than a larger one."

"Why, that would be…" her aunt began.

Elizabeth took the young lady's hand. "What my aunt is trying to say, Miss Darcy, is that is very kind of you to ask, but we ought to remain with my uncle. He is still in much pain, and besides, I would not wish… we do not want to disturb… the household."

"I understand," Miss Darcy said softly. "I wish I could do something to make your stay more enjoyable. It must be such tedium to remain in your rooms. I want to assure you that you are more than welcome to stroll about the house or the grounds. We truly do not mind."

Elizabeth felt her aunt and uncle's eyes fall on her. "Miss Darcy, you are very kind. But I think my aunt and I would prefer to remain near Mr. Gardiner."

"Here you are, Miss Darcy! I am so glad to have finally found you." The sound of a young lady's voice drew everyone's attention to the door. Elizabeth tensed when she saw that it was Miss Westerfield.

"Were you in need of something?" Georgiana asked.

"Oh, no," she said. "I merely wondered where you were. Mrs. Reynolds directed me here. Your brother is busy with his steward in the library, and I thought it would be nice to spend some time together. But I see you are engaged."

"I came to see how Mr. Gardiner was doing." Georgiana introduced Miss Westerfield to the Gardiners and explained a little about Mr. Gardiner's condition.

"I am so sorry to hear about your fall," Miss Westerfield said. "What does the doctor say?"

"Unfortunately, my husband cannot be moved, and traveling is out of the question for now," Mrs. Gardiner said. "The jostling of the carriage for even just a short distance could possibly worsen the injury."

"How unfortunate this must be for all of you, but I am certain Pemberley's staff is taking good care of you." Miss Westerfield clasped her hands.

"Indeed they are! I am being treated almost as if I were royalty," Mr. Gardiner said with a laugh, followed by a slight moan. "But I need to remember that even something as simple as laughing causes me great pain."

"We ought to leave so you can rest," Georgiana said. "Again, please do not hesitate to let us know if you need anything."

"Thank you, Miss Darcy," Mrs. Gardiner said. "It was a pleasure to meet you, Miss Westerfield."

Both young ladies smiled and nodded and slipped quietly from the room.

When they were gone, Mrs. Gardiner turned to her niece. "So that is Miss Westerfield."

Elizabeth nodded. "She is very pretty and seems most genteel."

"I do not think her exceptionally pretty," Mr. Gardiner said with a smile.

"Be kind, Edmund," Mrs. Gardiner said with a pointed look.

"Hmm?" her husband asked, shaking his head. "I truly do not see what Mr. Darcy would see in her... compared to our Lizzy."

"Oh, Uncle Gardiner, please. She is probably more suitable for him than I ever was." Elizabeth's brows unwittingly pinched in thought. *Whatever did he see in me? I certainly am not as attractive as she is.* His words at the Meryton Assembly struck her forcefully. *She is tolerable, I suppose, but not handsome enough to tempt me.*

What was it that had brought about a change in how he saw her? She shook her head, knowing she might never know.

Chapter 6

The next morning, when her aunt left to check on Mr. Gardiner, Elizabeth sat at the window looking out, hoping for another glimpse of Mr. Darcy. She told herself it was merely to see if Miss Westerfield was again accompanying him, but if she owned the truth, she really wanted to see only him. She shook her head, incredulous that such a thought crossed her mind, considering how she once felt about him.

The day before, she had not had any unexpected encounter with him prompting her to hide. She had only espied him from the window when he and Miss Westerfield set out walking. She could not justify the feelings for him that were building up inside of her. Her head and heart argued over who this man was and how she ought to feel about him. She did not want to see him, yet she desperately wanted to see him! She was a hopeless – and unreasonable – case!

At length, he stepped out into the courtyard, giving rise to the same feelings she experienced each time she had seen him since coming here. This time Miss Westerfield was already on his arm, and it appeared she was laughing. The beautiful young lady was looking up at him, and to Elizabeth's dismay, she felt a stab of envy. She crossed her arms tightly about her, as if that would crush the feelings that assaulted her, but to no avail.

She could not turn her eyes away from them. She watched as their chaperone stepped out again, and she thought back to the walks they had taken in Kent. Although they had been unplanned, they had been very much unchaperoned. She wondered if it was Miss Westerfield or Mr. Darcy who requested they be chaperoned. She watched until they disappeared from sight around to the front of the manor.

From everything she had seen and heard, it appeared as though his affections were now directed towards the young lady, and Elizabeth wondered if he was going to offer for her soon. It was likely the reason he had invited the family to Pemberley.

At length, she joined her aunt and uncle in his room. She felt restless, and her thoughts were in turmoil. She was unsure how much longer she would be able to endure staying here, having begun to recognize Mr. Darcy's true character and how wrong she had been about him. And now it was too late.

The doctor came by later that morning and was pleased with Mr. Gardiner's progress and his slight improvement and diminishing pain.

"It is not everyone who can sit idly by, even when I strongly adjure them to," Mr. Holmes said. "I can see that although you are in pain, it has lessened. So I shall now allow you to walk short distances. I want you to begin slowly. Feel free to start by walking about the room, and if your pain is not too severe, you can extend your walks down the hallway. You will need to be your own judge, as to whether doing so may cause you further harm."

"I most certainly can do that!" Mr. Gardiner replied, and with a laugh, he added, "Gladly!"

The doctor nodded. "First, let me observe as you take your first steps to see how well you endure it."

Mr. Holmes watched as Mr. Gardiner took a few tentative steps. "How does your back feel?" he asked.

Mr. Gardiner closed his eyes and slowly gave his head a nod. "It certainly hurts, but I can tell it is not as painful as before."

"Cracked ribs are indeed extremely painful. We shall leave the wrap around your chest and back for a few more days to help with support."

When the doctor left, Mr. Gardiner carefully sat down on the bed. "Oh, the joys of being able to move about!"

Elizabeth laughed. "I would have been one of those patients he was talking about who would not be able to obey his instructions. I cannot imagine lying prone in bed for so many days."

Mr. Gardiner took her hand. "Lizzy, if you were in as much pain as I was, I can guarantee that you would not wish to move about."

At that moment, Miss Darcy stepped in. "Mr. Gardiner! You are sitting on the edge of the bed! I saw Mr. Holmes leave. Has he given approval to move about?"

"He most certainly has, and I even walked a little about the room."

"I am delighted," she said.

"As we all are," Elizabeth said. "As much as we have appreciated all you have done for us, we are eager to leave and begin our journey home."

"I can fully understand that it must be difficult staying in someone else's home." She smiled at them. "It is not often that I have had to step into the role of Mistress of Pemberley, and I want to thank you for making it very easy for me." She clasped her hands and looked down. "I may not have the opportunity to do so much longer, for there is likely another who will soon..." She paused. "Well, I thank you for being so patient with me."

"That is very kind of you to say," Mrs. Gardiner said, stealing a quick glance at Elizabeth, giving her a sympathetic smile.

"I would hope all our guests – whether invited or here by accident – would display the same kindness and courtesy that you have towards me, my brother, and our staff."

"We would hope so, as well," Mr. Gardiner said. "Who would not, considering the excellent care and attention received?"

"Thank you," Miss Darcy said. "I hope you enjoy your day." She smiled and then looked at Mr. Gardiner. "And you. Mr. Gardiner, please have a care. I do not want to see you running through the halls on your first day back on your feet."

"Well!" he uttered in retort. "After paying her a compliment, the young lady thinks she can order me about!"

"It is for your own good!" Elizabeth said with a smile and turned to Miss Darcy. "Pay him no mind. I think he is getting a little restless and some short walks will likely do him a great deal of good!"

Miss Darcy smiled. "I shall check in later to see how you are doing. Have a delightful day."

When Miss Darcy stepped from the room, both the Gardiners turned to look at Elizabeth.

"How are you, Lizzy?" Mrs. Gardiner asked. "I know what you were thinking when she spoke of another becoming Mistress of Pemberley."

Elizabeth nodded briefly. "It is obvious Miss Darcy expects Miss Westerfield will soon become Mistress of Pemberley."

Elizabeth quickly turned and faced the window. "There is naught for me to do about it now. He offered it to me, and I turned him down." She hoped her aunt and uncle did not see the tears begin to well up in her eyes.

~~*

Darcy was in the library reading when a servant came in carrying a salver.

"Sir, a letter has come from the Inn at Lambton for the young lady who is here with her aunt and uncle."

Darcy looked up. "Thank you. Put it here." He pointed to the corner of his desk. "I shall see that she gets it."

"Yes, sir."

Darcy dismissed the servant and leaned back in his chair to finish reading his book. He looked at the small pile of books on his desk from which Georgiana's book had disappeared and then later miraculously reappeared. He shook his head, wondering if one of the maids had taken it to read. He could not imagine one of them doing such a thing, but it would explain its disappearance.

His eyes narrowed as he considered that ever since returning to Pemberley, odd things had been happening. First there was the bonnet floating leisurely down the stream, then finding out about the gentleman who had fallen, the noise in the infirmary room and the lavender fabric he could see on the other side of the bed, and then the book disappearing and then reappearing. He blew out a puff of air. Hopefully these odd occurrences would not continue, or at least he would discover a logical explanation for them.

He rubbed his temple as he considered Mrs. Wickham's condition. He had heard it had deteriorated during the night and that Wickham had finally arrived. He shuddered to think that the man was so near Pemberley again, although five miles away, in the home of his sister's family. It was certainly not the best timing for this to have happened, with Georgiana's returning to Pemberley after being gone so long, as well as the arrival of his guests. He ought to pay Mrs. Wickham another call, but he dreaded doing so with her son now there.

He stood up to stretch his legs and walked over to look out the window. A grey pall hung over the land, and it appeared that it might rain. It had been hot and dry lately, so he hoped he was right. He and Miss Westerfield had taken a shorter walk that morning as she feared the rains would descend and soak them.

"Fitzwilliam?"

Darcy turned around. "Hello, Georgiana. What can I do for you?"

"Nothing in particular. Where are the Westerfields?"

"Miss Westerfield is resting." He smiled. "I think perhaps our walks these two mornings fatigued her."

"And you so enjoy walking."

Darcy nodded. "Yes, but as it is something I have often done in solitude, it matters not whether she enjoys the activity to the extent that I do." He shrugged and rubbed his jaw. He suddenly saw an image of Elizabeth walking the grounds around Rosings with him. He quickly shook his head as if to dismiss the image from his mind.

"I am enjoying the book you picked out for me."

"Good. I am glad." He shook his head. "I am glad – as well as surprised – it made a reappearance."

She drew in a long breath. "I just came from visiting with the Gardiners."

Darcy nodded and smiled. "How is Mr. Gardiner faring? Has he seen the doctor yet today?"

"Yes. Mr. Holmes was just leaving when I stopped by. He gave Mr. Gardiner permission to walk short distances, taking care not to put any strain on his back."

"I am glad to hear that. I am certain he is eager to get up and about."

Georgiana nodded. "He was able to walk around the room and hopes to walk up and down the halls if he feels well enough to do so. I told them they are free to walk about the home, but they do not seem so inclined. I had a nice visit with them and their niece."

"Oh, that reminds me. I have a letter here for her that was brought over from the Inn at Lambton." Darcy walked over to his desk and picked it up. When he looked down at the letter, he abruptly stopped, his eyes widened, and he gasped.

"What is it, Fitzwilliam? Is something wrong?"

His heart pounded so strongly in his chest, he could barely move. He turned to look at his sister, attempting to formulate a single thought. He raked his fingers through his hair and then covered his mouth with his hand. He shook his head and lowered his hand. "I... I am a little confused." He looked up at Georgiana. "What is... what is the niece's name?"

"Miss Gardiner. Why do you ask?" She walked over to him. "Brother, what is it? What is wrong? I can see by your face that something is not right."

Darcy was silent for a moment, taking in slow breaths. Finally, he said, "Georgiana, I am well. But tell me, for I have not yet met the niece. How would you describe her?"

Georgiana looked at him curiously, but replied, "She looks to be about twenty years old, about my height, and has very dark chestnut hair. She is very kind, intelligent, and witty."

Darcy turned and walked to the window again. "And her first name? Do you know what her first name is?"

"Elizabeth, but I have also heard her aunt call her Lizzy." She walked over to her brother. "Can you tell me what is wrong? I am beginning to worry."

He silently held out the letter to Georgiana. "This is addressed to Miss Elizabeth Bennet."

She looked down at the letter. "I do not understand. We were all under the impression her name was..." Her eyes suddenly widened. "Fitzwilliam! Is this not the name of the young lady who..."

Darcy solemnly nodded.

"Perhaps it is another Miss Bennet with the same name."

Darcy shook his head. "Not unless another one also has a sister named Jane Bennet who lives at Longbourn." He pointed to the sender's name and address.

"There must be some mistake."

"I cannot see how it is a mistake. You have described Miss Bennet perfectly, and this... this..." He could not finish.

"You are certain it is her? This could be why she has been so reluctant to leave her room. She most likely did not want you to know she was here. What are you going to do?"

Darcy's jaw clenched. Finally, he said, "I do not know what I am going to do." His breathing faltered, and he shook his head.

"Brother, please take care. I know how distressed you were when she refused you. I was so worried about you."

"There is no need to fear that I am going to lose my heart again, Georgiana." He looked back down at the letter. "I cannot imagine going through that again."

"Are you going to take her the letter?"

He crossed his arms. "No, I am not. I cannot see her yet. I need to... I need to get out and walk or ride... or something. I need to think and regulate my thoughts and..." He drew in a long breath and did not finish. "You take it to her, but do not tell her what I said to you if she asks... which she probably will when she realizes that I most likely know." He looked at her intently. "Please, do not tell her that *you* know who she is." He paused. "It is for the best."

"What do I tell her?"

Darcy pounded his chin with his fist, and then put his hand on Georgiana's shoulder. "You may tell her I gave you the letter. That is enough."

"And what do you intend to do? I mean, about her being here?"

Darcy shook his head. "I suppose that depends on how she reacts to knowing I now know she is here. She will realize that when she gets the letter." He gave his sister a kiss on the cheek. "I shall be gone for an hour or two. I have much to think about and consider."

~~*

Elizabeth sat in her room reading, and a light tap at the door startled her. She had to stop fearing it was Mr. Darcy at every turn. Even so, she paused before opening it.

"Who is it?"

"Miss Darcy."

Elizabeth opened the door. "Miss Darcy! What a surprise!"

"Your aunt told me you were in here."

"And so I am. What can I do for you?"

Miss Darcy drew in a breath. "A letter came for you that

originally had been sent to the Inn at Lambton. They brought it here." She held it out to her.

Elizabeth looked at it and smiled. "Oh, good! It is from my sister. I have been waiting to hear from her." She looked at the address and chuckled. "No wonder it has been so long since I received a letter from her. Jane wrote the address wrong, and when it finally arrived at the Inn at Lambton, they had to forward it to me here."

Her eyes widened, and she suddenly gasped. "Oh, dear!" She placed her fingers over her mouth and turned away. She froze, unable to move as she stared down at her name.

"What is it?" Georgiana asked.

"Nothing, nothing." Elizabeth waved her hand through the air. "Miss Darcy, may I ask who… or how you came by this letter?" She attempted to ask in an indifferent manner, but she knew her voice cracked. She looked up at the girl attempting to read her expression.

"My brother asked me to bring it to you," Miss Darcy replied. "Why? Is something wrong?"

Elizabeth felt her face warm and she stood up and walked to the window. "No. No, it is just… Did he… did he say anything when he gave it to you?"

"Only that we had both been under the misapprehension that your last name was Gardiner."

Elizabeth gripped the sill of the window to help steady her. "Oh?" She took in a shaky breath and let it out in a nervous laugh. "I can understand how that could happen." Elizabeth shook her head. "That is all he said?"

"He said nothing more than that he was going to go out and walk or ride for a few hours as he had some things to think about."

"I see." Her hands trembled as she tried to determine what to do. She shook her head as her stomach knotted, and she felt numb. *What must he be thinking?* she wondered as she looked down at the letter again. *He now knows I am here.*

"I imagine you enjoy getting letters from your sister. I always wished I had a sister."

"She and I are… she is not only a dear sister, but a dear friend."

Elizabeth looked up and tried to smile.

Miss Darcy seemed to intently regard her for a moment and then said, "I shall leave you now so you can read your letter."

Elizabeth looked at Georgiana, attempting to smile away the distress that was likely written all over her face. "Oh, yes. Thank you, Miss Darcy."

Georgiana began to back out the door. "Good day, Miss Bennet."

Elizabeth gave her a resigned smile. As she stepped out, Elizabeth called out. "Miss Darcy!"

She turned. "Yes?"

"You said your... your brother has gone out?" She hoped Miss Darcy had not noticed the quaver in her voice.

Georgiana nodded.

Elizabeth straightened her shoulders, and with a renewed sense of determination, looked at the young girl. "I desperately need to get out and walk. I have spent too many days indoors. Do you think anyone would mind?"

Miss Darcy's face lit up in a smile. "Not at all! And if you do not mind my accompanying you, I would be more than happy to show you the gardens. They are lovely and are, in fact, my favourite places to walk."

"I should like that very much. We were on our way to see the grounds and the gardens when my uncle fell and thus were prevented from seeing them."

"Splendid! If you do not mind, I need to stay near the house. I am having a dress altered and will need to try it on once the alterations have been finished."

"I do not mind at all, Miss Darcy." She placed Jane's letter on her bed. "I shall read this later."

Elizabeth made a few quick preparations before going outside, steeling herself for an eventual encounter that was now inevitable. The two ladies stopped by Mr. Gardiner's room so Elizabeth could tell her aunt and uncle that she and Miss Darcy would be out walking. Elizabeth smiled at the look of astonishment on their faces.

When they stepped outside, Elizabeth breathed in deeply. "Oh, it is good to be outside. I have missed it." Surprisingly, she felt better already.

Georgiana tilted her head and looked at Elizabeth. "You would have been more than welcome to walk the grounds at any time, Miss Bennet. No one would have minded."

Elizabeth turned to meet Miss Darcy's gaze. "You are too kind. I just... I really did not want to impose."

Georgiana looked up to the sky. "I hope it does not start to rain. I would like to show you the main garden in the front of the manor, and then take you to the more private rose garden we have on the far side. It is a lovely place to sit... if you enjoy that kind of thing."

"I should like that very much."

They walked around to the front of the home and began strolling amidst the flowers and shrubbery. Elizabeth delighted in the variety of flowers and colours. Georgiana pointed out some of her favourites.

When they finished walking through the main garden, Georgiana suggested they hurry to see the rose garden as it looked like rain was imminent. At that moment, Mrs. Reynolds called out from the front door.

"Miss Darcy, they are ready for your fitting."

She turned to Elizabeth and grasped her hands. "Oh, I am sorry I cannot accompany you any further. If you would like to see the rose garden, it is just beyond that low row of shrubbery." She pointed in the direction she was to go. "There is a potting shed at one end. You cannot miss it."

"Thank you, Miss Darcy. I appreciate this very much."

Elizabeth hurried over to the rose garden, despite feeling the intermittent rain drops that had begun to sprinkle down on her.

When she approached the enclosed rose garden, she stopped. It was a delightful secluded area with benches scattered about. Again there was a variety of roses and colours, some in hues she had never seen before. The rosebushes radiated out in rows from a small pond, located in the centre. She began walking about, working her way through the garden as she admired the beautiful colours and leaned over to breathe in the delightful and myriad fragrances.

As the rain began to pelt her with larger, more frequent drops, she decided she ought to return to the house. At that moment, there was a crack of lightning, followed almost immediately by a loud boom of thunder, which seemed to unleash the waters from the heavens. Elizabeth thought momentarily to run for the house, despite the distance, but noticing the door to the garden shed was open, decided to take cover there.

She hurried over, and with her head down, she threw herself into the shed. She shook off some of the water and when she looked up, she saw a gentleman sitting there, facing away from her.

He turned quickly and looked at her. When his eyes met hers, she gasped and trembled.

"Mr. Darcy!"

Chapter 7

"Miss Bennet!" Mr. Darcy visibly started when he looked over and saw her, his eyes widening. His hand instantly jerked, causing something to fall to the floor. "Ow!" he said as he immediately grabbed his hand.

"Oh, no!" Elizabeth cried, seeing a stream of blood drip onto the floor. She frantically looked about, and seeing some folded cloths nearby, seized one, and hurried back. Her fingers adeptly wrapped the cloth tightly about the wound as Darcy carefully pulled his other hand away. "Oh, dear, I fear it may be a deep cut." She pressed the cloth against it and tried to order her thoughts. She took a deep breath as her head tilted up and her eyes met his intense gaze.

He brought his free hand tentatively over hers, which still held the cloth tightly. "I think I can manage from here," he said.

Realizing she was still grasping his hand, she released it quickly, stepping back. "Oh yes, certainly." Her fingers began to shake, and she clasped her hands tightly together. Her face warmed when she realized the man in front of her wore no coat, no neckcloth, and the sleeves of his shirt were rolled up his arm.

She did not know what more to say or where to look. He did not seem inclined to say anything but merely kept his gaze on her. She felt the intensity of his gaze and cast her eyes down. Noticing her wet dress, she gasped and pressed her hand to her neck. "Oh, dear! I must look a fright!"

Darcy started. "Pray, forgive me! My coat is over there, if you would like to… I would… I fear you will need to…" He lifted both hands and gave a slight shrug.

"Oh, yes! Thank you! I can get it." She gave her head a shake as she walked over to pick up his coat and threw it over her shoulders. "Again, I am so sorry. I seem to be causing injury at every turn." She pulled the coat around her.

"I think I will survive." His eyes narrowed. "Do you blame yourself for your uncle's fall?"

Elizabeth let out a soft moan. "I had turned back to look…" She felt a sudden warmth in her cheeks. "I had turned away and did not see that he had stopped at the top of the staircase. I collided into him when I stepped forward, and he fell down."

"I see."

Elizabeth's heart pounded so strongly, and coupled with the rain pelting down on the roof, she could barely hear herself think. "Mr. Darcy, I pray you will forgive my intrusion. I was looking at the gardens. Miss Darcy… your sister had been showing them to me, but she was called in, and I came over to see the rose garden. When it began to rain, I saw the shed and thought it best that I take cover in here." She paused and drew in a breath, wondering whether she was making any sense. Her thoughts seemed to be in a muddle, and more so, her words. "I am deeply sorry."

He nodded slowly, dropping his eyes back to his hand.

Elizabeth closed her eyes briefly and looked away. "I know you… I know you must have become aware of the fact that I was here when the letter was brought for me from the Inn at Lambton. No doubt you must have been surprised to discover I was here."

"I was."

"I know what you must be thinking…" she said softly.

"Do you?" He looked up abruptly, and his eyes met hers.

Elizabeth felt her stomach lurch at his words, and she could not find the strength or willpower to pull her gaze away from his. The biting tone of his voice and the challenging look on his face caused her breath to catch in her throat. She trembled and did not know if she was chilled from being wet or because of the way he was looking at her. If she only knew what he was thinking – and feeling – it would make things so much easier for her.

"Well, actually no, I do not. I… I can only imagine what you must be thinking, and I want you to know, Mr. Darcy, that I am so very sorry. I did everything in my power to discourage my aunt and uncle from coming here. My aunt grew up in Lambton, you see, and while we were visiting her friends there, she so much wanted to see Pemberley again. She had such fond memories, and…" Her voice trailed off.

"There is no need to apologize, Miss Bennet." He checked the wound again, seeing it was still bleeding. "Or should I say, Miss

Gardiner?" He lifted a brow as he glanced up at her.

Elizabeth grimaced. "I thought perhaps…" She shook her head. "I allowed that misapprehension in the hopes that my presence here would not be discovered."

"I see."

"Again, I am so sorry."

"And as I said, there is no need to apologize."

"No, I suppose not, but please allow me to apologize for startling you and causing this injury. I hope it is not serious."

"I think I shall live. It is a hazard of the job," he said, drawing in a quick breath.

"Job? What is it you are doing in here?"

He reached down and picked up the object that had fallen. "I am attempting to carve a piece of wood into what hopefully will look like a bird when it is finished."

"I have seen some wood-carved birds around the house. Did you do them?"

"They are not all mine, but I have made many of them," he said with a nod.

Elizabeth could not prevent the teasing smile that appeared, feeling somewhat more at ease. "I was not aware that wood carving was one of the fine accomplishments of an esteemed gentleman."

Darcy lifted his brow, and with it, his eyes to her. "An accomplishment, perhaps, but not necessarily that of an *esteemed* gentleman."

She felt her cheeks grow warm. She looked down at the piece of wood in his hands. "What kind of bird is this going to be?"

"A falcon."

"Ah, I think I can see it. Your work is superb." Elizabeth nervously knitted her fingers together as she looked back to the open door. Noticing the intensity of the rain, she let out a soft huff, knowing she would not be able to leave for a while. She turned back to Mr. Darcy. "If you do not mind my asking, how long have you carved wood?"

Darcy looked at the piece of wood he held in his hand. "Since I was about eight years old. A very wise gentleman used to carve wood, and I would often watch him. One day he asked me if I would like to learn, and I told him I would."

"I am impressed."

It was Darcy's turn to shrug his shoulders. "It has proven to be an excellent way for me to deal with the heavy burdens and responsibilities that came upon me at an early age. He was very wise, for he taught me that I must learn to control my actions with the knife, no matter how I was feeling on the inside."

Elizabeth looked away, realizing her unexpected appearance had likely caused him to lose control of the knife and injure himself. She slowly looked back at him. "It appears you were an excellent student."

"He was an excellent teacher."

Elizabeth watched his eyes darken. "Did he work at Pemberley? Was he one of the gardeners?"

Darcy pressed his lips into a thin line. Very softly, he said, "He was my father's steward."

Elizabeth's eyes widened. "Mr. Wickham?"

He nodded. "He tried to teach his son, as well, but even as a boy, Wickham was not interested in learning patience and self-control." He shook his head. "The late Mr. Wickham was a fine gentleman, but unfortunately, his son is nothing like he was." He looked at Elizabeth as if waiting for her response.

Elizabeth realized Darcy would not know if she ever read his letter detailing Wickham's character. She did not want to bring up the letter – or anything that happened in Kent – so she merely said, "It is unfortunate he turned out like he did when his father was so good."

Darcy drew in a long breath. "Unfortunately, he took on the less admirable characteristics of his mother." He shook his head. "She always wanted to live above what they could afford and was never satisfied."

"As does Mr. Wickham." It was silent for a moment, and then she said, "Did you carve the owl that is in the library? It is magnificent!"

He tilted his head and narrowed his eyes. "I did, but... you were in the library?"

"I..." Elizabeth's shoulders drooped, and she gave her head a resigned shake. "Yes, I was in the library. It is beautiful. What I would give to have…" She drew in a sharp breath as she stopped herself from continuing. She felt her cheeks warm again and hoped he would not realize what she was going to say. In noticing his stiffening posture, however, she was certain he had.

She struggled for something else to say. "You may as well know, Mr. Darcy. I was behind the middle wall of shelves when you brought your sister in to give her the book you had purchased for her." She shrugged her shoulders. "I am to blame for its disappearance. I was actually holding it in my hand."

"And you did not feel you ought to step out, announce yourself, and return the book to me so I could give it to my sister?"

A pang of guilt overtook Elizabeth. "I… I did not want you to see me," she said softly.

"I see." Darcy looked at the wound again and covered it back up quickly. "And then you replaced the book later so it was there again when I returned."

"Yes," she laughed nervously. "I could not keep it, knowing…" She nervously waved her hand.

Darcy began to nod his head. "So all along I believed I was imagining things… or not in my right mind."

"I am sorry." She swallowed as a lump formed in her throat. "If you do not mind my asking, in addition to the finished owl in the library, I noticed an unfinished bird on your desk sitting on some papers. Is that another bird you are working on?"

Darcy's eyes shot up, and his brows lowered slightly. He licked his lips and said, "It was going to be a… magpie."

"Truly? A magpie?" She smiled, but it quickly disappeared. "Why do you say it was *going* to be a magpie? Do you not intend to finish it?"

A frown appeared as he seemed to search for words. "I am not certain. I… I lost all inspiration to finish it."

"I see." Elizabeth laughed nervously. "My father calls me his magpie. He actually calls me his *Maggie-pie*. He gave me and each of my sisters the nickname of a bird. Jane, of course, is a dove, as she is such a sweet, serene, and peaceful young lady. He named me a magpie because he says I am a great deal like them. He claims that they are very intelligent and social birds." She shrugged and tried to give him a carefree smile, something she did not feel at all.

"So I understand." Darcy drew in a deep breath.

Elizabeth glanced away, hoping he did not notice the warmth she felt in her cheeks. She wondered what it was he understood. Was it that the magpie was intelligent and social... or that her father called her a magpie? At the moment, she did not feel intelligent at all, but was struggling to make sense of her words and the situation in which she now found herself.

"Now, if you do not mind my asking *you* a question, did you... could you perhaps also have been hiding behind your uncle's bed when I came in that first day?"

Elizabeth felt her face warm further with a deeper blush. "You... you saw me?"

"At the time, I was not certain what I saw, save for some lavender fabric on the other side of the bed near the floor... very much like that dress you are now wearing."

Elizabeth looked down at her dress and winced. "I suppose that was me. You see, I..."

"You did not want me to see you."

She silently nodded, feeling unsettled as his eyes locked onto hers.

He drew in a breath and a frown crossed his features as he dropped his eyes and fixed them on his wound. "And one more question... if you do not mind." He lifted his eyes to her. "Did you perchance lose a bonnet?"

Elizabeth dropped her gaze. "I suppose I did." She winced. "You see..."

Darcy lifted his hand. "No need to explain. It is enough for me to know there is a logical explanation for the odd things that have happened around here of late." After a moment of silence he added, "I shall have a maid return your bonnet to you later."

"Thank you," she said softly.

Elizabeth turned her eyes to the door to see torrential rain still pouring down. She pulled his coat tightly about her. "The rain... do you suppose it will let up soon?" She could not imagine how she would return to the house if it continued as it was.

"The forecasting of weather is *not* one of my accomplishments."

Elizabeth laughed softly. "No, I suppose not." The silence that followed seemed louder to her than the thundering of her heart within her chest or the pelting of the rain on the roof of the shed.

Darcy glanced down at his wound again. Blood still oozed from it in a few places.

"Again, I am very sorry," she said. "I should have returned to the house once it began to rain, but I was captivated by the garden." She paused and pressed her lips together. "The roses in particular are beautiful."

Darcy met her gaze. "Thank you." A small smile appeared but was just as quickly gone. "Now, Miss Bennet, I suggest we figure out a way to get back to the house across this increasingly sodden ground without drowning!" He walked to the door, braced his uninjured hand on the frame, and looked out. "It does not seem likely to end any time soon, and now there is an enormous lake of mud between us and the house."

He held out his injured hand. "Would you be so kind as to tie the ends of this cloth very tightly about my hand, making certain it is pressing down upon the wound?"

"Certainly," she replied, taking a step closer to him. "I can at least do that." Her fingers suddenly seemed unable to do even the simplest task, as she felt Mr. Darcy's eyes upon her. She could not help but wonder what he was thinking. He stood so close and was being so amiable. She did not deserve such civil treatment, especially after she had erroneously accused him of injustices and now caused this accident – *another* accident! She unwittingly let out a groan.

"You are not feeling faint, are you, Miss Bennet?"

"Not in the least!" she said with a nervous laugh. "I am the one who usually handles cuts and wounds in the family. My mother and my sisters all unfortunately grow faint at the sight of blood." She had no idea if she was speaking any sense or if he even cared.

When she had finished wrapping his hand, he thanked her, and he reached down and pulled out a pair of mud boots. "I keep these here, but unfortunately, there is only one pair." He sat down and began putting them on, taking care with his injured hand.

Elizabeth shivered again as she felt the air begin to cool. "I am not afraid of a little mud," she said with a slight chuckle. "As you… you may well recall when I walked to Netherfield."

Darcy lifted his eyes to her, an odd smile on his face. "I do. You were wearing a good amount of mud on your ankles and on the hem of your dress when you arrived."

Was he mocking her? Embarrassed, she said, "Well, it was for a good cause. At least, I considered visiting my sister a good cause."

"I suppose it was." He leaned over and picked up a rather large piece of heavy cloth. "But you have no need to worry about stepping in the mud today, Miss Bennet."

"And how am I to manage to make it to the house? Or do you intend to leave me here to fend for myself?"

Darcy's lips turned up slightly, and he gave one corner of the cloth to Elizabeth to hold, and he took the opposite corner in his other hand. "This oilcloth for the most part shall keep us dry." He drew up the middle part over his head. "And, no, I do not intend to leave you here or make you trudge across the grounds in the mud, as much as you think I might." He paused and looked intently at her. "Pray forgive me, Miss Bennet, but…" He suddenly gathered her up into his arms. "I intend to carry you!"

Her initial shock at being swept up into his strong arms took away her breath and all rational thought. She was jostled about slightly as he jumped and occasionally slipped through the slick mud, but he held her tight as he carried her towards the house.

Despite being somewhat sheltered by the large oilcloth, the rain still pelted her face, so she turned her face against his chest to shield it from the onslaught. When one wayward step almost brought them both to the ground, she quickly wrapped her arms about his neck, holding on tightly.

Surprisingly, Elizabeth was soon unaware of the pouring rain and the jostling of her body as he hurried across the grounds to the house. The only things she was mindful of were being held securely in the strong arms of Mr. Darcy and the feel of her face pressing against his chest.

He carried her up a short flight of stairs and stopped. Elizabeth could feel the heaving of his chest and the strong beating of his heart from the exertion. Hers was beating just as strongly, but for a completely different reason. She slowly lifted her head up and found him looking down at her. A tremor jolted through her as she found it impossible to turn away from his intense gaze.

"I think…" she began, her voice quaking, "that I can manage from here."

Darcy gently set her down and opened the door. "I am certain you can, but this is the servant's entrance, and it goes into the service areas and kitchen. It might be a little confusing to find your way through the house. If you wait while I remove my boots, I shall direct you back to your room."

"Thank you," Elizabeth replied, feeling sheepish and unsteady on her feet. She could only wonder what he thought of her being here and everything she had done that had interfered with his well-regulated life. At least he was treating her civilly. He really had no reason to do so.

Darcy took off his boots as Elizabeth slipped out of his coat, and she handed it to him when he stood. He led Elizabeth through the back rooms, around the kitchen, and finally to a large hallway, where he stopped.

"Miss Bennet, my sister informed me that the doctor has given your uncle permission to walk short distances. There is a small dining room that is not a great distance from his room. I shall have our dinner served there, and you and your aunt and uncle will dine with us this evening."

Elizabeth could barely think. Her heart still pounded from her encounter with him. "I thank you, but I do not…"

"Miss Bennet, this is not a request. I expect you to be there. You are guests in my home and have remained in your rooms far too long. I must insist on it."

Elizabeth swallowed; her mouth was suddenly extremely dry. "Yes, sir."

Darcy allowed a small smile and gave a satisfied nod of his head. "You may join us in the adjacent sitting room before the meal. I shall point the rooms out to you as we go so you will be able to find them later."

"Thank you," Elizabeth said softly.

They began to walk again and, at length, came upon the small dining room and then the sitting room, which he pointed out to her. As they approached her uncle's room, she could only imagine what her aunt and uncle would think when they saw him at her side. She unwittingly shook her head, as she had feared the worst in encountering him, but he had proven to be exceptionally and surprisingly gracious.

Mr. and Mrs. Gardiner both looked up when they entered her uncle's room. Their eyes widened when they saw Mr. Darcy with their niece, and it was a moment before either could speak. Elizabeth was grateful their initial response was somewhat subdued.

"Good day, Mr. and Mrs. Gardiner," Mr. Darcy said.

Mrs. Gardiner was the first to reply. "Good day, Mr. Darcy. It is good to see you again."

Mr. Gardiner then offered his greetings.

"Lizzy, we were worried about you when it began to rain and you did not return." Mrs. Gardiner walked over to her niece, putting her arm about her. "But for the most part, you are dry. I am glad."

"I did get caught in the rain." Elizabeth laughed nervously. She felt a warmth travel up her cheeks as she recollected being held in Mr. Darcy's arms. She could see the look of curiosity in her aunt's expression and knew she would have a lot of explaining to do once the gentleman left. "Mr. Darcy... assisted in getting me back to the house without getting too sodden."

"Thank you, sir," Mr. Gardiner said. "First, your generous hospitality to us since the accident, and now this. We are much obliged to you."

Darcy shook his head. "Think nothing of it." He drew in a breath. "I have made a request of Miss Elizabeth that you join my sister and me and our guests for dinner tonight. There is a small dining room just down the hall, and a sitting room on this side of it. Please come to the sitting room at your leisure. My sister and I will be waiting."

"Thank you very much!" Mrs. Gardiner said with delight.

"Mr. Darcy, we appreciate that very much!" Mr. Gardiner said. "But to assist in my walking, would you by any chance have a cane I could use?"

"I have a walking stick that I will have brought to your room."

"Thank you, sir."

"I shall leave you now and look forward to seeing you shortly."

Mr. Darcy nodded and then left the room.

Mrs. Gardiner took Elizabeth's arm and drew her into the room, closing the door behind her. "Now you must tell us everything, Lizzy. Do not leave out a single detail." She pointed to the chair. "I think you need to sit down, for I believe – at least I hope – that it will be a long story." She suddenly laughed. "I think I need to sit down, as well!"

"Here, Aunt, you take the chair."

"No, no. I shall sit next to Edmund on the bed."

Elizabeth sat down and smiled. For the first time since coming here, she felt at ease, no longer having to hide or fear being seen. She was still not certain, however, what Mr. Darcy thought about her being here, but she was grateful their initial encounter was over.

After she had finished summarizing what had occurred outside and had received a few teasing remarks from her uncle and raised brows from her aunt, Harriet came with the walking stick for Mr. Gardiner.

"From Mr. Darcy for Mr. Gardiner," she said.

"Why thank you!" he replied, running his hands over the smooth wood. "This is beautiful!" He looked over at Elizabeth, who had just told them about Mr. Darcy's hobby of woodcarving. "Do you think Mr. Darcy carved this?"

"He may have," she said. "In fact, I would not be surprised if this is the cane he is holding in his portrait." Elizabeth walked over to look at it. "It is an owl's head at the top. There is also a wood-carved owl in the library. He said he carved that one. I am certain he did this one, as well."

When they finished admiring the workmanship of the cane, Elizabeth proceeded to answer the multitude of questions her aunt and uncle had concerning her encounter with Mr. Darcy. When she had done that to their satisfaction, she thought it best to retreat to her room to ready herself for dinner with him, his sister, *and* the Westerfields.

Chapter 8

Darcy slowly walked to his chambers, looking down at his bandaged hand as he did. He could not believe that Elizabeth was in his home, had walked the halls, slept in one of the rooms, and strolled through Pemberley's gardens and grounds. He stopped and glanced out a window that overlooked the gardens. He wondered what she thought of Pemberley, and he could not help but wonder what she now thought of *him*!

He heard Georgiana playing her new instrument and set out in that direction. He came to the door and stood quietly until she finished playing.

"Brother?" She slowly turned on the piano bench.

Darcy smiled. "How did you know I was here?"

She tilted her head. "I heard you." She gave him a mischievous smile." I always hear you, as much as you try to sneak up on me."

"I sneak up on you because you always cease playing when you know I am here."

Georgiana lifted a brow. "Do I?" She smiled. "But I always begin again." After a moment, she asked, "How are you, Fitzwilliam?"

"I am well." He drew in a deep breath.

"Are you?"

He shook his head and shrugged. "I am still attempting to make sense of this."

"And by *this*, you mean Miss Bennet's being here?"

He silently nodded and walked over to her. He rested his elbows on the piano and clasped his hands, asking, "Georgiana, did you, by any chance, have anything to do with Miss Bennet being in the rose garden earlier?"

Georgiana rose and came to her brother's side, slipping her hand into the crook of his arm. "I cannot imagine what you are talking about." She looked up at him with a smile. "You saw her then?"

"I did." he said as he covered her fingers with his other hand.

"Did you have anything to do with it?"

"Well, I suppose I may have recommended we walk out to see the garden together, and when I was called in for a dress fitting, I may have suggested she continue on to see the rose garden."

"How did you know I was out there?"

"What makes you think I knew you were there?"

Raising a brow, he sent her a pointed look. "Georgie?"

She shook her head. "All right. You said you were going out for a while to either walk or ride because you needed to think. I knew that since it appeared that it was about to rain, you would likely do neither, but would go to the potting shed, instead, to do some wood carving. That is where you always retreat when you need time alone to think, is it not?"

Darcy looked at his sister incredulously. "Do I do that?"

Georgiana leaned her head against her brother. "You most certainly do, except when you are indoors, you are in the library."

He leaned over and kissed the top of her head. "You know me better than anyone else, Georgie."

She gave his arm a squeeze. "So what are you going to do?"

"Do? About what?"

She let out a laugh. "You know very well about what. I saw your reaction when you realized Miss Bennet was in the house. Your feelings for her are as strong as they were when you first wrote to me about her. Do you think her feelings for you have improved?" She lifted her brows encouragingly.

He let out a slow breath. "Things are not looking favourably in that quarter." He held up one finger. "Number one - she made a point of telling Mrs. Reynolds that while we were acquainted, it was a *trifling* acquaintance."

Georgiana gave him a wistful smile.

He held up a second finger. "Number two - she told me, as we waited out the storm in the potting shed, that she had tried to talk her aunt and uncle out of coming to Pemberley, and number three…" He held up his third finger. "She concealed her presence from me several times as she did not wish for me to see her."

Georgiana winced as she held up four fingers, prompting her brother to groan. "Four?"

She slowly nodded her head. "She led us to believe her name

was Miss Gardiner."

Darcy pursed his lips and was silent for a moment. "Indeed, and it was not a misapprehension on our part. It was intentional, on her part."

Georgiana seemed to ponder this and smiled. "If you ask me, I think this is all highly in her favour."

Darcy looked at her askance. "Whatever do you mean?"

Georgiana squeezed her brother's hand. "Fitzwilliam, most women would love to come here if only to see you, as they imagine themselves becoming the Mistress of Pemberley. They will plot and scheme to attract your attention any way they can."

Darcy laughed. "That is a rather interesting way to look at it, but I do not think this reasoning is at all in *my* favour."

"We shall have to wait to see on that account, but you have not answered my question. What do you intend to do?"

Darcy inhaled deeply and moved his fingers in a circular motion across the shiny, smooth wood of the piano. "I cannot be certain. With Miss Westerfield here, I do not think there is much I can do, but..." He brought up his other hand and fingered the wrapping on his wound.

Georgiana looked down and noticed it. "Oh, dear! What happened?"

He lifted his brows. "This? I suppose you could say Miss Bennet caused it."

Georgiana gasped. "How?"

"When she stepped into the potting shed to get out of the rain, I was about to cut away some wood on the bird I was carving. I looked up and was so stunned to see her, the knife slipped." He studied the cloth wound about his hand. "Instead of cutting into the wood, I cut into my hand."

"You are always so careful."

"Normally, but this... I was not expecting her to walk in at that moment. I was still... shocked from finding out she was here, and... yes... I did go to the potting shed to think. I needed to prepare myself for an inevitable encounter. I was pondering how I would act – how I ought to act if – and when – I saw her. It was then that she walked in. I was not prepared to see her and reacted." He looked down. "My hand suffered because of a sudden and unexpected move of the carving knife."

Georgiana smiled. "And perhaps a sudden and unexpected beating of your heart?" She laughed at her brother's grimace.

"I will have the doctor look at it when he comes tomorrow. In the meantime, I shall have it dressed more properly."

"Well, even though it was a *painful* encounter, I am glad you finally saw each other."

He chuckled. "Georgie, I do not want you to get any ideas about Miss Bennet and me."

"You are not going to give up before you find out how she feels, are you?"

"Not necessarily, but I must proceed with caution. I am not certain I can endure another…" Darcy drew in a breath and gave a quick shake of his head. "But I have invited her and her aunt and uncle to dine with us this evening. We shall eat in the smaller dining room, as it is an easier walk for Mr. Gardiner from his room." He turned to look at her. "I do not know if it was the wisest thing for me to do. I extended the invitation before I really thought it through. I did not take into consideration what torture this might prove to be for me."

"Torture? Do you mean if you find she still despises you?"

Darcy hung his head. "Even if she no longer despises me, she may not ever return my affection as I…" He gave his head a shake. "No, I ought to have left things as they were."

Georgiana leaned against his arm. "You mean leaving them to eat in their rooms and then for you never to see her again when they depart Pemberley? No, I believe you did the right thing, Brother."

"It does not bode well that the Westerfields are here. I do not know what to do about Miss Westerfield, especially with all the rampant rumours abounding, and from what I recollect, her father has quite a temper. I am not certain how *he* will react to having people in trade dining with us, and I have no idea what *her* expectations are, let alone her parents." He let out a loud huff. "I do not even know what *my* expectations are concerning her."

"Well, we shall handle that when the time comes."

"*We* shall?" he asked with a laugh.

"Of course. Oh, and Brother, as for Miss Bennet, I will do

everything in my power to make certain she hears only glowing reports about you." She poked her finger into his ribs. "And you had best be prepared to receive a great deal of praise this evening, which I know makes you exceedingly uncomfortable."

Darcy wrapped his arm about his sister. "Not when it comes from you, Georgie."

The young girl smiled and looked up at him. "I am curious about something. How did you and Miss Bennet get back to the house in all that rain?"

Darcy pursed his lips, thinking he need not tell Georgiana everything. "Very carefully." He grinned and tugged on a blond ringlet that framed his sister's face. "Now you ought to run along and dress for dinner."

Georgiana stood up on her toes and kissed him on the cheek. "I will have you know that while I was somewhat instrumental in directing Miss Bennet to the rose garden, I had absolutely nothing to do with making it rain when it did."

Darcy shook his head and laughed. "Go ready yourself for dinner, you little imp!"

He watched as Georgiana walked away laughing. His chest constricted as he considered everything that was pressing down upon him at the moment, all of them potentially affecting him – and his sister – in one way or another.

One of those things was taking a wife. He pondered what it might mean to him if he gave in to the leanings and yearnings of his heart. Elizabeth might never be prevailed upon to marry him, as she had so vehemently declared, no matter what he did. Was it worth putting his heart at risk again and receive yet another refusal from her? He had no idea whether she had even read the letter he had presented to her the morning after his disastrous proposal. From her comment acknowledging Wickham's disreputable behaviour, however, he suspected she had.

"I seem to have no ability to think rationally when Miss Elizabeth Bennet is near me," he reasoned. "What am I doing even considering this?" He turned from the piano and leaned against it. "And yet…" His heart suddenly leapt, and the slightest smile appeared on his face. "How can I not?"

~~*

When Elizabeth returned to her room, she sat down at a small dressing table. A smile threatened to appear as she took her fingers and aimlessly attempted to straighten her damp hair. Just as quickly, however, she dropped her hand over her rapidly beating heart. *Does he still have feelings for me, or is he merely being the gracious master of his estate to the Gardiners and me? He certainly did not have to invite us to dine with him.*

She studied her reflection in the mirror and sighed. *And what about the beautiful Miss Westerfield?*

Elizabeth stood up and walked to the dressing room, pulled out a soft blue dress, and held it up to her. Whatever the thoughts, reasoning, and feelings that had directed his actions earlier, she had to admit she had enjoyed it – probably more than she should have.

When she finished changing into the dress, she sat down and looked at the letter on her bed. "Oh, Jane! I nearly forgot about your letter." She let out a giggle. "If only I could tell you the reason for neglecting you. You would certainly not believe it."

She quickly opened it and began reading.

Dearest Lizzy,

How I miss you! How we all miss you! We trust you are enjoying your time with Aunt and Uncle Gardiner and are seeing many lovely sights in Derbyshire. We are all doing well, as are the Phillipses and the Lucases.

Recently, we have been kept busy and were entertained with several parties and engagements. This has provided great enjoyment for our mother and a diversion for our two youngest sisters. Lydia still harbours resentment towards Papa for forbidding her to go to Brighton, and Kitty, though relieved that Lydia was not allowed to go, is still brooding about not being invited in the first place. When the regiment left, our two youngest sisters complained continually about there being nothing to do; our recent engagements have helped alleviate that.

There was more general news about her family that Elizabeth read with great pleasure. It was good to have finally received a letter from her dear sister. But the last paragraphs of the letter caused Elizabeth some concern.

Lizzy, there is something I must share with you, and I really do not know what to do about it. The Gouldings' son, Arthur, has returned home from the navy. He did well for himself and is a Lieutenant Captain. He has been attending all the social engagements and is paying me a great deal of attention.

Mother insists that if he asks for my hand, I must accept it. She says she cannot tolerate another missed chance. I know she refers to Mr. Bingley's leaving and your turning down Mr. Collins. Oh, heavens, what would she do if she were to discover you also turned down another! Each day I fear that Mr. Goulding will come to speak to me or go to Father for his consent. It is not that I dislike him; he is very cordial and pleasant, but I do not love him.

Oh, Lizzy, when I used to think of marriage to Mr. Bingley, I had such feelings of eager anticipation. When I think of marriage to Mr. Goulding, I shiver in dread. I wish you were here to help me stand up to Mother. I do not think I will be able to go against her will in this. Father seems to have taken her side, saying he is a pleasant enough fellow and I ought to seriously consider it. He may be teasing – I never can tell, but I do not want to take the chance.

I hope you come home before any offer is made. I would feel so much more at ease about this if I had you standing beside me to advise me – and to stand up to Mother. I shall never love anyone as much as I loved Mr. Bingley.

I hope you are having a wonderful visit, and I look forward to your return.

Yours always,
Jane

"Oh, poor Jane." Elizabeth closed her eyes and shook her head. "Please do not do accept this man solely out of coercion! You must only accept a man's offer out of love, admiration, and respect!"

She placed the letter on the small table next to the bed and opened the door to join the Gardiners, almost colliding with her aunt.

"Oh, Aunt Gardiner. I was just going to join you."

"I came to ready myself for dinner and see if you needed any assistance."

"No, I am ready. I was just reading Jane's letter."

"And how is everyone faring?"

Elizabeth retrieved the letter and handed it to her aunt. "I shall let you decide."

As Mrs. Gardiner read the letter, a compassionate look touched her features. "Poor Jane. I know how difficult it would be for her to defy your mother."

"Yet she must!" Elizabeth said. "Mr. Goulding may have done well in the navy, but we have known him all his life. He does not have the kind, generous heart that Jane does. I even recollect him having a short temper. Does a man ever outgrow that?" She shook her head vehemently with a look of repugnance colouring her features. "He will never do for her!"

Her aunt replaced the letter on the table, and she took Elizabeth's hand. "Let us hope and pray he does not offer for her before we return. Try not to worry."

"How can I not worry about Jane when she is faced with this? I shall try not to, but it will likely be difficult." She stamped her foot. "If only it were me instead of her! I would have no qualms about turning him down, no matter what Mother said!"

Mrs. Gardiner chuckled. "Lizzy, I am grateful it is not you, for if it were to be known that you had turned down three offers of marriage, I can only imagine what people would think of you."

"Well, they shall never hear about the second, as long as Jane and you and Uncle Gardiner do not speak of it!"

"Our lips are sealed, dearest Elizabeth. You know that." She leaned over and kissed Elizabeth on the cheek.

Once both ladies were ready, Elizabeth looked at her aunt and smiled. "Shall we go? It might take Uncle some time to walk to the sitting room."

"Good thought, Lizzy."

When they stepped into his room, Mr. Gardiner was sitting on the edge of his bed, and he greeted them with a smile that lit up his face.

"Ah, here are my two favourite ladies, and how lovely you both look!"

"Thank you," they replied, returning the smile.

As they walked slowly to the nearby sitting room, Mr. Gardiner's wife and niece encouraged him to use the cane both to keep his balance and support his weight. He was walking farther than he had walked since the accident, and they were all concerned that he might do something that would make his injuries worse.

As they slowly approached the sitting room, they could hear voices, and Elizabeth surmised that Mr. and Miss Darcy were already there, along with the Westerfields. She heard Miss Westerfield's soft laughter several times before stepping in.

When they came to the door, she saw that Mr. Darcy was seated beside Mr. Westerfield and conversing with him. Mrs. Westerfield and their daughter were speaking with Georgiana. They all turned to them when they stepped in.

"Ah! Our other guests have arrived!" Darcy stood and walked over to them, smiling. "Welcome! How was the *long journey*, Mr. Gardiner? I hope it was not too strenuous."

"Oh, no, not at all." Mr. Gardiner chuckled and looked at the two ladies on either side of him. "I have the loveliest and finest caregivers a person could ask for." He leaned towards Mr. Darcy and added softly, "As well as Mrs. Reynolds. We have been spoiled by her."

Both men laughed as Miss Darcy approached them. She invited them to join them and take a seat. "If you would like some light refreshment before the meal, there is food and drink on the side table."

"Thank you, Miss Darcy," Mrs. Gardiner said. "Edmund, would you care for anything?"

"Thank you, my dear, but no. I believe the only thing I need is a chair." He looked at Mr. Darcy with a teasing raised brow. "I feel somewhat fatigued from the *long journey*."

As they joined the others, Darcy made the introductions. The Westerfields were apparently long-time acquaintances of the Darcys, and they currently lived in a town home in London a few blocks from his. He introduced Elizabeth as an acquaintance he had made while visiting a good friend in Hertfordshire, and she and the Gardiners, who were from London, had been on a tour of Derbyshire and his home when the accident occurred.

Darcy stood and waited for everyone to be seated. Being a smaller sitting room, there were fewer chairs and only one sofa, and Elizabeth, when faced with a choice of whether to sit in the adjoining chair to where he had been sitting or one on the other side of Georgiana, opted for the latter.

Mr. Gardiner took the chair beside the sofa, claiming the sturdier back would be kinder to his injuries, and his wife sat on the other side of Mrs. Westerfield, across from Elizabeth.

The ladies resumed their conversation, which apparently concerned the concerts and plays they had attended in London the previous season. Georgiana had only attended two, so the Westerfield ladies were more than willing to offer their praises and critiques of the half dozen or more they had attended.

When they finished speaking about the most recent concert they attended, Mrs. Westerfield looked at Mrs. Gardiner and Elizabeth. "Have you attended any noteworthy concerts or plays of late? Mr. Darcy said you live in London."

Mrs. Gardiner smiled. "We do live in town, but as we have four young children at home, we seldom have the time or energy to attend an evening event."

"I see," Mrs. Westerfield said. "Where are the children now?"

Elizabeth answered. "They are currently staying with my family in Hertfordshire. My elder sister, Jane, loves the children dearly and is always willing to watch them."

"I see," Mrs. Westerfield said and took a sip of tea.

"We were able to attend a concert in the park this past spring when Elizabeth's sister, Jane, was staying with us," Mrs. Gardiner added. "It was enjoyable, and the weather cooperated very nicely."

At her aunt's mention of Jane, Elizabeth unwittingly looked up and saw that Mr. Darcy was eyeing her. When he quickly looked away, she wondered if he had heard her sister's name mentioned, causing him to recollect their meeting in Kent when she accused him of interfering in Jane and Mr. Bingley's particular regard for each other.

Miss Westerfield turned to Elizabeth. "We spoke earlier about Miss Darcy's playing and singing and the new pianoforte her brother gave her as a gift." She turned and patted Georgiana's hand. "You are so fortunate to have such a devoted brother!" She turned back to Elizabeth. "Do you play and sing?"

"A little, but from all I have heard concerning Miss Darcy's proficiency, I fear I would play very ill in comparison."

Miss Westerfield clasped her hands, and a smile lit her face. "We must have our own little concert one evening while we are here."

"That is a wonderful idea," Mrs. Westerfield said. "It was at a musical soiree in town that Mr. Darcy first heard Angeline sing and play, and I am confident he was captivated with her performance." She smiled at her daughter, whose eyes turned to Mr. Darcy. "I believe he said that she sang as sweetly as an angel."

Elizabeth could not help but turn to observe Mr. Darcy, as well, and quickly looked back when she saw that he was looking in the general direction of both Miss Westerfield and herself. If he was looking at Miss Westerfield, the smile the young lady sent back to him was likely in return to one he directed to her.

Elizabeth looked at Georgiana, wondering if she would feel comfortable performing for this larger group of people. "What are your thoughts about having a small concert, Miss Darcy?"

She looked at Miss Westerfield and then back to Elizabeth. "I think I would be willing to play as long as I do not have to sing." She let out a breathy nervous chuckle. "I would feel less inclined to suffer any apprehension if I am only required to play." She then turned to look at her brother. "But perhaps we can convince Fitzwilliam to sing while I play. Most people do not know that he has a very pleasant baritone singing voice."

Miss Westerfield's eyes lit up with delight. "Oh, that sounds delightful! I had no idea he could sing."

When all eyes turned to Mr. Darcy, he looked over with a sidelong glance. "What is it you are saying? From the mischievous look on Georgiana's face, I presume she is scheming something that pertains to me."

"Oh, nothing mischievous," Miss Westerfield said. "Your sister was just telling us that you have a pleasant baritone voice, and if we have a little concert, you might be persuaded to sing while she plays." She lifted her brows as if in question.

Darcy frowned. "Georgiana knows that it is only on the rare occasion that I sing."

"Yes, but he always insists that I perform before others by playing *and* singing." She smiled playfully. "I believe he ought to, as well."

"Perhaps we ought not insist upon it," Miss Westerfield said, "if he does not wish to."

"And why should a gentleman who has a talent, not perform... when he expects it of his sister?" Elizabeth sent Mr. Darcy a challenging glare. "I am certainly in favour of hearing both Mr. and Miss Darcy perform." In all truth, she wanted to hear him sing, for there was nothing she enjoyed more than an agreeable masculine voice – especially a baritone.

He shook his head. "I doubt you would want to hear me sing."

"Yet, your sister claims you have a most pleasing voice," Elizabeth said.

She watched him send a pointed, yet teasing, glance at his sister, and he turned back to Elizabeth. "She is my devoted sister, and I fear she is biased."

"Oh, but sir, I am certain you deserve all of her praise," Mrs. Westerfield said.

"I cannot speak to that," Mr. Darcy said.

The party was called to dinner, bringing the conversation to an end. Elizabeth thought she saw him breathe out a puff of air in relief.

They stepped into the small dining room which had a table with eight chairs fitted nicely about it. Darcy looked at his sister and nodded, as if to encourage her to assume her duties. She took in a deep breath and smiled nervously, taking her seat, and the others followed.

As the meal was served, the initial conversation around the table was light and touched on many subjects. At length, however, it became more spirited as the topic addressed the Prince Regent and the Tory and Whig parties. Elizabeth, being a young lady and a guest, held her tongue, although if she had been better acquainted with the Westerfields, she might have been willing to express her views on these subjects, as her beliefs often went against Mr, Darcy's opinion. The Westerfields, and especially Miss Westerfield, seemed to agree with him on every subject.

Finally, after biting her tongue long enough, she offered, "I cannot agree with the staunch Whig dictates. To believe that someone in the lower classes cannot and should not attain to the same wealth and respect a landowner might possess is nonsensical." She shook her head. "Particularly, in regard to respect. A Whig may have the deference of others, but oftentimes has not rightfully earned it, and more often than not, does not deserve it."

Everyone around the table was silent, and Elizabeth thought she perceived a slight upward curvature of Mr. Darcy's mouth.

At length, Mr. Westerfield leaned forward to address Darcy. "Well, we are all entitled to our own opinions." He looked at Darcy. "Do you have hounds? I do not think there is anything that can compare to a good fox hunt."

"I do have hounds," Darcy said. "And I agree there is nothing more exhilarating."

"Oh, yes!" agreed Miss Westerfield. "Nothing so exhilarating. I have enjoyed watching many a fox hunt. It is always so exciting."

Mr. Westerfield looked at Elizabeth. "I believe you said you have a home in the country. Has your father hosted fox hunts?"

Elizabeth laughed. "Oh, no. My father has five daughters and loves to spend his time reading, so he has very little interest in it."

"Do you not have an interest in watching a fox hunt, Miss Bennet?" Miss Westerfield asked. "Many women do."

"I do not. I actually find it distasteful."

Everyone's eyes turned to Elizabeth. Darcy tilted his head as he looked at her. "And why is that, Miss Bennet?" he asked.

She met his eyes, which looked back intently at her. She forced herself to turn away, for she could not think clearly with him staring at her so. "I do not think it can be good for the dogs, which run avidly about, and the poor horses, which have to follow the dogs and jump fences, streams, and ditches, and go around trees and bushes. I am certain many a rider has fallen off."

"And he probably got right back on, eh, Darcy?" Mr. Westerfield asked.

"If at all possible," he answered. "Miss Bennet, the dogs love what they do. They are bred for that very purpose, and a horse must be well-trained to follow the rider's lead, so that the rider, who also must have excellent horsemanship skills, can guide the horse to accomplish those feats."

"A little bumping and bruising does little to dampen a gentleman's spirits while doing something he loves." Mr.

Westerfield declared.

Everyone murmured their agreement, even the Gardiners, and the table fell silent for a moment.

At length, Elizabeth said softly, "And then there are the poor foxes."

Darcy stared at his plate for a moment, his eyes widening. "The poor foxes?"

Elizabeth heard her aunt clear her throat slightly, and she felt a slight nudge coming from her direction. She picked up the napkin from her lap and dabbed her mouth. "Would you like it if you were being chased out of your home and had to run from a wild pack of dogs and horses and men to survive?" She shook her head. "I think not."

"You do realize, Miss Bennet, that foxes cause a great deal of damage to a farmer's crops and chickens. Without the fox hunt, their numbers would only grow." Mr. Darcy sent her a pointed look and began to rub his jaw with his hand.

"I do understand that, Mr. Darcy, as our home has suffered loss due to foxes. But for men to call this sport, when they do nothing but ride? They are not even the ones who kill the foxes; it is usually the dogs. I see no sport in this at all. If you must shoot a fox that is raiding your garden, so be it. But I find the whole idea of fox hunting as a sport distasteful."

Mr. Westerfield laughed. "Oh, but the sport is in the ride. As you yourself claimed, there is the skill of jumping over one obstacle after another. It is definitely a sport and most injuries are minor." He paused, and then turned his attention to Darcy. "What happened to your hand, Darcy?"

Elizabeth saw Mr. Darcy flinch slightly, dropping his hand slightly as he looked down at the wrapping. She felt her own cheeks warm at the question.

He pursed his lips and looked up again to meet Mr. Westerfield's questioning gaze. "A minor accident. It is of little concern." The chuckle following his reply seemed forced to Elizabeth's ears. "As you said earlier, a gentleman's spirits are rarely dampened when he is injured doing something he loves."

Elizabeth could not look at him. As she stared down at her plate, she considered this man who was becoming more and more a mystery to her as more and more of his character was being revealed. She thought she had known everything about him she cared to know. His passion for carving birds was certainly a surprise.

Mr. Gardiner spoke up. "While I have never participated in a fox hunt either, I am certain my niece would change her mind if she saw one first hand."

"Too bad it is not fox hunting season," Mr. Westerfield said. "I would love to see your hounds do their work."

"Even if it were hunting season, I would say the rains we had today would have precluded it."

Westerfield shrugged. "It is a shame. I know Angeline would have enjoyed it greatly."

She eagerly nodded. "Oh, I would, but perhaps there will be another time."

She smiled at Mr. Darcy, and Elizabeth knew exactly what she was thinking.

Mr. Westerfield pointed his fork towards the window, which had a sheet of rainwater running down it. "Speaking of the rain, that downpour certainly arrived unexpectedly this afternoon."

"We have been in great need of it. I am grateful," Darcy said.

Mr. Westerfield nodded. "But as I happened to be standing at the window in our chambers looking out, what do you think I saw?"

"What, Father?" Miss Westerfield inquired.

"Two people, a man and a woman, who were obviously surprised by the downpour." He turned his attention back to his plate, stirring around the food with his fork.

Elizabeth's insides tightened, and she held her breath as she waited in dread for him to continue. She stole a quick glance at Darcy, who in turn was eyeing the gentleman with a wary look.

Mr. Westerfield looked up. A scowl darkened his face, and he wagged his finger at Darcy. "I was truly shocked, Darcy, by what I saw."

Elizabeth looked down to her plate, wondering what might follow. She hoped – but highly doubted – that would be the end of it.

Chapter 9

Darcy shifted in his chair, wondering what Mr. Westerfield had seen and what he suspected. He recollected the severity of this gentleman's temper; while it did not flare often, when it did, it was fierce. "I am certain it was nothing. People get caught out in the rain all the time." He hoped to keep his voice indifferent, which was quite the opposite of how he was feeling.

"Well, although I could not see who it was, I could definitely see that a man was carrying a lady. They came from the potting shed down by the rose garden and had covered themselves with a large cloth of some kind, presumably to keep themselves dry." A sombre look overspread his features. "Or to conceal their identity."

Darcy's concerns over what his guest may have seen were somewhat eased. It appeared he had not seen that it was him holding Elizabeth in his arms. He stole a quick glance at her, as he warmed at the remembrance. She was sitting perfectly still, her face averted from him.

"They were coming from the potting shed?" Georgiana asked, her eyes wide as she looked across the table at her brother.

Darcy gave a very slight nod of his head.

"Indeed," continued Westerfield. "The one down by the rose garden. My guess is it was most likely secret lovers having a clandestine meeting."

Darcy's eyes widened at his guest's words as his insides roiled, feeling more concern for Elizabeth's apparent discomfiture than anything else. Although this time he did not turn to look at her, he could see that she was staring down at her plate. He reached for his goblet and sipped some wine as he determined what to say in response. Fortunately, Mrs. Westerfield spared him from the task.

"Oh, Frederick, you ought not say such things with young ladies present!" She sent him a scolding look.

Mr. Westerfield leaned back into his chair, stretching one arm out across the table and fingering the stem of his goblet. He glanced at the three young ladies. "My apologies." Then he looked at Darcy. "But you need to keep a tight rein on your servants." He shook his head. "This kind of behaviour should never be tolerated. You must always demand propriety."

As Darcy drew in a breath to speak, Elizabeth lifted her eyes to him. He could see they were filled with regret, and he could not help but wonder if she felt distress that someone had seen them. Or worse, did she feel such loathing towards him that she despised the idea that someone would even hint that she was his secret lover – albeit unknowingly? At length, he said, "I doubt it was as…" Darcy swallowed hard and continued, "…as imprudent as you assumed, Westerfield."

"Oh, I am certain my father did not imply that you do not have a tight rein on your staff, Mr. Darcy." Miss Westerfield smiled sweetly. "I am certain he spoke more as a generality." She looked at her father. "Did you not?"

"Of course." Mr. Westerfield shook his head. "I hope no one has taken offense."

Darcy politely nodded.

An awkward silence filled the room. It appeared to Darcy that the Gardiners felt as discomfited as did he, his sister, and Miss Bennet. Elizabeth must have told him of their accidental meeting there. He was also fairly certain Georgiana realized it had been Elizabeth and him. He truly hoped Mr. Westerfield had been oblivious to their identity, as he had declared.

As if intent to change the subject, Miss Westerfield looked at Mr. Darcy. "That brings to mind the time our family was visiting at Pemberley, and your mother warned us that it looked like rain, but we wanted so much to play outside." A smile lit her face. "Do you recollect what happened?"

Darcy nodded, unable to keep the smile from his face. "I do. How could I forget? We sneaked from the house and set out for the stables."

Miss Westerfield laughed. "Yes. I was seven, I believe, and you were eleven. Once at the stables, we saw a litter of kittens nestled in the hay, but we did not see their mother. I was intent on staying with them until the mother returned."

"And you sent me looking for a box we could put them in to

bring them into the house if she did not return."

"And before we knew it, the rains came," Miss Westerfield said. "A mighty deluge."

"The rains came, but not the mother. And little did we know that our own mothers were back at the house frantically looking for us."

Mrs. Westerfield shook her head. "I will never forget that! We determined that the two of you had run off somewhere. You were always going on adventures. I think one of the servants had seen you leave the house. We thought you would return when the rain began, but our concern grew when you did not come in as the rain intensified."

"I refused to leave the kittens there. Finally, the mother came in drenched from the rain, but as happy as she could be to be reunited with her kittens."

Darcy nodded. "We returned to the house as drenched as that cat was, to our own mothers who were happy to be reunited with us, but displeased we had not told anyone where we were going."

Miss Westerfield drew in a deep breath and sighed. "Little did we know how lucky those kittens were that we found them."

Darcy's eyes widened. He hoped she had not remembered, but apparently she had.

"Why do you say that?" Elizabeth asked.

"The next day we went back to see them, and just as we arrived, we found George Wickham carrying two of them away." She began to slowly shake her head. "When we asked him what he was doing, he had the nerve to inform us he intended to use them as target practice." Miss Westerfield shuddered. "He had a new gun he wanted to try out. I was so angry at him! I could not believe anyone would do such a cruel thing!"

Mr. Westerfield turned to Darcy. "I hear he has gone quite bad. It is a shame after all your father did for him."

"He was always so charming and such a fine looking man!" Mrs. Westerfield exclaimed. "But you combine those two traits, and I guarantee you some innocent young lady will suffer if captivated by his allure."

"I would not be surprised to hear he has ruined more than one young life," Mr. Westerfield added.

Darcy said nothing, keeping his eyes on his sister. She had grown pale and looked down. He then noticed something else. Elizabeth had also turned to her. She had not looked at *him*; she had looked at his sister with a look of compassion on her face. In the midst of this revelation and the pain it must have caused his sister, he felt a leap of joy inside. He was now confident Elizabeth had read his letter!

Elizabeth turned to Miss Westerfield. "Did you visit Pemberley often when you were younger?"

All talk of Wickham ceased as Miss Westerfield and her mother shared story after story about their visits at Pemberley and times the Darcys came to visit them at Alderbrook. The ladies carried the conversation, allowing Darcy to quietly listen – and further consider the unexpectedness of Miss Elizabeth Bennet being in his home. She had gently redirected the conversation away from Wickham, and for that he was most grateful.

It appeared his sister had handled the story about Wickham with very little apparent distress. While he had been able to see it, and he was certain Elizabeth had seen it, as well, no one else seemed to pay her any mind.

~~*

After dinner, the ladies were invited to join Miss Darcy in the sitting room, while the men remained in the small dining room for their after-dinner drinks.

The Westerfield ladies seemed more inclined to speak to Miss Darcy, mostly about her brother, and especially concerning his ability to sing. Elizabeth was content to listen, for Mr. Darcy's sister confirmed everything she had heard about him since coming to Pemberley. It was apparent by the look on the Westerfield ladies' faces that they were delighted to hear such praise for the man who might one day join their family through matrimony, while Elizabeth attempted to conceal her thoughts and feelings for that very reason. It would not do for her to give the appearance that she was interested in the gentleman, as well.

She could not help but think of the conversation about Mr. Darcy's and Miss Westerfield's early years. She felt a twinge of jealousy; they had known each other so long and had shared years of memories together. There was absolutely nothing about Miss Westerfield with which she could find fault. She seemed perfectly suited for Mr. Darcy – and she had likely never insulted him to his face with words she could never take back.

When the men returned, Mr. Gardiner expressed his wish to return directly to his room, as he was fatigued. Elizabeth was glad to take her leave of the others, as she found it difficult to be in the presence of the woman who would eventually be Pemberley's mistress.

As they walked back to their rooms, Mrs. Gardiner turned to Elizabeth. "Elizabeth, I hope you do not mind if I give you a little advice."

"You know that I respect you a great deal, Aunt, and appreciate any good counsel you have to offer."

Mrs. Gardiner drew in a breath, took Elizabeth's hand, and very kindly said, "A gentleman likes to be respected in what he says and does, and since we are guests, and Mr. Darcy is master of this house and our host, I believe you ought to take care in expressing your opinions when they go against his."

"But you know I always speak as I find."

"Yes, I know," Mrs. Gardiner said as she patted Elizabeth's hand. "But remember, he has other guests, as well, and his sister hinted that he might be settling his affections on Miss Westerfield. He most likely does not appreciate having someone – particularly a young lady – disagree with him at every turn when he hopes to make a good impression on a young lady and her family."

Elizabeth blew out a puff of air. She knew her aunt was wise, and she trusted her judgment, but she recollected all the times in Hertfordshire and Kent their conversations bantered back and forth. If he had disliked it so and found her impertinent because of it, why had he asked for her hand?

She turned to her aunt. "You are most likely correct, and I suppose I did become rather contrary to his expressed opinions on several subjects tonight."

"It is just a word of caution, Lizzy, for we would not want Mr. Darcy to regret inviting us to join him and his guests, now, would we?"

"No, I suppose we would not."

Mrs. Gardiner chuckled. "If you find yourself tempted to disagree with something, hold it in until you are alone with me, and then you can express your outrage to your heart's content."

When they reached Mr. Gardiner's room and stepped inside, Mrs. Gardiner closed the door. "Now, having said that, Lizzy, what were you thinking when Mr. Westerfield began speaking about seeing the couple run from the shed?"

Elizabeth's cheeks warmed. "I was mortified that he had seen Mr. Darcy and me and wondered at first if he knew it was us." She noticed the look on her aunt's face. "Truly, Aunt, there was really no other way to get back to the house. I was more mortified by what Mr. Westerfield insinuated than worried that he knew who it was. I cannot imagine how Mr. Darcy felt."

"Well, it appears Westerfield did not know who it was, and for that we can be grateful." Mr. Gardiner raised a brow at his niece. "Or would you have preferred he did realize who it was? Would it have made things easier if he knew it had been the two of you, and he packed up his belongings and his family in disgust and left Pemberley?"

"I really do not know what I want or do not want at the moment, Uncle, aside from sleep. I think I shall go to my room." She kissed them both and wished them a good night.

"Good night, Lizzy," her aunt said.

"Sleep well!" her uncle added.

Despite being fatigued, Elizabeth could not settle her thoughts enough to fall asleep. So much had happened. Had she truly just encountered him only today?

She considered her aunt's admonition to her and thought about the times she had countered his opinions – challenged him, even! She had found it exhilarating, if she owned the truth. He was intelligent and even kind in his responses to her, even when he did not agree with her. But if he disliked being confronted in such a manner, why did he eventually ask for her hand?

She rolled over in bed and dug her hands under her pillow, placing her head firmly down upon it. He seemed even more of an enigma to her than he ever had before, but despite that, she felt in great danger of having an ever-increasing fondness for the man she had cruelly refused to marry.

~~*

Elizabeth awoke after suffering through only a few hours of sleep, her mind still in turmoil. She had finally conceded that she could ill afford to upset or embarrass Mr. Darcy with her differing opinions. He was being gracious to her and her family, despite the abominable way she had treated him a few months back. He had been extending to them the most generous and gracious hospitality, more than she and her relations deserved or expected.

She would honour her aunt's request, and if she found herself at odds with a topic of conversation, she would hold her tongue so as not to provoke him or his guests. He deserved only the utmost respect. She could only hope she was capable of doing it!

Elizabeth walked to the window and looked out as the rising sun shone through a hazy mist. It appeared there would be no more rain, but it was still muddy outside; otherwise, she would have taken a walk. She would love to take a leisurely stroll across a meadow or run wildly through the woods as she attempted to sort out the array of thoughts and feelings assaulting her.

She sat quietly, waiting for her aunt to waken, and after they had dressed, they both went to see how Mr. Gardiner was faring.

He was still suffering from a little pain and stiffness, so they sent a message to Mr. and Miss Darcy by way of Mrs. Reynolds that they would remain in their room to break their fast instead of going to the dining room. Mr. Gardiner did not think he could make that long of a walk again so soon, so they thanked them for the previous evening and hoped that a good day of rest would be all he needed.

Mrs. Reynolds came by with both Elizabeth's bonnet and a message from Mr. Darcy. He hoped to see them again that evening in the small dining room if Mr. Gardiner felt up to it. Elizabeth could not help but feel a tinge of regret that he did not come himself.

The doctor came by later that morning, and while he was there, Elizabeth returned to her room. She opened the book she had picked up in Mr. Darcy's library and sat down to read. At length, there was a light tap on her door.

"Come in," she called out.

The door opened slowly, and Miss Darcy peered in. "I hope I am not disturbing you."

"Oh, no, I am only reading. Come and join me." Elizabeth pointed to a chair across from her. "What can I do for you?"

A pained look crossed Miss Darcy's face. "In truth, I am seeking a respite from Miss Westerfield."

Elizabeth's brows lifted in surprise. "Miss Westerfield? Why is that?"

Miss Darcy shook her head. "When my brother is occupied, as he is now, she always seeks me out."

"I see. She seems nice. Is there... is there something you dislike about her?"

"Oh, no. She is very kind and attentive... very attentive." She lifted her hands in frustration. "There are times I need to be alone, and she does not seem to understand that."

"Is now one of those times?"

Georgiana nodded.

"Could you not sequester yourself in your chambers for a short while?"

"Oh, I am certain she would seek me out."

Elizabeth could not help but smile. "You claim you wanted time alone, and yet you came here. May I ask why?"

Georgiana shrugged. "I feel as though I can talk to you. It is not..." Georgiana paused and twisted her face in thought. "I do not feel as though it is a lot of work and effort for me to talk to you. You make it easy."

Elizabeth laughed. "Truly? And you do not feel that way with Miss Westerfield?"

Georgiana pursed her lips, as if she were considering her words. "While Miss Westerfield is very kind, the only things she wants to talk about with me are my brother and Pemberley." She let out a puff of air. "I feel as though I am merely a source of information for her about them and she is not at all interested in who I am."

"I see." Elizabeth searched the young lady's face; she could readily see the desperate look of someone who wanted to be liked for herself and not for her brother or her home.

Miss Darcy looked down at her fingers, which she was nervously knitting together. "Miss Bennet, I want to apologize for the remarks Mr. Westerfield made last evening." She slowly looked up with a small smile. "My brother informed me how you sought refuge in the potting shed while he was there, and I realized he must have been the one who was carrying you, so you would not get wet and muddy. We are certain Mr. Westerfield is not aware that it was either of you." She reached out and placed her fingers on Elizabeth's hand. "We regret any discomfiture you might have felt last night when he gave his account of what he saw."

Elizabeth pursed her lips together and drew in a deep breath. "I own I felt somewhat disconcerted, as I am certain your brother did, but I know Mr. Westerfield did not mention it to cause any of us unease."

"My brother and I are both very sorry."

Elizabeth smiled. "I do not blame you, so there is no reason for the two of you to be sorry."

Miss Darcy stood up and walked over to window. She drew in a long breath before speaking. "I do not know if you are aware, Miss Bennet, but my brother invited the Westerfields to Pemberley because he is... he is considering asking for Miss Westerfield's hand." She turned and looked at Elizabeth with what seemed to be a studied expression.

Elizabeth felt her heart pound at hearing those words. "I... I had wondered whether that might be the case." She could not help but wonder if the young girl was giving her a cautionary warning and wished she knew whether Miss Darcy was aware of all that had happened between her and her brother. She lifted her eyes and tried to smile. "How do you feel about it?" She hoped the young lady had not noticed the quaver in her voice.

"She is kind and very pretty, but..." Georgiana came and sat across from Elizabeth on the bed. "I do not know if she is particularly suited for him."

Elizabeth smiled and took her hand. "You would likely feel that way about any lady he would consider marrying, for I suspect you feel that lady will be taking someone away from you whom you consider very special."

"I do love him dearly, but I do not want him making a

mistake."

Elizabeth drew in a breath. "It shows what a caring sister you are."

She shook her head. "He brought her here with the intention of getting to know her better. They have not spent a great deal of time together recently, you see." She drew in a breath. "While that was his main intention – and an engagement was certainly a possibility – rumours began swirling around the Ton that it was a settled matter and he would ask for her hand directly."

"Do you think she and her family are expecting him to offer for her?"

The young girl's eyes widened, and she nodded. "I do, but… I have said too much." She let out a nervous laugh. "As I said, for some reason it is very easy for me to talk to you."

Elizabeth forced herself to smile. "I thank you."

Georgiana seemed to search her face for a moment and then said, "I shall leave you now. Will we see you this evening?"

"We hope to be able to join you."

Georgiana stepped out, and Elizabeth pressed her hand to her neck. She closed her eyes as she considered Miss Darcy's words and wondered if she knew how her brother had once felt about her. She shook her head and began to walk about the room.

"No, I cannot assume he feels anything for me anymore!" She felt the sting of tears forming in her eyes and tried to hold them back. One tear, however, slowly made its way down her cheek. Wiping it away, she stopped at the window and gazed out.

The sun was winning its battle against the haze, and she looked forward to exploring more of Pemberley's grounds on the morrow. Hopefully everything would be dry.

Elizabeth joined her aunt and uncle after the doctor left. He had told her uncle the pain he was experiencing today was to be expected after the increase in movement and activity the day before, but admonished him to rest as much as he felt he needed. He assured them that he did not believe the pain was due to any further injury.

He also informed them that perhaps he might be fit to travel again in two to three days.

Mr. and Mrs. Gardiner were delighted to receive the news, but

Elizabeth could not fully rally her spirits. While it would be best for her peace of mind to leave, she found herself enjoying Mr. Darcy's company far too much and did not wish to be out of his presence. She knew once they departed Pemberley, she would never see him again, for he would likely ask for Miss Westerfield's hand. It was all she could do to keep her tears from spilling over.

~~*

After resting throughout the day, Mr. Gardiner felt he was up to walking to the dining room for the evening meal. They informed Mrs. Reynolds they would be joining everyone.

When they came into the sitting room, as they had the previous evening, they were greeted with smiles and laughter.

"We have just had Mr. Darcy's assurance that there will be a musical soiree two evenings from tonight." Mrs. Westerfield smiled and then looked at her daughter. "Angeline will sing and play, Miss Darcy will play, and Mr. Darcy has agreed to sing." She clasped her hands together. "Shall you delight us with your singing or playing, Miss Bennet? Mrs. Gardiner, Mr. Gardiner, will you be participants or observers?"

"Well, I…" Elizabeth began, and all eyes turned to her. "I will play and sing – as long as I have an instrument on which to practice."

Mrs. Gardiner waved her hand through the air. "Edmund and I shall be delighted to be observers, thank you. He would not be up to performing – he plays the viola, but I imagine it would prove too stressful for his back."

"In addition to the fact that I do not have my viola with me," he said with a laugh. "My dear wife did not think we had room for it on our journey."

Everyone laughed, and Elizabeth was grateful her uncle seemed to be doing so much better. She looked around the room and listened as everyone cheerfully talked about how delightful their small soiree would be. Save for Darcy, who seemed to be looking, but not seeing, his mind fixed on some completely different object. Perhaps he was wondering when he would ask for Miss Westerfield's hand. Or perhaps it was the urgent matter that had brought him home a day early.

~~*

During the meal, Elizabeth was on her best behaviour – at least according to her aunt's standards. While she was tempted to offer a contrary opinion on several occasions, she chose to answer with a polite nod, an affirming murmur, or complete silence. She did not trust herself to answer in a way she did not truly feel.

When the last course of the meal was being served, Elizabeth was ready for this charade to be finished. She realized she missed the banter she had had with Mr. Darcy back at Netherfield and Kent, but she would be obedient to her aunt's wishes.

At length, the subject of his library came up.

"It is a thing of beauty, Darcy," Mr. Westerfield said.

"Thank you. I am rather proud of the collection of books I have. I enjoy reading a variety of subjects."

"As should everyone!" exclaimed Miss Westerfield.

Elizabeth had to stifle the smile as she recollected the extent of Miss Westerfield's interest in the library seemed to be mainly to impress her guests one day as Mistress of Pemberley.

Darcy continued speaking with Mr. Westerfield, and therefore, she turned her attention to the conversation Georgiana was having with Miss Westerfield. Elizabeth suspected that the young girl knew of Miss Westerfield's lack of interest in reading. "My brother owns a very large collection of historical and biographical books." She shook her head and pinched her brows. "He insists that I read at least one a week to expand my knowledge. It is very important to him to be informed of the events and people of the past." She drew in a resigned breath. "I am convinced he shall one day also demand it of his wife and children."

Elizabeth's eyes widened, and she quickly looked down, but not before seeing Miss Westerfield's face grow pale.

"Does he truly?" she asked and then looked at Mr. Darcy.

Georgiana nodded. "Do you enjoy reading historical and biographical books? Some can be so large and so dull!"

"Well, I… not very often, but I believe I could."

Elizabeth looked up to see Georgiana smile and turn her

112

attention back to her plate. She was not certain, but it appeared that Georgiana had unnerved Miss Westerfield in laying forth these expectations her brother may – or may not – have. But if it was not something Mr. Darcy demanded, his next words seemed to indicate she was right – if only partially.

"I have a great many books of poetry in my collection. I believe everyone ought to have a great appreciation for rhyme. It is timeless and holds aesthetic value."

A chorus of agreement came from those at the table.

Mrs. Westerfield clasped her hands in glee. "Mr. Westerfield showered me with sonnets when we met. It was what made me fall in love with him – that and his ready smile and bright blue eyes." She looked at him and smiled, and then back to Mr. Darcy. "He even wrote some especially for me."

"Ah yes, poetry is the food of love," Darcy said, suddenly directing his gaze at Elizabeth. "What are your thoughts on poetry, Miss Bennet? Does it nourish and encourage love… or might it starve it away entirely?"

She was startled that he directed his question at her until she recollected their conversation at Netherfield about poetry. Was he inciting her to challenge his stated opinion on the subject?

"I think…" She paused and looked at her aunt, who was eyeing her warily. Turning back to Mr. Darcy, she said, "I think a sonnet will have whatever effect on love the person reading it desires."

Mr. Westerfield laughed. "Now that is a safe statement, and if that is the case, then it matters not whether the poems I wrote my wife were good or bad. She would have come to love me as long as she had the desire to." He lifted up his glass to Elizabeth. "So now we know."

Everyone laughed at his comment, except Elizabeth. She looked across the table at Mr. Darcy who was looking at her curiously, with a raised brow and lips pressed tightly together.

She shuddered as she realized he was looking at her much the same way he had in Hertfordshire, when she believed him to be studying her to find fault with her. She quickly averted her gaze, reached for her goblet, and took a sip of her wine.

Chapter 10

Elizabeth awoke the next morning as the first rays of light filtered into her room. Her aunt was still sleeping, so she rose quietly and walked to the window, hoping to see blue sky and sunshine. She pulled back the rose-coloured drapery and was granted her wish.

She dressed in a yellow muslin morning dress as quietly as she could, so as not to waken her aunt. Mrs. Gardiner began to stir, however, and finally sat up.

"You are awake already, Lizzy?"

"Yes, I woke up and could not sleep any longer. Pray, forgive me for waking you. I was hoping I would not disturb you."

"Are you going out for a walk?"

Elizabeth nodded. "It looks delightful outside, and I have not taken an extended walk around Pemberley since we arrived." She chuckled. "My attempts were always interrupted by something."

"All right, but do take your shawl… and do not get lost."

Elizabeth picked up her shawl and tossed it over her arm. "I will try not to get lost, Aunt. As large as Pemberley manor is, I doubt I will ever be beyond its sight."

Elizabeth walked out to the sound of her aunt's laughter.

When she stepped outside into the courtyard, she breathed in deeply. The air, after the rain two days ago, was fresh, yet cool, so she wrapped her shawl about her shoulders and began to walk. When she reached the large archway that took one out of the courtyard, she stopped to determine which way to go. She had already walked to the lake, stream, and gardens, so she considered exploring the nearby woods or perhaps the grassy meadow that extended beyond the lake.

She turned around and looked at the low ridge that rose behind Pemberley. "Ahh! It will give me a perfect view of all that Pemberley is!" Her heart fluttered at just the thought of its vastness, and she decided to set off in that direction.

Elizabeth quickly found a walking path with a gentle incline that was not any steeper than the one she walked at Oakham Mount. While muddy in spots, it was passable as long as she took care where she stepped. After some leisurely walking, she looked up and realized the summit of the ridge was higher than she had initially thought. Off to the side, however, was a delightful flat area which would provide a nice view of the prospect below.

She walked over and leaned against a tree, looking out over the manor, which was just below her. The view below of the sparkling lake, dense woods, and colourful gardens was magnificent. Her breath caught as she considered again that it all could have been hers. That thought had assaulted her at different times throughout her stay. She let out a sigh of admiration as she considered the stately home, the incomparable library, the dark polished wood of the furniture, the fine fabrics of the window coverings and upholstery, and the… gentleman. Elizabeth put her hand up to her neck, fingering the pendant she wore as she pondered all that had taken place since…

"Good morning, Miss Bennet."

Elizabeth started and turned in surprise, feeling a euphoric wave flood through her when she saw Mr. Darcy walking towards her. "Good morning," she replied with a smile. "Are you on your way up to the top of the ridge?"

Darcy shook his head. "No, I am actually on my way down from there."

Elizabeth looked up. "I thought I would attempt it, but I think this morning I will settle for this being my destination. It is a lovely view."

"It is one of my favourites." Darcy turned and pointed up to the top. "From up there you can view both sides of the ridge, but you are limited as to what you can see of Pemberley because of the overgrown shrubbery. This open ledge allows one to see so much more."

"Then that settles it. This is as high as I shall go…" She turned and looked at him with a teasing smile. "At least today."

They stood quietly, both gazing at the vista below them. Finally, Elizabeth said, "Does Miss Westerfield not wish to walk this morning?" She turned her head briefly towards Mr. Darcy, and then back. "I saw you go out with her before the rains came."

Darcy's shoulders rose as he took in a breath. "I do not think she is inclined to walk as far or as long as I wish to. My purpose in climbing up the ridge this morning was to see how the grounds fared in the storm. With the winds and heavy rains we received, I wanted to make certain no trees were down and there were no areas of flooding."

"I see. And was everything to your satisfaction?"

Darcy nodded. "Yes. At least all that I could see from up there. My steward will ride out later today to check some of the areas that cannot be determined from such a distance."

After a moment's pause, Darcy spoke again. "I am glad your uncle is improving."

"Thank you. I know he is grateful that he is now able to get up and about." Elizabeth pressed her lips together. There was a moment of silence again, and then she said, "It appears you have a lot of pleasant memories with Miss Westerfield."

Darcy shifted his weight from one foot to another. "Yes, our family acquaintance goes back many years."

"She is… she seems most amiable."

"Yes, she is exceptionally… agreeable."

Elizabeth felt a sudden wave of disappointment flood her, after having just felt such elation. She clasped her hands tightly when a tremor passed through her.

Darcy suddenly turned to face her. "May I ask you a question?"

Elizabeth looked up at him and mutely nodded.

Before speaking, he looked down and crossed him arms. When he looked back up, he asked, "Where were you last evening?"

Elizabeth started. "Pardon me? You saw me at dinner, as well as before and after." She shook her head. "I do not understand the meaning of your question."

His brows lowered, and he slowly shook his head. "I saw someone last evening that looked a great deal like you, but that young lady did not act at all like the Miss Bennet I know. I have my doubts that it was you."

Elizabeth could not stifle her laugh. "Unless I have a twin somewhere, you know very well it was me."

"All reasoning would have indicated it was you, but you… not once did you disagree with me – or anyone else – on any subject."

He leaned in towards her. "Even the subject of poetry, of which I know we spoke – and disagreed on – at Netherfield."

Elizabeth looked down sheepishly. "Yes, we did, and yes, I did agree with you on just about everything last evening."

"No, you agreed with me on *absolutely* everything," Darcy corrected her. "Not once did you challenge or argue with anything that was said."

Elizabeth nervously turned her gaze away from him and back towards the view. "I am far too outspoken. My aunt suggested I ought to respect you as our host and all that you have done for us, by not being so disposed to express any opposite opinions I may have."

Darcy let out a huff. "I see."

Elizabeth bit her lip and tilted her head as she looked back at him. "You appear to be displeased. Is that because I did not argue with you last night? Do you believe my aunt was wrong in advising me to keep my pert opinions to myself?"

"I can understand her concern. But I tire of hearing opinions – particularly those of ladies – that only agree with mine." Darcy drew himself erect and added, "I have often wondered who a lady really was, what they were really like, and what their true opinions on subjects were." He gave his head a shake. "It may come as a surprise that I rather enjoy a lively discussion, even if it is on the opposite side of an argument." He took in a deep breath. "For example, the Miss Westerfield I knew and remembered when we were younger was never afraid to challenge me or disagree with me. She no longer does that."

"I see," Elizabeth said softly. "Oh!" she said after a moment of silence. Her eyes widened as the import of his words forcefully struck her. She suddenly comprehended that while she had argued with him in Hertfordshire and Kent out of spite, he had welcomed her frequent and somewhat contentious discussions. She felt her face warm in a blush and looked down.

When she looked back up, he was staring intently at her. "Miss Bennet, if you will excuse me I ought to return. Enjoy your morning."

"Thank you."

He remained still, however, and said, "I understand your aunt's giving you such prudent advice. You may continue to abide by it if you wish, but…" He paused and pressed his lips together quickly. "I will not think poorly of you if you go against your aunt's counsel and disagree with me on occasion." He began to walk to the path, but stopped and turned back to her. "It is often through intelligent, differing discourse that one can grow in their understanding of another and perhaps be enlightened about their own faulty reasoning, beliefs, and even their… conduct."

Elizabeth smiled as she watched him walk away, feeling that her understanding of the man was becoming clearer with each passing day.

~~*

Later that afternoon Elizabeth joined her aunt in assisting Mr. Gardiner as he walked the length of the hall and back without his cane. He was not as sore this morning as he had been the day before and wanted to walk a little beyond the small dining room. As they came to one of the main hallways and turned, they heard music playing in the distance.

"I wonder if that is Miss Darcy playing." She looked at the Gardiners. "Since I earlier turned down her invitation to hear her play, would you mind if I go hear her now?" She bit her lip. "Besides, I need to decide what I am going to perform at the soiree. Perhaps I can select something while she is playing, and then practice when she is finished."

Mr. Gardiner took her hand and squeezed it. "You go on, my dear. Your aunt and I shall manage nicely."

"Thank you." Elizabeth turned in the direction of the music, knowing it was coming from upstairs. She followed the melodic sounds as she recollected the various rooms they visited on their tour five days ago. Had it truly been five days? So much had happened since then!

She came to the room and peeked in. Georgiana was facing away from her as she concentrated on her piece of music. Not wishing to startle her, Elizabeth remained silent until she had finished her piece. When the young girl finished, Elizabeth began to softly clap her hands.

Georgiana turned quickly, and a smile appeared on her face. "Oh, Miss Bennet! I thought perhaps you were my brother. He always sneaks upon me like that and then claps, whether I deserve it or not."

"Well, you certainly deserved it. You are delightfully proficient."

The young girl chuckled. "Thank you. I do enjoy it."

"Will you play another? And while you play, may I look through the music for something I might perform tomorrow night?"

"Certainly." Georgiana indicated to Elizabeth where she would find a good selection of music and walked over with her.

The two ladies perused the pieces of music together, and Georgiana quickly settled on one that she claimed she truly enjoyed. She returned to the piano while Elizabeth continued to look.

As she began to play, Elizabeth continued to look through the music, pulling out two pieces with which she was familiar. She read through each piece to familiarize herself with them, and then decided on one. She looked up at Georgiana with a smile and began to move her feet to the music. "Ah, a three-quarter piece. One can waltz to this if one is so inclined."

"Do you know how to waltz?" Georgiana asked, looking briefly from her music to Elizabeth. "My brother forbids me to learn until I am older."

Elizabeth laughed. "It is thought to be a scandalous dance by many. I only know enough of the steps to be a danger to some gentleman's toes if I were to dance it on the dance floor." She looked down at her feet as they moved in rhythm, forward, to the side, and then back again. She then lifted her hands as if she had a partner and continued.

She closed her eyes as she concentrated on the steps. She could imagine no one but Mr. Darcy as her invisible partner. When her hand was suddenly clasped, her eyes shot open.

"It appears as though you are without a partner, Miss Bennet. May I have this dance?" He gave a bow.

Elizabeth looked up into his smiling face and lost all ability to think, let alone dance. Her feet stopped moving, and she felt her cheeks grow warm. "I… I think not. I really do not know how to perform the waltz well."

"It is actually much easier than many of the country dances and all their steps one must learn. I was watching you and could readily see you know the basics. Shall we?"

Elizabeth felt his hand lightly press into her back at her waist as he took her hand in his other. She suddenly knew why many considered it an inappropriate dance. She could not imagine dancing so close to just any gentleman. The fact that it was Mr. Darcy gave her pause to consider just how much her opinion of him had improved, for she was greatly enjoying it.

He slowly began to move to the music. "Would you not agree that neither of us perform well for strangers?"

Elizabeth instantly recollected the conversation they had at Rosings, but before she could think of a reply, he added in a soft voice, "But then, we are not strangers, are we?"

Elizabeth dared not look at him. She felt her face warm as she considered the import of his words and swallowed in an attempt to moisten her dry mouth. As he began to move to the rhythm of the music, she struggled to command her feet to move in the proper direction, but instead, she tripped.

"Just follow me," he said reassuringly.

Elizabeth tentatively placed her left hand above his shoulder, just barely touching it. She kept it there until a turn prompted her to grasp it tightly to prevent herself from falling. No, this was not at all like country dancing, which was faster and with very little contact with one's partner other than holding hands.

When she finally felt comfortable enough to look up at him, and she was better able to regulate her thoughts, she asked, "How is it that you know the waltz, Mr. Darcy? Many consider it quite scandalous." She laughed softly. "Even your sister told me you will not allow her to learn it."

"Georgiana is too young. And I only came to learn it because my aunt – Colonel Fitzwilliam's mother – forced the two of us to learn because she felt it would soon become widely acceptable and popular in England." He shook his head. "We surmised it was so she could have partners with whom to practice. Her husband refuses to learn."

"I see." Elizabeth said with a soft laugh.

She was all too aware of how close he was to her. With every turn they made, Mr. Darcy pressed his hand gently against her back and closed his hand more firmly around hers to guide her. While she had enjoyed being held in his arms when he had carried her in the rain, she now felt a great delight that she did not want to end. At length, she realized he was humming to the music, and she smiled as she realized he did, indeed, have a very pleasant baritone voice.

Elizabeth drew her head back and asked, "Do you always hum when you dance? I do not recollect that you were humming when we danced at the Netherfield Ball."

"Was I humming just now? I did not realize it."

"You were, and your sister is correct. You do have a very nice voice."

"I thank you, and no, I rarely hum when I dance."

"You must be enjoying your sister's playing."

"Yes... she plays superbly," he said softly as the music came to a stop.

They stood silently watching each other, still in the position of a waltzing couple. They quickly stepped apart when they heard the sound of footsteps hurrying away from the door.

Darcy took in a quick breath and rushed towards the door, looking to his left and then right when he reached the hall. He shook his head as he walked back into the room. "Unfortunately, I did not see who it was. It was most likely a servant walking past."

His pinched brows told Elizabeth he suspected differently.

Elizabeth looked up and attempted to make light of the situation despite the onslaught of feelings and seeing in his features a reflection of those same emotions. "Thank you for the dance, sir. You are an exceptional instructor."

"You are an exceptional... student."

"I had... I had better return to my room to see if my aunt and uncle have need of anything to ready themselves for dinner. Thank you." She turned to Georgiana. "Thank you for allowing me to hear you play, Miss Darcy... and for the music." She retrieved her piece of music with shaking fingers. She knew it would be futile to practice the piece now. "I shall return later to practice."

As Elizabeth hurried out of the room, she looked down at her hand, which Mr. Darcy's fingers had enfolded. Despite its trembling, it felt warm to the touch, and she placed it gently over her heart.

~~*

Darcy stood still for a moment after Elizabeth stepped from the room. He was silent as he looked down at the hand he had wrapped around hers. It still felt warm, and he brought it up to his face, covering his lips and jaw.

Darcy turned back to face Georgiana, who came and stood beside him. He smiled at her as his feelings for Elizabeth assaulted him.

"You enjoyed dancing with her, did you not?" she asked.

"I should never have…"

"But you did, and I can readily see that you still have strong feelings for her."

Darcy looked down at the hand that had cradled hers and grasped it with his other hand. "I own… I do have feelings for her, but…"

"Why can you not admit you still love her and you will never love Miss Westerfield as much as you do Miss Bennet?" Georgiana shook her head. "Miss Westerfield is kind and sweet and pretty, but you do not love her."

Darcy took in a deep breath. "If only it were that simple."

Georgiana straightened her shoulders and swallowed. She had never spoken to her brother in this fashion, but she felt strongly about this. "I know love is never simple, and I know you asked for her hand once and she refused you, but I believe you are so afraid of being hurt by her again that you do not see that her feelings for you have improved."

Darcy waited to answer as he gathered his thoughts. "They may have improved but that does not mean she loves me."

"And you will do nothing to secure her love?" Georgiana shook her head. "I believe your actions and words towards her – or your inaction and silence – are an indication of how much or how little you really love her and are willing to sacrifice for her." She drew in a deep breath. "Do you not see that she is likely just as afraid of allowing herself to love you as you are her? She already turned down your offer of marriage once, and it is likely she fears you would not give your heart to her again."

Darcy's mouth went dry.

"I watched both of you as you danced. There was something that was very evident to me, and I personally believe it was a strong sense of love and devotion." She reached up on her toes and kissed his cheek. "I shall leave you now, Brother. I need to get ready for dinner and shall leave you to think on it." She tilted her head. "Will you promise to do that?"

Darcy leaned over and kissed the top of his sister's head. "I promise, Georgiana."

He watched her leave and then closed his eyes. He could still feel the sensation of holding Elizabeth and twirling to the rhythm of the music as he waltzed with her. His brows lowered, and he let out a long breath. Could Georgiana be correct? Had Elizabeth's feelings for him improved? He could only hope.

Chapter 11

Elizabeth determined that she would keep her differing opinions on matters being discussed to herself this evening, despite now knowing how much Mr. Darcy enjoyed them. She would not incite any disagreements, engage in any bantering, or challenge anyone's assertions, but would either remain silent or cheerfully agree with what was being said, as her aunt had advised. She wanted to respect her aunt's caution.

As she and the Gardiners gathered in the larger dining room to eat, however, she realized there had been no need for her to have made such a resolution. It ended up being a very quiet meal with sparse conversation.

The Westerfields said very little. Mr. Westerfield had no teasing remarks, Mrs. Westerfield offered no compliments, and Miss Westerfield's formerly frequent smile rarely appeared on her face. Elizabeth was uncomfortable, as she realized one of them likely had witnessed her dancing with Mr. Darcy, and now all were aware of it. Just the thought brought a rosy tint to her cheeks, feeling both exhilaration at being in his arms and discomfiture that she had been seen in the arms of the gentleman the Westerfields believed would be making an offer to their daughter.

Mr. Darcy made several attempts at conversation, but only succeeded in getting a response from Mr. Gardiner. The two of them seemed to be the only ones interested in conversing.

Elizabeth had not informed her aunt and uncle about their spontaneous waltz. She was fairly certain they would not have approved of it, especially since they suspected Mr. Darcy's intention was to ask for Miss Westerfield's hand. She also wondered about their views of the waltz, especially when danced by two people who had no understanding between them, despite its becoming more acceptable in society.

After the meal, the party moved to the small parlour, where they again had little conversation. At length, Mr. and Mrs. Gardiner excused themselves, citing Mr. Gardiner's fatigue.

Elizabeth rose with them and excused herself, as well. They thanked Mr. and Miss Darcy for a lovely meal and evening, said good evening to the others, and walked to the door. As Elizabeth trailed behind her aunt and uncle, Mr. Darcy came to her side and joined her as she stepped out of the room.

"Must you leave, Miss Bennet?" he asked softly.

Elizabeth noticed her aunt turn back, giving her a quizzical look as the couple continued to walk away. Elizabeth looked down, feeling the nearness of Mr. Darcy unsettling to her composure. "I think I must. It has been a long day."

Darcy turned his head slightly towards the room and then back to her. "I know you are concerned that one of the Westerfields saw us dancing. I beg you please not to worry yourself. If they mention it, I will reassure them that it was just a dance."

Elizabeth's mouth felt dry as she gazed up at his encouraging gaze, although it did nothing to reassure her. She tried to smile. "Good night, Mr. Darcy." She curtseyed and turned, walking away.

"Good night, Miss Bennet."

Elizabeth heard the long release of his breath and then footsteps as he returned to the room.

~~*

Darcy walked back into the sitting room, noticing the silence and awkward looks of his guests and Georgiana. He sent his sister a questioning glance, and it was returned with a slight grimace. He had only been out of the room a few minutes; he hoped their guests' silence had not distressed her.

"Ah, you have returned. I fear, good sir, that we are fatigued, as well. If you do not mind, we are going to retire to our rooms. Good evening to you both." Mr. Westerfield stood and reached for his wife's hand, saying no more. After helping her to her feet, he assisted his daughter in rising.

"Thank you for a delightful day and delicious meal," Mrs. Westerfield said with a small attempt at a smile.

They said their goodnights and walked out. The solemn expressions on Miss Westerfield and her mother's faces convinced Darcy they were either unhappy with Mr. Westerfield's decision to retire early or displeased with *him*, having seen him dancing with Elizabeth. He suspected the latter.

When they were gone, he turned to Georgiana. "Did anything happen in here while I was in the hallway?" He walked towards her and took her hand. "Did they speak of anything?"

Georgiana shook her head. "They said nothing." She rolled her head, letting out a sigh. "I fear I do not fare well when no one is inclined to converse. I had no idea what to say to them, especially since I believe that it was one of them who had seen you and Miss Bennet dance." She looked up at him. "Even though you were only out of the room a few minutes, it felt much longer to me as I struggled to know how to begin a conversation with them."

Darcy pressed his lips together and then softly said, "I am sorry."

There was a moment of silence between them, and Georgiana finally spoke. "To own the truth, I felt little compulsion to try to converse with them."

Darcy's brows lifted quickly. "Truly? Why is that?"

Georgiana looked down at her hands as she rubbed her fingers together. She finally looked back up. "Because if I had to choose which of the two ladies I would want for my sister, it would have to be Miss Bennet." She drew in a long breath. "Miss Westerfield is sweet and kind, but I have not felt that she is interested in getting to know me at all. Miss Bennet, on the other hand, truly seems interested in who I am and does not just consider me the younger sister of Mr. Darcy of Pemberley."

She stood up and took her brother's hand as he regarded her intently. "The Gardiners are likely to depart Pemberley very soon. I would suggest you do something before they do!"

"And what would you have me to do?"

She gave a slight shrug of her shoulders. "At least try to determine what Miss Bennet's feelings for you might be." She released his hand and smiled. "I shall leave you now. Good night."

Darcy watched his sister walk towards the door. "Good night, Georgiana."

~~*

126

The next morning Darcy set out early for a walk. Having slept little because of the thoughts that had assailed him, he had tossed and turned most of the night. Dreams – or was it merely vivid recollections – of holding Elizabeth as they danced, and her hand in his – pushed away all other thoughts and concerns. As he aimlessly walked Pemberley's grounds, he knew what he wanted. Georgiana's thoughts and wishes from the previous night mirrored his own. But could he risk being rebuffed by Elizabeth a second time?

There were storm clouds on the horizon, and he hurried his steps. He would not return to the home, however, for he needed to walk to clear his thoughts, and he hoped he could sort them out before the rains came. He set out in the direction of the woods.

As he walked, he thought back to the previous night, pondering all that had occurred, but particularly, his sister's words. He wanted nothing more than to give in to the leanings of his heart and attach his affections to Miss Bennet. The mere thought exhilarated, as well as unsettled, him. The love he had for Miss Bennet was as strong as it had ever been, but her rejection at Hunsford and the pain it caused him were still as deep as a fresh wound.

He looked down at his hand, where he had cut himself with the knife when she had entered the potting shed. It was mostly healed, but it would likely leave a scar. He knew that no matter how much time would pass since that fateful day in Kent, he would likely have a permanent scar on his heart. The wound on his hand was healing; however, his heart had not.

Darcy drew in a deep breath and let it out slowly as he turned to the path that would take him into the woods. As he stepped within the canopy of trees, he looked up to see the small specks of blue sky peeking through the plethora of leaves. The light along the path dimmed as the trees grew thicker and the clouds began to obscure the morning sun. There was silence except for the chirping songs of the birds and the crunching of twigs beneath his boots.

He walked only a short distance when he suddenly stopped, finding himself face to face with the young lady who held his heart in her hands and kept his thoughts captive. She had been standing still, looking at something just off the path.

He nodded and smiled. "Miss Bennet, this is a surprise."

She laughed, saying, "You know me well enough, Mr. Darcy, to know I love walking."

"Are you returning from the woods?"

"I thought I might enjoy walking through the dense shelter of trees, but I discovered I could not see the house from here and feared I might get lost, so I decided against it."

"It is easy to get lost in them." Darcy glanced back towards the house, which he could not see.

"Yes, I would imagine."

"What specifically drew your attention?"

"I… I was watching the magpie over there." She nodded her head to the right. "I was hoping to see another, for…" She looked down. "It is a silly…"

"*One is for sorrow,*" Darcy said.

"Yes! I despise that rhyme, although when I see but one magpie, I always look around with the hope that I will see another. *Two is for mirth,*" she said with a laugh, and then gave a shrug when the lone magpie flew away. "I guess it is only to be one." She turned back to Mr. Darcy. "I shall be on my way."

He squared his shoulders. "Miss Bennet if you wish, you may accompany me. I thought I would walk into the woods this morning." He paused and then added again, "If you wish." He held his breath as he waited for her reply. He felt if she declined, all his heartfelt hopes for this woman would be dashed.

"Yes, I would like that very much."

Darcy's breath released, along with a smile of relief. He felt a surge of exhilaration. At first, the two walked in silence. Darcy's mind reeled with thoughts about how he might convey to Elizabeth that he had taken her accusations about him to heart and had come to the stark realization that in many ways she had been correct. He wondered if it would make any difference at all in how she viewed him. He carefully pondered his words to ensure they would not be as provoking as the words he spoke to her at the parsonage. As he was about to begin, Elizabeth spoke.

"Did the Westerfields say anything to you after my aunt and uncle and I left last night? Was there something that had upset them?"

Darcy stopped and turned to her, readily seeing the concern in her eyes. "They did not speak of seeing us dancing together, if that is what you mean, and I chose not to bring it up."

"I see."

As he looked at her, he realized how close he was to her, yet still so far. Unfortunately, the Westerfields being at Pemberley – and the reason he invited them – presented him with a dilemma. While he had not specifically articulated to them his reason, it was assumed he was going to propose to Miss Westerfield, and he did nothing to correct that assumption. "They really did not speak of anything. They returned to their rooms immediately after you and the Gardiners left." Darcy inclined his head towards her. "I would not let it distress you, Miss Bennet, for if Mr. Westerfield had come to believe there had been any impropriety between us, we would have heard about it from him. He has quite a temper, and he is not one to be…"

"Well, is this not astonishing? Can I really believe my eyes?"

Darcy and Elizabeth abruptly turned towards the all-too-familiar voice and found themselves face to face with George Wickham, whose wide eyes and twisted lips displayed his astonishment at seeing the two of them together at Pemberley.

"What are *you* doing here, Wickham?"

Wickham's eyes narrowed in disbelief. "Now, why would you ask that? I believe it was you, Darcy, who encouraged – nay, demanded – Colonel Forster to send me home so that I could be at my mother's side as she bid farewell to this life. I rode day and night to get here, albeit reluctantly." He leaned back against a tree and turned his eyes to Elizabeth. "But I might wonder what *she* is doing here!"

"It is none of your business!"

"Hmm. If I had known Miss Bennet was here, I would have been much more willing to come."

Darcy felt his anger rise seeing the look he gave Miss Bennet, and he glared back at him. "I told you that you were never to come to Pemberley again!"

"Ah, not quite, for you said I was never to come near the house again." He glanced about him and gave a casual shrug. "I cannot even see the house from here."

"Why are you walking these woods, then?"

"You know I am a curious creature, and I gave in to that curiosity." He smiled slyly. "Now I am so glad I did. This is so much more than I expected."

"I have no interest in your curiosity or expectations, Wickham, and I demand you leave!"

Wickham crossed his arms defiantly. "Not so quickly! How could I have missed this? How did I not know? Rumours in Lambton have it that you had invited a young lady and her family to Pemberley, and that you are soon to ask for her hand. I merely hoped for a slight glimpse of this young lady to see for myself who she was." He began to shake his head. "I confess I thought it would be a young lady with a grand fortune and exceptional connections, and I wondered if I might possibly be acquainted with her. But to discover it is none other than Miss Elizabeth Bennet of Longbourn is unbelievable." He shook his head and then turned his eyes to her. "What you must have concealed from me, Miss Bennet, when you told me about your trip to Kent and your encounter with Darcy." He let out a huff. "You must have also kept it from Lydia, for she certainly would have informed me about this attachment had she known."

"Mr. Wickham, I fear you are severely mistaken." Elizabeth's face paled, and her voice quavered. "I am not..."

"You have no idea of what you are speaking!" Darcy said heatedly.

"No?" He lifted a brow. "Darcy, you look shocked that someone in your employ might whisper some gossip. Well, even though you expect loyalty amongst your staff, there is nothing more appealing to a lowly maid than sharing gossip – especially about someone like you."

"That is enough, Wickham!"

Wickham shrugged. "I imagine you want to know who began the rumour, but that is something I cannot tell you. I heard it from my mother, weak as she is, who heard it from someone who likely heard it from someone else." He paused. "Speaking of my mother, I am rather disappointed you have not asked about her. Do you not care how she is faring?"

Darcy fought his impatience with Wickham that warred against a concern for the widow of his late father's steward. He steeled himself and asked, "How is your mother?"

"She is not well, and I doubt she will survive the week. But I think the news I now shall bring back to her that I know the young lady in question will certainly delight her enough to give her an extra day's strength." He looked down. "Of course, she will use her last breath to convince me I need to marry." He let out a sarcastic laugh.

"As both of us have tried to tell you, Mr. Darcy has no intention of asking for my hand!" A look of distress flooded Elizabeth's face. "I am here with my aunt and uncle, and my uncle suffered an accident when we were touring the home. That is the only reason I am here."

Wickham stared at her in silence, as if trying to comprehend. "Well, my eyes can see very well, and when I came upon you, the two of you look exceptionally… warm and friendly with each other." He shook his head and smiled smugly. "But if that is the case, and Darcy has no intention of asking for your hand, I apologize for the error." He looked at Darcy. "But there is still the rumour. So who is it if it is not Miss Bennet?"

When Darcy said nothing, Wickham shook his head. "I am appalled by your behaviour, Darcy. You are apparently entertaining hopes of asking one lady to marry while…" He nodded at Elizabeth with an arched brow. "…while enjoying the company of another!"

Darcy could barely breathe as he considered how this man had destroyed what had started out as a very enjoyable walk with Elizabeth. He could not imagine how she *felt*, and now that she knew everyone was expecting him to offer for Miss Westerfield, he wondered what she *thought*. He felt a sudden tremor course through him at the thought that she might feel relief. "Wickham, you need to learn to ignore the rumours, and I would hope you do not intend to spread them around further than they already have been." Darcy kicked the dirt with his boot. "Now I have asked you once and I ask you again to remove yourself from Pemberley!"

Wickham paused and looked pointedly at Elizabeth. "Miss Bennet, you appear quite distressed." He let out a sarcastic laugh.

"Pray, forgive me. But I cannot help but wonder if your distress might be due to the fact that you were hoping he would ask for your hand." He shook his head. "Or could it be that the very thought of him asking for your hand is the cause of your distress?" He turned to leave, but stopped and looked back. "Either way, you must realize that he likely considers himself too far above you to even consider it." He gave one last glare at Darcy and as he turned away, he said, "Good day."

Darcy and Elizabeth remained still and silent as they watched Wickham walk away laughing. Finally, Darcy said, "Come, let us return to the house."

Elizabeth tried to appear unaffected, but since Wickham had readily seen her distress, she was certain Darcy noticed it, as well. He apologized for Wickham's unexpected appearance and allegations, seemingly as distraught as she was over it.

"There is no need for you to apologize for *him*," Elizabeth said in a shaky voice.

They continued to walk in silence, and at length, Elizabeth spoke. "I know Mr. Wickham's unexpected appearance unsettled you. Do you worry about Georgiana with him around?"

Darcy drew in a breath and clasped his hands behind him as he walked. "I do not fear that Georgiana will have any of the feelings she believed she had when she was with him at Ramsgate, but I fear what *he* might resort to. He harbours a great deal of resentment towards me, and nothing is beyond him. He is not to be trusted." He paused and then spat out, "Never!"

"I do not know your sister very well, but in the time I have been here, I have come to believe that she is a strong young lady."

Darcy turned and looked at Elizabeth. "Thank you. Georgiana would appreciate your belief in her character." He paused and drew himself erect. "That means a great deal to me, as well."

Elizabeth tried to smile, but her heart weighed heavily on her. She did not feel equal to the task of examining Darcy's comments regarding Wickham's erroneous allegations. She could ill afford to cling to any hope that his intentions towards Miss Westerfield had changed. She was in an impossible situation and could only regret that she had not known of his goodness and character when he offered for her in Kent.

She turned her head slightly so that she could just see him walking at her side. She wanted to reach out to reassure him and console him. She had to resist the urge to slip her hand through his arm and lean against him – for her comfort, as well as his. The way things stood between them – and to own the truth, she really had no idea where they stood – she knew any such actions might be construed by him as a desperate measure to touch his heart. She wished she could leave him in no doubt that her feelings towards him had changed, but she could not. Not with Miss Westerfield here at Pemberley and expecting an offer from him.

When they had almost reached Pemberley's courtyard, Darcy paused. Elizabeth looked up at him and noticed a melancholy expression on his face. As he looked at his home, he seemed sad.

"Is something wrong?" she asked. Her hand reached towards him, but she brought it back down before touching his arm, as she longed to do. "Except for having your day ruined by Mr. Wickham."

He ran his fingers through his hair, and it was a moment before he answered. "There are times I look upon Pemberley and all it has given me, all it has to offer, and all the dreams I have had for it, and I suddenly find myself at a loss to know where I am going, and… and sometimes, even who I am."

Elizabeth's mouth went dry, and she could not help but think the words with which she had censured him in her refusal of his offer had wrought some of these feelings. She could hardly have credited them as having had such an effect on him. She glanced down, feeling a great deal of remorse, and she wished she could apologize for them.

They started walking again, and she glanced away as a tear slid down her cheek. She tried to surreptitiously wipe it away and decided now was as good a time as any to offer some sort of apology for the harsh words she had spoken to him. "Mr. Darcy, I…"

Darcy came to an abrupt stop again. "What is going on?"

Elizabeth looked up at Darcy and then followed his gaze to the front of Pemberley, which had just come into view. "It appears as though two carriages are being loaded."

"It looks like the Westerfields' carriages." He turned and looked at her with a frown. "Pray, forgive me, but I must find out what is happening." He searched her face. "The courtyard entrance is an easy walk. Would you mind terribly if I see to my guests?"

Elizabeth nodded. "Not at all. I shall find my way back without any difficulty."

"Thank you," he said with a nod of acknowledgement. He turned and walked hurriedly — and then ran — to the front of the house.

Elizabeth watched him leave and was assaulted with innumerable feelings. Could she entertain even an ounce of hope that the Westerfields were departing? If they were, did this mean Mr. Darcy would now be free? She frowned. Or would he try to make amends to the Westerfields if they were leaving because someone witnessed him dancing with her? She gave her head a shake. She felt a slight tinge of guilt that she hoped he would not.

She remained where she was and watched as he reached the carriages and began speaking with Mr. Westerfield. He then walked over to Miss Westerfield and spoke to her. As Elizabeth watched, she realized that she could find no fault with Miss Westerfield. The young lady was beautiful, kind, and had been a long-time friend of his. She felt another tear roll down her cheek as she considered the young lady who — unlike herself — was highly accomplished and had a good fortune and high connections. Her own situation in life paled in comparison.

Chapter 12

Elizabeth walked slowly into the courtyard and sat down on a bench. She tilted her head back, staring up at the sky, which had lost much of its blueness to an increasing number of clouds moving in. A single raindrop from a dark cloud overhead dropped on her cheek, mingling with a tear that trailed down her face. She reached up to wipe them both away.

She could not order her feelings. Wickham's sudden and unexpected appearance had ruined what could have been a lovely walk. If she and Mr. Darcy had been able to talk – honestly – about how things stood between them, then perhaps the Westerfields' departure would be looked upon favourably by them both. But she could not be certain that his feelings for her now were still what they had been in Kent.

When the raindrops began to increase, she hurried into the house and walked to her uncle's room. As she neared the door, she heard voices and stepped in to see Miss Darcy with her aunt and uncle.

"Miss Darcy, this is a pleasant surprise. How are you this morning?" As soon as the words were out of Elizabeth's mouth, she could readily see a look of distress on the young girl's face. "Is something wrong?"

"I have been trying to find my brother. Something has happened, and I am not certain what I ought to do."

Mrs. Gardiner put her hand on Miss Darcy's shoulder and explained further to her niece. "Apparently the Westerfields are leaving. Miss Darcy thought they seemed disturbed about something, but they would offer no reasons for their unexpected departure."

"Your brother has gone to them. We… I saw him walk to the front just as the Westerfields were about to board their carriage."

A sigh of relief escaped Georgiana's lips. "I am so glad. I would not wish to have them leave without his seeing them first."

"Did they say something was wrong?" Mrs. Gardiner shook her

head. "I cannot possibly imagine them to be unhappy with anything here."

Georgiana lifted her eyes to Elizabeth, and they exchanged a brief glance.

"I am certain it was nothing serious." Elizabeth hoped she sounded more convinced than she felt. "Perhaps something came up that required their attention elsewhere."

"Yes, perhaps…" Georgiana gave a small curtsey. "I ought to join him. If you will please excuse me…"

"Yes, certainly!" Mr. Gardiner said. Once she was gone, he looked up at his niece with a sly smile. "So could it be perhaps that the beautiful Miss Westerfield has decided Pemberley and Mr. Darcy are not good enough for her?"

Elizabeth shook her head. "I doubt that." She could not get rid of the feeling that she might be responsible for what was now taking place, and she felt a weight of guilt upon her.

"Well, we must not conjecture," Mrs. Gardiner said. "Perhaps Mr. Darcy will tell us later, but in the meantime, let us make the most of our time left here. With Edmund's mobility improved, we ought to make plans to return home. I would like to visit one more friend in Lambton before we leave, so I will send off a note to her to see if I may pay her a call on the morrow." She looked at her husband and smiled. "Do you think you will be able to manage without me for a few hours if I do so?"

"I am certain I shall manage somehow!" he replied with a hearty laugh. "What could go wrong?"

~~*

Darcy hurried towards the front of the house, hoping to get there before the carriage pulled away. He was not certain what prompted the Westerfields' decision to leave, but he had his suspicions. He hated the possibility that Miss Westerfield may have been hurt if she or one of her parents had seen him dancing with Elizabeth. He and Angeline had always been such good friends. His stomach lurched, however, as he considered that if he had asked for her hand, he would be marrying a young lady he did not love. At the moment, he could not decide whether he felt relief they were leaving or guilt that it was because of his actions.

He was out of breath when he reached the front of the house. He slowed down and brushed himself off as he approached them. He was grateful he would be able to speak to them before they departed.

"Are you leaving?" Darcy asked. "Is something wrong?"

Both ladies looked silently at Mr. Westerfield who replied. "Not necessarily wrong, sir, but it appears our expectations were not in accordance with yours."

Miss Westerfield dipped her head down, but not before Darcy noticed a tear trailing down her cheek.

"I am... I must beg your forgiveness. I regret if there has been a misunderstanding." Darcy knew what that understanding had been, even though he had never expressed it explicitly.

"No need to apologize." He looked at his wife and daughter. "We must hurry so we can make progress on the roads before the storm begins." He looked up. "It appears to be moving to the south." He turned back to Darcy and said, "Good day, sir." He motioned for the ladies to prepare to board the carriage just as Georgiana joined them.

Darcy looked at her. "Georgiana, the Westerfields are leaving."

"I am so sorry to see you leave. I hope... I hope you enjoyed your stay."

Miss Westerfield stepped up to her. "I enjoyed getting to know you now that you are a lovely young lady." She reached out and took her hand. "Goodbye."

Georgiana attempted to smile. "Goodbye."

Miss Westerfield looked at Darcy and took in a ragged breath. "I enjoyed reminiscing about our times together when we were young." Tears pooled in her eyes, and she quickly choked out, "Goodbye, and thank you." With that, she quickly turned and stepped into the carriage.

"Goodbye, Miss Darcy, Mr. Darcy," Mrs. Westerfield said. "You have been most hospitable during our stay."

"It has been our pleasure," Darcy said.

It was now only Mr. Westerfield who stood opposite Darcy. "I always admired your parents, Darcy, and I hope... I hope you will live up to their good name."

Darcy's mouth went dry, and he slowly nodded. "I do try."

"Well, goodbye."

As he stepped up into the carriage, Darcy walked up to the door. He looked in and gave Miss Westerfield an apologetic look. "God speed and have a safe journey."

Darcy and Georgiana watched silently as the carriage pulled away. Georgiana tucked her hand through her brother's arm and looked up at him. "Did they give you a reason for their sudden departure?"

Darcy gave his head a quick shake. "No, but I am certain it was because one of them saw me waltzing with Miss Bennet." He let out a long breath. "But I am truly surprised, as I would have expected more of a set down by Mr. Westerfield than what I received." He kept his eyes on the carriage. "I remember him as having a strong temper. That, I do not understand."

"Perhaps it was something else." Georgiana looked up at him. "Brother, despite your strong feelings for Miss Bennet, you are not pleased with this outcome. I can see it in your face."

He opened his mouth and then closed it. His eyes flickered with indecision as he considered his words. "I am grieved that they likely find my character unprincipled and, therefore, consider me not worthy of the Darcy name."

Georgiana tugged at his arm. "Oh, I am certain that is not the case. They could not think that."

Darcy drew himself erect and put his hand over his sister's. "It matters not. They are gone, and…" He shook his head. "I am not grieved by their departure but for my part in their decision to leave."

Georgiana smiled. "But now you can confess your feelings for Miss Bennet – honourably!" She let out a small laugh.

"Yes." Darcy's face remained stoic. After a moment he said, "But Georgiana, there is something I must tell you."

"Is something wrong? Have you already spoken to her and she is not willing to receive your affections? I can see in your face that something else is disturbing you."

He patted Georgiana's hand. "I encountered Miss Bennet while out walking, and I was about to confess my unchanging feelings for her when…" He paused and pressed his lips together.

"Georgiana, George Wickham has returned. He was in the woods."

Georgiana's face paled and she cast her eyes down. "He is... here?"

Darcy felt the anger surge inside of him just thinking about it. "Yes, to see his mother before she dies, with which I cannot find fault." He fisted his hands at his sides. "However, I was greatly displeased he had come near Pemberley, and... I had just encountered Miss Bennet while out walking, and he saw the two of us together." He gave his head a brisk shake. "Apparently he had heard rumours about a young lady being at Pemberley that I was intending to ask to marry me. He made the assumption that it was Miss Bennet."

"He said as much?"

"Yes. She, of course denied it, as did I."

"But of course, you would both deny it to him." She shook her head. "You must talk to her!"

"I am not certain it would be wise, considering the supposed object of my affection just departed." He let out a huff. "Besides, I have business with my steward I must see to."

"If not now, then later. I will send for her to meet with me in the small parlour before the meal. You can come by, and I can conveniently leave to allow the two of you to talk."

Darcy chuckled and grabbed her chin, lifting it up. "I never knew you to be so conniving and manipulative, Georgie."

She gave him a wide smile. "Neither did I, but I rather like it!"

Darcy let out a laugh, partly out of relief that he would finally be able to speak with Elizabeth. "As do I!"

~~*

It was several hours before Wickham returned to Lambton. After encountering Darcy and Miss Bennet, he had walked to the place in the woods where he could furtively look out onto Pemberley. As he stared down at it, his face did not reflect admiration of the beautiful stately manor, only anger and bitterness.

He picked up a rock and threw it in the direction of the home.

"Why could it not have been mine? He loved me as a son!" He shook his head. "If only his true son had died, I am certain he would have made me the heir." He sneered. "Or if I had succeeded in eloping with young, pretty, and innocent Georgiana…"

He spent about an hour there, pondering the significance of encountering Miss Bennet and Darcy. When he could not account for it, he returned to Lambton to visit some old acquaintances before finally returning home.

When he finally reached his sister's home, he entered. He saw no one, and it was deathly quiet.

"Mother?" Wickham called out. "Mother? Alice? Is she still with us?"

Alice answered from the back room. "Of course, she is still with us. I do not know why, but ever since you arrived, she seems to be more alert."

He walked into his mother's room, and a smug smile appeared. "It is my charm."

"I doubt that. She has been waiting for you to return." Alice stood up so he could take the chair by his mother's side. "You really ought not leave her at a time like this."

"Ah, but being gone provided me with some very interesting news!" He waggled his brows.

"Well, she has some, as well! She wants to tell you herself, and I wondered if you would return in time to hear it from her own lips."

Wickham stood at her side and looked down at her. "Mother? I have returned. What is it you want to tell me?"

"She is so fatigued, I doubt she will be able to speak the words."

He looked at his sister. "Is it some inheritance she is bestowing on me? I hope she will have something to give me."

Alice shook her head. "You know Mother has nothing to pass on to you, and if she did, it would go to me for all I have done for her the past several years."

"Then what is it she wants to say to me? I hope it is not a death bed wish for me."

"No, it has to do with Mr. Darcy."

Wickham rolled his eyes and let out a huff. "I really have no wish to hear about *that* man, and if it is about his inviting a young lady to Pemberley with the intention of asking for her hand, she already informed me of that." He shook his head. "Although I now wonder how accurate it was."

"Well, it pertains to that lady, but it is something new that has come to light."

They both had to shake their mother a few times before she wakened. She opened her eyes and looked at her son, a smile slowly appearing. She brought her hand up and cupped his cheek.

"Ah, my George. I am so glad you are home." Her weary eyes started to close.

"I am, as well, Mother. Now I hear you have some interesting news."

Her eyes shot open. "Oh! I do! It is about Mr. Darcy!"

Wickham drew back at her sudden and unexpected burst of energy. "Go on, dearest Mother. I am listening."

She closed her eyes as she took in a deep breath.

When she seemed to doze off again, he took her hand and squeezed it. "Mother? What news do you have?"

She stirred and looked at him for a moment, as if to gather her thoughts. "The young lady… who had been brought to Pemberley with her family…" Mrs. Wickham reached out her hand to try to grasp the cup of tea at her bedside.

"She wants a sip," Alice said.

Wickham took the cup and helped her take a sip. "Yes, go on. The young lady…"

"She… and her family have left Pemberley… apparently distraught over something." She paused again and briefly closed her eyes.

"Truly? Miss Elizabeth Bennet has left Pemberley?"

"Who is Elizabeth Bennet?" Alice asked.

"Is she not the one everyone is saying he is to marry?"

"No…" With her eyes still closed, Mrs. Wickham lifted a finger and slowly wagged it. "She is from that family… that used to visit." She opened her eyes slightly and peered out at her daughter, waving her hand for her to continue.

"Miss Westerfield," Alice said. "He was going to ask for

Angeline Westerfield's hand in marriage."

Wickham's eyes widened. "Miss Velvet Sheen Angeline?"

Alice nodded. "The very one." She shook her head. "Although, I do not think she liked you calling her that."

Wickham leaned back against the wall and crossed his arms. "Ah, but she had unbelievably velvet skin, and her hair had a delightful sheen to it." He looked down at his mother. "You said she and her family left because they were distraught? Do you know what caused the distress?"

His mother, weary from the discourse, looked at her daughter to continue.

"Apparently there is another young lady at Pemberley who was seen privately dancing with Mr. Darcy."

"No..." Mrs. Wickham said impatiently, but weakly. "Not dancing... *waltzing*."

"Apparently they were *waltzing* together while Miss Darcy provided the music for their little private dance."

A wicked smile appeared on Wickham's face. "Well, this *is* interesting! Miss Elizabeth Bennet waltzing with Mr. Darcy; I am surprised."

Alice lowered her brows. "Who is Miss Elizabeth Bennet?" She shook her head. "And you said *you* have some news. What is it?"

Wickham licked his lips and turned to face his mother. "Indeed, I do, for I saw them..." He paused and then continued. "I saw Darcy walking alone with Miss Elizabeth Bennet into the woods." His brows lowered, and he gave his head a quick shake. "They did not see me at first, and as I observed them, it appeared they had more than just a casual acquaintance. If you know what I mean." He lifted a brow and let out a long, satisfied breath.

"Truly?"

"But I cannot imagine him risking everything with Miss Westerfield for..." His brows pinched. "Miss Bennet!"

Alice's eyes opened wide and her jaw dropped. "Who is this Elizabeth Bennet?"

"She is a young lady I met when the Militia was stationed in Hertfordshire, in a little village called Meryton. She lived nearby. She is one of five daughters, who are – all of them – only out to gain rich husbands. They will do anything to snare a gentleman with fortune. Her eldest sister almost immediately attached herself to a young gentleman of fortune who had only recently moved into the neighbourhood." He looked at his mother with a raised brow. "This gentleman also happens to be the good friend of Darcy."

"Go on," Mrs. Wickham said, her eyes wide.

"Her two youngest sisters were unabashedly flirtatious towards all the soldiers." He sent his mother a reassuring glance. "There was no need to worry, Mother. I behaved myself around them." He waved his hand. "I understood the family had no fortune whatsoever."

His mother gave him a sad smile. "If only you had been given what the late Mr. Darcy promised you."

Wickham scowled. "Darcy is not half the man his father was."

"So Miss Elizabeth Bennet is an acquaintance of yours?" Alice asked.

"Yes. I knew her and her family quite well."

"What is she like?" Mrs. Wickham asked with a frown.

"I would say that she is fairly intelligent, and I now will add that she is conniving. I would surmise she likely did not want Darcy to escape her grasp. She claimed her uncle injured himself while they were taking a tour of Pemberley, and they were forced to remain there." He let out a laugh. "They likely planned the whole thing before they even set out!"

"But she and Mr. Darcy… Are you certain they were alone in the woods?" Alice asked. "I cannot imagine him doing anything improper. There was no one there acting as their chaperone?"

"Oh, they were certainly alone, and there was no chaperone. They were completely out of the view of the house." He shook his head. "I cannot say what their intentions were – but my guess is they were headed into the woods for a clandestine meeting."

"That sounds so unlike him!" Alice said. "Are you certain?"

"I know what I saw. The highly esteemed Mr. Darcy is not as honourable as people think. His being seen waltzing with Miss Bennet and then the Westerfields leaving has certainly confirmed his character." He shook his head. "I have to confess I am shocked, but not at all surprised, knowing what I do of the young lady and her sisters."

Mrs. Wickham closed her eyes again. "Mr. Darcy was very kind when he visited." A look of distress filled her aging features. "Everyone considers him to be a most upright gentleman."

"Well, we know otherwise, do we not? Remember what he did to me?" Wickham spat it out. "His true character will be found out."

His mother responded with a frail sigh. "And I always had hopes that he would single Alice out as his wife."

"As if he would! You are fortunate he did not!" Wickham said, looking sharply at his sister.

She smiled. "I would have considered myself very fortunate, George, but I knew he would never single out a young lady who was only the daughter of his steward." She let out a breathy sigh. "Besides, I am perfectly happy with Michael. He has been a very good husband."

Mrs. Wickham smiled faintly. "But I saw how you looked at him when he came to see me."

A blush covered Alice's cheeks. "It is only because he is still so handsome."

"His father was always so honourable." Mrs. Wickham let out a long sigh. "I thought his son would turn out the same."

George suddenly drew himself erect. "Well, he did not. You look tired, Mother. I am going to sit in the parlour for a little while."

Mrs. Wickham closed her eyes and nodded. "Yes…"

"And Mother," Alice said. "If you do not mind, now that George has returned, I need to visit someone." She looked at her brother. "Let George know if you need anything."

"I will be here." Wickham gave a satisfied grin. "Feel free to go. Do not worry about Mother."

Wickham and his sister left their mother's room. "Thank you for staying with her. I am going to visit Ellen for a while."

"Always my pleasure," Wickham said with a sly smile. "You and Mrs. Abbott may visit as long as you please."

"I will not be gone too long." She gathered a few things. "Her daughter Harriet now works at Pemberley, and she will know what is and is not true."

Wickham laughed as he watched his sister leave the house. "A daughter working at Pemberley! This is even better! Since there is nothing Mrs. Abbott loves to do more than gossip, these rumours about Darcy and Miss Bennet ought to spread through Lambton and back to Pemberley itself in no time!" He sat down in a chair and began rubbing his jaw. "Perhaps I should have made their walk into the woods more scandalous. I could have added some additional details." He shook his head. "No. I did not even have to lie about what I saw." He chuckled. "Darcy's true actions will end up being his downfall this time."

Chapter 13

Elizabeth spent the afternoon with her aunt and uncle in the small sitting room. She read in a distracted manner, looking up at every sound of approaching footsteps. While she was curious to find out why the Westerfields departed so suddenly, she was also eager to see Mr. Darcy. She wondered what he might be doing or thinking. Her uncle reminded her that he was a man with many responsibilities and was likely taking care of them. Later in the day, she received a request from Miss Darcy to join her in the parlour.

"How kind of her. Perhaps her brother is with her." Mrs. Gardiner lifted her brow teasingly.

"Or perhaps she is bored and desires some company," Elizabeth answered her. "But I shall gladly go find out." She could not keep from smiling. She truly enjoyed spending time with the young girl.

As Elizabeth set out for the small parlour, her spirits soared more than they had since she first arrived at Pemberley. While she had initially been fearful of encountering Mr. Darcy, she had been surprised to find herself disappointed when she found out everyone thought the beautiful young lady who had come to Pemberley would soon receive an offer of marriage from him. She also found herself consumed with admiration, respect, and strong feelings for the gentleman she had once despised. She gave her head a shake as she realized this was the first time since coming to Pemberley that she had been able to entertain hopes that he might still have those ardent feelings of love for her.

When she came to the parlour, she saw that Miss Darcy was already there. A smile appeared on the young girl's face.

"I am delighted you came. Would you care for some refreshments?"

"Tea would be splendid, thank you."

Once the tea was poured, Georgiana turned back to Elizabeth. "I am sorry I was not able to come see you after I left this morning. I had some things I needed to do."

"I believe that included practicing on the pianoforte." She paused and smiled. "I heard you playing."

"Yes, that was me." She laughed softly. "I was working on a difficult piece. You may have heard me make several mistakes."

Elizabeth gave her a reassuring smile. "I can honestly say I did not hear one."

"You are too kind." She drew in a deep breath. "It was a song I had been practicing for the musical soiree that we were going to have."

Elizabeth pursed her lips and then said, "I suppose we will no longer be having one."

Georgiana shook her head. After a brief moment of silence, she said, "We are still not certain why the Westerfields left so abruptly."

Elizabeth stood up and walked over to the window and looked out. "Perhaps one of them saw your brother and me... dancing." She turned and looked back at Georgiana. "I would be deeply grieved if I had been the cause of some misunderstanding."

Georgiana smiled. "Pray, do not put any blame on yourself. After all, it was my brother who asked you to dance." Her smile suddenly disappeared. "I hope he did not make you feel uncomfortable. Oh, I hope you did not think he acted in an improper manner. I am certain he did not mean to."

Elizabeth felt her cheeks warm. She wanted to reassure the young girl that she did not think ill of him for his actions, but she had to admit she had not even told her aunt and uncle about it. "I do not think any less of him."

"It gave me great enjoyment to play and watch you dance, and... I believe my brother enjoyed it, as well. He told me he rarely dances, and chooses not to dance the waltz at all when one is played at a ball. He thought you were a delightful partner."

Elizabeth felt her heart swell, and she returned to her chair. "I am certain he was exaggerating," she said nervously.

"No! I assure you he was sincere." A look of admiration filled her eyes. "He is always sincere – and honourable – in all he says and does."

Elizabeth smiled, and then turned to see Mr. Darcy enter.

"Ah! Here you are, Georgiana. Good afternoon, Miss Bennet."

"Mr. Darcy." Elizabeth said with a nod, but immediately tilted her head away, hoping her suddenly warm cheeks would not be noticed by him. She had not expected to see him so soon and was caught by surprise, although she had to admit it was a pleasant one.

"Oh, Fitzwilliam! I am glad you are here. Would you be so kind as to entertain Miss Bennet while I see to a few things?"

Elizabeth watched as Miss Darcy hurried towards the door before he could answer. The young girl was looking back and smiling, so she did not see a manservant enter. The two collided.

"Oh!" Georgiana exclaimed. "Oh, excuse me. I did not see you."

A note in the servant's hand dropped to the floor, and he apologized as he leaned over and picked it up. "An urgent message just arrived for you, Mr. Darcy. There was a young man who dispatched it, and he is awaiting your reply."

"He is awaiting my reply?" Darcy's brows lowered as he took the letter. Georgiana came to his side, looking at him anxiously as the colour drained from his face.

"What is it?" she asked. "Is something wrong?"

He nodded as he rubbed his jaw. It was a few moments before he answered. "The Westerfields encountered a heavy downpour of rain, and the carriage slid off the road, turning onto its side."

He drew in a deep breath. "Miss Westerfield suffered some minor injuries, but her father and mother were more gravely injured." He pursed his lips as he read more of the letter. "They have been taken to a manor in a small village that she estimated was about a five-hour carriage ride from Pemberley. She has no acquaintances there, and apparently their other carriage carrying the valet, maids, and much of their luggage, continued on, unaware of the accident." He let out a long puff of air.

"Oh, that is terrible!" Georgiana slowly shook her head. "What is to be done?"

Darcy looked up at his sister. "She has asked me to come. There is no one else she knows who would be able to get there in a timely manner. She is frightened and alone."

"What shall you do?" Georgiana asked. "This is grave, indeed."

Elizabeth stepped forward and spoke gently. "If I were Miss

Westerfield, I would greatly appreciate a good friend coming to my aid and assisting me in any way they could." She paused and fought a wave of tears that threatened to spill. "I think… I think perhaps you ought to go to her."

Darcy looked up and seemed to search her face. She gave him an encouraging smile, accompanied by a quick nod of her head.

He seemed to struggle with his decision. He turned and asked the servant, "Did the person delivering this say how long it took him on horseback?"

The servant nodded. "It took him almost three hours, due to the condition of the roads."

Darcy looked down at the letter again. "Ask the young man to wait for me, and I will accompany him as he returns." He drew in a deep breath and let it out in a quick breath. "Have my horse saddled and ask my valet to pack a small satchel of clothes. I will send word if I need more things sent to me."

"You are going, then?" Georgiana asked, a look of distress colouring her features.

Darcy put his hands on her shoulders. "I am. I should be able to get there before nightfall." He looked up at Elizabeth. "Pray, forgive me, but I believe I must go."

"As you should." Elizabeth gave him a nod of encouragement.

"Are your aunt and uncle in their room?"

"I was with them last in the small sitting room."

"I shall stop by there and take my leave of them." He looked at Elizabeth and then turned towards the door. He suddenly stopped and looked back at her. "You will… I hope you and your aunt and uncle will remain at Pemberley until I return. I am…" He drew in a breath. "I am not certain how long I will be, but I hope you will be able to do so."

Elizabeth fought back the tears that were filling her eyes as she nodded, feeling all the weight of disappointment upon her. "If it is at all possible. It will, however, depend upon my aunt and uncle."

Darcy nodded, and his eyes narrowed as he looked at his sister. "Georgiana, with Wickham back, you are not to go outside alone – even to the gardens to pick flowers. Do you understand?"

Georgiana consented with a nod, and he then turned to Elizabeth. "Miss Bennet, I would strongly admonish you not to take any walks about the grounds for the same reason."

"Certainly."

"If you will excuse me, then. I am terribly sorry." Darcy said no more, and Elizabeth and Georgiana silently watched him turn again and walk out the door.

~~*

It was a quiet dinner as everyone felt the import of all that had occurred that day, beginning with the surprising departure of the Westerfields, to word of their accident, to Mr. Darcy's decision to go be of assistance to them. In addition, Elizabeth could not stop thinking about her walk in the woods that had, for a short while, been most pleasant, but which had ended up being frightfully disconcerting when they encountered Mr. Wickham.

Miss Darcy seemed to feel unequal to the task of being Mistress of Pemberley without her brother at her side. Elizabeth did what she could to encourage the young girl, despite feeling a great weight of disappointment pressing on her.

After the meal, they gathered in the small sitting room, but her aunt and uncle did not remain long. Elizabeth decided she would stay a little longer with Miss Darcy. It was a decision she later came to regret.

They had been visiting for a short while and talking about a variety of things – the weather, London, balls, and dancing. At length, Miss Darcy looked at Elizabeth with wide eyes.

"May I ask you something, Miss Bennet?"

"Certainly," Elizabeth said with a smile.

The young girl bit her lip and drew in a long breath. Finally, she asked, "Have you ever been in love?"

Elizabeth was taken aback and chuckled softly as she considered her answer. "I… I cannot say that I have ever truly been in love, although I have greatly admired someone."

"Oh, I see." A look of disappointment flooded the young girl's face.

Elizabeth tilted her head. "Why do you ask?"

It was a moment before Miss Darcy spoke. She seemed to search Elizabeth's features, and finally said, "Last year… I thought

I was in love." Her voice quavered.

Elizabeth's heart began to pound as she wondered whether she was going to tell her about Mr. Wickham. She could not let her know that she already knew.

Miss Darcy averted her eyes. "But I was so wrong."

Elizabeth reached over and took her hand. "While I have never been in that position, I have been wrong several times in my life about so many things, and I... we need to learn from those mistakes and grow." She squeezed her hand and released it. "You are a very wise young girl."

A glimmer of light appeared in the young girl's eyes. "Thank you. I hope I learn from my mistakes."

Elizabeth wondered if Miss Darcy was bringing this up because her brother told her he had seen Mr. Wickham. She pursed her lips and then said, "I perceive that you are a young lady with much strength."

"Oh, I do not feel strong at all! There are times I feel like I want to run and hide!"

Elizabeth laughed. "As I did when I did not want your brother to know I was here."

Georgiana tilted her head. "Why did you feel you needed to hide from him?"

Elizabeth opened her mouth and then closed it as she considered how to answer. Finally, she said, "I had not been particularly kind to him when we last saw each other, and I felt he would have thought me impertinent for encroaching upon his home, considering how I had treated him."

"Oh, I am certain he would not have thought any such thing."

"Well, I was pleasantly surprised to find that he treated me with all civility when we did encounter each other. She reached out and took Miss Darcy's hand. "There are times when *everyone* feels afraid, but I know *you* will be strong when you need that strength."

"I hope so," she answered softly.

And I know that as you grow and mature, you will eventually find the young man who is best suited for you."

Miss Darcy smiled. "Oh, but I think I already have."

Elizabeth's eyes brightened. "Have you? And who is this gentleman?"

She swallowed deeply. "He is actually a friend of my brother's. He is amiable and has a lively personality, and yet he is gracious and generous. He and his sisters had planned to join us at Pemberley this past week, but unfortunately, circumstances prevented them from doing so."

Elizabeth felt a tightening of her stomach. "And may I ask who this gentleman is with whom you have found favour?"

A shy, but sweet smile lit her eyes. "His name is Mr. Bingley."

Elizabeth clasped her hands tightly, and her eyes widened in surprise. "Mr. Bingley?"

"Are you acquainted with him?"

Elizabeth nodded. "Yes, he lived…"

"Oh, yes, now I remember. My brother stayed with him at Netherfield Park, and that is where he met you. You lived in the same country neighbourhood, I believe."

Elizabeth felt her cheeks warm as she wondered just how much the young girl knew. Was she even aware that her sister and Mr. Bingley had formed a strong attachment? "Yes, our home, Longbourn, is just three miles from Netherfield Park."

Miss Darcy leaned in. "Do you not think he is an admirable gentleman?"

Elizabeth made an attempt to smile, despite her increasing anguish over hearing such news. "I do. I do not think one can find a finer gentleman."

Miss Darcy fingered the material of her dress. "I know my brother has long had a wish for me to settle my affections on him."

"Has he? But you are still so young," Elizabeth said. She knew she had no right to discourage her, but this was distressing news to her.

"Yes, I know." She bit her lower lip and drew in a breath. "But I cannot help but think I will never find another who is so perfectly amiable and kind."

Elizabeth tried to smile as she pondered this. Did Mr. Bingley return the partiality? Had he truly lost all affection for Jane? She dared not think about what it would mean for *her* to consider loving Mr. Darcy if his sister married Mr. Bingley. It would be devastating for Jane.

~~*

Darcy left Pemberley and followed Hughes, the young man, as their horses pounded towards a small, unbeknownst-to-him village where the Westerfields had been taken. The accident had occurred on the main road, and apparently this village was the closest place to take the injured to receive medical care. He hoped the care would be sufficient to be of help. A tightness gripped his chest. He hoped her parents would recover. He could not imagine what Angeline would do if she lost one – or both – of her parents while she was alone and so far from home.

In the three hour long journey, he contemplated not only Angeline's present circumstances, but pondered what Elizabeth's feelings for him might be. Every hopeful glance, word, and smile she recently had given him quickly evaporated into something he told himself he had only imagined or misinterpreted. Would he ever have the opportunity to speak honestly with her?

At length they came upon the overturned carriage. Hughes stopped to point it out to Darcy. It had fallen down into a ditch and was not easily seen from the road.

"Who found them? Did someone come upon them?" Darcy asked the young man.

"Mr. Lloyd Kingston, of Wakespur Manor, happened by. The young miss had been able to climb out of the damaged carriage. Kingston and his driver saw her and stopped. They put her in the Kingston carriage, wrapped her in a blanket, and then pulled her parents out. Unfortunately, the coachman and footman did not survive the accident."

Darcy's head dropped. "This is grievous, indeed!" He straightened and looked at the young man. "How much farther is the village?"

"We are not four miles from the village, but it is an additional two miles to Wakespur Manor, where they were all taken. I am a stable hand there. I grew up in Derbyshire and know the area well, so they dispatched me to take the missive to you."

"You did well, Hughes. Thank you. Let us be off, then."

They two men mounted their horses and sped towards the

manor. As they rode, Darcy's thoughts were in turmoil. He was grateful that they had been taken to a manor and not just an inn. He had never heard of this Mr. Kingston or Wakespur Manor, but he hoped he would approve of both. For Angeline's sake.

When at last they arrived and the manor came into view, Darcy saw that it was moderate in size, but appeared to be in good condition – at least on the outside. They walked up to the front door, which opened as they stepped up. The butler, aged and feeble, extended his hand in a welcome.

Hughes made the introductions and then said, "I shall take the horses to the stable and attend to them."

"Thank you," Darcy said, giving him a nod. He looked at the butler. "How are the Westerfields?"

"There is little change. The doctor is more concerned with the gentleman, as he has not yet awakened. Mrs. Westerfield has opened her eyes and is able to speak. She is very weak, however, and is very concerned for her husband."

"And Miss Westerfield?"

"She is understandably distraught. If you come into the sitting room, sir, I shall send for her. She is with her parents and has not left their side since arriving. I know she will want to come and acquaint you with all that happened."

He was shown into the sitting room, and after the butler sent a maid after Miss Westerfield, he informed Darcy some food and drink would be brought in shortly. Darcy thanked him and sat down. After a moment, however, he stood and began to pace. His legs were sore from riding so long, and he could think better on his feet. He stretched out his arms and then clasped his hands on top of his head, arching his back.

"Good evening, sir," a voice from behind startled Darcy.

He turned, and found himself looking into the face of a well-dressed young man, about the same age as himself. "Good evening," Darcy said, extending his hand. "Fitzwilliam Darcy."

"I am Lloyd Kingston, and I welcome you to Wakespur Manor. I am sorry that it is under such dreadful circumstances."

Darcy was rather surprised that the Master of Wakespur was young, as he had never heard of him, and now with the young man standing before him, realized he had never seen him about Town.

"Thank you, sir. I appreciate all you have done for the Westerfields."

"I believe they are getting good care. The doctor has seen them and will return in the morning. I have provided Miss Westerfield with a maid to assist her and her mother with anything they need." He swallowed. "I do want all things to be done with propriety.

Darcy was about to express his thanks when he heard a familiar voice.

"Fitzwilliam!"

Darcy turned to see Angeline running towards him. "I cannot believe this has happened!" Tears ran down her face, which had several cuts and bruises. She reached out her hand, and Darcy took it in his.

"I am grieved you are going through this. I came as quickly as I could." He gave her hand a squeeze. "How are your parents?"

Her hand trembled in his. "We can only wait. It is my father who has the more serious injuries. Mother shall likely rally in time, but, oh…" Her sobs filled the room, and she leaned her head against his chest.

Darcy lifted his eyes to see Kingston studying him. Kingston likely believed, by her actions and calling him by his Christian name, that there was an agreement between the two. *He* knew, however, both were attributed to the dire situation in which she found herself. In order to maintain a modicum of propriety, he gently stepped away from her and said, "Miss Westerfield, come sit down and tell me what happened."

Darcy escorted Miss Westerfield to a chair as refreshments were brought in. He pulled a handkerchief from his pocket and placed it in her palm.

"Miss Westerfield, would you care for something to eat or drink?" Kingston asked.

"Thank you," she said softly, wiping her eyes. "I have been unable to eat or drink anything since I arrived." She took several breaths. She turned back to Darcy. "Now that you are here, I think I shall be able to eat a little."

After being served, Miss Westerfield proceeded to tell him what had happened.

"It had begun to rain very hard, and the sky had grown very

dark. We could tell by the movement in the carriage that the road was very muddy and slick. My father mentioned that it likely had been raining most of the day." She drew in a shaky breath and wiped her eyes. "Suddenly we heard the horses whinny, and the carriage seemed to slide one way and then the other." She looked down and seemed to be gathering her thoughts. "I saw my mother look at my father with eyes wide in terror, but he tried to reassure us both, grasping our hands tightly. It was then that..." She closed her eyes and choked in a breath. "It was then that the carriage slid again, began to tilt, and it came crashing down on its side. Then, it was silent except for sound of the rain still pelting down."

As Miss Westerfield took a bite of cake and a sip of her tea, Mr. Kingston spoke. "It was soon after that my carriage came upon theirs. My coachman noticed Miss Westerfield on the side of the road. He jumped down and called out to me to see to the young lady while he freed the horses, who had somehow been able to remain upright. I brought Miss Westerfield to my carriage and covered her with a blanket. She told me that her mother and father were still in the carriage, but they were not responding to her attempts to waken them."

"I was so grateful they came along, yet I was so frightened for my parents. He and his coachmen pulled them from our carriage and put them in his." Tears began to fall again. "Our coachman and the footman who had been riding with us... they both died." She began to sob.

Darcy gently took her hand. "And what of your other carriage with your maids, valet, and luggage? Did they not see you?"

Miss Westerfield sniffed. "We had stopped earlier to dine, and as the weather did not look threatening, I convinced my parents to stay a little longer to allow us the time to walk along the street to look in the shops. My father sent the other carriage on ahead. They have no idea where we are and what has happened to us." She closed her eyes. "It is my fault this happened. I was the one who wanted to linger. The two carriages should never have been separated."

Darcy adamantly shook his head. "It is not your fault, Miss Westerfield. You could not have known this would happen."

"No, but I know my brother will blame me. I have sent a

156

message to him. Hopefully he will come directly when he receives it."

There was silence for a moment, and then Darcy asked, "May I see your parents?"

"Oh, yes! They will be... I mean, my mother will be pleased you came." She shook her head and trembled. "But she is so weak."

"I shall have a room prepared for you, Darcy." Kingston spoke quietly to one of the maids before escorting them up.

As they walked to their room, Angeline held onto Darcy's arm tightly. Darcy knew she needed his support, but he also could not help but wonder again why the Westerfields departed when they did – and as they did. Miss Westerfield did not at all seem upset with him. It could be because she had other concerns on her mind, but he was not certain. He wondered if he would discover the reason while he was here. That was the main reason he had agreed to come – as well as being encouraged to do so by Elizabeth. He shook his head as he wondered whether Elizabeth's suggestion for him to leave had been out of concern for Angeline or had she merely wanted him gone.

Chapter 14

Elizabeth awakened the next morning as the sun's first rays of light touched the sky and peeked through the window coverings in her room. She climbed out of bed and walked to the chair by the window. She sat down, pulled back the curtain, and looked out. Her eyes felt heavy and dry, despite the tears that had filled her eyes throughout the night. She had not slept well at all. Her insides were in knots as she pondered what might have happened when Mr. Darcy arrived at his destination last night. Did he speak with Miss Westerfield and clear up any misunderstanding or misapprehensions she may have had? Would the situation in which she found herself with both of her parents injured cause him to feel such compassion for her that he asked for her hand? She gazed out towards the woods, where she and Mr. Darcy had walked, and she felt a sharp pang as she thought back to their walk together, wishing it had not been first interrupted by Mr. Wickham and ended by seeing the Westerfields departing.

Then there was the surprising news Miss Darcy had shared with her. So, her brother still had designs on keeping Mr. Bingley from Jane and encouraging an attachment between Mr. Bingley and his sister.

Elizabeth began to rub her forehead, realizing this would prevent any attachment she might desire with Mr. Darcy. She could not do that to her sister. If Jane were to hear that Miss Darcy was attached to Mr. Bingley, she might give in to her mother's wishes and marry Mr. Goulding.

She let out a soft moan.

"Lizzy? Are you awake?" Mrs. Gardiner sat up in the bed. "What time is it?"

Elizabeth shrugged. "The sun is up, so I am up."

Her aunt laughed. "Yes, and you have always been that way, even as a baby, which your mother considered to be ill-mannered of you."

Elizabeth murmured an affirmative.

"Lizzy, are you unwell?" Mrs. Gardiner stepped out of bed and walked over to her niece. She placed an arm about her shoulders and leaned in. "Are you displeased that Mr. Darcy has left?"

Elizabeth blew out a puff of air. "I can hardly blame him when I encouraged him to go." She clasped her hands and looked down at them. "I…" She didn't finish, but turned to her aunt. "Mr. Darcy did not know when he would be returning, and I know Uncle Gardiner is eager to return home." She looked back out the window. "Perhaps we need to make plans to take our leave."

"As a matter of fact, we were talking about that very thing last evening when we returned to our rooms. Lizzy, he wants to leave within a few days. We have already been gone longer than we planned."

"I am well aware of that."

Mrs. Gardiner picked up a brush and began brushing Elizabeth's long, chestnut tresses. "I will be going to visit a few friends today. Perhaps when Mr. Darcy arrived to check on the Westerfields, he found them to be greatly improved and will return home later today."

"Yes, perhaps he will."

~~*

Elizabeth tried to rally her spirits and encourage Miss Darcy, who seemed a little less troubled by her brother's departure, but still slightly unsure. But when the young girl needed to pay a call, Elizabeth returned to her uncle. He was resting in the small sitting room.

"Now I do not want you to feel as though you need to spend your time with me. I am doing well."

Elizabeth smiled. "I know. I have been enjoying Miss Darcy's company, but she needed to visit someone."

"So with her gone and your aunt visiting her friend, you are stuck with me." He let out a laugh, but the smile quickly disappeared. "I know your aunt talked with you this morning about our leaving soon."

Elizabeth nodded and then turned her head as she took in a halted breath. "I knew it would likely be soon."

He chuckled. "I am certain your Mr. Darcy will have returned by the time we need to leave."

She pressed her lips tightly together. At length, she said, "He is not my anything. It is probably best that we leave as soon as possible."

Her uncle leaned in towards her. "Now, Lizzy, why would you say that?"

"I truly have no idea what he thinks of me... or if he thinks of me at all."

"Oh, I am certain..." He paused as Mrs. Reynolds stepped into the room.

Her carriage was stiff, and instead of a smile, she wore a tight-lipped frown.

"I am here to inform you that... unseemly rumours have been circulating around Lambton and amongst the staff here, that..." She gave a pointed look at Elizabeth. "That my Master and you, Miss Elizabeth, have been seen together in some rather disreputable situations."

"What?" Both Elizabeth and her uncle asked at once.

Mrs. Reynolds continued as if she had not heard them. "There is talk that the two of you were walking unaccompanied into the woods together yesterday, and that you were seen dancing together in the music room a few days ago." She straightened her shoulders and lifted her head. "I have spoken with Mr. Brooks, the butler, and we are both concerned for our master's character."

Elizabeth felt her face warm, but before she could reply, she turned at the sound of hurried steps approaching the room. It was her aunt. "Elizabeth! I cannot believe that rumours about you and..." She paused when she noticed Mrs. Reynolds. "Oh! Good day, Mrs. Reynolds."

"So you heard them, too," Mrs. Reynolds declared. "I am sorry, but with Mr. Darcy being from home, Mr. Brooks and I have made the difficult decision to ask you to leave Pemberley at once."

"But can we not hear from my niece to find out if any of this is true?" Her uncle looked at Elizabeth. "Tell her, Elizabeth, that you have never been in the woods alone with Mr. Darcy. And danced with him? These must all be lies."

Elizabeth closed her eyes and looked away. She knew the

warmth of her face was likely revealing to them what they did not want to believe. "I own we did dance…"

"The waltz, as I understand," said Mrs. Reynolds.

She nodded and drew in a breath. "Yes, Miss Darcy was playing a three-quarter piece, and I was moving in the steps to the waltz. Mr. Darcy came in and…" She suddenly felt dizzy. "Yes. We danced the waltz."

"And the woods? Lizzy, do not tell me you were walking into the woods with him?" her aunt asked. "Alone?"

Elizabeth reached out her hand to a nearby table to steady herself. "I had been out walking by myself and encountered him."

"But did you continue to walk with him *into* the woods?" Mrs. Reynolds' brows lowered.

Elizabeth mutely nodded. "Very briefly, but I assure you, we did nothing indecent." She suddenly looked up. "Almost as soon as we had begun walking together, we encountered Mr. Wickham!" She searched Mrs. Reynolds's face. "Certainly, you know he is capable of spreading vicious stories. He likely began spreading rumours about us and made it out worse than it truly was, much like he had done about Mr. Darcy in Meryton."

Mrs. Reynolds slowly shook her head. "You have confirmed by your own words the nature of these rumours."

Elizabeth sent her aunt and uncle a pleading look. "You must believe me that nothing improper occurred between us. If any there are any rumours hinting at indecency between us, they are nothing but lies!"

Mrs. Reynolds drew her shoulders back. "As does happen when rumours begin spreading, but I still must ask you to depart at once." She shook her head. "While it cannot be confirmed, it is being suggested that your actions with my Master led the Westerfields to depart so abruptly."

Elizabeth turned her eyes to her aunt, who nodded. "Yes, Lizzy, that is what I was told by my friend in Lambton, as well."

"There is nothing more to be said. I will send a maid and manservant to your rooms to help you pack up your belongings and arrange for your driver and carriage to be brought around directly."

"But can we not wait for Miss Darcy to return? She certainly will…" Mrs. Gardiner began.

Mrs. Reynolds shook her head. "This does not concern the young girl. As I have the reputation of my Master to protect and uphold, this is the only option. I am deeply sorry."

"Yes!" Elizabeth said suddenly, and then continued softly, "Yes, we will leave. I agree. There is nothing more to be said about it." She looked at her aunt and uncle. "Come. We have much to do to get ready." She then looked at Mrs. Reynolds. "Thank you for all you have done for us." With tears filling her eyes, Elizabeth turned to walk back to her room. She swallowed down a lump in her throat and shook her head as she thought of the lone magpie she and Mr. Darcy had seen yesterday. "One is for sorrow…" she said softly, a tear trailing down her cheek.

~~*

Darcy slept fitfully throughout the night, despite the fine room and comfortable bed. His thoughts frequently had gone to the young lady and her family in the room down the hall. He had a deep concern for the welfare of Angeline and her parents, as well as their suffering the loss of their coachman and footman. The two men had likely served them for many years.

But he had also thought deeply about the other young lady and her family at Pemberley. Miss Elizabeth Bennet. Did he dare hope that she would ever come to return his love? He pondered what it had been about her that had drawn him to her, despite all his arguments against her suitability for him.

And of the two ladies, which one would give him the greatest happiness? He knew on the one hand, the intensity of his feelings for Miss Bennet had not dissipated. She had touched his heart, and despite thinking he had gotten over her, when he found out that she was at Pemberley and then saw her again, it had all come rushing back.

Miss Westerfield was a genteel, kind, beautiful, and accomplished woman, whose fortune and connections would complement his, thus making her a suitable match. She had been a long-time acquaintance, a friend that he had long admired. But did he love her? He shook his head. No, he did not.

He got out of bed and dressed, hoping he would find Mr. and Mrs. Westerfield improved. But more than that, he hoped Angeline's brother would arrive, or some family member, so he could return to Pemberley – and Elizabeth.

He returned to the sitting room, where he found freshly baked breads, fruit, coffee, and tea awaiting him. He was pouring himself some coffee when Mr. Kingston entered.

"Good morning, Darcy. I hope you slept well."

Darcy gave a shrug. "Not well, but I doubt anyone did, with the events that took place yesterday."

"We do not stand on ceremony in this house, so help yourself to some food. I've had some taken up to Miss Westerfield and her mother."

"I am certain they will appreciate it."

Kingston sat down and crossed his leg over one knee. "So tell me, Darcy, how is it you are acquainted with the Westerfields. It was apparent last night that you know Miss Westerfield well."

Darcy took a sip of his coffee before answering. "We have known each other since our childhood. Her parents were good friends with my parents." He looked down at the dark liquid as it caught reflections of the light and suddenly thought of Elizabeth's hair. He shook his head. "She and her family had been visiting Pemberley. They just left yesterday morning."

"I see." He looked down at his fingers, which he was tapping on the arm of the chair. "Do you... Is there an attachment between the two of you?" He slowly lifted his eyes.

Darcy swallowed. "No, she... no."

Kingston waved his hand. "I did not mean to offend."

"No offense taken. She wrote to me to come, which I did because she was distraught. She knew I could arrive here more speedily than any of her family or other acquaintances."

Kingston stood up and walked to the sideboard and picked up a piece of bread. "She seems most amiable and agreeable... especially under such dire circumstances." He quickly took a bite.

"That she is," Darcy replied with a chuckle.

"I do not get to London often. I prefer to stay here, away from the crowds, so my acquaintances amongst the Ton are few."

Darcy nodded. "I prefer Pemberley to Town, as well, but I

enjoy some of the amenities London offers, so I put up with the crowds and putrid air in order to attend the theatre, concerts, and the like."

"Do you know if… does Miss Westerfield enjoy being in town?"

Darcy looked at him with a raised brow and more than a little interest. "I know she spends the season there and is often seen at the theatre or balls."

Just then a servant stepped in and addressed Kingston. "You wished to know when the doctor had arrived. He is now on his way to their room."

"Thank you, Martin." He glanced at Darcy. "Hopefully we will receive some good news about her parents."

Darcy nodded. "Indeed."

A moment later, Miss Westerfield joined them. "I thought I would come down while the doctor is seeing my mother and father."

Darcy could readily see her sunken cheeks, red and puffy eyes, and pale skin, which indicated she had not slept well. "Please, have a seat, Miss Westerfield. Can I get you something?"

She waved her hand through the air. "I do not think I could eat anything. Food was brought to our room, but I do not have the appetite for it." She looked down as she wiped away a tear that rolled down her cheek.

The two men glanced at each other with concerned looks. "Miss Westerfield, I know you are deeply concerned for your parents, but I want to assure you that they will receive the best care with Mr. Aubring."

Miss Westerfield looked up and smiled. "I thank you. And again, I thank you for all you did yesterday for us. We are much indebted to you."

Kingston stood up. "I only did what anyone would have done."

Darcy watched him and thought he looked uncomfortable with the praise.

"If you will excuse me, I have business with my steward this morning. I will have someone apprise me of what the doctor reports." He nodded towards the maid who stood by the foods. "Rebecca will remain here so there is no hint of impropriety." He gave a shrug. "Not that I am worried, but I am particular that way."

"Yes, thank you, Mr. Kingston."

"Always best to be wise in that area," Darcy followed.

Once Mr. Kingston was gone, Miss Westerfield lifted her reddened eyes to him. "Again, I cannot thank you enough for coming. My mother told me she was certain you would, but I had my doubts, especially when we..." She paused and drew in a hitched breath. "I know our sudden departure must have left you with many questions."

Darcy leaned towards her and clasped his hands in front of him. "I will admit I was surprised to find you were leaving, but I... I also had my suspicions as to what prompted your family's decision to leave."

Miss Westerfield began to stroke the nape of her neck, and then said in a trembling voice, "I saw you and Miss Bennet waltzing."

Darcy closed his eyes and looked down. "I am grieved you saw that."

"I heard Miss Darcy playing, and I set out for the music room to listen, and maybe practice a little for the soiree when she finished." She paused and wiped away another tear. "As I approached, I noticed a young maid peeking in at the door. When she saw me, she quickly walked past me, raising her brows and looking at me as if there was something significant going on. When I came to the door and looked in, I immediately understood what her expression meant."

"You *and* one of our maids saw us. Do you know which one of our maids this was?"

She shook her head. "I do not know her name. She is very young and has tight red ringlets about her face."

"I think I know the one." Darcy looked over at the maid who stood with them in the room. He was certain she was far enough away so she could not hear, but he knew the subject of their conversation could readily be misconstrued.

Darcy lowered his voice. "I have no excuse for what I did. It was a spontaneous decision on my part, for when I heard the music and looked in, much like you did, I saw Miss Bennet moving to the steps of a waltz." He turned back to look at her.

"So I joined her in the dance."

After a moment of silence, Darcy said, "I would imagine you told your parents…"

"I was not certain what to do, but I knew I could not tell my father." She shook her head. "I do not like a confrontational scene, and I knew if I told him, there would be one." She paused. "So I told my mother. She and I are very much alike, and she advised me *not* to tell Father."

Darcy was stunned. "You did not tell him?"

She swallowed hard. "You have seen my father's bursts of anger. He is very strict on matters of priority, and he is not one who likes to see someone deceived or hurt, especially someone in his family."

"And especially his daughter," Darcy added softly. "I knew someone had to have seen something. That night, I noticed something not quite right."

"My mother and I decided to tell Father that I believed we were mistaken in what we had assumed was the reason for our invitation." Her cheeks filled with a rosy blush. "We had come to believe that you…" Her voice trailed. "We were guilty of accepting as being true rumours that you… you intended to offer for me."

Darcy turned his head and felt his stomach tighten as he listened to her words.

"I also told Father that my feelings for you had changed." She suddenly stood up and turned away. "I told him that I discovered that you and I had few interests in common." She turned back. "Mother suggested to him that we should leave." She let out a nervous laugh. She shook her head as another tear escaped. She quickly wiped it away. "There was one thing, however, that I did not tell Mother." She swallowed hard. "I knew that you were… that you were deeply in love with another." She looked up at him.

Darcy's eyes widened in surprise. "You… knew?"

"You seem surprised. I readily noticed how you looked at Miss Bennet and seemed to enjoy the banter you had with her. Ladies notice this kind of thing." She paused and drew in a breath. "I knew you had known her before, if only briefly. I have known you my whole life, and yet you never looked at me that way, or seemed to enjoy talking with me, as much as you enjoyed talking with her." She paused for a moment. "It was difficult, at first, to comprehend. I tried to reason that this young lady had come to Pemberley to ensnare you, that her uncle's fall and injuries may have been part of her plan all along to throw herself into your path. I thought perhaps you would come to see the truth of that and push aside any feelings that you had begun to develop for her."

Darcy stood up and began to pace about the room, wondering what he should tell her. Finally, he stopped and said, "You are right in that my feelings for Miss Bennet are very strong, and I have harboured such feelings since almost the first time I met her." He shook his head. "But Miss Bennet would never use any arts and allurements to try to ensnare me. In truth she had a... she had rather strong dislike of me."

Miss Westerfield's jaw dropped. "She disliked you?" She shook her head. "I did not see dislike at all in her expression as she looked at you. In fact, I only saw admiration and fondness for you."

Darcy gave a shrug, despite feeling his heart leap. "Truly? I cannot answer to that, for she disliked me immensely and made no effort to hide it." A small smile appeared. "In fact, when she found herself having to remain at Pemberley due to her uncle's injury, she did everything in her power to prevent me from seeing that she was there." His brows pinched. "No, she would have never used any form of arts, manipulation, or any such thing to attract my attention."

"I see." Angeline reached out her hand. "Pray forgive me for being so wrong about her."

"Miss Westerfield, I..." Darcy was unable to finish, as the doctor joined them.

"Miss Westerfield, if you would return to the room, we can discuss your parents' condition."

She turned to Darcy. "I must go to them. I shall let you know how they are doing." She started to walk away, but stopped. "You are a good man, Fitzwilliam." She looked like she was about to say more, but instead, she walked away.

Darcy watched her until she had disappeared down the hall. He drew in a breath. "She is an admirable woman who will someday make a fortunate gentleman very happy." He leaned his head back and closed his eyes. Instead of seeing Angeline, however, he saw Elizabeth in the darkness. Elizabeth, who was willing to challenge and confront him, brought liveliness into his life, and stirred him to depths he had never known.

He thought of the bird he had begun to carve when he overheard Mr. Bennet at the Netherfield Ball telling someone how he called each of his daughters by the name of a bird, depending on its characteristics. He particularly remembered that he called Elizabeth a magpie. He thought how appropriate that was, for the bird is one of nature's most intelligent, social creatures. He had begun to carve it in February when he returned to Pemberley for a month. He had futilely tried to put her out of his heart and mind after leaving Netherfield, but try as he might, he could not. He had told himself that this little bird he was carving was merely a memory of the woman who unwittingly touched his heart. When he returned from Kent, however, after receiving such a brutal refusal of his offer of marriage to her, he had no desire to finish it.

Now, however, there was a thread of hope that when he returned to Pemberley, he would discover that Angeline's observations about Elizabeth and what her feelings towards him might be were correct. He could only hope that today Angeline's brother or someone in his stead would arrive and he would be able to set off for home directly. That thought gave him great delight.

~~*

Later that afternoon, Darcy took a walk about the grounds. It was a very nice home, and the gardens and landscape were stellar. He had not seen Angeline since she left him to go with the doctor, but he had received word that her mother was improving and her father had begun to show signs of responsiveness.

As he returned to the house, he encountered Kingston. "I hear there is some improvement in both Miss Westerfield's parents," Kingston said. "I am glad."

Darcy clasped his hands behind him as he walked. "Yes. That is good news." He looked at him. "I know that Miss Westerfield expressed her gratitude to you, but I want to thank you, as well.

There could have been more lives lost than their coachman and footman had it not been for your willingness to stop and lend assistance."

"I was happy to do so."

Darcy again sensed Kingston was uncomfortable with the praise.

"Look, someone is arriving." Kingston's eyes narrowed. "Could it be someone from Miss Westerfield's family?"

Darcy looked towards the house, seeing a young man dismount from his horse. "I believe that is her brother, James." He felt a wave of euphoria as he contemplated finally being able to return to Pemberley. As he and Kingston hurried to greet the young man, he said, "With his arrival, I shall be taking my leave immediately. I actually left guests at Pemberley, who – much like your guests – were staying because the gentleman had been injured."

"I must say I am surprised by your leaving so soon, but now I understand why, having guests waiting for your return." He stopped and turned to him. "I know that Miss Westerfield greatly appreciated your dropping everything to give her comfort and support when she most needed it. Despite the distance there is between Pemberley and Wakespur, you were the closest person she could think of to ask to come." He paused. "And for that, *I* thank *you*."

Darcy nodded, and the two walked towards the young man. Kingston assured him he would have a stable boy saddle his horse.

Darcy greeted James Westerfield and made the introductions. It was apparent he had been informed that his parents and sister had left Pemberley without an engagement being procured, for he did not mention anything to Darcy about it. The three men spoke briefly, and then Kingston showed Westerfield to his family. Darcy returned to his room to pack up the few things he had brought with him.

He then returned to the Westerfields' room and stepped inside, greeting Mrs. Westerfield, and walking over to her husband. He was asleep, but Darcy could see more colour in his face than he had the night before. This was a good sign. He then went up to Angeline.

"I know you are being well cared for, and now with your

brother here, I will be taking my leave."

She reached out and took his arm. "Allow me, please, to see you out." As they stepped out of the room, she continued, "Again, I must thank you for coming. I know you did not have to."

"I could not leave you alone, and I was grateful to find that you were in good hands."

"Yes, Mr. Kingston has been very kind."

Darcy stopped and looked at her. "Miss Westerfield… Angeline… I thought I should tell you that the rumours you had heard about my intentions regarding you did have a basis of truth. I had invited you and your family to Pemberley so that we could become reacquainted with each other… in order to…" He paused. "Forgive me. I am ill-equipped to speak of things of the heart." He shook his head. "I was pleased to discover that you are still the excellent young lady I remember. But…"

Angeline looked up at him with a tilted head. "But you are in love with Miss Elizabeth Bennet."

Darcy pursed his lips and nodded. He placed his hand over hers. "I apologize for any grief I may have caused you."

"I own that my disappointment was great, but I shall soon recover." She then looked up at him, and with tears glistening in her eyes said, "If it is within your power to secure her affections, I wish you and Miss Bennet great joy."

"That means more to me than you can imagine."

She gave a small smile, blinking away a tear that trickled down her face. "Now, having said what I did earlier about Miss Bennet and what I perceived her feelings for you were…" She quickly wiped away the tear and drew in a shaky breath. "If I am mistaken, I would be more than delighted to receive your addresses again." She placed her hand on his arm. "Goodbye, Fitzwilliam."

Darcy lifted her hand and kissed it. "Goodbye, Angeline."

Chapter 15

Elizabeth could not speak as she and her aunt gathered their belongings for their journey back to Hertfordshire. She fought back tears, which insisted on falling despite her attempts to prevent their escape. Her aunt questioned her over and over again, as to why she was so willing and insistent to depart.

"Lizzy, certainly you want to try to clear your name. I would hate to think people will look upon you as someone whose actions destroyed the hopes and dreams of another."

Elizabeth shook her head. "We must go."

"But we ought to wait for Miss Darcy. She will know what to do."

Elizabeth closed her eyes for a moment before answering. "Miss Darcy is very young and does not need to be put in the position that would force her to contradict her housekeeper. I will not do that."

In truth, Elizabeth hoped Miss Darcy would return before they left, if nothing more than to give her a proper farewell. She had enjoyed Georgiana's company, despite what the young girl had told her the night before about her feelings for Mr. Bingley.

Once they were packed, Mrs. Reynolds escorted them out to the courtyard, where their carriage awaited. As they passed maids and servants, several glanced at her as if they believed all the rumours that were being spread about her – even ones that most likely had been exaggerated.

As they stepped up into the carriage, Mrs. Reynolds's features softened. "I want to assure you that this is not something I wanted to do, but something I felt I needed to do. I had some food packed for your travels, and I trust that you will have a safe journey home."

"Thank you for everything," Mrs. Gardiner said.

"Yes," agreed her husband. "We are grateful, indeed."

Elizabeth murmured a soft, "Thank you," that was swallowed up in her choked sobs.

They rode in silence as the carriage drove out of Pemberley's gates. As they traversed the woods, Elizabeth remembered the elation of stepping into them with Mr. Darcy, as well as feeling the shame of knowing that stories were being spread throughout Lambton and Pemberley concerning that walk. As the carriage approached the turn on the road that would give them their final view of Pemberley, she watched intently until they turned and it was gone. She then closed her eyes, tucked her head against the side of the carriage away from her aunt and uncle, and let her tears fall unrestrained as she considered she would never see it – or *him* - again.

At length, she stirred when she heard her uncle ask if anyone was hungry. While she was not in the mood to eat, she was hungry, and readily took a piece of fruit.

"Thank you," she said.

Her aunt smiled at her. "Ah, Lizzy, how I wish I could remove all your pain and distress."

Elizabeth returned a small smile and then turned her eyes to gaze out the window. "In time, I am certain I will recover."

"I wish we could have stayed – even just one more day." Mrs. Gardiner let out a long sigh.

"We do not even know when Mr. Darcy will return."

"No, Lizzy, I suppose not," Mrs. Gardiner said softly.

"And it matters little, for there is something I discovered last night from Miss Darcy."

Both her aunt and uncle turned sharply to her. "What?" they both asked.

"She told me that her brother has hopes that she and Mr. Bingley will marry."

"Miss Darcy and Mr. Bingley? But she is so young!" Mrs. Gardiner said. "Certainly Mr. Darcy does not wish for them to marry now."

"Yes, she is young, but whether or not her brother wants it now, she believes herself to be in love with him." Elizabeth cast her eyes down. "Even if Mr. Darcy were to follow me to Longbourn, declare his unending love for me, and ask me... again... for my hand, I could not marry him. Imagine what that would do to Jane, how grieved she would be that my husband's

172

sister was going to marry the man she once loved – and still loves."

Her aunt and uncle exchanged glances.

"But Lizzy, you cannot forego your happiness in light of something that may not even happen."

"I could never do that to Jane," she insisted.

"This is not sound, Lizzy," her uncle said. "You are putting yourself in a hopeless situation. For what happens if Mr. Bingley returns to Netherfield and declares his love and devotion to Jane? What will you do then?"

"What do you mean?"

"If Mr. Bingley were to do that, you would still have to refuse Mr. Darcy, for then *he* would be marrying the sister of the woman who took Mr. Bingley from his sister."

Mrs. Gardiner took Elizabeth's hand. "You are making this too difficult, my dear. If the two of you love each other, that is what is most important. You need to think of yourselves and not worry about anyone else."

Elizabeth groaned and took the last bite of fruit. She hugged her arms about her. "At this point, I have no idea whether I do love him... or whether he loves me."

Mrs. Gardiner smiled. "Oh, I think you know very well that you love him, and from what I observed, I am fairly certain the gentleman is still in love with you!"

Elizabeth took in a shaky breath and turned her gaze to the window. "Of that, I cannot be certain."

~~*

Georgiana had three visits to make to some elderly tenants and was eager to return to Pemberley. She would have paid a call on Mrs. Wickham had her son had not come back. She had not seen the woman in years, as she was not a tenant of Pemberley, but rather lived with her daughter in Lambton.

Mrs. Annesley would have normally accompanied her, but since she was away, Georgiana was accompanied by Margaret, one of the older maids. She was someone who had a jovial countenance, and Georgiana enjoyed her company. She also assisted the cook in buying meat from the butcher and purchasing other items needed for meals. After their visits, the carriage stopped in Lambton, and Margaret stepped out to purchase some meat.

"I shall stay in the carriage," Georgiana said.

"As you wish, but I will need Adams to help me carry things out." She pointed to the coachman.

Georgiana smiled. "I shall just be here resting."

In truth, the young girl was eager to return to Pemberley to see if there was any word from her brother.

She leaned her head back and had just closed her eyes when the door opened. Her first thought was that she dozed off or they had finished making their purchases in surprisingly quick order. When she opened her eyes she flinched, for she was staring into the face of George Wickham. She felt herself grow weak.

"What… what are you doing here? You really ought not… You need to leave!"

He tilted his head. "I noticed the carriage and then saw that you were inside. It has been far too long since we have seen one another." He smiled and slowly scratched his jaw. "Have you missed me as much as I have missed you?"

Georgiana trembled, looking out on the street, hoping for the maid and coachman to return. She turned back. "No, I have not. My brother… my brother has warned you to stay away."

"From Pemberley, yes, but I can walk down this street as freely as any other."

Georgiana swallowed hard, drawing back her slender shoulders. "I insist that you leave immediately!"

A slow look of dejection filled his face. "And I always thought you to be so kind. Have you not any words of sympathy for my loss? My mother died no more than an hour ago." He cast his eyes down. "I am so grieved."

Georgiana closed her eyes, and then opened them, looking right at him. "I offer you… and your sister and her family my… the sympathies of my brother and me. I pray you will be comforted in your loss."

Wickham smiled. "There! I feel so much better." He casually leaned against the open door and began cleaning his fingernails. He slowly looked up at her with a single brow lifted. "So what can you tell me about all the rumours that are rampant around here concerning your brother and… let me see if I have this right. There is a rumour regarding him and Miss Angeline Westerfield. Mmm, she was a beauty. Something about the possibility of him asking for her hand? And then there have been several rumours about him and Miss Elizabeth Bennet, who, I believe stirred up a bit of jealousy, prompting the Westerfields to depart suddenly and without any notice." He leaned in. "What have you to say about these things?"

Georgiana could barely breathe, and her heart pounded fiercely. "I… I have nothing to say. Rumours are nothing but…"

"But then there is the shocking rumour about him and Miss Bennet alone in the woods. Does your brother often go walking with young ladies unaccompanied? In the woods?" He shook his head. "I thought him better than that."

"Wickham, get away from the carriage at once!"

Georgiana closed her eyes in relief at the sound of the coachman's voice. His commanding voice was all that was needed to make Mr. Wickham step away from the carriage.

Adams put the large bundle he was carrying into the carriage and looked up. "I am so sorry, Miss Darcy. We never should have left you alone." He turned his head towards Wickham's retreating figure. "The nerve of that man!" He looked back at her and shook his head. "Your brother will be very displeased."

When Margaret joined them, Adams told her what had happened. She stepped into the carriage and sat down next to Georgiana, taking her hand. "I know your brother has told the staff that Mr. Wickham is not a man to be trusted and was not to come near Pemberley. He also informed us that he was back in the area, but I had not a notion that he would be so brazen as to approach you. I am deeply sorry." She pursed her lips and let out a long sigh. "I hope me and Adams don't lose our jobs over this. I don't know what I'd do."

Georgiana placed her still-trembling hand over the woman's. "My brother will do no such thing. Please do not worry."

The look of worry did not leave the maid's face, and she began to twist her fingers.

"Truly, Margaret. Please do not let this concern you."

"Oh, but my dear, there is something else that happened in there, and I fear your brother is going to be even more upset."

Georgiana knit her brows. "What?"

"We encountered Mrs. Harper – the blacksmith's wife – inside, and she inquired whether the rumours about your brother and some lady – or some ladies – were true." She shook her head and let out a long sigh. "Oh, dear! There is talk everywhere about them."

Georgiana turned and looked out the window. Unfortunately, what Mr. Wickham had said about the rampant rumours were true. She closed her eyes. No, her brother would not be happy about this at all.

~~*

Darcy was elated to be on the road headed back to Pemberley. He looked forward to seeing Elizabeth again and was grateful for the clear skies as he pushed his horse as hard as he thought prudent. The roads were still damp, but not as muddy as they had been the day before. He would make better time and hopefully arrive at Pemberley before dusk.

He smiled when he saw Pemberley appear before him at the bend in the road. It was a view that gave him much joy, knowing he was finally home. Today, however, there was even greater reason to rejoice. He would find the time – make the time – to tell Elizabeth he still loved her. A slight tremor deep within brought him to the stark realization that he was still not certain of her feelings for him. He would cling to Angeline's conviction that Elizabeth had strong feelings for him. But were they strong enough?

He brought the horse into the courtyard, and seeing no one, threw the reins around a post. He would send one of the servants after a stable boy to care for the horse. He looked at himself and scowled at the dirt and sweat that covered him. He knew he would have to bathe to make himself presentable before seeing Elizabeth.

Some of the staff nodded at him as he passed them, hurrying through the hall towards his room. He waved to Mrs. Reynolds as she came around the corner from the other direction.

"Ahh, Mr. Darcy, I am so glad you have returned. There is…"

"Mrs. Reynolds, I must ask you to fetch my valet and have him draw me a bath. I need to clean up, and then I will go see Miss Bennet and the Gardiners."

"Ah, sir…" Mrs. Reynolds began, deep lines of worry running across her brow. "About them. There is something I must tell you."

"What is it?" His long legs came to an abrupt halt.

"Sir, they have left."

Darcy's jaw dropped. "Forgive me, but did you say they have left?" He could feel the huge weight of disappointment crash down upon him. "Why?"

He watched his housekeeper's face grow pale. "Sir, I think it best we go to your study… or the library so I can explain in privacy."

"No, I would prefer to know right here."

She shook her head. "No sir, there are enough rumours rampant about you, and I do not want anyone to overhear us."

"Rumours?" Darcy scowled and began walking. "Come, then!"

His long, hurried strides easily put him ahead of the older woman, who was forced to take quicker steps to keep up with him. When they reached the study and walked in, Darcy turned, crossing his arms. "Now what is the meaning of this? Why did they leave?"

Mrs. Reynolds spoke in a soft, slow voice. "Rumours have begun circulating about you and Miss Bennet, both within the very walls of Pemberley and in Lambton." She drew in a long breath. "I thought it was prudent – for her reputation and yours – that they leave directly."

His eyes darkened as he slowly shook his head. "Please do not tell me you *asked* them to leave."

Mrs. Reynolds seemed a bit taken aback, but she straightened her shoulders and faced him squarely. "The rumours were such that I did not feel it prudent for them to remain."

"What sort of rumours?"

"First there was the rumour that you and Miss Bennet had danced a waltz in the music room together."

"Is that all? Heavens, it is true, and there was nothing improper about it. Georgiana was there. She was the one playing the piece!" With a frown etched on his face, he gave his housekeeper a pointed look. "Was this justification to ask them to leave?"

"Perhaps not, but the Westerfields' sudden and unexplained departure brought about a second round of rumours. It was supposed that one of the Westerfields had seen you and Miss Bennet dancing, and they were greatly offended, so they left."

Darcy began to rub his jaw and was silent for a moment. "As a matter of fact, I did speak with Miss Westerfield about their sudden departure. She admitted she had seen us dance, but she claimed she had not told anyone." He suddenly looked up at Mrs. Reynolds. "Do we have a young maid employed at Pemberley who has red curly ringlets about her face?"

"Yes, sir. That would be Harriett Abbott."

Darcy groaned. "Is her mother Mrs. Abbott, the woman who is known about Lambton for her tendency to spread rumours and gossip?"

Mrs. Reynolds. "She is, sir. We had hoped, however, that Harriett would not follow in her mother's footsteps when we hired her."

"Well," Darcy said as he sat down. "At least I have an idea where these rumours began." He gave a pointed look at Mrs. Reynolds. "But I do not think them serious enough to ask our guests to leave. Would you be so kind as to bring Harriett to me?"

Mrs. Reynolds put up her hand. "Before I do that, I must inform you of one last rumour."

Darcy's eyes shot up. "What would that be?"

"Apparently, you were... you and Miss Bennet were seen walking alone in the woods together."

"This is absurd!" He pushed himself out of the chair and walked to the window, trying to control the swell of anger threatening to consume him. "There was nothing scandalous or even rumour-worthy in that walk!" He took a moment before turning back to the woman who had been Pemberley's housekeeper since before he was even born.

"Where is Georgiana?"

"She went out earlier to pay some calls. She returned and went directly to her chambers."

Darcy's fists clenched. "So she was from home when all this transpired?"

"Yes, sir."

"Is she aware of this?"

"No, sir. I have not had the opportunity to tell her."

Darcy walked to his desk and braced his hands on the back of his chair. "Please find Harriett and bring her to me." He looked up at Mrs. Reynolds. "I will need to speak to you, as well, when you return with her."

"Yes, sir." Mrs. Reynolds replied, as she walked out the door. Her shoulders sagged as she breathed out a long sigh.

When she walked out of the room, Darcy raked his hand through his hair, feeling as though he had stepped into a nightmare, instead of the joyous dream he had been anticipating. "Could things get any worse?" He leaned against the wall of the study and closed his eyes.

"Fitzwilliam, I am so glad you have returned! There is something I must tell you."

Darcy opened his eyes to see Georgiana hurrying towards him, a pained look on her face. "I am not particularly glad to be home."

Georgiana nodded. "You have heard about the rumours?"

He nodded. "Were you aware that Mrs. Reynolds asked the Gardiners and Miss Bennet to leave because of those rumours?"

Georgiana's eyes widened. "Oh, no! I cannot believe it!"

"Neither can I, but it is done." He looked at her sadly. "And I had been so looking forward to seeing her... Miss Bennet." He paused and then asked, "How did you come to hear of the rumours?"

Georgiana pursed her lips and cast her eyes down.

"Georgiana?"

"I... encountered Mr. Wickham in Lambton."

Darcy felt a shudder jolt through him. "He did not approach you, did he?"

"He did. I was in the carriage while Margaret stopped to buy some meat from the butcher. Adams went with her to help her carry it back out to the carriage."

"They left you alone in the carriage? You should not have even gone into Lambton."

"I was only left alone for a few minutes."

"I do not care how short a time it was. Look what happened in only a few minutes! Must I get rid of all my staff for their incompetence?"

"All the staff?"

Darcy took in a breath to calm himself. "The rumours. You said you had heard about them."

She nodded. "Mr. Wickham mentioned something…"

"Oh, I would wager he did!"

"And then Margaret said the butcher informed her of some rumours that were being spread about Lambton."

"Well, in your absence and mine, Mrs. Reynolds decided it was her duty to ask the Gardiners and Miss Bennet to leave, as she… Miss Bennet… was the object of the worst of these rumours. Mrs. Reynolds claimed it was to protect me and my name." He dropped his head back. "Does she not realize I am more concerned with protecting Elizabeth's name than my own?"

Georgiana stumbled towards him and fell against him, wrapping her arms about him. "This grieves me as much as it must grieve you." She drew her head back and looked up at him. "I can see you are angry; please do not do anything you will come to regret."

He let out a soft huff. "Such as release Mrs. Reynolds, Margaret, Adams, and Harriet from their duties?"

"I know you would not dismiss Mrs. Reynolds. You must realize she is not aware of what your feelings for Miss Bennet have been. I am certain she was only doing what she felt was right."

"Yes, I know."

"But how was Harriet involved?"

"I believe she was the source of two of the rumours. She likely mentioned to her mother that she had seen Miss Bennet and me dancing, and she had noticed the Westerfields' sudden departure. But the rumour of Elizabeth and me in the woods…" He rubbed his jaw, suddenly noticing that it felt rough from not having had a shave since yesterday. "Wickham saw us together, but I had only just encountered her when he saw us." He paused. "And while the thought of letting all my staff go has some appeal to me to appease my anger, no, I will not. Save, perhaps for Harriet."

Georgiana's brows narrowed, and she steepled her fingers, placing them up to her lips. "But I seem to recollect that her mother is good friends with Mr. Wickham's sister. I wonder…"

There was a tap at the door, and Mrs. Reynolds stepped in. "Harriet will be here shortly, sir."

Georgiana put up her hand. "Could my brother and I have another moment together in privacy, please?"

"Certainly." She stepped out, closing the door behind her.

"Fitzwilliam, I know you are angry, grieved, and greatly disappointed, and I can understand that. But consider Harriet. I have often spoken with her, and I do not believe she would do or say anything with ill-intent. I believe she just mentioned some things she saw here to her mother, who then took it upon herself to spread the rumours."

"But she should not have!"

"No, perhaps not. But do you not think we could now use her to help squelch some of those rumours? Allow her to remain on staff, but inform her of the truth of what happened and how important it is to not to speak to others of what happens here – especially if she wants to keep her job."

"And the rumour Wickham likely started? I am certain he told his sister he saw us together in the woods. She told Mrs. Abbott, who then told…" He shook his head. "Everyone!"

She stepped closer and took her brother's hand. "Yes, but people in Lambton know Wickham – and they know *you*. Once they discover it was Wickham who started it – and likely embellished it, they will think no more about it."

"You are such a sweet optimist, Georgiana." He paused and stood up. "I shall allow Harriet to remain on staff with the strict warning that one more infraction and she will be gone." He leaned over and kissed the top of his sister's head. "Now, is there anything else you want to say before I speak to her?"

A forlorn look crossed her face. "Mrs. Wickham died earlier today."

Darcy raised a brow and took a few moments to reply. Finally, he said, "I am sorry for their loss." He braced his arms against the desk. "Well, I think I have had enough distressing news for the day."

Georgiana smiled. "I think I have, as well."

Darcy tilted his head at his sister. "You know that you are very wise for your young age."

Chuckling, she replied, "That is exactly what Miss Bennet told me."

This prompted Darcy to smile. "And why did she tell you that?"

Georgiana's smiled faded. "I told her about how once I had been very wrong in thinking I loved a person." She quickly shook her head. "I did not tell her his name or give her any details, but she told me she thought I was very wise."

"I am glad she thinks so, as well."

"Yes." Her eyes lit up. "I then told her about how I now have strong feelings for another, much finer gentleman."

Darcy drew in a halted breath. "You are referring to Bingley, are you not?" He stood erect and motionless. "Did you... did you give her *his* name?" He felt as though his heart stopped beating in the few moments before she replied.

She nodded. "Yes, I did, for I knew she was acquainted with him and thought she would be most pleased!"

Chapter 16

It was not often that Darcy had to speak harshly to someone in his employ, as most of his staff knew exactly what he expected from them – in what they were to do and not to do. It was even rarer that he had to speak with Mrs. Reynolds about something she had done. In fact, he could not recollect ever having to do so.

She was very apologetic, as he had expected she would be. She was also surprised when he confessed his admiration for Miss Bennet. Upon hearing that, she was effusive in both her compliments about the fine lady and in expressing her distress over her actions.

Darcy reassured her that he understood why she had asked their guests to leave, and if it had been someone other than Elizabeth, he would have completely agreed and supported her actions. He apologized for not acquainting her with the whole situation sooner. By the end of their discussion, each insisted upon taking the blame for it.

Before she left, Mrs. Reynolds said, "Mr. Brooks and I will speak to the staff about this, sir."

"No, this is not something I would want my housekeeper and butler to handle." Darcy's brow furrowed as he looked down. "I prefer that you leave that uncomfortable confrontation to me." He glanced up at her. "I want to look into each of their faces as I speak to them. I will ask, however, that the two of you stand by my side when I do."

"Yes, sir," Mrs. Reynolds said. "I understand. Shall I send in Harriet now?"

Darcy nodded and waited for his housekeeper to bring the young girl to him. He watched as she came nervously into the room.

"Come, sit down," Darcy said. "There is something I need to discuss with you."

After he spoke with her, Harriet seemed genuinely penitent that her actions had caused such turmoil, and she promised she would never do it again. She was grateful she was not released from her job. Her family was financially distressed, and the money she earned by working at Pemberley was desperately needed. Darcy agreed to let her stay but warned her if she ever spoke of anything like this again – even to her mother – she would be dismissed immediately. She was most appreciative for the second chance, and he left it to Georgiana and Mrs. Reynolds to discuss the situation further with her in an attempt to restrain the gossip in Lambton and prevent it from happening again.

When he spoke with Adams and Margaret, he strongly reprimanded them for leaving Georgiana alone, but he admitted that due to the circumstances and his sister's desire to remain in the carriage, there was little else they could have done.

Later, with his housekeeper and butler flanking him, Mr. Darcy spoke to the entire staff. Not everyone had been complicit in spreading the gossip, but all were noticeably ill at ease as they stood before him. He held himself erect, with his head held high, as he spoke in an even tone with carefully measured words. He wanted them to fully realize his disappointment in them, but he also wished to show them he had nothing of which to be ashamed. He hoped he had succeeded in both.

After speaking with the staff, Darcy retreated to his library for a much needed respite from all that had transpired during the past twenty-four hours. He told himself he needed time alone to think and read. However, he knew he would not be able to concentrate on a book, and his thoughts would only be of Miss Bennet.

He sat down at his desk and leaned back in his chair, closing his eyes. He wondered what he could have done differently to prevent this. He had experienced every possible emotion in the past twenty-four hours. He was fatigued and could not order his thoughts. These were the first moments he had had alone since first hearing that Elizabeth had been asked to leave, and his concern for her weighed heavily on him. It was not only the fact that she and her aunt and uncle had been asked to leave Pemberley, but that she had been implicated in the gossip. He could not imagine what she was thinking or how she felt.

When he opened his eyes, they fell upon the unfinished magpie lying on the desk. He tentatively reached for it but drew his hand back. It had remained untouched since his return from Kent.

A light tap on the door drew his attention away from the bird. He turned to see Georgiana. "May I come in?"

Darcy waved her into the room. She was as concerned for him as he was for her. It was obvious that she was deeply grieved by all that had happened. He could discern by the look on her face that she was still troubled.

"I am sorry to intrude, but I neglected to inquire about the Westerfields earlier. So much has happened, and I completely forgot to ask how they were faring."

"That is perfectly understandable." Darcy began tapping his fingers on the desk. "Mrs. Westerfield had already begun to improve by the time I arrived, and Mr. Westerfield began responding this morning. Miss Westerfield's brother arrived earlier today, so I felt that I could leave." He gave a slight shrug. "I had no idea of the upheaval awaiting me at home."

"I am so sorry," Georgiana said as she sat across from him. "What are you going to do?"

"About the rumours?" Darcy looked at his sister and was silent for a moment. "If they only concerned me, I would likely do nothing. I care little about what is said and believed about me, and the people whose opinion I care about know me well enough to not believe gossip – or at least not spread it further." His voice trailed off.

Georgiana lifted her brow. "But...?"

"But..." he paused, "...this also involves two young ladies who do not deserve what is being insinuated about them. Fortunately, Miss Westerfield is not aware of the gossip that pertains to her, but unfortunately, Miss Bennet is." He dropped his head. "I need to think on this and determine what I ought to do. I cannot imagine what Miss Bennet must think of me now, considering how she once felt about me." He drew in a long breath. "I am certain she was mortified that she and her family were asked to leave. I have written to Mr. and Mrs. Gardiner expressing my regrets."

"Did you say anything else?"

He gave Georgiana a pointed look. "What else would you have wanted me to say?"

"You could have said that to make up for the humiliation they must have felt, you would like to invite them and Miss Bennet back to Pemberley." Her smile was wide. "And that you would like to get to know their niece better."

Darcy let out a huff.

"Oh!" Georgiana said pounding her hands onto her lap. "I wish I had been here to prevent this from happening!"

Darcy shook his head. "It matters not. It was all my fault. Every one of these claims being made was for the most part true, and they were the result of my actions, and my actions alone."

Georgiana stood up and leaned across the desk. "No, Fitzwilliam! You cannot blame yourself."

"Why should I not?" Darcy leaned forward. "I gave in to the leanings of my heart. I should never have waltzed with Miss Bennet or taken a step further with her into the woods alone." He shook his head. "I suppose we could blame the magpie." He swallowed hard as he picked up the unfinished wood carving, turning it around as he examined the unfinished piece.

Georgiana shook her head. "What do you mean? Is that what this bird was going to be?"

He nodded mutely and then looked down, pursing his lips. "As I came upon Elizabeth, she was staring at something off the path. It was a lone magpie, and she was looking for another." He lifted his eyes to his sister. "One is for sorrow…"

Georgiana nodded knowingly. "Two is for mirth, three for a funeral, and four for a birth."

When her brother said nothing, she said, "It means nothing."

"I know. I do not believe in such things. But it was immediately after seeing that bird that everything began to happen. We encountered Wickham, the Westerfields left, they had an accident…"

Georgiana sighed. "The gossip began to spread, and Mrs. Reynolds asked Miss Bennet and her aunt and uncle to leave."

Darcy's jaw clenched. "And Wickham approached you in Lambton." He shook his head. "I am so sorry you had to come face to face with him."

The young girl tried to smile. "It was not all that bad. In a way I am glad it happened."

Darcy's brow lifted. "In what way?"

"I felt nothing for him. I felt no pangs of lost love, or regret, or even embarrassment."

Darcy reached over and took her hand. "I am so very glad. I had hoped he had not said anything to distress you."

"He only seemed eager to inform me of the gossip that was going around."

Darcy answered with an edge in his voice. "I believe he was delighted to hear what was being said about me and was happy to contribute to it."

When her brother said no more, Georgiana reached over and took the bird he still held. "Why have you not finished this bird? Were you unhappy with how it was progressing?"

"No, it was coming along splendidly." He took in a deep breath and closed his eyes. "When I was in Hertfordshire – it was actually during the Netherfield Ball – I overheard Mr. Bennet talking to someone about how he had named each of his daughters after a bird that suited their personality. He called Elizabeth a magpie because she is intelligent and very social – just like the bird." He chuckled. "I began to carve it when I returned to Pemberley in February. I had no idea that I would ever see Miss Bennet again, I just wanted a..." His voice trailed off.

Georgiana ran her fingers along the roughly carved back of the bird. "A memory of her."

Darcy nodded and continued, "When I returned to Pemberley last week, I knew I could not bring myself to work on it after what happened in Kent. I brought it in here and began working on another bird in the potting shed."

Turning it over in her hand, she said, "I do not know how you do it. Your woodcarvings are wonderful."

"The late Mr. Wickham taught me how to look at a piece of wood and visualize the bird that lay within. The task was then to carve away the wood that did not belong." He paused for a moment. "I found that piece of advice very useful as I carved each bird."

Georgiana turned it around in her hand and looked at it through narrowed eyes. She shook her head. "I could never do what you do."

"You have no need to. You are proficient in music, which is a more suitable accomplishment for a fine lady." He took it from her. "But look here," he said as he pointed to the piece of wood. "Can you not see that this is its long tail and here its head is held high?"

Georgiana shook her head and smiled. "Regretfully, I cannot, but I encourage you to finish it. I think you *need* to finish it." She stood up and walked over to kiss his cheek. "I shall leave you now to rest. Please try not to worry."

"Thank you," he said as he watched her leave the library and close the door behind her.

A frown suddenly appeared as he thought about his life. He wondered whether it was possible to carve away those parts of him that did not suit the man he wanted to be, the man he thought he was, and more importantly, the man Miss Elizabeth Bennet could possibly fall in love with. He let out a groan as he wondered what – if anything – could be left intact.

~~*

Two and a half days of wearisome travel brought Elizabeth and the Gardiners to Hertfordshire. Despite her uncle's healing and improvement at Pemberley, the long days of the jarring carriage ride proved uncomfortable, and at times, downright painful for him.

Elizabeth's thoughts were in turmoil as they silently drove towards Longbourn. She wondered how, on such a beautiful summer day with the sun shining bright and the sky as brilliant blue as a glistening sapphire, that she could feel such misery. Her mood was dark and grey. It ought to be raining, she thought, for then her tears would fall more freely.

She knew her aunt and uncle were aware of her anger, grief, and confusion over the events that took place at Pemberley. But it was the possibility that Mr. Darcy could return to Pemberley engaged to Miss Westerfield that tormented her most. As they drew near home on their final day of travel, she had convinced herself that she would likely never see him again, and might possibly hear of an engagement between them before long.

Elizabeth was grateful when they began passing familiar scenery. The thought of seeing Jane again banished all the invasive thoughts that had been plaguing her. She needed Jane's calm and comforting presence, but *she* needed to be there for *her*, as well. She did not know if there might be an engagement already between her and Mr. Goulding or whether one would be forthcoming. Was her sister still grieving for the loss of Mr. Bingley? Elizabeth gave her head a quick shake. She did not want to tell her about Miss Darcy's feelings for him. She *could not* tell her!

The travellers agreed they would not burden the family with the reasons they left – that they had been asked to leave. Since they had stayed longer than they had planned, their unannounced arrival would not be questioned.

The first view of the small neighbourhood in which the Bennets lived brought a sense of relief and delight to Elizabeth – the first such feelings in several days. She kept her face to the window as they passed the cottages and farmland on the outskirts of Meryton. They soon reached the main street and passed the inn, the Assembly Hall, and the familiar shops that lined it. A few familiar faces going about their everyday business made her realize she was truly home, prompting tears to pool in her eyes.

When the carriage came to a stop in front of Longbourn, those tears finally fell. Elizabeth was eager to see her family and quickly wiped them away, so she would not be questioned when she greeted everyone. Lydia and Kitty hurried out first, followed by Mary, and then Mrs. Bennet.

Elizabeth stepped down from the carriage, and one by one she was drawn into her family's arms. She received a brief hug and short greeting from her two youngest sisters. Mary's hug was short, but her greeting was longer and seemed more sincere.

Mrs. Bennet welcomed her daughter back with a hug and a pat on her back, and then she began to lament. "I was worried from the moment you left that something dreadful would happen, and look, I was right! My poor brother!" She turned to Mr. Gardiner and walked over to him with her arms extended, but Mrs. Gardiner stepped between them.

"I am afraid his back is still sore, so let us save the hugs until he feels better."

"Oh, yes, certainly. But Pemberley! You were able to stay at Pemberley! Was it beautiful? I am certain it was. But did they treat you well? I have wondered whether they would. I imagine that if Mr. Darcy had been there, he would have cared little for your well-being."

"We were treated quite well," Mr. Gardiner assured her.

Elizabeth turned and saw her father approach. He came up to her and wrapped his arms tightly about her. "I have missed you, my Maggie-pie." There was a catch of emotion in his voice. "It is good to have you home."

At the mention of her nickname, her breath hitched.

When Mr. Bennet pulled away, he noticed the frown on his daughter's face. "Now what is this, Lizzy? Are you not pleased to be home? I imagine Longbourn is nothing compared to Pemberley, eh?"

She forced a smile. "Yes, of course I am delighted to be home! And I am so happy to see you." Looking around, she asked, "But where is Jane? Is she not here?" She hoped her sister was not with Mr. Goulding.

The shouts and cheers of rambunctious children drew everyone's attention as the four Gardiner children dashed from the house, followed by Jane.

Mr. Bennet gave his head a nod in her direction. "She had the task of gathering up the children and bringing them out to greet their parents. I believe a few were napping." He chuckled. "She has had the singular responsibility of keeping the children as quiet and as far away as possible from your mother." After a pause, he added, "And she has done a remarkable job."

Elizabeth rushed towards Jane, and they embraced in a tight hug. Elizabeth put her head down on her sister's shoulder and suddenly was unable to hold back her tears. She began to sob, which prompted Jane to squeeze her tighter.

"Are you unwell, Lizzy? Is something wrong?"

Elizabeth drew back and her lips turned up in a small smile. "I am just glad to be home. I have missed everyone, but you, especially."

"I have missed you, as well." Jane replied.

As the family made their way to the house, Lydia talked of how dull the neighbourhood was since the militia's departure, but Kitty added that there had been many opportunities to dance. Jane commented on how the Gardiners' children had provided much animation in the home, but Mrs. Bennet complained that she was not used to such noise and running around. Mr. Bennet said the news in the neighbourhood was that the Lucases were looking forward to welcoming their first grandchild near the end of the year, and while Mrs. Bennet did not seem particularly pleased with that news, she gushed that Mr. Goulding had been particularly attentive towards Jane.

The two older sisters exchanged a glance, with Elizabeth lifting a single brow in an enquiring manner. She took Jane's arm, and the two fell behind.

"Tell me, Jane. Has anything happened since you last wrote? Mr. Goulding has not asked for your hand, has he?"

Jane shook her head. "Fortunately he has not." She suddenly grimaced.

"What is it?" Elizabeth asked.

"I fear I behaved badly."

Elizabeth could not hold back her laughter. "You? I strongly doubt that."

"Oh, but I did." She leaned close and began to whisper. "I could readily see that Mr. Goulding did not enjoy having the children around when he came to visit." She winced and looked down. "So I told the children..." She paused and slowly looked back up.

"Yes?"

"I told the children that he loved to play with them, and whenever he came by they ought to engage him in their games."

Elizabeth's eyes widened. "Did you truly? And what happened?"

Jane smiled. "He endured them for two days and has not been back since."

Elizabeth laughed. "Well, he deserves to stay away if he does not enjoy children, especially when you love them so very dearly!"

"I know that once they are gone, he will resume his visits, and I fear..."

Elizabeth took her hand and squeezed it. "If he returns with the intent to ask for your hand, I will stick to you so tightly, nothing will be able to separate us." Shaking her head she said, "Just let him try to get you alone. I will not have it!"

Jane smiled. "I am so glad you are home, Lizzy."

Elizabeth sighed. "I am glad to be home, as well."

For the remainder of the day, Elizabeth and her aunt and uncle answered every possible question several times about how Mr. Gardiner fell, what Pemberley was like, whether Mr. Darcy was as disagreeable as he had been in Hertfordshire, and what they had seen and done on their trip.

Later that evening, Elizabeth and Jane said goodnight and went up to Jane's room where they could have some privacy to talk.

"I can see something is weighing on you, Lizzy," Jane said with a look of concern. "I know you are tired and have been traveling several days, but did something happen at Pemberley? What did Mr. Darcy do and say when he saw you?" She tilted her head. "I know you must have felt awkward when he saw you were there."

Elizabeth leaned her head back. "Oh, Jane, I was mortified, but not just because he saw me, but because..." She let out a long breath.

"What?"

"I fear *I* behaved badly – or at least, I acted like a foolish child."

"You? What did you do?"

"I tried to keep my presence from him. I acted so unbecomingly. I... I actually hid several times when he came near."

Jane's eyes widened. "Truly?"

"Our poor aunt and uncle did not know what had become of me. I was not acting like myself, but they did not know everything that had transpired between us."

"That he had proposed and you had refused him?"

"Yes." She took Jane's hand. "I finally told Aunt Gardiner. And when your letter was delivered from the Inn at Lambton, and it was addressed to me, Mr. Darcy saw it. It was then he realized I was there."

"Oh, Lizzy! I am so sorry. I had no idea..."

Elizabeth laughed. "Of course you had no idea. How could

you?" She shook her head. "He was bound to find out eventually."

"What did he say? What did he do?"

"He was very polite, he treated me with the utmost kindness, and I felt quite ashamed."

"Do you think he still loves you?"

Elizabeth's shoulders lifted in a small shrug. "Well, I cannot answer that, for he had invited another family to Pemberley, and it was believed that he was going to ask the young lady, Miss Westerfield, to marry him."

"Oh, dear. But you do not love him… do you?"

Elizabeth's lips pursed as she pondered this. "My estimation of him improved greatly while I was there. I saw things I had never seen, and heard things about him that indicated he was very much unlike what I had thought him to be."

"But he is to marry another?"

"Of that I am not certain.

Jane sighed. "Did you… while you were there, did you hear anything of… Mr. Bingley?"

Elizabeth felt her heart begin to pound. She did not want to lie to her sister, but she could not tell her about Miss Darcy and her confession.

Finally, she said, "We came to understand that he and his sisters had been expected at Pemberley, but he had made a last minute change of plans." Elizabeth saw her sister try to smile.

"It is all for the best," Jane said. "I would not want him to feel any obligation to even inquire after me."

A mischievous gleam lit Elizabeth's eyes. "I would have been more than happy to tell him there was a suitable young man who had singled you out. I would have watched his reaction very carefully."

"I am certain you would," Jane replied. "Did anything else happen while you were at Pemberley?"

"There were some… wretched things that happened…"

Jane's brows lowered. "What kind of things?"

"Jane, you must promise not to speak of this to anyone. I do not want this to be generally known."

"Lizzy, you are frightening me."

"No need to be frightened, but I think you will be surprised."

Jane reached for her sister's hand. "What happened?"

"Mr. Darcy and I encountered each other on a walk the day before we left, and we began to walk in the woods."

"Alone?"

Elizabeth nodded. "We had actually walked several times alone when we were at Hunsford."

Jane's eyes widened. "You never told me that."

"Well, there had been nothing exceptional in those walks. Unfortunately on *this* walk, we encountered Mr. Wickham. Of course he was surprised to see me at Pemberley, but more surprised that Mr. Darcy and I were walking together alone."

"I imagine he would be surprised."

"He proceeded to allude to things about us that both Mr. Darcy and I vehemently denied." Elizabeth pursed her lips.

"That horrible man!"

"Then the Westerfields abruptly left and were later in an accident, Mr. Darcy departed Pemberley to go to them, and then we heard there were... rumours, gossip... about him and me." Elizabeth took in a deep breath and closed her eyes.

"Lizzy?"

"Mrs. Reynolds, his housekeeper, was concerned about what was being said about us, and to protect his reputation, she asked us to leave."

"To leave Pemberley?"

Elizabeth slowly nodded. "Neither Mr. nor Miss Darcy were there, and since our uncle's injuries had improved, we decided not to question it, but to come home." She closed her hand over Jane's. "So we did not leave Pemberley on good terms. I do not know what Mr. Darcy will think once he returns home to find out everyone was talking about us."

"All because of Mr. Wickham?"

She looked down, shaking her head. "No, he could not have known everything that was being said about us, but he likely contributed to it." She quickly wiped away a tear. "Oh, Jane, I came to admire Mr. Darcy – the man I once loathed. I cannot bear to think I may not see him again."

Jane leaned over and wrapped her arms about her. "Oh, Lizzy, I know exactly how that feels."

Elizabeth looked into her sister's face. She knew immediately Jane spoke of the heartfelt feelings she still held for Mr. Bingley, and she felt her sister's grief as deeply as she felt her own.

Chapter 17

Jane had been correct. Once the Gardiners and their children departed to a tearful farewell, Mr. Goulding paid a call at Longbourn. Elizabeth wondered whether he had been stealthily hiding nearby so he could see when the Gardiners and their children finally left.

Mr. Goulding was very much like Elizabeth remembered, both in appearance and temperament, although it had been several years since she had seen him. He was not particularly handsome, but neither was he unattractive. There was something about his smile that did not sit well with her. She studied his face as he talked to Jane, asking her how she was, and apologizing for not coming by recently.

Elizabeth realized his smile appeared to be frozen in place. It never left his face, never widened or lessened, and did not reach his eyes. She was certain it was not sincere.

When he inquired of Jane whether she would like to take a turn about the grounds, Elizabeth replied for her. "Oh, Mr. Goulding, that is a lovely idea! It is such a delightful day! We would love to."

His look of both surprise and disappointment pleased Elizabeth immensely.

As they stepped outside, Elizabeth took Jane's arm, holding her close. She looked at Mr. Goulding and smiled. "I understand our little nieces and nephews took a great liking to you."

He let out a nervous laugh. "I cannot say they took a great liking to me, but they seemed intent on occupying my time whenever I visited."

Elizabeth smiled. "A sure sign of their approval." She tilted her head. "And did you enjoy your time with them? Jane certainly enjoys their company. I do not think she has ever met a child she does not like." Jane sent her a cautionary look, but Elizabeth continued. "I do not know if I shall ever marry, Mr. Goulding, but I have often told Jane I will be just as delighted to be an aunt to her ten or eleven children."

Mr. Goulding coughed. "Ten or eleven…"

"Oh, yes! What a lively household that will be." She chuckled as she noticed him grimace. "She will be an excellent mother who will take an eager interest in her children's welfare and spend a great amount of time with them." She paused and then added, "And with the children's father, of course."

The gentleman seemed at a loss for words. Elizabeth was pleased with the outcome and noticed that Jane felt the same, as she betrayed the smallest smile.

Once talk of children and all their merits had ceased, Mr. Goulding's comfort seemed restored, and he participated more in the conversation. It caused Elizabeth to wonder whether he was completely dismissing all that she had said about Jane's love for children.

When he finally took his leave, Elizabeth leaned against a tree and gave Jane a solemn look. "He may be more difficult to sway away from you than I had anticipated. He is likely so taken by your beauty and charm that he will agree to put up with anything just to have you for his wife."

"Oh, Lizzy, do not say such things."

"Well, he shall not have you. I shall forbid it. If he thinks he only has to secure our father's blessing, he will be surprised."

"Do you think Father will give his blessing if he goes to him? Do you think he will compel me to marry him?"

Elizabeth shrugged. "If Mother has any say in the matter, he might. I am not certain he will feel he can oppose her a second time. It was bad enough when he went against her wishes when Mr. Collins proposed."

Jane leaned against the tree next to Elizabeth. "I am so glad you are here and stayed by my side when he came. Do you think he would have proposed if you had not been there?"

A chuckle escaped Elizabeth. "It is possible that he might propose no matter if you are alone with him or are in a roomful of people." She stopped, and her eyes grew big. "Oh, Jane! Can you imagine if he were to decide to propose to you in front of our whole family?" She shook her head. "That would be unfortunate, indeed!"

The two sisters began to laugh. It felt good to Elizabeth, as it had been several days since she had been able to truly laugh. She hoped this was an indication that her grief and despair no longer had a grip on her.

~~*

Darcy had spent a good amount of time with his steward, and as he finished meeting with him on this pleasant summer day, he hoped to have some leisure time to himself. Unfortunately, there was one more thing he had to do. Mrs. Wickham's funeral was in two days, and he needed to address this matter directly.

As he rose from his desk and prepared to leave, Georgiana walked into the library. "Fitzwilliam, may we talk? You have been so busy the past few days, I feel as though I have rarely seen you."

Darcy sent her a look of regret. "I know, and I am sorry for my neglect of you." He sat down and extended his arm for Georgiana to sit. "Unfortunately, my assistance was required in order for Mrs. Wickham to have a proper funeral and burial."

Georgiana sat down, her jaw dropping. "You willingly gave them financial assistance?"

"I did, but I did not do this for Wickham, his mother, or his sister, but for the late Mr. Wickham."

"I see. Well, I hope she appreciates it."

Darcy tilted his head and smiled. "Who? The late Mrs. Wickham or her daughter?"

Georgiana chuckled. "Both, I would imagine."

There was silence between brother and sister, and then she finally spoke. "Have you thought of what you might do once all this has passed?"

"Do about what?" he said, lifting a single brow.

She crossed her arms and gave her head a shake. "You are impossible."

"If you are referring to Miss Bennet, I have barely had time to think of her."

"Indeed?"

He pursed his lips. "Save for all the times during the day I see something that reminds me of her."

Georgiana reached over and picked up the unfinished magpie.

"Such as this?"

Darcy nodded silently.

"Are you going to finish it?"

Darcy let out a frustrated laugh. "Perhaps when I have some time, which I do not see in the immediate future."

"But Miss Bennet…"

Darcy shrugged. "What would you have me to do? I certainly cannot go to Hertfordshire. Not knowing for a certainty how she feels…"

"You could write to her."

Darcy sent her a reproachful look. "I am not going to write to her. You know that would not be proper." Darcy glanced down quickly, hiding a grimace, knowing he had not too long ago done that very thing.

They sat quietly again, until Georgiana said softly, "*I* could write to Miss Bennet." A small smile appeared.

"And tell her what, exactly?"

Georgiana shrugged. "That we were both grieved by what happened and hope that our paths might cross again someday… soon." She smiled.

Darcy's head lowered, but he lifted his eyes to his sister. "Is that all you intend to say? I will not have you pouring out words of love in my stead."

"I will not disclose the leaning of your heart towards her, Fitzwilliam. If you wish, you may read the letter before I send it."

Darcy smiled. "I will insist upon it!"

~~*

Two days later, Darcy walked down the long staircase towards the front door, attempting to loosen his neckcloth, which felt uncharacteristically tight. He saw Georgiana approach him, and he smiled.

"I can see that you would prefer to do anything but attend this funeral."

Darcy pressed his lips in a forced smile. "I do it for the memory of the late Mr. Wickham. He was a good man, and she was his wife."

"But the people you will be forced to see, knowing what they think and have been saying about you."

"It is better that they see me and not think I am hiding away in shame at Pemberley. Yesterday, I went to the parsonage in Lambton and met with the vicar, the magistrate, and a retired naval captain – all excellent men from the area – who gave me their assurances that they would do everything in their power to prevent the spread of further rumours."

"And did you go speak with Mrs. Abbott?"

Darcy nodded. "I did. The vicar and his wife accompanied me."

He had set out for Lambton the day before with a single purpose, which had been to hopefully destroy the rumours and protect the characters of both Miss Angeline Westerfield and Miss Elizabeth Bennet. He could not help but think it would likely be one of those two ladies who would become his wife.

"What did she say?"

"She said she was very contrite and promised to hold her tongue in the future. She even said she would do what she could to stem the spread of any more rumours about me, as I was so generous in not letting her daughter go."

"But today you will see so many more people, some of whom may still be spreading rumours."

Darcy placed his hands on his sister's shoulders. "This is nothing new for me. I have often had to face many people while rumours have run rampant about me. As I said before, I care little about what most of these people believe about me."

She looked up slyly. "But you do care about the opinion of *some* people."

He paused before answering. "Yes, there are a few people whose opinion matters, yet they are the ones I trust are not spreading gossip about me and are, in fact, doing what they can to stop the rumours."

Georgiana reached up and straightened his neckcloth. "I do not know how you do it. I would find it so difficult to face people who were spreading falsehoods about me."

Darcy placed his fingers under her chin and lifted it up so she was looking at him. "And I have told you time and again, I will do whatever is in my power to prevent you from ever having to go through that."

He saw the tears begin to well up in her eyes and felt a tug on his heart. "Do not worry, Georgiana."

She shook her head. "Oh, but sometimes I do. If Mr. Wickham is inclined to spread rumours about you, how do I know he will not spread the same about me?" She crossed her arms and looked down. "And most of it would be true."

Darcy drew in a deep breath. "He will say nothing about you because he fears what I can do to *him*. Besides, he only wishes to harm me. I do not think he has it in him to do something that would bring harm to you."

The footman brought Darcy his gloves and hat, and as he put them on, he said, "Once this funeral is over, I am certain George Wickham will be gone."

Georgiana nodded and said, "It is hard to believe there is a funeral on such a beautiful day as today."

Darcy shrugged. "We cannot schedule these things. And yes, I would much rather be out riding or walking in the woods…" He paused and drew in a slow breath as a memory of Elizabeth and him walking into the woods suddenly struck him. He continued, "…than going to a funeral, but I shall do my duty."

He kissed the top of Georgiana's head. "I must be going so I am not late. I will see you when I return."

As Darcy rode towards Lambton's church, he stared out the window of the carriage, seeing little. His thoughts, however, continued unabated. As he forced himself to do yesterday when he went into Lambton, he must look people directly in the eye, hold himself erect, and try to appear composed and congenial. He would offer more than the usual civility. He needed to display an air of being unaffected by what people had been saying about him. If only it had not involved Miss Bennet and Miss Westerfield. Right now, however, he felt most of his agitation could be attributed to having to face Wickham. He reminded himself that once the funeral was over, that man would likely be gone, and – he hoped – would never return.

He also thought about Mrs. Abbott's final words to him. She had told him, "I'm not making excuses for what I did. It is something I have done most of my life." Her weathered and worn face looked up at him with shame and regret. "My life is so very plain and simple, Mr. Darcy. I believed the only way people would find anything I have to say interesting would be to share – no, I shall call it what it is, gossip – about other people's lives. It was very wrong of me to speak about you as I did, and I promise I shall try to do better in the future."

Darcy could not help but recollect a time when he had spoken unfavourably about someone. He shook his head as he pondered how he could have done such a thing, degrading Misses Jane and Elizabeth Bennet and their family to Mr. Bingley and his sisters. Yes, he had also forwarded his thoughts to others, including Elizabeth, herself! By doing that, he had likely destroyed all his hopes and dreams.

As his carriage traversed the small streets of Lambton, people glanced his way, occasionally muttering something to their companion as they recognized the Pemberley livery. There was no sense conjecturing what they might be saying about him, so he kept his head forward until he arrived at the church.

As the church came into view, his thoughts turned to Elizabeth. The pain he had first felt upon hearing she and her aunt and uncle had been asked to leave, was almost as strong as when he had received her harsh refusal. If she were to welcome his addresses now and agree to marry him, how would she feel about living so near to a village that had been spreading rumours about her? How would she feel about the staff at Pemberley that had come to believe she had behaved inappropriately with him?

He pursed his lips and shook his head as he recollected her words to him at Rosings. *There is a stubbornness about me that never can bear to be frightened at the will of others. My courage always rises at every attempt to intimidate me.*

Amongst all the ladies of his acquaintance, Elizabeth would not despair over idle rumours and gossip. He drew in a breath. He had never considered that the lady he married might also become the object of such accounts along with him. He had always assumed that sort of nonsense would cease, and there would no longer be an interest in him. But as he had promised Georgiana, he also would do everything in his power to protect his wife from having to endure such a thing. Somehow he had to make certain there was no longer any thought of impropriety on Elizabeth's part, especially amongst this staff. He did not want them thinking - even in their own private thoughts – that she had formed a scheme to ensnare him with her arts and allurements, driving Angeline away. He was just not certain how to effectually do that.

As the carriage came to a halt, he then thought of Angeline. Her sensibilities were more fragile, and she would likely find it difficult to deal with being the object of rumours and gossip. He had seen in her a strength that had surprised him, but she was still vulnerable and would likely feel all the mortification and pain rumours and gossip could bring.

He rubbed his chin as he considered that since Angeline now knew how he felt about Elizabeth, would she settle for being his second choice if Elizabeth still had no desire to marry him?

He was suddenly struck with a clear realization. When he thought of marrying Angeline, it came from his head. When he considered marrying Elizabeth, it came from his heart. He shook his head. "No," he said softly to himself. "The thought of marrying Elizabeth is coming from my heart *and* my head!"

He gave his head a shake and pondered this as he drew in a breath, stepped out of the carriage, and steeled himself for what might come.

Darcy saw several people with whom he was acquainted, acknowledged them with a nod, and then walked towards the church. It was such a pleasant day; people were congregating outside. He saw Alice, George's sister, and her husband, Michael Jacobson, and walked over to them.

"Good day, Mr. Jacobson, Mrs. Jacobson." He turned to Alice. "My deepest condolences in the loss of your mother. I know she will be greatly missed."

Alice smiled. "Thank you for coming, Mr. Darcy. She was very fond of you and appreciated your visits in her final days. You have been very good to us. Thank you for all you have done."

He assured them it was his pleasure, wished them well, and upon hearing a groan behind him, turned to find Wickham standing behind him.

"I am surprised you came," Wickham said with a sneer. "It must be difficult for you to face these people knowing that they no longer hold you in such high esteem." He shook his head, while grinning maliciously. "I found some of those rumours hard to believe myself."

Darcy's face darkened. "Some of which were started by you," Darcy said in an accusing whisper. "I have nothing of which to be ashamed. I did nothing wrong. Miss Westerfield and Miss Bennet did nothing wrong."

"Well, it is much easier to protest after the fact than to behave properly in the first place, is it not?" Wickham sneered at him and then turned his head. "Ah, a long-time friend." He walked away without another word.

Darcy's fists tightened, and he stood a moment as he collected himself. He hoped what he told Georgiana was true – that the man would leave once the funeral was over. As long as Wickham was still in Lambton, there would likely be no end to the gossip – that man would be more than delighted to supply it.

At length, the people began to quietly enter the church. It was a solemn occasion, and while it was mostly men in attendance, Mrs. Jacobson entered on the arm of her husband. She occasionally dabbed a tear away, but seemed to bear up well under her grief.

Darcy walked in with the others, taking a seat towards the back. It was stifling in the church, and Darcy again reached up to loosen his neckcloth. He hoped it would be a short service so he could return to Pemberley directly. Fortunately, the procession to the cemetery was not a great distance. As he waited for the funeral service to begin, his mind drifted to Elizabeth and what she might be doing. What was she thinking about him and all that happened to them? What ought he do about it? Was there anything he could do about it?

He was grateful when the funeral service began, for eyes were no longer upon him, tongues no longer wagging. He noticed something, however, that seemed odd. As the clergyman began to speak he noticed Wickham's sister and her husband looking about them. They were not paying attention to what was being said. He wondered what it was that they were looking at. Or *who* were they looking for?

Darcy's insides lurched, and his heart began to pound when he realized he did not see Wickham. He began to look about, as well.

Both he and Wickham were tall, so he would have readily seen the man if he were in the church. He watched Mrs. Jacobson shrug her shoulders and turn her attention back to the clergyman in the pulpit, but Darcy could not do the same. If Wickham was not here, where would he have gone?

As the clergyman began to pray, and heads were reverently bowed, Darcy stood up, took another quick glance about the church, and quietly stepped out. Once outside, he hurried to his carriage and called out for his driver to take him back to Pemberley at once.

Upon seeing one of the merchants leading a saddled horse down the street, Darcy rushed over to him. "May I use your horse? I have need of your horse! It is of utmost importance!"

"My horse?" he asked. "But what am I to do without him?"

"Are you in need of him now?"

"No, but I will be."

"My carriage and horses will remain here for your use. When I send your horse back, they will be returned to me. If you need anything, take my carriage while I am gone."

The man's eyes lit up. "You will allow me to ride in your carriage?"

"Yes! Hurry, man! Make your decision."

"Of course! Take my horse!"

"Thank you!" He looked at his driver. "See if you can find the magistrate and send him to Pemberley at once. He is likely attending the funeral." Without waiting for a response, Darcy mounted the horse and quickly urged it into a full-speed gallop away from the small village.

His heart beat as thunderously as the horse's gait as he made his way to Pemberley. He tugged at his neckcloth until he was finally able to remove it, and he flung it to the ground. While he made good progress with the man's horse, it felt like it was taking forever for him to reach Pemberley.

When the stately manor finally came into view, he tried to determine where Wickham might be if he had indeed come here. He determined his best course of action would be to find Georgiana first to ensure her safety. He still had some distance to go and gave the horse another nudge to get him there sooner.

Chapter 18

Elizabeth and Jane stepped into the house after spending some time outdoors, as the weather was so fine. They found their mother reading a letter that had just been delivered.

"Did you receive a letter? Who is it from?" Elizabeth asked.

"It is not for me, Lizzy. It is for you!"

"If it is addressed to me, why you are reading it?" Elizabeth gave her head a shake of disbelief and let out a frustrated sigh as she rushed over to her.

"You surely do not expect me to wait for you to come inside to find out what the letter is about when it is from Pemberley!"

Elizabeth's heart jumped. "From Pemberley?"

"Yes, from Miss Georgiana Darcy."

Elizabeth snatched the letter from her mother's hands. She dreaded what news her mother may have just discovered.

"I believe you said Georgiana Darcy is Mr. Darcy's sister?"

Elizabeth looked down at the letter, grateful it was fairly brief. "Yes, she is Mr. Darcy's younger sister."

"Is she as proud as that gentleman is? I imagine she is."

"No, not at all." She shook her head. "And Mr. Darcy is not as proud as we all believed him to be."

Mrs. Bennet chuckled. "Ah, perhaps you think so now that you have seen his grand home. I am certain he is still very proud."

Elizabeth tapped the letter against her palm. "If you do not mind, Mother, I am going to go up to my room to read it."

"Do what you must, but she does not say much... I do not understand why she is so grieved over something the housekeeper did while she and her brother were away."

Elizabeth closed her eyes, wondering what she ought to say. It was Jane who spoke instead.

"You remember, Mother, that your brother fell down the stairs and needed medical assistance? That happened while the Darcys were from home."

Elizabeth quickly nodded. "Yes! That must be what she is

referring to – Uncle Gardiner's fall and subsequent injury."

Mrs. Bennet wagged her head back and forth. "I did not forget! Of course I did not forget that! It consumed my thoughts the whole time you were away. I was so worried about him. I thought he might suffer and die, and you and your aunt would have to travel back here alone, and… Oh, never mind! But what was this unnecessary mortification?" She pinched her brows. "And why would you have hard feelings against them?" She shook her head. "They must have neglected my brother or exhibited excessive pride!"

Elizabeth began mumbling. "No, Mother. Mrs. Reynolds, the housekeeper…" She took in a breath as she attempted to come up with something to satisfy her mother's curiosity. "She… there were some things that happened in the nearby village that took up Mr. Darcy's time, and she felt we ought to… she suggested we leave so he would not feel obligated to entertain us." She winced and stole a glance at Jane, hoping that would be the end of it.

"But Edmund's injuries!"

"By that time, my uncle's injuries were much improved, so we decided that would be the proper thing to do. He was eager to get home, and we had stayed much longer than we had anticipated."

"But this is so strange. So the housekeeper suggested you leave, did she?"

Elizabeth nodded. "Yes, but there are no hard feelings at all. None."

"I see," Mrs. Bennet said. "I am glad you saw it that way. I would have been mortified."

"It was nothing, Mother. Truly."

"But who are the Westerfields? And what about this accident?"

Elizabeth's heart skipped as she wondered what Miss Darcy could have said about them.

"They were the family visiting while we were there. I am certain we told you about them. They had an accident after leaving Pemberley."

She could only imagine how her mother would feel if she knew the whole truth of everything that had occurred. "Now, if you will excuse me, I shall go up and read Miss Darcy's letter.

Elizabeth hurried upstairs and went into her room, closing the door behind her. She walked over to her bed and sat down. Indeed, the letter was short, and while she was eager to read what Miss Darcy had to say, she had been more determined to escape her mother's relentless questions and speculations.

Dear Miss Bennet,

I hope you had a comfortable journey home and that you and your family are well. My brother and I are doing well and trying to keep busy. He always seems to have something to do. With all our guests now gone, I have been spending time practicing on the pianoforte. I hope someday to hear you play and sing.

My brother and I were most aggrieved that you and your aunt and uncle suffered a great deal while my brother and I were away. We regret that your experience at Pemberley began with such a calamity and ended with such unnecessary mortification. Our housekeeper felt she was doing what she must, but Fitzwilliam and I were saddened that you had been subjected to such treatment.

Mrs. Reynolds has been the housekeeper at Pemberley for over thirty years, and she has always had our best interest at heart. She felt that she did what she had to do, and while her motives were pure, if either of us had been there, we would never have even considered it. We regret that we were not able to take a proper leave of you and your relations.

You might be wondering about the Westerfields and what happened when my brother went to see them after the accident. I can tell you that they are all are making an excellent recovery. And as for the matter that prompted their early departure, my brother assured me that all is well. He and Miss Westerfield have settled everything between them to his satisfaction.

I enjoyed getting to know you and hope if we meet again, there will be no hard feelings towards us.

Georgiana Darcy

Elizabeth closed her eyes as they filled with tears. "So they have everything settled between them," she said softly.

She put her finger to the letter and stroked back and forth over the name Fitzwilliam. So he is engaged. She read the last line of the letter again and wondered if she would ever meet either of them again. If they did, she would have to prepare herself for the inevitability that Mr. Darcy would have a wife.

~~*

With her brother away at the funeral, Georgiana felt restless. It was such a pleasant day, she gathered some scissors, a pair of gloves, and a basket, and set out for the gardens. With the flower gardens in full bloom, there would be many colourful and fragrant flowers from which to choose to put in vases. She had several favourites and stopped to sniff them as she walked past, then clipped the stems of the prettiest ones, placing them in the basket.

As she walked about, a breeze wafted across the garden carrying a mixture of fragrances that tickled her nose. She looked down into her basket and smiled at the yellow, orange, pink, and deep red colours. These would be much enjoyed in the sitting room. She hoped the fragrant flowers would bolster her and her brother's spirits.

She glanced towards the rose garden, and as she walked, she put on her gloves so she would not prick her finger on a thorn.

When she reached the garden, she walked around at first, content to just look, and occasionally take in the scent of a rose. She wanted to select only the most beautiful roses to cut. They needed to be deep in colour and perfect in shape. She bent down to cut the stem of a fragrant yellow-orange rose, followed by ones that were deep pink, rosy pink, and bright red. When she felt she had picked enough flowers to fill one of the larger vases, she sat down on a bench and took off her gloves, placing them in the basket. She then carefully picked up what she thought was the prettiest rose she had chosen. It was yellow, as bright yellow as the shining sun on this beautiful day. She brought it to her nose and closed her eyes as she drew in the perfumed scent.

She was placing it back into the basket when a familiar voice called out her name, causing her to flinch. The thorn on its stem pricked her finger, and as she pressed it to her lips, she looked up. Her heart began to pound when she saw George Wickham walking towards her. Her cheeks grew warm, and she shuddered.

"What... what are you doing here?" she demanded, swallowing

hard. "Why are you not at your mother's funeral?"

He continued to saunter towards her, shaking his head. "Boring affair," he said.

Georgiana's eyes narrowed. "That is so wrong. You ought to be ashamed of yourself. How will you face anyone again, knowing that they are aware you did not honour your mother with your presence?"

Wickham lifted a brow and waved a hand through the air. "My dear, Georgiana, funerals will not bring the person back, and if that is all I have to be ashamed of, I guess I am doing rather well."

He took a step closer to her, prompting her to stand up and retreat a step. "You ought not be here."

"Yes, so your brother often reminds me." He looked at his finger nails and swiped across the tips with his thumb. "Or perhaps I should say he *warns* me." He casually glanced up. "He is at the funeral, by the way."

Georgiana shuddered, and she found herself tightly gripping the pair of scissors in the basket. "I know he is there, and that is where you should be."

He laughed. "Oh, but you should have seen him! I know he was trying to appear unaffected by the gossip that has been spread about him, but I have known him as long as anyone. I could see that he was uncomfortable amongst the stares and whispers."

Georgiana looked about her to see if anyone was nearby, but she saw no one. "His only reason for being uncomfortable would have been because he had to see you." Georgiana turned towards the house. "If you will excuse me."

Wickham did a short side-step to block her path. "Not so fast, my pretty little one. When I saw you in Lambton, I had not finished saying all I wanted to say to you." He shook his head. "Some people are so ill-mannered. How dare they think they can interrupt me and force me to leave when there was so much more I wanted to tell you?" He scuffed the dirt with his boot.

"You should leave now if you know what is good for you, Mr. Wickham."

"Georgiana, what is this *Mister* Wickham? You know me as George. I have always been George to you, and I treasure that you always felt comfortable enough to call me that. There are no formalities between us." He took another step towards her, and Georgiana took another step back.

Georgiana wished she knew what to say to him. Words never came to her when she needed them most. She felt both fear and anger building inside her. She wanted to let him know exactly how wrong she had been about him, how wrong he had been about her, and how she now felt about him.

He lifted a brow and smiled. "You can come with me now, Georgiana. There is no one to stop you. You know this is what you have wanted this past year." He took a step closer, one arm reaching out to her. "We are much closer to Gretna Green now than we were when we were at Ramsgate. It will be a much easier journey."

The young girl's eyes widened and then darkened. "You take me for a fool, but I am not! Being with you is the very last thing I would ever want!" She drew in several nervous breaths. "And as for your name, you are not worthy to be called George, after my good father, or Mr. Wickham, the name bestowed on you through *your* good father!" She shook her head in disgust. "Both my father and yours would be ashamed of what you have become."

Wickham drew back in mock surprise. "Is this truly the same little Georgiana that I came to admire? My! What liveliness and pluck you have! I would never have guessed you capable of it!" He looked upon her with a sinister smile. "But I rather like it."

Georgiana swallowed as she watched him take another step closer. Her hands gripped the scissors, but she wondered if she would be able to do anything with them.

When he took the few steps to bridge the distance between them, he grabbed her arm, and the basket and the flowers fell to the ground. She held onto the scissors, however, and when he rushed towards her, she struck his arm in defence. Despite the vile curse indicating his pain, the small cut did nothing to stop him. The next thing she knew, he had grabbed her hand and pried the scissors from her fingers.

"Now, Georgiana, is that any way to treat a long-time friend?" His expression was solemn, and he regarded her through half-closed eyes. "Come, my sweet. You are going with me!"

When Georgiana tried to scream, he covered her mouth with

his hand and pulled her away from the garden.

~~*

Upon finally reaching Pemberley, Darcy brought his horse to a halt, dismounted, and looked about him quickly, before looping the reins about a post. He hurried inside.

"Georgiana?" he called out. "Where is Georgiana?"

Mrs. Reynolds came from another room. "Why, Mr. Darcy, you are returned early from the funeral. It cannot be already…"

"Where is Georgiana?" he interjected sharply as called out her name again. He looked at his housekeeper. "Do you know if she is in the house?" His eyes were wide, and he looked about wildly. "Quickly! You must tell me! Where is she?"

"She is not inside, sir. I believe she went down to the gardens to pick flowers to fill some vases in the…"

Darcy spun around and hurried for the door, leaving the housekeeper perplexed and with her mouth open.

His long legs took him quickly to the garden in front of Pemberley. He looked about him, panting, but could readily see there was no one around. From his vantage point, he could see the rose garden, but saw no one there, either. His chest constricted as he wondered whether he was too late. Had Wickham already encountered her? He gave his head a shake; he refused to believe she was in danger. He raced to the rose garden, chest heaving, and concern etched deeply on his face.

He thought he heard a muffled scream which spurred him on. He was out of breath when he reached the rose garden, and looked around, but still he saw no one. With fists clenched, he began walking around the path that circled the roses. He looked in every direction and suddenly noticed some movement beyond the garden shed on the other side of the shrubbery.

He sprinted over, and when he saw Wickham dragging his sister, trying to force her to go with him against her will, he let out a fierce growl and rushed towards them. "Let her go, Wickham!"

Wickham looked up, and upon seeing Darcy, seemed taken by surprise, but his grip remained tight. He held up the pair of scissors in a threatening manner.

Darcy's insides roiled as he looked into his sister's face. Her complexion was ashen, and her eyes were wide with fear. "Let her go, Wickham. This is between you and me."

Wickham's face twisted in anger; his eyes bulged. "It's always been about you and me." He pointed the blades at Darcy. "But one thing you don't realize is that I have never wanted it to be about you and me. I have never wanted anything to do with you."

Darcy's heart pounded as he took in the situation. He carefully took a small step forward. "And yet you come asking me for money, you attempt to undermine me at every turn, and you harass my sister."

Wickham shook his head quickly. "I would have no need for you or your money if you had given me the same respect your father had for me. *You* are the one who undermined *me*." When Georgiana tried to squirm out of his grasp, Wickham jerked her back towards him.

Darcy fisted his hands and glared at Wickham. "You know that your reasoning is completely unsound. One does not gain respect if their actions are not worthy of it." He took another step towards him. "Now, let her go, Wickham."

"No! I intend for her to be mine!"

Darcy drew in a breath in an attempt to calm himself and tried a different approach. "Wickham, the magistrate will be here shortly."

Wickham laughed. "He is likely sitting in the church listening to the boring sermon the clergyman is giving."

"You are a disgrace to your very own mother!" Darcy had to make sure he did nothing to risk Georgiana's safety. "As soon as I realized you were not at the funeral, I had someone go after the magistrate. He is likely on his way now."

"You see?" Wickham's voice whined. "You give me no respect!"

"No, *you* do not see, Wickham. You have not earned my respect or anyone's respect. What are people thinking even now that you are not at your own mother's funeral?" Darcy took another small step towards him. "Release my sister at once."

Wickham cocked his head and looked down at Georgiana. He turned the scissors, pressing them into her cheek. He sneered as he said, "What do you think would happen if sweet little Georgiana ended up having to live her life with her pretty face all scarred? Shall we see?"

Darcy saw his sister tremble, tears forming in her eyes. His mind whirled with what he ought to do as he saw the fear in her face. Even if someone came upon them, Wickham could inflict terrible damage just with the pair of scissors he held in his hand.

"You know you do not want to do that, Wickham. Let her go, and we can discuss this."

Wickham gave a nonchalant shrug. "What happens to her is of no consequence to me."

Darcy watched his sister's face as realization struck her of what Wickham had just said and what he might do. She shuddered, closed her eyes, and her head and shoulders drooped. Her movement drew Wickham's attention away from Darcy, who took the opportunity to quickly lunge at him, pulling Georgiana from his grasp. He grabbed Wickham's hand which held the scissors, and with every ounce of strength he had, he threw Wickham to the ground.

Georgiana screamed when she saw Wickham point the scissors at her brother. Darcy held Wickham's arm extended out, pushing his wrist as far away from him as possible. Both men vied for control over the other, but it appeared they were equally matched.

As the men tumbled about, Wickham was able to wriggle out of Darcy's grasp, and he rolled away, quickly rising to his feet. He pointed the scissors towards him and bent over as Darcy jumped to his feet holding his arms out to prevent the scissors from hitting him where they could do serious harm.

Darcy suddenly had an opportunity and grabbed Wickham's shoulders, and with a grunt and a shove, sent Wickham tumbling to the ground. The man landed face first onto the roses that had fallen out of Georgiana's basket. Wickham let loose a howl of pain, and when he turned and looked up, blood was dripping in several places from thorns that pierced his skin.

"You will pay for this!" he exclaimed, wiping his hand across his face, which was now smeared with streaks of blood and dirt. He stood up and charged forward, with his arm raised and the point of the scissors facing Darcy. As Wickham lunged, Darcy ducked out of the way and pushed his body into Wickham's stomach. Both men again fell to the ground.

Darcy tried several times to pull the scissors out of Wickham's hand as they rolled about, but the man had his fingers tightly locked in and around the handles. He gritted his teeth as it took every ounce of strength to keep the blades away from himself.

Wickham was able to escape from Darcy's grasp and rolled away. He stood up and came towards him, anger etched on his face. Darcy jumped to his feet and swung, landing his punch just below Wickham's chest. It seemed to knock the breath out of him, and Darcy was able to grab the blade of the scissors, but still could not pry them from Wickham's hands.

Darcy could barely hear Georgiana screaming over the pounding of his heart and the sounds of their fighting. He looked over at her, and she seemed unable to move. She screamed for them to stop and for someone to come help.

He wondered why no one had yet come to intervene, but then realized they had likely only been fighting a short time. It seemed like an eternity.

The men were on their feet again, their arms outstretched and each holding the scissors, as both men attempted to gain the advantage. Darcy was growing fatigued, but knew he could not let up. If he had believed Wickham was as dangerous as he was now showing himself to be, he never would have kept the man's character from those he met. His thoughts went to Hertfordshire and the small neighbourhood around Meryton that had been so deceived by him, including Elizabeth.

Thoughts of Elizabeth and Georgiana spurred him on. He again slammed his body against Wickham's, causing the men to stumble backwards, and the two fell to the ground again, the scissors pulled down between them.

Wickham's arm moved in towards Darcy as the two men continued to grapple, and then cries of pain rang out.

Georgiana rushed towards her brother and Wickham. She looked down and frantically screamed for help. A pool of blood spread out between the two men, who were lying unmoving on the ground.

Chapter 19

Darcy tried to take in a breath, but his chest felt constricted, and he was doubled up in pain. He slowly opened his eyes, and his hand touched his shoulder. The pain was sharp and intense, and he felt blood oozing out. He lifted his head and looked about, trying to catch his breath and assess his injuries. He looked down and saw that blood covered his shirt. He pressed his hand tightly over the wound Wickham had inflicted with the blade of the scissors. He hoped it would stay the bleeding.

He looked up and saw his sister running off, disappearing around the front of the gardening shed.

He struggled to sit up and was about to call for her to come back, but stopped himself. He closed his eyes, as the pain and dizziness swept through him again. He knew that if she had seen the two of them with severe injuries and the pool of blood beneath them, it would have assaulted her sensibilities. He looked over at Wickham's motionless body and found it difficult to swallow. His heart pounded in his chest as he wondered if Wickham's wounds were fatal. He wondered if he had killed him.

His mind could barely recollect what had taken place between them as everything had happened so quickly. He knew that as they had struggled for control of the scissors, Wickham sliced into his arm beneath his shoulder, and then he punched Wickham in the stomach with his other hand. Despite Darcy's pain and struggle to take a breath, he felt such a surge of anger and strength that he grabbed the scissors and slowly began turning the pointed ends away from him and towards Wickham.

As they had struggled, they both fell. Darcy could still barely breathe, and as they hit the ground, Wickham let out a cry of pain. He surmised the man must have fallen on the blade of the scissors.

Darcy looked around him, hoping to see help come. He then saw Georgiana running back.

"Georgie..." It came out in only a whisper.

She rushed over to him and pressed a cloth onto his wound. "I do not think it is a deep cut, but it is bleeding quite a bit." A look of worry crossed her features. "Do you think you can keep pressure on it? I am going to see what I can do for Mr. Wickham."

Darcy's eyes narrowed as he turned to look at Wickham. "Georgiana, I doubt Wickham..."

A cry of pain from the man interrupted him.

Georgiana nodded. "I saw him hit his head hard against the ground, and he has a deep wound. I am going to do what I can to stop the bleeding."

She turned and kneeled beside Mr. Wickham, rolling him over. He moaned again.

Georgiana let out a soft gasp, and Darcy saw her shudder. She took one of the cloths she carried and pressed it against his wound, which was located in his chest. "Be still, Mr. Wickham. You have a serious injury."

Wickham slowly opened his eyes. His face did not display any recognition or awareness of what was happening.

When he closed his eyes again, Georgiana shook him and fortified herself with a deep breath. "You can do this, Mr. Wickham. I know you can. Do you hear me?" She pressed down on the cloth harder as more blood began to escape.

"Georgiana, I do not think it is any use. He appears to have lost a great amount of blood already." Darcy was amazed at his sister's determination to help the man who had more than once attempted to harm her. He tried to move closer to her, but a wave of dizziness stopped him.

The sound of approaching voices brought a great sense of relief to Darcy. He turned his head to see several people running towards them.

"Mr. Darcy!" Mrs. Reynolds cried out, rushing over to him. "You are injured! Let me help!"

Darcy shook his head. "Go to Wickham. I doubt there is much to be done, but I want Georgiana removed at once. She is not equal to the task of..."

"No, I will remain!" Georgiana looked down at her patient as he struggled to open his eyes. "Ah, there you are, Mr. Wickham. You must try to stay awake! I will do everything in my power to help you!"

Wickham opened his mouth, but nothing came out. He slowly closed his eyes again.

"Mr. Wickham! George! You must keep your eyes open. George! I know you can do it!"

One of the men gently moved Georgiana away so he could apply pressure to the wound, which was still bleeding profusely. The young girl remained at his side, however.

Darcy's jaw was clenched in both pain and indignation as he watched Georgiana show compassion towards this man who was continually threatening harm and giving offense. Could she still have feelings for him?

Wickham weakly lifted a hand. "Georgiana..." It fell back to the ground. With eyes closed, he mouthed the words, "I am sorry."

"Do not talk. You have been cut, and I think you hit your head against the ground when you fell." Georgiana paused and drew in a breath. "Be still. It is for the best."

Darcy saw the smile the man gave his sister. It sickened him, and he felt the urge to order everyone away and let him die.

"I would have never..." Wickham was unable to finish his thought.

"I know," Georgiana said softly. "You must save your strength."

More men arrived, including the local magistrate, who rushed over to Darcy and bent down. "Can you tell me what happened?"

Darcy took in a breath and closed his eyes. He felt weak, but he knew he had to tell the magistrate what had happened. "Wickham stole away during his mother's funeral. When the service began, I noticed he was gone and suspected he would come here. We... we have recently had some words. When I came upon him, he was attempting to talk Georgiana into running off with him. When she refused and I showed up, he threatened both of us." Darcy nodded toward the pair of scissors, whose blades were covered in blood.

"My sister had been cutting flowers, and he grabbed the scissors from her. We began to scuffle, and he stabbed me in the shoulder with them, but I grabbed his hand and turned the blades away from me. As we fell to the ground, he hit his head and fell on the blade of the scissors, causing his injury."

The magistrate nodded and looked over at Wickham. "The man will likely spend a good amount of time in jail… if he survives."

Darcy leaned back and closed his eyes as others tended to him. But his concern was not for himself, not for Wickham, but for Georgiana.

~~*

Darcy sat at his desk rubbing his shoulder. It had been almost a week since the fight, and his wound was still covered with a bandage and was noticeably painful when he touched it or when he moved that arm. It oozed occasionally, causing him to wonder if it would ever heal.

He leaned back and closed his eyes, wondering if he had done the right thing in allowing Wickham to live the remainder of his life in Lambton with his sister instead of in jail, as the magistrate had wanted. The man had suffered a near-fatal wound, but due to Georgiana's strength and fortitude, he had survived.

He would never be the same, however. Because of his severe head wound, he was now limited in his ability to communicate and do the simplest of things. His left arm would never regain its full mobility, and it was believed that with his great loss of blood, his heart may have been damaged. He would likely never be able to leave the house on his own.

For that, Darcy was grateful. The man would never again entice a young girl, would never mount up gambling debts and leave without paying them, and… Darcy shook his head. He would never tell another lie about him. He owed Georgiana his life, and he owed Darcy his freedom – as limited as it was. To help Wickham's sister, who now had the unfortunate task of caring for her brother, Darcy had repaid many of Wickham's debts in Meryton, Brighton, and those he had accrued in the short time he had been in Lambton.

As he pondered this, a letter was brought in.

He thanked the servant and looked down at the blotted address, smiling. "Ah, Bingley, you must have received my letter."

He had written to his friend several days ago, giving him an account of what had recently happened. He assured him that he and Georgiana were doing well and there was nothing to worry about. He had debated what to tell him about his guests. Bingley had known Miss Westerfield was coming, but did not know about Miss Bennet's presence here. He grimaced; he had decided to keep that fact from his friend. He had briefly told him about the Westerfields leaving, their subsequent accident, and giving assistance to them. He had made no mention of the rumours that had begun to circulate, the reason they departed, or the conjectures many had made about his reasons for inviting her.

The situation with Bingley was complicated, even more so now that his own sister had grown quite fond of him.

He opened the letter and leaned back in his chair as he began to read.

Darcy,

I can barely comprehend what you and your sister had to endure at Wickham's hands. I am so grateful that you were not more seriously injured. The horror! The wickedness of that man! The...

Darcy could not read the last word for it had not been blotted.

I hope this does not come at a bad time for you, but my heart has been doing battle with my loyalty to you, and I can keep it from you no longer. I have to confess to you that my reason for not coming to Pemberley with my sisters was not so much Caroline's objections (although that was a large part), but due to my own reluctance.

Darcy, your sister is a very sweet girl, and I have only the fondest feelings for her. I would never do anything to hurt her, but I fear my heart is still strongly attached to Miss Jane Bennet. Despite your words of caution about what her feelings towards me were — or were not — last year, I cannot put her out of my mind.

Therefore, I am resolved to return to Netherfield in the next week or two. I hope you can convey to Miss Darcy my affection for her. Explain to her that it is of a brotherly nature, and that I hope that she will one day find someone who suits her better than I do.

I shall remain at Netherfield as long as necessary to ascertain Miss

Bennet's feelings. Hopefully, I will be able to discover that she still has the ardent admiration for me I believed she once had. I hope she does not think ill of me for leaving as I did last November and for not returning. If you are so inclined, feel free to join me there. My sisters will not be accompanying me.

Your friend,
Bingley

When Darcy had finished reading the letter, he slowly put it down. He moved his sore shoulder about, trying to determine how much pain remained. The movement was tolerable, but the wound itself still stung sharply. He rang for Mrs. Reynolds, and when she arrived, he asked her to send Georgiana to him.

When she came in, Darcy nervously smiled. He extended his hand to the chair next to his and drew in a breath. "Georgie, there is something we need to discuss."

"Yes? What is it?"

"We have spoken little of what happened that day when Wickham came here."

Georgiana folded her hands and placed them in her lap. She looked down at them for a moment and then looked back up.

"Do you... are you upset he was not arrested and put in jail?"

Her brows pinched as she considered this. "I understand he will be limited in what he is able to do and would probably have..." She took in a shaky breath. "He probably would have died in prison."

Darcy pursed his lips together. "Georgie, you... what you did for Wickham, helping him like you did..."

"You were surprised by my actions and want to make sure I do not still have strong feelings for him." She smiled. "Am I correct?"

"Yes. I wondered what prompted actions that were so... unlike you."

She looked down at her hands again and smiled. "It is just as Miss Bennet told me."

Darcy shook his head. "Miss Bennet?" He felt his mouth suddenly go dry.

Nodding, she replied, "She said she believed I would be strong when I needed to be. I had to be strong for both him and you.

221

You had the strength to hold the cloth to your wound to stop the bleeding, but Mr. Wickham…" She bit her lip. "He was not strong enough to do much of anything, and…"

"And?"

Georgiana looked away briefly. "And I knew that you would regret having Wickham die at your hand." She turned her eyes back to her brother. "I wanted to spare you whatever guilt you might have felt later."

Darcy was silent for a moment. "Georgiana, you were strong beyond anything I would have ever imagined." He drew in a breath. "So you have no lingering feelings for the man?"

"None whatsoever," she said adamantly.

"Good. I am glad." He paused and picked up the letter he had just received. "Georgie, there is something else I need to talk to you about, and I…" He leaned towards her. "This may be another one of those times you need to be strong."

~~*

Elizabeth was perturbed by Mr. Goulding's continued visits. Since she had returned home, he had taken neither the subtle nor the blatant hints that her sister was not in the least interested in his attentions. She knew it was a matter of time before he asked for Jane's hand, or at least went to her father to receive his blessing and consent. She had to find out whether he had gone to him yet. She went to her father's study and found him alone and apparently in a contented mood.

"Father," she said as she stepped in and closed the door behind her. "May I speak with you?"

"Certainly!" He waved her in.

Elizabeth stood and grasped the back of a chair. "Has Mr. Goulding approached you about his intentions regarding Jane?"

Mr. Bennet drew in a deep breath and leaned back in his chair. "No, he has not, which has your mother vexed beyond measure."

"Good!" Elizabeth said quickly. "I am glad! But, do you know what you are going to say to him when… if he does?"

Mr. Bennet's brows lowered. "If you are here to give me your opinion on the matter, you can get in line."

"Mother has spoken to you…"

Mr. Bennet was nodding before she had finished asking her question.

"I can imagine what she has said."

"And do you expect me to defy your mother in this? As I did for you with Mr. Collins?"

Elizabeth gave her head a firm shake. "I most certainly do!" She sat down across from him, leaning forward. "Jane does not love him – her heart is untouched – but she is too kind to dismiss his attentions."

"Yes, yes. He is an odd fellow."

"Then you will refuse to give your consent?"

He lifted a single brow and pursed his lips. "You know what your mother will do, if I refuse."

"That can be dealt with."

"Do you know how long she remained angry with me after you turned Mr. Collins down?"

"Is she not still angry with you?" Elizabeth said with a teasing laugh.

Mr. Bennet slowly nodded. "Occasionally, the subject still comes up."

Elizabeth grimaced. "I cannot bear to think of Jane wedded to that man."

Mr. Bennet let out a long breath. "Neither can I, and each time he leaves after a visit, I thank the good Lord that he did not seek me out."

Elizabeth smiled. "I knew you would be sensible about it."

Mr. Bennet shook his head and wagged his finger. "Now, I have not agreed to anything, my Maggie-pie. I am the one married to your mother and must live with her the rest of my years."

Elizabeth felt a sting of pain as the image of a magpie came to her mind. She briefly closed her eyes as they threatened to fill with tears.

"Come, Lizzy. You know I will do what I can for dear Jane."

She looked up quickly, blinking her eyes to rid them of the tears. She reached across her father's desk and took his hand. "I know, Papa. I know, and I greatly appreciate it."

A servant came in and placed some letters in front of her

father. He then turned to Elizabeth. "And a letter for you, Miss Elizabeth."

Her eyes lit up, and she smiled as she took it.

"Who is it from, my dear?"

"Aunt Gardiner. And at least this time, Mother did not get it and read it first!"

"Your mother does that, does she?"

"Unfortunately, she does!"

As her father opened his mail, she opened hers and began reading it.

My dearest Lizzy,

I thought I ought to write and let you know how we are doing – in particular, your uncle. He is much improved, has begun to work a little, and is feeling less and less pain. I still encourage him to take things easy, but he does not always take my advice – or if he does, he does so begrudgingly. But enough teasing. Lizzy, there is something rather serious I need to convey to you.

It pertains to Mr. Darcy. I received a letter from my friend in Lambton. She told me that he was seriously injured..."

Elizabeth gasped and looked up suddenly, her heart pounding. "Papa, would you excuse me? I need... I would like to read this letter in my room."

Her father waved her on as he studied his own mail. "As you wish."

She hurried up the stairs, fear gripping her. She threw herself down onto her bed and opened the letter again with shaking hands.

He was seriously injured in a fight with Mr. Wickham.

"Mr. Wickham!" Elizabeth bit her lip, and she felt an uneasy churning in her stomach.

Apparently, during Mrs. Wickham's funeral, Mr. Darcy noticed that Mr. Wickham had left the church. For some reason, he suspected he might have gone to Pemberley, so Mr. Darcy returned home, where he found that man with his sister. From what people are saying (and you know how people love to gossip, but I think this is truly what happened), Wickham hoped she still had a fondness for him after spending all her childhood with him. He tried to entice her to go away with him, but she refused (thank goodness!), and when Mr. Darcy arrived, Wickham threatened him with a pair of scissors Miss Darcy had brought out with her to cut some roses. They scuffled, and both men were stabbed as they rolled about on the ground.

Elizabeth's hand went over her mouth, and she held her breath as she continued to read.

Mr. Darcy received a deep cut in his arm near his shoulder, and I am told he is recovering well. We can be grateful for that. Mr. Wickham was more seriously injured. He also sustained a cut which was deeper and a little closer to his heart. While both men were bleeding profusely, Mr. Wickham lost a critical amount of blood and also suffered a severe head injury. It was the quick thinking of Miss Darcy that probably saved both men. She rushed to the gardening shed and grabbed some cloths. She tended to her brother first, and when she determined he had the strength to press the cloth against his wound, she went to Wickham. Apparently it was a gruesome sight, but she persevered, holding the cloth tightly against his wound and trying to talk to him to bring him through it.

Her screams had alerted others to what had happened, and several people hurried to them. In addition, before Mr. Darcy left the funeral, he had sent someone for the magistrate to come directly to Pemberley. He suspected Mr. Wickham might try to do something, and he was right. Mr. Wickham's injuries proved to be so dire that he will never be able to return to the Militia and will likely need constant care. Mr. Darcy chose not to have charges pressed against him as he considered the man's condition would be punishment enough for his actions. His sister in Lambton now has to care for him.

We can be grateful Mr. Darcy is mending well.

I wanted to let you know, dearest Lizzy, that my friend also told me that while the rumours about you are still going around, they are not as rampant. Wickham's actions have taken over people's thoughts and tongues. Unfortunately for Mr. Darcy, the rumours still revolve around him, but in a different manner. But as my friend tells me, he has had to live with rumours and gossip most of his adult life. It was just unfortunate that some of those recent rumours involved you.

And I neglected to tell you that Mr. Darcy wrote to us after we returned home, apologizing for all that had taken place. He was deeply grieved that we had been asked to leave Pemberley and hoped that we would understand. He particularly wanted me to express his regret to you, Lizzy.

Lizzy, if I may be so bold, both your uncle and I are of the opinion that if ever your path crosses again with Mr. Darcy's, let it be made known to him — more apparent to him — that your feelings for him have changed. We know it is something that will have to be done prudently, but do not leave him uncertain, if you perceive that he might still care. We truly believe he does.

I hope you are doing well. I miss your smiling face and lively conversation. Say hello to everyone for me.

With love,
M. Gardiner

Elizabeth swallowed hard, grateful for the news that Mr. Darcy was recovering. She pounded her fist as she considered Wickham's vicious deeds. If she had received word only that Mr. Darcy had been seriously injured, she would have worried about him day and night. She cared nothing of the rumours about her, hoping only that he was doing well.

She was also grateful her mother had not intercepted this letter, for she would have had a difficult time explaining how she had been included in the rumours that involved Mr. Darcy.

She fell back onto her pillow and closed her eyes as a tear escaped. She could not imagine what both Mr. Darcy and his sister were feeling, especially after what Mr. Wickham had done. She shook her head. Mr. Darcy had found his way into her heart, and she did not know how to regulate the strength of her feelings for him. She felt that she had come to love him. But it was so much more than love. She felt compassion, concern, admiration, and respect for him. Yet, it was an impossible situation, and one in which she had little hope for a happy resolution.

Chapter 20

Elizabeth and Jane sat in the parlour listening to Mr. Goulding give an account of his naval experiences. Elizabeth believed he was making himself out to be more of a hero than he had actually been, and she found his chronicle too long, dreadfully dull, and on occasion, far too gruesome. She felt Jane might faint at any moment, but he did not seem to notice and continued on as if nothing were wrong. She believed he truly thought she and her sister were enjoying his extravagant tales and thinking even more highly of him with each narrative.

Whether it was in successfully fighting off French soldiers or marauding pirates who jumped aboard, proficiently manning the vessel during a severe storm, or firing a cannon and sinking a French frigate with a direct hit, he was always the one who saved the day. Jane and Elizabeth sat very close to each other, their shoulders touching, and their eyelids becoming heavier with each unbelievable story.

Mr. Goulding had come to Longbourn that day wearing a wide smile on his face, wider than normal, and Elizabeth found herself blatantly staring at his mouth, wondering how long he would speak with his smile frozen in place. She felt certain he had come to ask for her sister's hand and, although dismayed by the thought, she was determined to prevent it at all costs. She would do whatever it took to save Jane from a most uncomfortable situation and disagreeable future.

When Mrs. Bennet came downstairs after resting in her room, she looked rather startled when she saw the gentleman in the parlour. "Oh!" she exclaimed, shaking her head a few times as if she had not yet fully wakened. "Mr. Goulding! You are here! How good it is to see you!"

He gave a deep nod. "Thank you, Mrs. Bennet." He paused, and then asked, "Would you be so kind as to allow Miss Bennet and me some time together outside? It is such a lovely day!"

Elizabeth felt Jane tense and heard her gasp. She looked

straight up at Mr. Goulding and said, "Jane and I would be happy to accompany you outside."

"You will do no such thing!" Mrs. Bennet scolded, but just as suddenly, she shook her head and smiled. In a much kinder, softer voice, she said, "I... There is something I must have you do, Lizzy. Come with me! Allow Mr. Goulding some time alone with your sister."

Elizabeth was horrified as her mother marched over to her and pulled her off the sofa upon which she and Jane sat. She glared at her mother. "Mother, I must remain with Jane!"

"You will come with me!" Mrs. Bennet's eyes widened, sending her second eldest daughter a look of reprimand, and she then looked up and smiled sweetly at Mr. Goulding. "Now, off the two of you go!" She waved her hand at the couple.

Jane's face grew pale, and she sent a pleading look to Elizabeth, who returned her sister's look with a stern warning in her eyes. She mouthed the words, "Say no!" while shaking her head.

When the couple had stepped outside, Elizabeth faced her mother. "How could you do that? If his intention is to ask for Jane's hand in marriage, she will be terribly distressed. You know she does not love him, and she certainly cannot marry him!"

"Lizzy, your obstinacy is too wearisome for me. You will never marry if you remain critical of every man you meet. Allow Jane to give me some peace of mind that at least one of my girls will marry well. It is something *you* refused to do!"

Elizabeth pursed her lips to hold her tongue for a moment, wishing her father had not left. She wondered if her mother planned this event to take place while he was from home. "Mother, I sympathize with your concerns, but marrying Mr. Goulding would *not* be marrying well. He is not at all suitable for Jane. They do not have the same interests, he is dreadfully boring, and he does not even like children. Certainly you must realize this."

Mrs. Bennet waved her hands through the air. "Well, those are of no import! I know of many couples who have differing interests. She will learn to ignore his stories. As to children, most gentlemen do not like them, at first. They either come to like them when they marry and have some of their own, or they leave them to the care of their wives and nannies."

Elizabeth closed her eyes and shook her head.

Her mother continued, "I am going back up to my room, but I shall be watching out my window, so you had better not step out there. Jane and Mr. Goulding will come back in when they are finished." She turned to walk away, but then stopped and looked back. "I warn you, Lizzy. I will not have you interfering in this matter! I have been waiting for this for a long time and have been disappointed more than once!" She gave Elizabeth another pointed glance.

When her mother had gone upstairs, Elizabeth walked to the front window and pulled back the drapery. She looked out but did not see them. She hurried over to the side window, where she saw Jane sitting on a bench. Mr. Goulding was walking around it, occasionally stopping to talk. Jane was sitting very still, staring straight ahead, and her hands were clasped in her lap.

Elizabeth leaned against the window sill and sighed. "Oh, Jane, just tell him no. Just tell him no! Please think of yourself, and do not worry about what Mother will do or say."

After watching them for several minutes, she finally decided to go out, knowing that it would take her mother some time to return downstairs if she was still intent on stopping her. Besides, they had been out there long enough. If he had not yet proposed, he was taking far too long.

She walked to the front door and opened it, but was startled to see a gentleman standing there, looking away from her. When he turned around, her eyes widened in astonishment and delight.

"Mr. Bingley! What a surprise this is!"

"I hope I have not come at an inopportune time. Would you..."

Elizabeth stepped outside, a smile brightening her face. "On the contrary, Mr. Bingley! You have come at a most opportune time!" She took hold of his arm and began pulling him to the side of the house. "But I must have you come with me! Hurry along!"

Mr. Bingley followed Elizabeth, a perplexed look on his face. "Can you tell me where we are going and what we are...?" He stopped when he saw Jane and Mr. Goulding.

He paused and turned to Elizabeth with an apparent look of

distress. "It appears… Are we… disturbing something?"

"No, I think not!" She turned and called to her sister. "Jane! Look who has just arrived!"

When Jane turned her head and saw Mr. Bingley, she slowly rose to her feet, nervously tucked a loose strand of hair behind her ear, and then brought her fingers to her lips. Elizabeth could tell she was affected by seeing Mr. Bingley, and she hoped Mr. Goulding noticed.

As Elizabeth and Mr. Bingley approached, it was apparent to Elizabeth that her sister was trying to hold back tears. "Oh, please do not let us be too late!" she said in a hushed whisper.

"Are we… Are we interrupting anything?" Bingley looked from Jane to the gentleman standing next to her.

"Yes!" Mr. Goulding replied with a sharp nod of his head.

"No," Jane said softly.

"Good," Mr. Bingley said with an uncertain half-smile. He turned to the gentleman. "I do not believe we have been introduced."

"Oh, pray forgive me!" Jane looked at Mr. Goulding but could do little more than that, so Elizabeth made the introductions.

"Mr. Goulding, while you were in the navy, Mr. Bingley moved into Netherfield Park. He has been away quite some time but has now returned. Mr. Bingley, Mr. Goulding grew up in the neighbourhood but has been gone the past few years. He was at sea when you moved here last year."

The men exchanged a quick handshake as they eyed each other in an awkward silence.

When no one seemed inclined to speak, Elizabeth turned to Mr. Bingley. "We had not heard you had returned to Netherfield. How long have you been back in the neighbourhood?"

"I just arrived. This very afternoon." He looked at Jane and let out a nervous laugh. "While I knew for a few weeks that I was returning, I was not certain when that would be. When all my business in town was finished, I decided to set out at once. I actually returned without letting anyone know, so the staff remaining at Netherfield is at this moment trying to get everything in order." He then shook his head. "I do not think they are pleased with me."

Elizabeth believed her sister was making every effort to appear composed, but she could see the look of distress mixed with hope on her face, so she gave Mr. Bingley a wide smile. "While they may not be delighted, we certainly are. This is probably the most delightful news we have had in some time!" She looked at Jane. "Is that not true, Jane?"

Jane nodded, her eyes not moving from Mr. Bingley's face.

After another silent pause, Elizabeth asked, "Mr. Bingley, did your sisters accompany you?"

"No, they were otherwise engaged. I am here alone."

Elizabeth smiled at that news, as well as at Mr. Goulding's look of consternation, as his eyes moved between Jane and Mr. Bingley. The two reunited lovers contentedly gazed at each other, which must have left him rather perplexed. Elizabeth was certain Jane had never smiled so sweetly, so serenely, and so delightfully while in his presence. If only she could speak!

It appeared, however, that Mr. Goulding was not yet ready to yield. "Mr. Bingley, Miss Elizabeth, if you would be so kind as to give Miss Bennet and me another moment together... just a little bit longer. There is something of great import I need to ask her."

Elizabeth crossed her arms. "Mr. Goulding, you have been outside with my sister for a good ten minutes, and I would imagine if there had been something important you wanted to say to her, you would have already said it by now."

"But I…"

Elizabeth drew him aside and spoke in a soft voice. "In case you are wondering, Mr. Goulding, I do not think any of us are interested in what you wanted to say." She nodded to Jane and Mr. Bingley. "As you can see, Jane and Mr. Bingley are exceedingly fond of each other and have not seen each other in a very long time. I would suggest you take your leave now before you make a fool of yourself."

Mr. Goulding looked back at the couple and shook his head several times. It appeared to Elizabeth that he was trying to determine if they did indeed have a partiality for each other. His brows lowered, and Elizabeth was delighted to see that he apparently recognized the affection Mr. Bingley and her sister had for each other. She felt a great sense of relief, until he turned to

Elizabeth, his lips forming again into an unchanging smile. He took a deep breath and said, "I have often thought you were quite pretty, and I would find it perfectly agreeable to get to know you better. Would you, Miss Elizabeth, allow me to pay a call and visit *you* on the morrow?"

Elizabeth's eyes widened, and she drew back. "Pray, forgive me, but I would not. Not tomorrow or the next day or even a month from today." She paused and gave him a small smile. "If you remember me at all, Mr. Goulding, you will recollect that I can be direct, and so I must be now. We have known each other our whole lives, and I do not think you and I are at all suited."

Mr. Goulding seemed at a loss for words at Elizabeth's harsh honesty, but he took her not so subtle hint and departed without saying goodbye or looking back. She watched Jane and Mr. Bingley and could see that their feelings for each other had never diminished. She was delighted to see that Jane had at last found her tongue, and the two were talking with great animation. It gave her great joy to know Jane would now be able to marry a man she truly loved.

She felt a tug at her heart. At least one of them would.

Elizabeth glanced up at her mother's window and saw her watching. She gave her a big smile and walked behind Jane and Mr. Bingley as they returned to the house. Her mother may have had other ideas in mind for this warm summer day, but Elizabeth was certain she would not argue with Mr. Bingley replacing Mr. Goulding in her plans.

She was indeed happy for Jane, but... She shook her head. She could not help but wonder several things. First, what had prompted Mr. Bingley's return? Knowing how easily persuaded he had been by Mr. Darcy last year, had he felt it necessary to obtain his approval before returning? She also wondered what Mr. Bingley's feelings were for Miss Darcy. What might Mr. Darcy think of his coming immediately upon his arrival to visit Jane, and what did this mean in regards to Miss Darcy and any affection she had for him?

Elizabeth let out a long sigh. She would worry about those things later. Mr. Bingley had returned, Jane was very happy, and there was no dreaded engagement between her and Mr. Goulding.

She pinched her brows, wondering what Mr. Goulding could have been saying all that time he was out there with Jane, but grateful he had not hurried his proposal. She could not help but chuckle, as Jane likely sat there demurely listening to all he had to say – while quietly dreading the question she believed he would eventually ask. Elizabeth, on the other hand, had no qualms about letting him know how both she and her sister felt.

~~*

If Mrs. Bennet was disappointed that Mr. Goulding had been displaced by Mr. Bingley, she never mentioned it. It was as if that first gentleman had never been considered suitable for dearest Jane. She seemed to have the opinion that Mr. Bingley had always been the one who would be the most favourable match.

Elizabeth spoke to her father about the proposal that almost happened, and they both concluded Mrs. Bennet had schemed to bring it about. Mr. Bennet had mentioned to his wife several days earlier that he would be running an errand on that particular day, and she must have strongly advised Mr. Goulding to visit Jane precisely when her husband would be from home. She must have been fairly certain her husband strongly objected to an engagement between the two, even though she was eagerly in favour of it.

When Elizabeth asked Jane what Mr. Goulding had been talking about all that time they had been outside together, Jane replied that he had once again been speaking of his accomplishments and all the advantages he could offer someone. Jane confessed that she had been able to redirect this conversation several times by asking the right questions and getting him to speak further on a particular subject. She was proud of herself, making him believe her appraisal of him was continually growing and improving with each account he gave. Elizabeth was proud of her, as well.

Despite her curiosity, Elizabeth did not speak to Mr. Bingley of a possible attachment to Miss Darcy. He made a slight reference to her and his friend one day when Jane told him that Elizabeth and her aunt and uncle had spent a good amount of time at Pemberley because of their uncle's injury.

"Oh! To think that I might have seen you there, if only we had come!" Mr. Bingley shook his head. "There were several things, however, that kept us from going to Pemberley at that time."

Elizabeth readily noticed an awkward glance away but he quickly recovered. "It would have been a delightful surprise to see you," she replied.

"Yes, despite those difficulties prompting our decision not to go, I would have enjoyed seeing you, as well."

Elizabeth believed he truly meant it, but she wondered what those difficulties were that had kept them from coming. She surmised now that it was likely due to his sister, who did not wish to see Mr. Darcy singling out Miss Westerfield. Since Jane had not informed him that she had hidden from Mr. Darcy on several occasions, she only replied, "At least we all have been reacquainted here." She knew that if Mr. Bingley had come to Pemberley as was originally planned, she would have instantly cast aside her mortification of Mr. Darcy seeing her, for the sole purpose of finding out what Mr. Bingley's feelings were for Jane.

Elizabeth enjoyed watching the ardent admiration Jane and Mr. Bingley still had for each other. It was apparent they were equally taking great delight in each other's company. She felt confident they were well on their way to an engagement.

To their youngest sisters, however, Mr. Bingley's return to Netherfield only meant the possibility of another grand ball.

"Jane, you must inquire whether Mr. Bingley plans to give another ball. There has never been a grander ball than the one held at Netherfield," Kitty said.

"Yes, he must!" cried Lydia. "But it shall not be so grand this time unless the militia returns. Imagine how dull it will be with no officers!"

Elizabeth shook her head, and then Mary offered her opinion. "It is just as well the militia are gone. The soldiers were far too great a temptation to several young ladies in the neighbourhood." She gave both her sisters a reproachful, pointed look.

Lydia's shoulders rose in exasperation. "You make it sound as though there was something improper about spending time with them. They were always civil and proper towards us."

Kitty nodded. "They were exemplary gentlemen!"

Lydia laughed. "Oh, especially Mr. Wickham! How I miss him!"

Elizabeth looked up and exclaimed, "Mr. Wickham!"

"Yes," Lydia replied softly. "What about him?"

Her brows lowered, and she pursed her lips. "I fear… Lydia, there is something I must tell you about Mr. Wickham that you may find distressing." She drew in a breath, wondering what she should say.

"What?" Lydia asked. "Tell me! Has something happened to him?"

Elizabeth nodded. "He has been gravely injured."

Lydia's eyes widened, and her hand flew over her mouth. "Oh, no! Is he going to die?"

"I do not think so, but…"

"I imagine he was injured doing something impressively heroic. I am certain he was doing something quite brave. Did he get shot protecting us from the French? Did he rescue someone out of the hands of a fierce enemy?" She leaned in, eager to her Elizabeth's response.

Elizabeth would not tell her everything; she would not give any details, especially regarding Mr. Darcy's involvement in the incident. She would, however, tell her youngest sister enough to reveal Mr. Wickham's despicable character and actions in case they ever encountered him again.

"No, Lydia, in fact, it was quite the opposite." She drew in a breath. "I know this will be difficult for you to hear, but I tell you this in order to make certain you know the type of man he is."

When she had finished telling her sisters just enough to paint a picture of his character, Mary assured her sisters she had been sceptical of his character all along, Kitty appeared to be truly grieved that she had believed him to be a proper gentleman, but Lydia insisted there had to be more to the story than Elizabeth had been told.

"Were you there, Lizzy?" she asked. "Did you witness what he did?"

"Well, no, but…"

"You see?" She pounded her fists in her lap. "You never know what people might say about someone whose reputation they want to injure."

"No, Lydia. His character has been confirmed not only in this instance, but in others, as well. I am so glad Father did not allow you to go to Brighton, for who knows what difficulty you would have found yourself in if you had continued to trust him."

Lydia's shoulders sagged. "But Mr. Wickham was so much fun and so handsome! I cannot believe it!"

"I fear you must, Lydia."

A challenging look flashed in her eyes. "I believe you once thought well of him, Lizzy."

Elizabeth let out a sigh. "I did, Lydia, so you see I am not always capable of judging a character correctly." She slowly shook her head. "I was wrong about him, and I have learned many difficult lessons in that regard. In some instances, I have greatly regretted my initial estimation of a person." She walked over and took her youngest sister's hand. "It is in the realization and acknowledgment of our mistakes that we learn and grow. Sometimes that realization comes too late. I tell you this in order to spare you from having to go through anything like that."

She squeezed Lydia's hand and then turned away. She could not help but wonder if she would ever get over her pain and regret for incorrectly judging Mr. Darcy's character.

Chapter 21

Elizabeth always accompanied Jane on her visits to Netherfield to see Mr. Bingley as his sisters had not yet joined him to act as proper chaperones. On this day, he was not yet ready to see them when they arrived, so they were shown into the sitting room to wait for him.

To occupy her time at Netherfield and allow time for Mr. Bingley and Jane to get reacquainted with each other, Elizabeth would either find a book to read from his library, work on some needlework she had brought along, or play the pianoforte.

They had been sitting for quite some time waiting, and Elizabeth decided she would like to go into the parlour to play the pianoforte while they waited.

Jane smiled. "I think that is a splendid idea."

"Do you have a preferred piece you would like me to play?"

Jane's shoulders rose in a sigh. "Something light and cheerful. The other day, your playing was so heavy and dreary."

Elizabeth shrugged her shoulders. "Much like I was feeling, I imagine."

"Oh, Lizzy…"

"I am feeling much better today. With each passing day, I feel my spirits more uplifted." As Elizabeth walked towards the other room, she said, "I promise to play something you will enjoy."

She walked into the next room to the instrument and looked through the small selection of music. She was certain that in the two weeks she had been chaperoning her sister, she had played almost every piece of music available to her.

She was delighted to find a familiar piece that she had not yet played, and quickly looked over the piece to reacquaint herself with it. For the most part, it was easy enough to play, with the exception of one difficult section, but it was a light and cheerful tune. "I only hope I can play it with the gaiety it requires," she said softly to herself.

Elizabeth sat down, and with a grand gesture, she lowered her fingers onto the keys. They readily moved up and down the keyboard as she played the piece, pausing only occasionally to turn the pages of the music.

She closed her eyes as she played through the easy parts of the music that she knew. She swayed as she allowed the music to pour over her. She considered for a moment that the tune was indeed lifting the sense of grief and despair that had been weighing her down.

When the more difficult section approached, she opened her eyes and quickly looked to the page, seeking her place. She turned the page and found it just as her fingers hesitated.

She smiled when she heard Jane and Mr. Bingley talking. In actuality, it was Mr. Bingley she heard, for he was always so gregarious, and his voice easily carried through the sitting room into the parlour. Elizabeth decided she would finish the piece and then join them. As she concentrated on her fingering through the difficult section, she sensed someone behind her. Ah, Jane had come to her rescue to turn the page.

When the hand came out from her side, however, it was a gentleman's hand. His fingers grabbed the corner of the music and turned the page at just the right time.

Not taking her eyes from the sheet of music, she said, "Thank you, Mr. Bingley. I had not known you were able to read mus…" Her fingers faltered, and she gasped when she noticed the scar on the hand in front of her. She stopped playing, jerked her head around, and found herself gazing into Mr. Darcy's face!

"Please continue, if you wish," he said with a nod towards the keys.

Elizabeth felt the need to turn away, her cheeks growing warm and her eyes beginning to glisten with tears. But at the same time, she felt incapable of finishing the song, for her fingers were too shaky to obey her commands. She stared at the music, trying to make sense of the jumble of notes on the page, as well as his being here. She did not know what to say to him. Should she acknowledge his engagement and wish him joy? Should she inquire after his injuries? Ask him about his sister?

It was useless. She took in a deep breath and said, "I fear you turned the page for no reason, Mr. Darcy. This part of the song is far too difficult for me. But I thank you all the same."

She began to stand, despite feeling that her legs were too shaky to support her. She suddenly felt his fingers press lightly onto her shoulder. "Please continue." He turned another page and pointed. "Here, begin here. This is an easier section."

She mutely nodded and placed her fingers back on the keys, just as he sat down on the bench next to her. She began playing, and he kept his fingers holding the corner of the page. They remained silent until he had turned it.

"Miss Elizabeth, I want to apologize for all you endured at Pemberley. I regret that your visit there began and ended so dreadfully."

"Mr. Darcy, there is no need. Your sister already apologized for both of you in the letter she wrote to me."

"But I feel I must, for the mortification you must have suffered when Mrs. Reynolds asked you to leave, and knowing you were the object of rumours being circulated amongst my staff and the villagers in Lambton."

"You are certainly not to blame." She struggled to continue playing but found the fingering challenging again, not because the music was difficult, but because Mr. Darcy was sitting at her side. Her feelings were stirred as she felt his shoulder touching hers, her knee occasionally brushing his as she attempted the footwork, and his masculine scent filling her senses. She inwardly scolded herself for enjoying it far more than she should have. She could not allow her heart to be so easily touched, when she was uncertain of his feelings for her, let alone that he might have become engaged.

She could tell he was looking at her intently and heard him draw in a breath. "But I am a great deal responsible for the nature of some of those rumours. If I had acted more…" He paused and shook his head. "If I had acted in a more… gentlemanlike manner and done only what was proper, there would have been nothing about which to spread gossip and rumours."

Elizabeth continued to play, but then she placed her hands in her lap, comprehending the meaning of his statement. She had brutally accused him of acting in an ungentleman-like manner when she refused his offer of marriage.

"Pray, forgive me. I was not paying attention to your place on the page."

Despite Elizabeth's pounding heart, she smiled. "I have finished the piece, sir."

Darcy let out a breathy chuckle. "Oh, yes." He quickly stood up.

With him no longer in such close proximity to her and the song finished, she was able to think more clearly. "I would not have you be so hard on yourself for what happened. It was certainly not your fault that our trip began with a fall, and at the end of our stay, your housekeeper was doing only what she felt was in your best interest."

"I would still ask that you accept my apology for all that happened."

Elizabeth stood, gathered up the music sheets with still shaking fingers, and held it against her. "If you insist, then I certainly accept your apology."

"Thank you," he replied.

Elizabeth suddenly thought of her aunt's letter and her admonition for her to let him know of her feelings if she were ever to encounter him again. She knew if he were engaged, expressing the affection and admiration she had for him would not be proper, but there was something she could do.

"Mr. Darcy, if this is a time for apologies, then I must offer mine to you."

"There is no need for you to apologize for anything."

"Oh, sir, but indeed there is." She took a breath and placed one hand on the pianoforte to steady herself. "I must apologize for the words I spoke to you in Kent. I was so very wrong about many of the things of which I accused you. Pray, forgive me for my disrespect."

Darcy let out a long sigh. "There was much you said that I deserved…"

Elizabeth tilted her head as she looked up at him. "Mr. Darcy, I willingly forgave you when I did not see the need for *you* to apologize, and now I only ask that you do the same."

He pursed his lips and smiled. With a low bow of his head, he said, "Miss Elizabeth, I would be delighted to accept your apology."

They stood silent for a moment merely looking at each other. Elizabeth tried to determine if he harboured any of those feelings he had for her at Kent or if he had come to Netherfield with the sole purpose of apologizing. Her biggest question, however, was whether or not he was engaged to Miss Westerfield.

Finally, Mr. Darcy asked, "Shall we join Bingley and your sister?"

Elizabeth nodded, and they walked into the sitting room. Elizabeth greeted Mr. Bingley, gave a quick smile to Jane, who had a wide smile of her own, and she took a seat on the other side of her sister. Her heart still pounded, and she was still unsteady, so she was grateful to sit. She grasped the arm of the sofa as she watched Mr. Darcy sit down in the chair next to her.

"We did not know you were coming, Mr. Darcy," Jane said.

"Oh? I wrote Bingley to inform him I was on my way, but I am certain he had other things on his mind." He leaned forward and clasped his hands as he directed his gaze to his friend and then back to Jane.

She blushed as Mr. Bingley let out a laugh.

"He expects me to remember everything he writes, and he likely also expected a reply, which I knew would arrive at Pemberley only after he had departed." Bingley paused. "At least I wrote to tell you I was returning to Netherfield." Bingley straightened his shoulders as if he was proud of himself that he had at least done that. Elizabeth wondered if he was steeling himself for a set-down from his friend for acting without seeking his counsel on the matter first. If a set-down was coming, it would likely not be done in front of the ladies.

Elizabeth stole a glance at Mr. Darcy, however, and pleasantly surprised to see a smile on his face. So Mr. Bingley had not felt the need to get Mr. Darcy's approval before coming back, which was certainly in Mr. Bingley's favour. And it was apparent that Mr. Darcy had no objection to his coming back. At least, none that she could readily see.

After some general talk about the neighbourhood, Jane and Mr. Bingley began talking quietly together. Mr. Darcy leaned against the back of the chair and winced. He began rubbing his fingers along his shoulder.

Elizabeth saw his grimace of pain in that quick movement. "Are you still in pain from your shoulder injury, Mr. Darcy?"

His brows lowered. "You are aware of what happened?"

Elizabeth nodded. "Yes, my aunt received a letter from her friend in Lambton who told her what happened. She wrote to tell me of it." She gave her head a brisk shake. "I hope you have not suffered too greatly."

"It occasionally lets me know it is still healing."

"Oh, but the nerve of that man!"

Darcy's face grew sombre. "He suffered life-altering injuries, and my only regret is that his injuries were at my hand, due to my uncontrollable anger, despite his deserving it. My anger was so..." His jaw clenched and he shook his head. "He is not worth any further mention."

"No, of course not." Elizabeth paused, sensible of the fact that he did not want to talk about Mr. Wickham.

They partook of refreshments as they continued in conversation, with Mr. Bingley and Jane interspersing their hushed discussion with soft laughter, frequent smiles, and an occasional blush. Mr. Darcy and Elizabeth, however, spoke only of trivial matters. There was no banter between them, no encouraging smiles, and to Elizabeth's dismay, no revelations made of the subject which was foremost on her mind.

At length, Bingley looked up. "It is such a delightful day, why do we not take a stroll out on the grounds?" He looked at Jane expectantly.

The others all agreed it was a wonderful idea.

As they walked towards the front door, Bingley and Jane led the way. At the last moment, however, Darcy turned to Elizabeth.

"If you will excuse me, I need to retrieve something. Would you please wait here for me?"

Elizabeth nodded and turned to Jane. "We will catch up with you."

Darcy was but a few minutes, and Elizabeth was surprised he had a coat over his arm.

She laughed. "Are you expecting a sudden storm to come upon us?"

He looked down at her with a smile. "Unexpected, sudden

storms have been known to happen."

She pursed her lips. "Indeed."

When they stepped out, Elizabeth saw that Bingley and Jane were walking towards the garden on the south side of the house. "There they are."

Darcy put up a hand to stay her. "And so let us walk *this* way." Darcy pointed in the opposite direction.

"But…"

He glanced over at his friend and Jane as they disappeared around the corner of the manor. "Miss Elizabeth, I am of the opinion they would like some time alone." He lifted a brow for emphasis.

"Oh!" she exclaimed. "Is he…?"

Darcy nodded.

She let out a nervous laugh. "I would not wish to interrupt them, then."

They walked towards a small grove of trees, and Darcy led her to a bench. When she sat down, he seated himself next to her, placing his coat on the other side of him.

She drew in a breath. At least one of her concerns could now be properly addressed.

"Mr. Darcy, if you do not mind my asking. I came to understand from your sister that she had a fondness for Mr. Bingley. What will this mean for her if my sister agrees to marry him?" In addition to his answering the question about his sister, she also hoped she would discern his thoughts on the matter.

"*If* she accepts him? Is there any doubt your sister will accept him?" Darcy gave her a teasing smile.

"No," she said with a soft laugh. "There is no doubt."

Darcy's face grew sombre. "Georgiana did believe she was in love with him." He clasped his hands and leaned forward, looking straight ahead. "She told me that she had informed you of her feelings for him, and I knew that would afford you no pleasure." He drew in a breath. "It is true that I had thought if Bingley was willing to wait a few years to marry, he and Georgiana would make a highly suitable match." He turned his head to look at Elizabeth. "It was another wrong assumption on my part. He would have been good for her, but…" He looked down at his hands. "But she would not have been good for him."

"Mr. Bingley mentioned that he wrote to tell you he was coming to Netherfield. Was he asking for your permission to do so?"

Darcy slowly turned his head. "Do you think he needed to seek my permission?"

Elizabeth's brows rose, and she tilted her head. "It seems that he has, on several occasions, been easily swayed by your opinion and often looks to you for advice."

Darcy stretched out his legs and leaned his head back. "He has, but I regret that my counsel was not always in his best interest." He turned and looked at her. "He wrote and told me he was returning to Netherfield, and no, he did not ask my permission."

Elizabeth smiled. "I am glad to hear that."

"He also informed me in his letter his reasons for not coming to Pemberley. It was due to the expectations that both *his* sisters and I had regarding Georgiana and him, as well as Georgiana's growing affection for him. He did not return the partiality she felt for him."

This was eye-opening to Elizabeth, and she was delighted to hear that Mr. Bingley had made these decisions himself.

Very softly, she asked, "Does your sister know about his feelings for Jane?"

Darcy nodded. "She does now. I informed her before I left. She is young, and while she was a bit hurt and confused, I know she will come through without too much difficulty."

She wondered again of Miss Westerfield, and finally said, "In the letter from your sister…" She felt her fingers begin to tremble and clasped them together. "She wrote that Miss… Miss Westerfield and her family were doing well after the accident."

Darcy leaned forward, clasping his hands. "She was spared injury, but her parents were both gravely hurt; her father more than her mother. By the second day I was there, there had been improvement in both of them, her brother had arrived, and I had deemed them in good hands at Wakespur Manor under the care of Mr. Lloyd Kingston and his staff." He turned and looked at her. "He is the one who came upon them after the accident and took them to his home. He did all he could to ensure their comfort and recovery."

"I am glad." Elizabeth's brows knotted, as she did not know how to ask what she wanted to know – what she *needed* to know. She certainly could not come right out and ask if he was engaged. She finally decided to ask him about their departure.

"I know everyone was surprised about their sudden departure." Her face grew solemn. "Was it because one of them saw us dancing together?"

His shoulders rose as he drew in a breath. "Miss Westerfield saw us. She informed her mother, but they decided not to tell her father, as he would likely have become upset and caused a contemptible scene. The two ladies decided they would make their sentiments known to Mr. Westerfield that..." He turned to Elizabeth and shook his head. "They had believed I had invited them to Pemberley with the intention of asking for her hand in marriage."

Elizabeth held her breath as he spoke.

"While that was not something I explicitly expressed, I had invited them with the intention of getting to know Miss Westerfield better... with that in mind."

"I see."

"But I soon realized I could not marry her." He looked down as he shook his head. "She and I talked about the misunderstanding when I visited her and her family at Wakespur Manor. She was very gracious about it."

Elizabeth felt as though she could finally breathe with the weight of uncertainty no longer upon her. She looked at him and smiled. "I imagine she must have felt disappointed, however."

Darcy turned and studied her face. "Do you?"

They sat quietly for a moment, and then Darcy nodded towards the path in front of them. "Look! There is a magpie!"

Elizabeth turned her head in that direction and began to shake her head. "Oh, dear! There is only one!" She let out a nervous laugh. "This cannot be good, especially when Mr. Bingley is proposing to Jane!"

"I am certain seeing only one will not make any difference..." He stopped as a second magpie flew down to join it.

"Ah!" Elizabeth exclaimed. "One is for sorrow, two is for

mirth!" She let out a nervous laugh. "Now I can rest assured that all will go well!"

Darcy smiled and lifted his coat, pulling something out from underneath it. Elizabeth gasped to see that it was the finished carved magpie.

"You finished the magpie!"

Darcy nodded. "I had a lot of time on my hands as I recovered from my wound. Carving the wood was not easy in the beginning due to the pain, but I was eventually able to finish it." He paused and held it out to her. "I would like you to have it."

"Me?" Elizabeth reached out and took the bird, admiring the detail with her eyes and fingers. She looked at him and smiled. "It is beautiful. I am curious, however. How was it that you came to carve a magpie?"

Darcy shifted in his seat, looking straight ahead. "You know I carve birds."

"Yes, but I wondered why you chose the magpie."

He paused a moment and then turned to her. "At the Netherfield Ball, I overheard your father telling someone you were his magpie. Since I had never carved a magpie before, I knew it was something I had to do."

"But then you left it unfinished in the library."

"I began it in February when I was at Pemberley for a short while. When I returned last month, I did not think I could finish it." He paused, and then softly added, "After what happened in Kent."

Elizabeth felt a heavy weight upon her. "I see."

He turned to look at her. "After seeing you again at Pemberley, however, I knew I had to finish it."

She cradled the bird in her hands as she lowered them into her lap, her fingers shaking. She looked down at it and said, "Mr. Darcy, as I said, it is beautiful, but I cannot take it. It belongs at Pemberley."

"Perhaps it does."

Elizabeth had a teasing retort, but when she looked up and met his gaze, the intense look in his eyes soared through her. "I... I do not understand."

"I would hope... that someday you would bring it back to

Pemberley with you."

Elizabeth gave her head a shake. With a nervous smile, she asked, "Are you inviting my aunt and uncle and me back to Pemberley?"

"While the Gardiners are invited to return to Pemberley at any time, my thoughts were of a different nature. I had hoped you – and you alone – might return to Pemberley with it."

Elizabeth opened her mouth, but no words came forth.

"Miss Elizabeth, my reason for coming to Hertfordshire was twofold. First, I wanted to... I *needed* to apologize to you for what happened at Pemberley. Secondly..." He drew in a breath and let it out slowly. "I came to determine whether... whether there might be any possibility..." He looked down and clasped his hands tightly. He then turned and looked up. "Miss Bennet, please allow me to be direct." He swallowed. "I came to ascertain whether your feelings for me are what they were in Kent, or... whether they had improved. My feelings have not changed."

Despite Elizabeth's eyes stinging with the threat of imminent tears, she began, "Sir, I have..."

He put up a hand to stay her. "Please allow me to express my sentiments before you answer."

Relief washed over her, grateful to know she would have a few moments to gather her composure. Her rapidly beating heart, stirring feelings, and wave of exhilaration, however, warred with her lack of composure to immediately speak her mind.

"I had determined while you were at Pemberley that I still loved you and would never love another." He drew in a breath. "When Bingley told me he was returning to Netherfield, I knew I had to come to see you again."

When he paused, Elizabeth opened her mouth to reply. Darcy pressed his fingers lightly to her lips. "Please allow me to finish."

Elizabeth shuddered, despite the brevity of his touch.

"I have had much time to think, and I determined that it would serve no purpose to guess what your feelings were solely by observing your manner towards me. Therefore, I must inquire whether your feelings have changed and if you might welcome my..." He drew himself erect and took in a breath. "Would you be willing to spend time with me if I were to remain at Netherfield...

with a view towards your determining whether you might..." He shook his head. "Pray forgive me. As you know, I am not particularly adept at discerning one's feelings, especially a lady's; neither am I practised at speaking articulately on matters of the heart."

Elizabeth was moved by the depth of emotion visible in his eyes and reflected in his voice, and she could feel his tension in how rigidly he held his body. She wished so much to assure him that her feelings had changed and were greatly improved.

"Yes," she said softly.

"Pardon?" Darcy swallowed. "Is that *yes* in agreement that I am not adept at speaking articulately or ...?"

"On the contrary, Mr. Darcy. My *yes* refers to my feelings having changed; in fact, they are greatly altered for the better. If I am not mistaken, you ventured to say you would like to know if I would welcome your continued presence here, and yes, I would very much enjoy spending more time with you."

Darcy let out a long sigh, and his body noticeably relaxed. A small smile appeared. "I am delighted to hear that."

Elizabeth returned his smile. "I only recently came to discover that you are someone who deserves to be held in the highest esteem." She cast her eyes down as her cheeks warmed in a blush. "Even before you returned to Pemberley, my opinion of you had greatly improved in hearing about you from your housekeeper, your sister, and..." She paused and looked up. "And before that, in your letter."

She noticed him start when she said this. "Yes, I read your letter and took much of it to heart. I realized at once my error in judging your character in the manner I had, and I felt considerable regret – and admiration for you – by the time we finally came face to face." She pursed her lips together. "I have discovered a great deal about you since Kent and while at Pemberley, and I know there is much more I look forward to learning about you."

They gazed at each other silently, and Elizabeth thought he was about to kiss her when she heard Jane calling her. She pulled back from Mr. Darcy and watched her sister and Mr. Bingley come around the corner of the house.

Jane hurried over to her. "Elizabeth! I have wonderful news!

Chapter 22

After wishes of congratulations to the newly engaged couple, Elizabeth and Jane determined they should return home to share the news with their family. At Elizabeth's suggestion, the two men remained at Netherfield. Elizabeth did not want Mr. Darcy to witness her mother's expected outburst.

As they travelled home in the carriage Mr. Bingley always had available for them, Elizabeth eagerly listened to Jane relate how he had proposed.

Unlike Mr. Goulding, Mr. Bingley did not waste any time in setting forth the question. Jane had answered immediately in the affirmative, and the couple spent the rest of their time together discussing details on when the wedding might take place, when – and how – he would inform his sisters, and whom they ought to invite.

When Jane had finished her joyful account, Elizabeth pulled out the magpie from underneath her shawl and showed it to Jane. "Mr. Darcy gave this to me earlier."

"A magpie!" Jane exclaimed! "He carved you a magpie! It is beautiful!" She turned to her sister. "Why did he carve a magpie?"

Elizabeth smiled as she ran her fingers over the smooth wood. "When he was here last year, he overheard Papa telling someone he calls me his magpie – Maggie-pie – and he began carving it in February. When he returned to Pemberley after I refused his offer of marriage, he did not think he could ever finish it. That is why I saw it unfinished."

Jane's eyes widened. "But he *did* finish it! Elizabeth, does this mean…"

Elizabeth put up her hand. "He has given me the magpie and sought my consent to remain here to allow us to further our acquaintance."

"Does he intend to court you with a view towards marriage?"

"I believe so, but he…"

Jane wrapped her arms about her sister. "Oh, Elizabeth! I am so happy! Charles will be delighted to hear this, as well! One of the things we talked about was his growing suspicion that Mr. Darcy was quite fond of you."

Elizabeth's brows rose. "He had his suspicions, did he?" She laughed. "It may very well be that at this moment Mr. Darcy is informing him of the same thing. He did not want to say anything to him until he determined whether I would welcome his addresses."

"Oh, Lizzy! What a wonderful day this has turned out to be!"

Elizabeth leaned over and hugged her sister. "It certainly has!"

~~*

When Mr. Darcy accompanied Mr. Bingley to Longbourn the following day, he was received warmly and with much gratitude by the Bennet family for all he had done for the Gardiners and Elizabeth while at Pemberley. Mrs. Bennet was effusive in her thanks to the gentleman. Mr. Bennet expressed his sincere appreciation of Mr. Darcy's excellent care of his daughter and her aunt and uncle.

"It was my pleasure, sir."

After that first visit, however, Mrs. Bennet seemed to have forgotten all about what Mr. Darcy had done for her family and spent much of her time expressing her delight that Mr. Bingley would be joining their family. She mentioned several times how pleased she was that Jane would still remain close to Longbourn, and she talked constantly about the wedding.

This allowed Elizabeth to converse quietly with Mr. Darcy, and with the passing of each day, she felt she knew him better. She became convinced that, instead of the *last* man in the world, he was now the *only* man in the world she could be prevailed upon to marry.

On the men's third visit to Longbourn, Mr. Bennet called Elizabeth into his study when the gentlemen took their leave.

"Yes, Father? Did you want to see me?"

He nodded and pointed to the chair. "Please, have a seat." He lit his pipe and leaned back as his daughter sat down.

She folded her hands in her lap. "What is it?"

After drawing on the pipe, he set it down, and slowly blew out the smoke. "I must admit, Mr. Darcy has me quite intrigued."

Elizabeth let out a nervous giggle. "Does he?"

He placed his elbows on the table and clasped his hands. "Darcy has been here on three separate occasions, and I own I have become suspicious of the time and attention he is bestowing on my favourite daughter." He eyed her pointedly.

"I do not know of what you speak."

Mr. Bennet laughed. "Come now, Lizzy. This is your father to whom you are speaking. Certainly we are grateful to him for all he did for you and the Gardiners when you were forced to remain at Pemberley. I am beginning to sense, however, that the man is not all we believed him to be from last year." He looked at her with a single brow lifted.

Elizabeth cast her eyes down. "He is not, Father."

A small smile appeared on Mr. Bennet's face. "I am glad you feel that way, because I have surreptitiously left my study and silently peeked into the parlour several times this week. I have watched Jane and Bingley in quiet conversation with each other, as well as you and Mr. Darcy." He shook his head. "I have determined that you were either tolerating his presence for the sake of Jane and Bingley, feeling a sense of gratitude towards him for all he did for you and your aunt and uncle, or…" He leaned in towards her. "I began to wonder whether you were truly taking pleasure in his society." He lifted his eyes. "Which is it, dearest?"

She smiled. "You are very observant, Father."

He shook his head. "I do not know if I am observant or simply curious, but my greatest concern is for you, my dear. I would not wish for you to be hurt if Mr. Darcy does not return the affection I see you have for him, although…"

"Although?"

He steepled his fingers and pressed them against his lips. "In observing that gentleman, I am of the opinion he has just as much affection for you." He picked up his pipe and drew in a breath of smoke. "Am I correct in any of this, or am I just being a foolish father?"

Elizabeth smiled. "You are very discerning, Father. You always have been. We are… we both have grown extremely fond of each other." She reached out her hand, and her father immediately took it.

"Has he proposed, Elizabeth?"

Her brow furrowed as she wondered how she ought to answer this. Her father would laugh at her if he knew she had already turned down a proposal from him. He would likely tease both her and Mr. Darcy relentlessly. She gave her head a small shake as she determined he did not need to know that.

"There has been a hint of that intention on his part, but since coming here, no, he has not asked for my hand."

Mr. Bennet nodded. "You will answer yes if... when... he asks?"

Elizabeth's eyes widened with a smile. "Will you give him your consent?"

They looked at each other and both nodded and said, "Yes!" at the same time.

Mr. Bennet stood up and came around his desk. He took Elizabeth's hand and pulled her to her feet. She could see tears welling in his eyes.

"Are these tears of joy, Papa?"

He let out a long sigh. "I fear they are tears coming from the realization of what this will mean. Oh, you will be delightfully happy and content, and very well off, I dare say." He began to shake his head. "But you will be so very far away."

"You can come to Pemberley at any time to visit us and stay as long as you want." Her eyes widened with mischievous glee as she looked up at him. "He has a library full of books. You will be able to read to your heart's content."

"You know you may never get rid of me," he said with a chuckle.

"I will worry about that when the time comes." She smiled. "And London is not very far. When we are in London, you and Mother can visit us. It is only a half day's journey."

Mr. Bennet gave his head a quick shake. "You know I detest London. Your mother shall visit you in London. I shall visit you at Pemberley." He drew back. "Your mother! Heavens! What will your mother think of this? Does she have the same suspicions as I do?"

"I do not think she has the slightest notion of the mutual affection we have for each other."

Mr. Bennet laughed. "When she finds out, we shall never hear the end of this!"

"I cannot imagine what she will say or think." She chuckled softly. "Presently, she thanks me for keeping him occupied so Jane and Mr. Bingley can have some time alone together."

"Well, this will certainly come as a delightful surprise to her, but I fear she may be overwhelmed by the myriad feelings this will evoke." He stepped towards his daughter and gave her a quick hug. "Oh, well! Now, off with you while I ponder this astounding state of affairs."

~~*

One morning, about a week after Bingley and Jane became engaged, he and his friend were conversing with Jane and Elizabeth in the sitting room at Longbourn. Despite the early hour, Mrs. Bennet had dozed off in a nearby chair, and the remaining Bennet daughters were sitting across the room. Darcy suddenly rose.

"As it is such a pleasant day, would anyone care to step outside for a stroll?"

Jane's eyes lit up. "Oh, that would be…"

Bingley took Jane's hand. "I think I would prefer to remain indoors. Would you mind terribly if we do not go out with them?"

"Oh, of course not," she replied demurely.

Mrs. Bennet lifted her head. "Elizabeth, you enjoy walking. You go with him." She began frantically waving her hand directing them towards the door. "Go on, now!"

Elizabeth looked at Mr. Darcy to see his reaction to her mother's actions, and her heart leapt when she noticed the twinkle in his eyes and the smile on his face. She turned back to her mother and said, "Yes, Mamma."

When they stepped outside, Darcy offered his arm. "Your mother seemed eager to give us this opportunity to be alone. Does she have any suspicions about my intent?"

Elizabeth laughed. "On the contrary. She is more concerned

about Jane and Mr. Bingley having time alone. I think she was perturbed that we have remained at their side all morning."

Darcy gave a nod. "She does not suspect at all?"

"Not at all."

His brows pinched. "I would think she would look for every possible reason to hope that I had attached my affections to you."

Elizabeth shook her head and let out a sigh. "To own the truth, I doubt she believes I could attract the attention of someone like you." She tilted her head so that it brushed his shoulder. "I am her least favourite, you see, and in her eyes, my worth is only good enough to secure a Mr. Collins."

Darcy grunted.

"My father, on the other hand, began suspecting on the third day of your coming to Longbourn."

"Did he? And... did he make his feelings on the matter known to you?"

"He did. He is delighted with the attention you are bestowing on me."

As they strolled farther from the house, he led her towards some trees that lined the drive up to Longbourn. He turned to face her and took her hand. "Miss Bennet... Elizabeth, I..."

Their attention was suddenly drawn to the drive by the sound of a carriage.

"Who can that be?" Elizabeth asked. "It is certainly too early for a..."

Elizabeth stopped and gasped, as Darcy's eyes widened.

"My aunt!" he exclaimed.

"Your aunt?" Elizabeth asked at the same time.

When the carriage stopped, Lady Catherine de Bourgh's imposing figure stepped out. She halted when she noticed her nephew and Elizabeth standing nearby. She marched purposefully over to them.

Darcy took a few steps forward. "Aunt Catherine! This is a... surprise!"

"Good day, Lady Catherine," Elizabeth said. "What... what brings you to Longbourn?"

Lady Catherine made no reply, other than to study the couple, her face colouring a deep shade of red. Her eyes turned to

Elizabeth. "Miss Bennet, there seems to be a prettyish kind of wilderness on one side of your lawn. I wish to take a turn in it, if you will favour me with your company." She looked at her nephew. "Alone!"

Elizabeth stole a quick look at Mr. Darcy, who began shaking his head.

"There is nothing about which you need to talk to Miss Bennet," he said. "Tell us why you have come. Perhaps I can help you."

"I came here to speak with Miss Bennet!"

"Then you will speak to both of us."

Lady Catherine remained silent for a moment and then finally drew her shoulders back and turned. "So that is how it is to be, is it? Then come with me!"

Elizabeth and Mr. Darcy exchanged a look of concern, and made to follow her.

As soon as they entered the copse, Lady Catherine stopped and turned to face them.

"You can be at no loss to understand the reason of my journey hither. Your own hearts, your own consciences, must tell you why I have come."

Elizabeth looked at her with unaffected astonishment.

"Indeed, you are mistaken, Madam. I am not at all able to account for the honour of seeing you here, unless it is to visit your nephew." She glanced at Mr. Darcy, readily noticing the pallor of his skin.

"Miss Bennet, you ought to know that I am not to be trifled with. A report of a most alarming nature reached me two days ago. I was told that not only your sister was on the point of being most advantageously married, but that you, Miss Elizabeth Bennet, would, in all likelihood, be soon afterwards united to my nephew!" She glared at him furiously.

Darcy fisted his hands and clenched his jaw. "Aunt Catherine…"

"I felt certain that it had to be a falsehood, but to ascertain the truth of it, I instantly resolved on setting off for this place." Her voice shook in anger. "And what do I find upon my arrival?" Her eyes bulged. "The two of you together!" She waved her hand from

Elizabeth to her nephew. "This is not to be borne!" She stepped towards Darcy. "Do you no longer retain the use of your reason? Has this woman used her arts and allurements to draw you in?" Her eyes narrowed as she glared at Elizabeth. "*She* has made you forget what you owe yourself and all your family!"

"Your accusations could not be further from the truth, and I resent your coming here and insulting Miss Bennet with such claims!"

Lady Catherine's eyes remained fixed on Elizabeth. "Tell me, Miss Bennet, has he, has my nephew, made you an offer of marriage?"

"Your ladyship has declared it to be impossible."

Lady Catherine continued. "Let me be rightly understood. This match, to which you obviously have the presumption to aspire, can never take place." She turned to Darcy. "*You* are engaged to my daughter. Is Miss Bennet aware of this?"

Before he could answer, Elizabeth replied, "I am aware of the engagement you and your sister *wished* for their two children, and if your nephew honours that engagement, you can have no reason to suppose he would make an offer to me."

Lady Catherine looked at Darcy. "Have *you* so easily forgotten this engagement that you have had since your birth?"

"How could I *ever* forget such a thing since it is continually thrown before me when I am in your presence? But it is not something Anne or I ever wanted. What my mother said when I was an infant has no bearing on my life now."

"Are you lost to every feeling of propriety and delicacy?" She turned back to Elizabeth. "You will be censured, slighted, and despised by everyone connected with my nephew! Your alliance will be a disgrace; your name never mentioned by any of us."

"Lady Catherine," Elizabeth said, "Those would be heavy misfortunes, indeed, but the wife of Mr. Darcy would have such extraordinary sources of happiness attached to her situation, that she could, upon the whole, have no cause to repine."

Elizabeth noticed Mr. Darcy turn to her and smile.

"Obstinate, headstrong girl! I am ashamed of you. You, a woman of inferior birth, of no importance in the world, and wholly unallied to the family, do you pay no regard to the wishes of his friends? Both my daughter and nephew are descended on the maternal side, from the same noble line; and on the father's, from respectable, honourable, and ancient families. Their fortune on both sides is splendid. And what is to divide them? The upstart pretensions of a young woman without family, connections, or fortune. This is not to be endured! If you were sensible of your own good, you would not wish to quit the sphere in which you have been brought up."

"In marrying your nephew, I should not consider myself as quitting that sphere. He is a gentleman; I am a gentleman's daughter; so far we are equal."

"True. You are a gentleman's daughter. But who was your mother? Who are your uncles and aunts? Do not imagine me ignorant of their condition."

"Whatever my connections may be," Elizabeth said, "if your nephew does not object to them, they can be nothing to you."

Darcy shook his head, taking in a deep breath. "Aunt, you are being completely unreasonable!"

"*I* am not the one being unreasonable!" She turned her attention back to Elizabeth. "Tell me once and for all, are you engaged to my nephew?"

Elizabeth drew in a long breath and stole another look at Mr. Darcy. As angry as his aunt was, he looked angrier. "I am not."

Lady Catherine seemed appeased by her answer. She turned to her nephew. "And you, will you promise me, never to enter into an engagement with this woman?"

A scowl darkened Darcy's face. With clenched fists and jaw, he replied emphatically, "I will make no such promise!"

The woman, whose face was flushed in fury, pounded her cane on the ground. "How dare you defy my wishes, mine and those of your mother? I thought you reasonable and honourable." She let out a groan of exasperation. "I refuse to leave until you have given me the assurance I require!"

"I certainly will not! You may intimidate others with your unreasonable demands, but you cannot intimidate me, and it is very apparent you do not intimidate Miss Bennet!" He drew in a breath. "Our conversation here is finished!"

Her eyes bore into her nephew. "Not so hasty, if you please. I am by no means done. In addition to all the objections I have already urged, I have still another to add. I am no stranger to the rumours and gossip that were spread around Lambton and Pemberley. First it was said that you had invited the Westerfields to Pemberley to offer for their daughter. I was seriously displeased! But then it was said that an inconsequential lady of lower rank, no fortune, and meagre connections was seen engaged with you in indiscreet situations, causing the family to depart. As she was apparently from Hertfordshire, I must deduce that this woman was none other than Miss Bennet! Heaven and earth! What are you thinking, Nephew? Are the shades of Pemberley to be thus polluted? "

Darcy was silent for a moment. Elizabeth could see he was struggling to regulate the outrage he felt. He drew in a long breath. "Aunt, whatever rumours, gossip, and lies you may have heard, I can assure you that Miss Bennet and I never acted with impropriety. Never! Now, Aunt, I would suggest that you leave!"

"This is insupportable!" She turned to Elizabeth. "If my nephew will not give me the assurance that he will obey the claims of duty, honour, and gratitude required of him, I must obtain it from you!" She shook her finger at her. "*You* must promise me that if my nephew asks for your hand in marriage, you will refuse his suit! Will you promise me that?"

Darcy quickly stepped in front of Elizabeth and held up his hand to his aunt. "I have asked you kindly to leave, but if you are intent upon hearing Miss Bennet's answer to your last question, allow me to ascertain it from her." Without waiting for his aunt to reply, he turned around and took Elizabeth's hands in his.

"Miss Bennet, it seems as though my aunt is in dire need of having an answer to her question. You know it is a question I have wanted to ask you myself, so…" He lowered himself onto one knee. "Miss Bennet, I love you deeply and ardently, and would be delighted if you would become my wife. Would you do me the honour of accepting my offer of marriage?"

Elizabeth was surprised at Mr. Darcy's boldness to defy his aunt in her very presence. She gave him an encouraging smile that infuriated the woman even more. His aunt glared at Elizabeth with a threatening look, but Elizabeth could only see the tender look of love and admiration – mixed with hope and a little desperation – in Mr. Darcy's eyes.

"I would be… delighted to accept your offer and become your wife."

"Insolent girl! The two of you are a disgrace!" She spun around and spoke over her shoulder. "You can be assured you will never be allowed at Rosings, your marriage will never be acknowledged by your family, and I will do everything in my power to make certain you will regret this – both of you! I shall know how to act!"

She stormed away, and Darcy slowly rose to his feet. It was a moment before he spoke. "This was not how I planned to propose." He shook his head. "I am delighted you answered yes, but I was worried that the *unusual* mode of my declaration would not be conducive to an affirmative reply."

Elizabeth smiled and watched the carriage drive away. "I own that it gave me great delight in silencing your aunt on the subject." She tilted her head at him. "I can see you are still quite angry."

Darcy swallowed and only nodded.

"How do you think she knew…?"

Darcy put up his hand. "I am not ready to talk about her yet."

"Come," Elizabeth said as she took his arm. "Let us walk."

They walked in silence. Elizabeth could tell by his rigid bearing that he was furious and would likely find it difficult to compose himself for some time. They walked aimlessly away from the house for some time, and when she felt him relax, she stopped, withdrew her arm from his, and faced him.

"Are you feeling better?"

He walked over to a tree and leaned against it, scuffing the dirt with his boot. "I fear it will take me some time to come to terms with what my aunt just did." He gave her a small smile and reached out to take her hand, giving it a firm squeeze. "But Elizabeth, I do feel somewhat appeased. Having you by my side has helped immensely."

His voice trembled, and Elizabeth wondered if it was from gratitude towards her or anger towards his aunt.

Elizabeth drew closer, looking down at her hand which was still in his. "I am glad."

"I regret that you saw the very worst of my aunt… and me. She was unforgivably rude to you, and I do not know if I will ever forgive her for all she said." His chest heaved as he took a breath. "There is only one other person who brings out that much anger in me." He lowered his head. "I have always struggled with staying composed around my aunt... and *Wickham*."

Elizabeth continued to look at his hand holding hers. It was so much bigger and stronger than hers, yet so smooth. His fingers dwarfed hers; his fingernails were spotless and perfectly trimmed. Despite his lingering anger, she felt safe.

She lifted her eyes to him. "We all have people like that in our lives."

Darcy suddenly chuckled. "My only enjoyment in this encounter was watching you stand up to my aunt without any hesitation." He shrugged. "It was because of that I knew you would accept my proposal in front of her." He leaned over and kissed her forehead. "I was convinced you would enjoy imparting the one final straw that would break her unreasonable demands."

Elizabeth leaned in towards him with a smile. "I believe you have come to know me quite well." She tilted her head. "You did not find me too impertinent?"

"On the contrary, but Elizabeth, you must oblige me with one more thing." His gaze dropped to her lips, and Elizabeth parted them as she felt a thrill of anticipation.

Instead of leaning down and kissing her, however, he got down on his knee again and took her hands. "Miss Bennet, since I know you are a young lady whose courage rises at every attempt to intimidate her, I must ask you again if you will consent to be my wife. I want to be certain that your answer reflects nothing more than your desire to be married to me, and not a wish to silence my aunt." He squeezed her hands and looked up at her expectantly.

Elizabeth smiled. "This, sir, is not a difficult question to answer. As I said before, I would be delighted to be your wife."

Darcy stood and drew her close, wrapping his arms about her. This time, when his eyes dropped to her lips, he lifted his hand and touched them lightly with his finger. Then he leaned down and pressed his lips to hers. They remained undisturbed in an embrace, in the quiet of the copse, knowing that once they returned to the house, he would go to her father to get his consent, and she would go to her mother. There would be nothing but chaos ensuing.

Chapter 23

Elizabeth walked at Darcy's side as they made their way slowly back to the house. She paused each time she sensed another wave of frustration course through him. He would shake his head, let out a breath, and then smile down at her.

Just before they reached the house, Darcy stopped and turned to her. "I want to reassure you, Miss Bennet... Elizabeth, that your acceptance of my proposal has given me the greatest joy. I do feel it, despite my euphoric feelings being assaulted by anger at what my aunt said and did." He brought her hands up to his lips and kissed them. "I only wish I could have…"

Elizabeth, in turn, grasped his hands and kissed them. "We are engaged, and that is all that matters. Think nothing more of your aunt or the manner in which you proposed."

Darcy closed his eyes briefly and drew in a deep breath. He looked at her and shook his head. "I doubt there is any other woman who would have borne up as well as you did under her attack. I am deeply grieved and sorry."

Elizabeth smiled. "Fitzwilliam, it is not your fault."

They quietly stared at each other. Elizabeth sensed that he was drawing strength from her. She could see his face become increasingly calm the longer he looked at her. His jaw and fists were no longer clenched, his brow no longer furrowed, and the slightest smile appeared.

"You did not accept my proposal – my two proposals – because of my library, did you?"

The teasing glint in his eyes reassured her that he was well on his way to putting the encounter with his aunt behind him.

She could tease him back but quickly decided against it. "My acceptance of your offer of marriage was based solely and completely upon the fact that there is no finer man I know than you, and I love you so very deeply."

His smile deepened, and he wrapped his arms about her and leaned down to touch his forehead to hers. "You have made me the happiest of men." He looked towards the house. "Shall we go in?"

"Are you ready to face my family so soon after facing your aunt?"

"Mm. I might need a little more fortitude." He brought his lips to hers in a kiss. His arms tightened about her, as if he were pulling every ounce of strength from her that he could. After a few moments, he pulled away and said with a smile, "I believe I am ready, now."

When they reached the house, Mr. Darcy immediately went to see Mr. Bennet to obtain his consent to marry Elizabeth. She, on the other hand, returned to the sitting room to tell her mother and sisters that she was now engaged to Mr. Darcy. Upon hearing the news, Mrs. Bennet seemed unable to comprehend that Mr. Darcy had proposed to her second eldest daughter.

"He wants to marry *you*? But how can that be? He is Mr. Darcy!"

Elizabeth smiled as she tried to make her mother understand. "And I am to be *Mrs.* Darcy. He asked me to marry him, and I said yes."

Jane walked over and placed her hands on her mother's shoulders. "Mother, is this not splendid news? Are you not delighted?"

"Of course, I am, but it is all so strange!"

Charles beamed and came to Jane's side. "There can be no better news than hearing that my good friend is to marry my bride's sister."

"Oh!" Mrs. Bennet suddenly stood up, waving her hands. "But now we have to plan *two* weddings! Oh, my nerves! I am already quite undone as it is!"

Jane smiled at Elizabeth. "Lizzy, what would you think if we had one wedding; if we get married together?"

"A double wedding?" Elizabeth asked.

Jane nodded and turned to Charles. "What do you think, Charles? Would you mind?"

He laughed. "I do not care how many weddings take place that day. The only thing I care about is that I will be married to you at the end of it."

Elizabeth clasped her hands together. "I think that is a wonderful idea!" Her face suddenly grew serious, but with a hint of mischief. "Oh, but we do not know what Father will say. What if he does not give his consent? Fitzwilliam is in with him now." She shrugged. "He may refuse."

Mrs. Bennet's eyes narrowed, and she began marching towards the door. "He had better not refuse to give his consent! I am going to go to him directly, and…"

"Ah! Here you all are!" Mr. Bennet said as he entered the room with Mr. Darcy at his side. "Will you look who came in and asked for my consent to marry my Lizzy?"

"What did you say?" Mrs. Bennet asked. "You had better have given him your consent!"

"No worries there. I did, indeed, very happily give my consent."

Mrs. Bennet clapped her hands and squealed, as Elizabeth walked over to join Mr. Darcy. She slipped her hand around his arm, wrapping her fingers about it. She enjoyed being able to do something so simple without having to give it a thought. She looked up at him. "Jane suggested that we marry the same day as she and Charles. Would you be willing to share the day with them?"

Darcy nodded. "I was actually hoping that we would."

Elizabeth looked at her mother. "It appears as though you still have only one wedding to plan!"

~~*

The two newly engaged couples spent some time conversing with the family. Mr. Bennet was quiet, but his wife made up for his reserve with her bursts of eager anticipation mingled with overwhelming vexations. Everything would have to be perfect, and she was certain something would go wrong. Mary also observed quietly. She had no virtuous words to offer them, and Elizabeth contemplated whether her younger sister was speculating on her own prospects, wondering if she would find a gentleman worthy of her convictions. Kitty and Lydia began speculating, as well, but to Elizabeth's dismay, it was on all the fine gentlemen that would likely be thrown into their paths due to their two sisters' husbands.

At length, Elizabeth suggested the two couples step outside for a stroll. She had noticed that Fitzwilliam had grown quiet in the midst of all the raucousness and knew he needed a respite from it. Everyone readily agreed.

As soon as they cleared the doorway, Fitzwilliam took Elizabeth's hand in his and entwined his fingers with hers. His hand was warm and strong, and she felt such elation at his touch. She purposely kept their pace slow, and they soon fell farther and farther behind Charles and Jane. There were things she wished to talk about and preferred to do it in private.

When they were a good distance away, Elizabeth looked up at him. She decided she would initially address those subjects that would be easy for him to discuss. "When do you think your sister will come?"

"I will write to her tonight and have her come in a week's time."

"I look forward to seeing her again."

"And she, you, I am certain."

Elizabeth took her other hand and wrapped her fingers about his arm. "How do you think she will take the news of our marriage and…" She looked up to him. "And being in Mr. Bingley's presence now that he is engaged to my sister?"

Darcy pressed his lips in thought. "At first, she may feel awkward seeing Bingley, but I…" He let out a chuckle. "I think her happiness at seeing us engaged will overpower any other feelings she may have."

"She will be pleased, then?"

He nodded. "She is very fond of you."

Elizabeth smiled and leaned her head against his arm. "I am glad. I am fond of her, as well."

"I know Bingley will not experience any awkwardness around Georgiana. His feelings were never as engaged as hers were, and he likely is not aware of the extent of her feelings towards him." He gave a shrug. "I have wondered how much of her affection was the result of my… my…" He swallowed and let out a long sigh. "My interference and trying to influence her."

Elizabeth stole a glance up and noticed his grimace. "You were only doing what you thought was good for her. You knew Mr. Bingley well and thought he would suit her."

He gave his head a slight shake. "If I had known *him* as well as I should have, I would have realized his love for Jane was strong, as strong as..." He turned and took both of Elizabeth's hands in his. "I never once thought to attribute to Bingley's feelings for Jane the depth of undying love *I* felt for *you*."

Elizabeth pressed her finger to his lips. "You have reprimanded yourself enough. Everything has turned out as it should, and I do not want to hear any more about it."

He grasped her hand and kissed the tips of her fingers. He lowered his hands and placed them about her, pulling her close. "If you insist, my dearest, loveliest, Elizabeth." He gazed into her eyes and then leaned down and ardently kissed her.

After a few moments, he drew away. "As much as I regret having to end that kiss, I believe I must. There is another matter I wish to discuss that pertains to my sister."

"What is that?" Elizabeth could barely attend to his words, so affected was she by his kiss. She hoped she would be able to think clearly as he spoke.

"Bingley has written to his sisters, and they will be arriving shortly. You can imagine their dismay at the news that he is now engaged to Jane, and..." He paused.

Elizabeth smiled. "Oh, poor Miss Bingley! What will she do when she finds out *we* are engaged?"

Darcy touched Elizabeth's cheek and twirled a stray curl about his finger. He smiled and gave a small shrug. "I do not know. We shall find out, soon enough."

Elizabeth tilted her head. "But you said this also pertains to your sister."

"Yes. Would you allow me to bring Georgiana with me whenever I come to visit? I do not want to leave her alone with Miss Bingley, if I can help it." His fingers stroked down her cheek, and he left them resting on her cheekbone. "I would prefer to spend time alone with you, but I have to think of her."

"I would be delighted to have her join us."

"Good. I am glad. If she has to be alone with anyone, I think she would prefer being with you, as well."

Elizabeth leaned her head into his hand. "And… what of your aunt? How will this affect her, your extended familial relationships, and especially Miss de Bourgh?"

"I have seen her angry before. My family – her brother and my cousins – have all witnessed her tirades and know how unreasonable she can be. I am not worried about them, and she will soon get over it. I believe Anne will insist she apologize. Believe it or not, my aunt will do anything to indulge her daughter." He chuckled. "Anne is quite the manipulator, where her mother is concerned."

"Is she truly?"

Darcy nodded. "Her sedentary lifestyle is her own preference. She is not particularly sociable and prefers seclusion over inclusion. She never wished to marry and only looks forward to the day when Rosings is hers." He gave a shrug. "I know she does not want a rift in our relationship."

"I am glad to hear that."

"It may take some time for my aunt, however. I doubt they will attend the wedding, but I can guarantee that in a few months, my aunt will either write us a letter, or…" He lifted Elizabeth's chin with his finger. "Or she will show up at Pemberley, unannounced, just as she did here." He leaned down and kissed her lips. "She will act as if nothing ever happened."

"She will not apologize for her actions?"

"Oh, she will, if you want to call it an apology, but only because of Anne. She will twist her words so that we know she still believes she was right." Darcy took in a deep breath and looked up. "But…" He paused.

Elizabeth tilted her head. "But, what?"

"I fear that before she changes her opinion, she may try to cause us more distress with the rumours." He shook his head. "Unfortunately, she has a few friends who live near Pemberley, and she may try to incite more rumours or gossip through them." He shook his head. "There is one family in particular that she knows quite well. They live on the other side of Lambton and have many Lambton residents in their employ." He let out a groan. "This acquaintance has always kept her informed of any rumours and gossip pertaining to our family that spread through the village."

"So that is how she heard about the rumours." Elizabeth sighed. "And I am certain she discovered that you were in Meryton visiting me from Charlotte, who likely heard it from her parents."

Darcy nodded. "It seems she has spies everywhere." He chuckled. "I am surprised that your mother never suspected anything if such rumours were being spread about the neighbourhood."

She laughed. "I think she has been so focused on Jane's wedding, nothing else was of interest." She shook her head. "Besides, she was incredulous when I told her about our engagement. If she had heard any gossip about us, she likely believed it to have no basis in truth."

Darcy cupped his hand against Elizabeth's face. "While I care little for the rumours that have always circulated about me, I care greatly when they affect someone I love. I do not want you to be distraught by any gossip that is still circulating when we return to Pemberley."

Elizabeth gave him an encouraging smile. "I will just have to prove to Pemberley's staff, your neighbours – including your aunt's friend – and the people in Lambton that I love and respect you. Hopefully they will see by my actions that they have no need to concern themselves about my character."

"Elizabeth, I want to assure you that my staff will treat you with the utmost respect, despite what circulated amongst them. I will demand it of them."

Elizabeth nodded. "I am certain they shall. But all I truly care about is having *your* love and respect."

"Which you do, most ardently!" He drew in a breath. "I hope you will know that as a certainty!" He placed his hands about her waist and drew her close to him. "Elizabeth Bennet, you are everything I have ever wanted as my wife, to share my home and family, to love and to cherish all the days of my life." He wiped a tear that escaped down her cheek and then pressed his lips to the tear-stained trail. In a whisper, he said, "You have made me the happiest of men." He then touched his lips to hers, and she responded by wrapping her arms about his neck.

~~*

A few days later, Jane and Elizabeth sat in the parlour after the gentlemen left, and they began to discuss their wedding plans. Their maid, Sarah, came in and told Elizabeth her father requested to see her.

Elizabeth excused herself and went to his study. "Yes, Father. Did you wish to see me?"

"I did. Come in and take a seat." He motioned to the chair across from him.

"What is it?"

He removed his glasses and began rubbing the bridge of his nose. "I am of a mind, Lizzy, to do something you might find silly."

Elizabeth laughed. "And what is that?"

"Now that I am finally gaining some sons, albeit sons-in-law, I must find suitable birds to match their personalities."

Elizabeth's eyes widened and mouth fell open. "Truly? And have you determined what the two birds will be for the gentlemen?"

"Well, now, Lizzy, this is where I need some advice. I have chosen Mr. Bingley's bird. I have done much thinking about it and believe he is much like a wren."

"A wren?"

He nodded. "Indeed!"

She laughed. "How is he like a wren?"

"They are cheerful and sociable. Much like the magpie, but the magpie has the added trait of being intelligent. I do not think he is as intelligent as you. No, I *know* he is not. The wren also flits about here and there. Yes, I think the wren suits him fine."

Elizabeth tilted her head. "All right. And what have you decided for Mr. Darcy?"

"Ah, now here is my dilemma. You must help me out here. My first thought was that he was a great deal like a peacock. You know, proud as a peacock. What say you to that?"

Elizabeth vehemently shook her head. "That will not do. I have told you he has no improper pride and certainly not the ostentatious pride that is associated with a peacock. No, a peacock will not do." She laughed. "I can think of a few *other* people that would qualify as a peacock, however!"

"Hm. I am certain you can. I am of the same mind that the esteemed Mr. Darcy is not a peacock. Next, I considered the eagle, for they soar high above and look down on everyone. They are strong, have a majestic and regal air about them, and are confident and decisive. What say you to that?"

Elizabeth's brows pinched. "Certainly better than the peacock, but I do not think…"

"No, I agree. Now here is my third choice, and it is my favourite. I hope you will approve."

"What is it?"

"The owl. Think, Lizzy, he has an air of quiet mystery about him, soaring alone silently at night." He lifted his brows. "Do you not think that is the perfect choice?"

Elizabeth nodded. "It does seem to suit him well."

"Good, good! For the owl is also wise, and since he has chosen you to be his wife, I would have to say that he is the wisest man I know!"

Elizabeth chuckled. "Then an owl, he is!"

~~*

The plans for the wedding were kept simple yet elegant, due not only to Jane and Elizabeth's desire to keep their mother's nerves from becoming unbearable, but because Mr. Darcy did not want anything too extravagant. This, however, caused Mrs. Bennet such vexation, for she was of the opinion that the man must have only the finest and most elaborate wedding.

A number of compromises were finally settled on, and after several days of Mrs. Bennet voicing her opinions and woes regarding the wedding plans, Jane and Elizabeth decided to leave her out of the decision making. They did everything, allowing their mother only to think she was heavily involved in the preparations, as she would experience nervous flutterings and spasms regardless.

The biggest disappointment for Mrs. Bennet was that they would not be going to London to have her daughters' wedding dresses made by the finest modistes. Meryton had excellent seamstresses, and Jane and Elizabeth were able to find the satins and laces for the gowns they each selected.

Elizabeth was grateful Georgiana arrived at Netherfield before either of Mr. Bingley's sisters. She knew once they arrived, she would be subject to their company on occasion, and at the moment, she looked forward to spending time with just Mr. Darcy and his sister.

The two ladies greatly enjoyed each other's company. Darcy often sat back with a smile on his face as he watched his two favourite ladies converse with each other. He told Elizabeth he strongly felt that she knew how to bring out the best in his sister. His heart overflowed with love and joy.

Caroline Bingley and the Hursts arrived one afternoon when Jane and Elizabeth were at Netherfield. Caroline entered the sitting room, where they were all gathered. Upon seeing her brother and Jane, she approached them, giving both of them a feeble embrace. She turned and noticed Georgiana and rushed over to her with her arms outstretched.

"Oh, my poor girl! I hope you are bearing up well under what must be a grave disappointment." Although she spoke in a hushed voice, the others in the room had been able to hear her. She had yet to notice Darcy and Elizabeth, who were sitting behind her in the corner of the room.

"I am doing quite well, Miss Bingley. I am delighted for Mr. Bingley and Miss Bennet."

She gave her a sympathetic smile. "You are a brave young lady. I know this must be difficult for you."

Georgiana shook her head. "Not at all."

"Well!" she said, clasping her hands and spinning around. "What is there to…?" She stopped when she saw Darcy and Elizabeth. She gulped and drew back.

"Oh! I beg your pardon, I did not see you sitting there."

Darcy stood. "Good afternoon, Miss Bingley."

"Hello, Miss Bingley," Elizabeth said.

Caroline's lips twitched. "How good to see you again, Mr. Darcy… Miss Elizabeth."

Elizabeth was fairly certain Miss Bingley had not wished to

include her in her greeting.

"Well, is this not a pleasant gathering?" She looked about her as if she did not know what to say. Finally, she addressed Elizabeth. "Miss Elizabeth, now that we have arrived, I believe your chaperoning duties are no longer needed for your sister. Louisa and I shall be more than happy to chaperone them."

Elizabeth's brow arched. "I am certain you would, but I am not here to chaperone them."

"Oh?" A smile appeared and then promptly faded.

Darcy reached over and took Elizabeth's hand. "You might say, Miss Bingley, that we are chaperoning each other, for…" He looked at Elizabeth and smiled. "Elizabeth and I are also engaged."

Miss Bingley's eyes widened, and she seemed unable to speak. "You… are… engaged?" She shook her head. "To each other?"

"Yes! Is that not wonderful?" Georgiana asked. "There is going to be a double wedding."

"I see." Miss Bingley took in a hitched breath, attempted to smile, and offered a weak, "I wish you both a life of… joy."

Darcy and Elizabeth looked at her with wide smiles.

"Thank you!" Darcy replied.

"I am certain we will," Elizabeth said with great satisfaction.

Chapter 24

Jane and Elizabeth walked down the aisle of the church on the arms of their father. The church was filled with family and close friends of Bingley, Darcy, and the Bennets, but Elizabeth saw none of them. Her gaze was fixed on the men standing at the front. She smiled at the picture of contrasts these two good friends made.

Charles stood in a casual stance, occasionally rocking back and forth on his heels. He rubbed his hands together several times, and a smile lit his expressive face as he gazed upon his bride.

Fitzwilliam held himself erect, hands at his side, and his face seemed to radiate a steadfast contentment. The only movement she detected was the occasional shifting of his weight from one foot to the other.

Elizabeth sent him a smile, this man, who on their first meeting had claimed, "*She is tolerable, but not handsome enough to tempt me.*"

How that slighting remark had offended and hurt her. She had laughed at him upon overhearing his slight, and it had greatly affected her initial opinion of him. When did his feelings for her improve? When did hers?

As they drew closer to the front, his words on another occasion struck her. "*My temper would perhaps be called resentful. My good opinion once lost, is lost forever.*"

She gave her head a slight shake. How was it that he had not lost his good opinion of her when she refused his offer of marriage? He had been angry, hurt, and had certainly not been expecting a refusal. Yet, he had been willing to overlook not only her refusal, but the vitriolic words she had flung at him.

Perhaps it all began for him when she had stayed at Netherfield when Jane was ill. In their discussion about women's accomplishments, he had said, "*All this she must possess, and to all this she must yet add something more substantial, in the improvement of her mind by extensive reading.*" He seemed to enjoy stimulating conversation, discussion, and banter, and he knew she read profusely. While she had not all the accomplishments that Miss Bingley praised and exhibited, he seemed to consider reading as one he admired most.

Just as she was almost within reach of her intended, his words that had surprised her most came to mind. *"I certainly have not the talent which some people possess of conversing easily with those I have never seen before. I cannot catch their tone of conversation, or appear interested in their concerns, as I often see done."*

They had spoken about this very thing the day before. She had supposed him to be a gentleman of the world, who was adept at conversing with anyone and everyone, and yet he was not. What she had believed to be pride was, in truth, reserve. He was a man who did not wish to be displayed in front of everyone, and yet, here he was, standing at the front of Longbourn Church, with all eyes upon him.

"Keep your eyes on me," Elizabeth had told him. "Do not look out at the people. This is our day. We are the only two that matter."

Darcy had lifted a brow. "And perhaps the vicar?"

Elizabeth had nodded. "Yes, we certainly need the vicar."

"And Bingley and Jane, for I know both of them would be greatly disappointed if they were excluded."

"Yes, I suppose they are important, as well."

Darcy dipped his head. "And your father, for without his consent, we would not be marrying."

Elizabeth pinched her brows. "I am not so certain. If he had refused to give you his consent, I am certain I would have been able to convince him otherwise." She had laughed. "I do know how to get my own way with him."

Darcy had laughed with her. "Is this a foretelling of what I can expect? Do you have secret devices which you intend to employ with me to ensure you get your own way?"

"That is something we shall have to see." Elizabeth's voice held a hint of laughter. "Now, my dear Fitzwilliam, if you choose to look at any of those other important people during the wedding, so be it, but I shall be looking only at you."

He had leaned over and kissed her lightly. "And I shall be looking only at you."

She and Jane reached the front of the church, and they stepped towards their grooms. As the vicar began delivering the wedding message, the words Fitzwilliam had spoken to her just before he left the parsonage when she had refused his offer of marriage came to her. *"Please accept my best wishes for your health and happiness."*

Neither of them had any idea that their health and happiness would be bound together a few months later as they were joined in matrimony. Elizabeth almost laughed aloud as she considered how much had changed since then. She would never have believed that she could love someone as much as she loved him now.

They spoke their vows of commitment to each other, and she stole a glance up at him. When he met her gaze and smiled, she let out a contented sigh, just as they were pronounced husband and wife.

~~*

Elizabeth knew the wedding breakfast would be difficult for her husband. Now that they were married, his preference would have been to depart at once. She laughed as she considered that Mr. Collins and Charlotte had done exactly that after their wedding ceremony. Their journey to Kent was a mere fifty miles of good road. Elizabeth and her husband would be making the journey to Pemberley, which would take several days.

She thought of Charlotte and shook her head. A letter from her had expressed her regret at not being able to attend the wedding. Both her husband and Lady Catherine had been adamant that witnessing such a disgraceful alliance would be akin to committing a most grievous sin.

To keep her husband and patroness placated, Charlotte had not argued their point. She sent Jane and Elizabeth her warmest congratulations and told Elizabeth that if there were any opportunity for reconciliation between Mr. Darcy and his aunt, she would greatly enjoy seeing her if they came to visit Rosings.

Elizabeth enjoyed visiting with friends and family during the wedding breakfast. Colonel Fitzwilliam made a point of expressing his family's regrets that they were unable to attend but gave the couple their full support. He added his promise that they would do whatever it took to mend the breach between them and Lady

Catherine.

Mr. and Mrs. Gardiner could not have been more pleased that Pemberley would now be their niece's home. Mr. Gardiner took the credit himself, for he claimed if not for his back injury, they would have departed Pemberley with no opportunity at all to encounter Mr. Darcy.

Miss Bingley and her sister kept to themselves, and on more than one occasion, Elizabeth noticed them rolling their eyes or shaking their heads. When they seemed intent on trying to get Georgiana alone, Colonel Fitzwilliam came to the rescue, drawing the young girl away with some supposed business. She would be going to London with him, where she would join Mrs. Annesley and await word from her brother that they could return to Pemberley.

At length, Fitzwilliam suggested to Elizabeth that they take their leave. He knew it would be a lengthy goodbye, as sisters, mother, father, aunts and uncles, and friends would require many words and tearful hugs. His suspicions were proved correct, as it was another hour before they finally stepped into Pemberley's carriage to set off for the inn where reservations had been made for their first night.

As they journeyed toward Pemberley, they talked of inconsequential things. Darcy held Elizabeth's hand and frequently raised it to kiss her palm, or leaned over to kiss the top of her head or her cheek. When she inclined her head towards him, he was delighted to press his lips to hers.

After about an hour on the road, the carriage stopped, and Elizabeth drew back and looked out. They were at an inn.

"We are stopping already? I hope you do not think I am hungry. We left the wedding breakfast no more than an hour ago."

"We have not stopped to eat but will be staying the night here."

Elizabeth's eyes widened. "But we have such a long journey to Pemberley. I would think you would want to travel through dusk."

At that moment, the door to the carriage opened, and Darcy put up his hand. "Would you give us a few moments, please?"

When the door closed, he turned to face Elizabeth.

"You are of the opinion I want to spend my first day of marriage riding in a carriage all day? Why would you think that?"

He sent her a teasing look.

"Oh." She laughed, and her cheeks grew rosy. She looked out the window and then back to him. "But I have had no time to begin to feel the least bit nervous!"

He looked at her with an intense gaze and took her hand in his, placing his other hand over it. "Are you nervous?"

A dizzying tremor coursed through her, and her pulse quickened. "I think... any bride on her wedding night has a right to be nervous."

He leaned forward. "My dearest Elizabeth, you are not afraid, are you?"

She gave him a smile. "On the contrary. It is not so much *fear* about tonight, but rather... *uncertainty.*"

"Good. For there is nothing of which to be afraid, and by tomorrow all your uncertainty will be gone." His voice was husky, but spoke to her of understanding, admiration, and trust.

He placed his fingers under her chin and lifted it. Very slowly he drew near and kissed her again, a soft, tender kiss that made her heart beat even faster.

He suddenly drew back, letting out a breathy sigh. He pointed towards the window. "I hope you like the inn. I stopped here on my way to Hertfordshire to see how suitable it would be."

Elizabeth looked up at him through lowered brows. "Mr. Darcy! Are you telling me you came to Hertfordshire with the *certainty* that I would accept your offer of marriage?" She gave him an arch glance.

Darcy took her hand again. "On the contrary. It was not so much *certainty* that you would answer yes, but rather... *hope.*"

This time Elizabeth brought his hand up to her lips and kissed it.

Darcy's face grew serious. "I confess when I came to you in Kent, I had the mistaken and prideful confidence that you would accept me." He shook his head. "I was so wrong..." He paused and gave his head a quick shake. "We have been apologizing frequently, of late. But I must offer one more apology to you."

"There is no need..."

He pressed his fingers lightly against her lips. "Oh, but there is. My offer of marriage to you was appalling in its reason, foolish in its judgment, and insulting to your character, worth, and sensibilities. I had come to you expecting you to accept my offer. It was very wrong of me, and I can only feel a great sense of gratitude that despite my arrogance, insolence, and ineptitude that day, today we are married."

Elizabeth was tempted to protest, but she knew he would continue to press her to accept his apology. "Fitzwilliam, I accept your apology, but I would like to add something."

"What is that?"

"Today we are not only married, but blissfully, contentedly, and most agreeably wed." She leaned over and pressed her lips to his. "Do you not agree?"

"I do with all *certainty*."

Elizabeth laughed and shook her head. "Shall we go in?"

Darcy's smile was wide. "*Certainly!* That is something I am most eager to do!"

~~*

The leisurely journey to Pemberley took a week, with a few stops off the main road to more scenic areas. It was relaxing for them as they enjoyed spending time together walking, reading, and getting to know one another in the joyously intimate ways only a husband and wife truly in love experience.

When the majestic Pemberley house came into view, Elizabeth felt a thrill seeing it for the first time as her very own. Her eyes filled with tears as she considered how blessed she was with both the man at her side and the home they now called their own.

The carriage drew up to the house where two straight lines of servants had come out to greet them. Mr. Brooks and Mrs. Reynolds stood in the centre. As Elizabeth stepped out, she suddenly felt all eyes upon her. She did not discern any critical or judgmental expressions, but she suddenly realized what it must be like for her husband to enter a crowd where all eyes fell upon him. She could see why he disliked it immensely.

Introductions and reintroductions were made. There were many servants Elizabeth had seen, as well as many she did not recollect seeing during her stay. Mrs. Reynolds immediately came to her side. "Mr. Darcy has requested that he show you around the home, first. You are familiar with the main floor and some of the second floor, but he would like to show you to your rooms." Her smile held a hint of nervousness. "Once you are settled in, I would request a short tête-à-tête with you, if you please."

"I would be delighted, Mrs. Reynolds." She smiled warmly, hoping to assure the housekeeper she held no resentment towards her for asking them to leave.

The couple stepped inside, and Elizabeth looked around. She could not believe how different it looked. Just as the view of the manor itself had seemed much more majestic knowing it now belonged to her, the interior of the home was just as appealing. She had gazed upon it before, as an outsider, as one who did not belong. While she appreciated all she had seen, she was now in awe that it suited her immensely.

Once they had stepped away from Mr. Brooks and Mrs. Reynolds, Fitzwilliam whispered to her. "I know Mrs. Reynolds likely wants to apologize profusely to you."

"I could see it is weighing heavily on her." She slipped her hand through his arm. "I shall be very kind to her and give her all the reassurance she needs that I harbour no ill-feelings towards her."

"Thank you. She also will want to talk to you about selecting a lady's maid. She will have some ideas."

"And I will be glad to consider them."

They took a leisurely stroll through some of the upper floor rooms, some of which Elizabeth had seen and some of which she had not. When they came into the library, she sighed.

"Did I ever tell you how beautiful your library is?" She walked about, once again in awe of all the books. "If ever you cannot find me, Fitzwilliam, I would suggest you look here first."

He laughed. "Then I shall never lose you, for I shall be in here, as well."

There was one hallway of rooms that Darcy pointed out as guest chambers. She had no need to see each one now, but was curious how they were decorated. She might stroll down the hall someday just to see for herself.

They turned down another hall and soon came to their chambers. When they stepped in, Elizabeth was rendered speechless. The first room they stepped into was quite immense. The furniture was made of light wood, and the patterns were florals and light pastels. A light-coloured stencilled wall-covering hung on one wall. She rightly assumed this room was hers. There was a small bed, a vanity, and a desk and chair by the window. Darcy opened a door, and she saw that it had a large dressing room and spacious closets.

"Do you like it, Elizabeth?"

"It is…" She turned to him. "I can barely summon up the words to describe how I feel about it. It is beautiful."

"I am glad you approve."

She walked around, touching the silken and plush fabrics and smooth woods. Her husband watched her, enjoying her delight. "If there is anything you do not like, do not hesitate to mention it. We will make any changes to it you want."

"Fitzwilliam, I cannot think of anything I would want to change. She walked over and looked out the window. "It is a magnificent view, as well." She turned back to him. "I am not certain I will ever want to leave this room."

"Well, I certainly hope you will want to leave it and join me in mine." He looked at her teasingly. "At least on occasion."

"I suppose I shall… but only if your room and view are as delightful as mine." She returned his teasing smile.

"Come. I shall let you decide for yourself."

They walked through the dressing room and through another door. Elizabeth looked about her in awe. The furniture was constructed of dark heavy wood, the colours were deep and rich, and the patterns were bold stripes. The bed was larger than any she had ever seen, and her first thought was that she might get lost in it. A silk damask wall covering of a hunting scene hung on one wall. While the two rooms were completely different, they were equally beautiful.

As Elizabeth admired both his chambers and the view from the window, they heard the servants in the dressing room unpacking their belongings.

Fitzwilliam closed the door to his chambers and walked over to Elizabeth, placing his hands on her shoulders. "Mrs. Reynolds is overseeing your belongings being unpacked. Once they have finished, she will remain to visit with you. I know she would like to get the choice of your lady's maid taken care of directly. She will serve you in that capacity until one is decided upon."

"That is not necessary," Elizabeth protested. "I had to share Sarah at Longbourn with five other ladies."

He gave her a pointed look. "This is not Longbourn."

Elizabeth swallowed, her mouth suddenly dry. "Yes. You are right."

"I am going to change and then go to the library, where my steward is awaiting me. You are free to do whatever you would like when you have finished with Mrs. Reynolds. You can rest in here, explore more of Pemberley, or join me in the library in about an hour."

"I would like that very much," Elizabeth said. She came up to him and stood on her toes, bestowing a brief kiss on his lips. "Thank you, Fitzwilliam, for everything."

Darcy shook his head. "No, Elizabeth, I thank *you!*" He leaned down and pressed his lips gently against hers. As the kiss deepened, he wrapped his arms about her, holding her tightly against him as if his very life depended upon it.

~~*

Elizabeth met with Mrs. Reynolds and assured her there were no resentful feelings towards her for her actions in requesting she and her aunt and uncle leave Pemberley. As the housekeeper helped Elizabeth change, they discussed the different servants whom she felt would serve Elizabeth well as her lady's maid. It was decided that each lady Mrs. Reynolds deemed suitable would wait on Elizabeth for a day, and then she would decide which would suit her best. There was more to discuss in terms of her now being Mistress of Pemberley, but Mrs. Reynolds felt that it would be best to acquaint her with all it involved over the course of a few days.

Once Mrs. Reynolds left, Elizabeth sat in her chair and gazed out the window. "Of all this I am now mistress!" she said with a wide smile. "I could not be happier."

An hour later, Elizabeth retrieved a small wrapped package that had been placed in one of the drawers and went to the library to join her husband. He greeted her as she walked in.

"Are you finished with your steward?" she asked.

"Yes. Did you and Mrs. Reynolds have a good discussion?"

"Oh, yes. She was very apologetic about asking us to leave, and then reassured me that I will have all the respect the Mistress of Pemberley deserves. We talked about what I would need in a lady's maid, and she told me a little about how things are done here. I can see that she is going to be very thorough."

"So she taught you everything you need to know about Pemberley?" He stood up and walked over to her.

"Hardly. She said it is likely to take several days."

"It will likely take several weeks, if not months." He nodded to her hand. "What do you have there?"

She walked over to the table that held the carved owl and pulled the carved magpie out of the wrapping, placing it next to it.

"Ah, the magpie. Are you certain that is where you want it?" Darcy asked. "You do not want it in your chambers?"

"This is perfect." She looked at him with an arched brow. "Do you not know about the owl and the magpie?"

Darcy rolled his eyes. "Oh, no. Is this another folk tale with some unreasonable message attached to it?"

"On the contrary!" Elizabeth laughed. "My father has chosen the owl as the bird that represents you. Quiet, mysterious, and oh, so very wise."

"Truly?"

"And so it only makes sense that those two birds, which represent the two of us, should be together all the days of our lives… in the library at Pemberley."

Darcy wrapped his arm about her and kissed the top of her head. "I am grateful he did not choose the peacock for my bird."

Elizabeth laughed. "To own the truth, he briefly considered it, but we both agreed it would not do."

"I will thank him the next time I see him!" His smile did not seem to come from the depths of him.

"Fitzwilliam, is something wrong?"

He stared silently for a moment. "My steward just informed me that my aunt has already begun to make absurd accusations against us. She has notified her acquaintances here that I acted disgracefully, flagrantly, and…" He blew out a breath, shaking his head. "And that I acted dishonourably by breaking off an engagement with her daughter and marrying someone so far beneath me, someone not worthy to be Mistress of Pemberley – as she claims her daughter would have been."

"I see."

He pressed his lips tightly and drew Elizabeth close. "I will not have it! I will not! I will speak to Mr. Brooks and Mrs. Reynolds later about addressing the servants again. I know there are servants working here who have family members that work for my aunt's acquaintance. This must cease!"

Elizabeth placed her hands on his shoulders. She could see his anger and wished he would not worry so about her. "They will eventually come to see the love and respect we have for each other. I am certain of that. We will not let a few idle rumours destroy the joy we have. Eventually they will cease."

She gave him a smile and leaned her head against his chest.

As they stood together, a servant stepped in with the mail.

"Pardon me, sir, but this mail was just delivered."

"Place it on my desk, please." He looked down at Elizabeth. "Will you excuse me a moment?"

As her husband sat down at the desk to sort through his mail, Elizabeth began to stroll around the library looking at the books.

"Are you looking for anything in particular to read, Elizabeth?" he called to her.

"I do not even know where to begin. There is far too great a selection. I could easily take five to ten books to bed with me each night to read if I could." She sent him a teasing glance.

Darcy lifted a brow. "I would hope you would rather…" He stopped and shook his head. "I wonder what this could be."

Elizabeth watched as he opened the letter and began reading. He cradled his jaw with his hand, occasionally shaking his head, and letting out a questioning murmur. At length, he looked up. "Elizabeth, I have just received the most astonishing letter."

"What is it? Who is it from?"

"It is from Miss Westerfield."

Chapter 25

Elizabeth hurriedly walked to her husband's side. "From Miss Westerfield? What does she say?"

Darcy rubbed his jaw. "I am astonished, somewhat confounded, and just a little incredulous."

She gave him a teasing glance. "Is she berating you for your choice of wife? Did she read of our marriage in the papers and cannot believe it is true?"

"She *did* read about it in *The Times*, however she sends us *both* wishes of congratulations and great joy." His brows pinched. "But that is not what surprises me."

"What is it, then?" She placed her hands on his shoulders and leaned down.

He looked up at her. "She is to marry Kingston, the gentleman who found them after their accident and took them to his home and cared for them."

"Had they been previously acquainted?"

"No. That is why it is so unexpected. It seems far too soon for them to have truly formed an attachment."

"Do you not approve of him?"

He laughed. "From the little I spent in his company, I cannot say if I approve or not. He seemed to be kind and generous, perhaps a little strict on propriety."

"Did you not mention that Mr. Westerfield was much the same way?"

"He is." His brows lowered. "Hopefully he is not as prone to displays of anger as Mr. Westerfield." He drew in a breath as he looked down at the letter again. "She writes that she and her family remained at Wakespur another three weeks after the accident, and the two found they had much in common." He gave his head a shake. "After leaving Wakespur, they went to London." He looked up at Elizabeth. "Kingston apparently followed." He tapped the desk with his fingers. "When I was there, he told me he does not care for London and rarely goes." He looked up at

Elizabeth and smiled. "He must have found London more to his liking with Miss Westerfield at his side." Darcy paused and pinched his brows in contemplation. "Now that I think of it, I believe he was a fair way towards being in love with her even when I was there."

"She is beautiful, kind, and very accomplished."

Darcy nodded, but Elizabeth could see a slight frown appearing.

"Fitzwilliam? Is there something else?"

"There is." He slowly looked up. "She writes that after their wedding, they will be spending a month in London before setting out to the Lake District."

Elizabeth leaned in towards him, tilting her head. "And...?"

"She wonders if... she would like to know if she and Kingston could stop here for a few days on the way."

"Here?"

He nodded. "I know this is highly unexpected, and I would not want to put you in an awkward situation with her." He looked back down. "I will tell her we are unable to accommodate them."

Elizabeth walked to the chair across the desk and sat down. "You will do no such thing! You will write to her and tell her that she and her husband are more than welcome!"

"Elizabeth, are you certain?"

A smile graced her face and she reached for his hand. When he took it in hers, she said, "Fitzwilliam, you have said on more than one occasion that you wished there was some way you could diminish any lingering rumours or sentiments people may still have about you, me, and Miss Westerfield. If there are those who still attribute the Westerfields' sudden departure to any questionable arts and allurements I may have employed, what better way to show them that is the furthest thing from the truth?" She placed her other hand over his. "We shall welcome the Kingstons as very close acquaintances, and everyone shall see how well we get along."

Fitzwilliam pondered this for a moment. At length, a smile of realization lit his face, and he slowly began nodding his head. "Elizabeth, I believe you are right. There is great wisdom in what you say." He looked at her intently. "Hopefully the rumours will have diminished by the time they get here in two months, but if there are still any lingering doubts, this would certainly settle the matter." He stood up and walked around the desk, drawing her up. "I could not have devised a better plan than this, no matter how hard I tried."

"If you do not mind, Fitzwilliam, I would like to be the one to write to her inviting them to come. I want to be certain she knows I welcome her wholeheartedly and look forward to their arrival." She tilted her head. "Would that be agreeable to you?"

"It would."

"I also am of the mind to inform her of the rumours about us that circulated around Pemberley and Lambton. I believe she ought to know. She cannot not know of them, as you were not even aware of them the last you saw her."

"I agree. You might mention to her that you think if the servants see that the two of you have the most amicable friendship, it will undoubtedly silence any further unwarranted speculation about what happened."

"I will." She lifted her gaze to him. "But Fitzwilliam, there is still the matter of your aunt's inciting rumours about us through her acquaintances here. What can be done about those?"

Darcy pressed his finger to Elizabeth's nose. "I give her one month to make amends with us – in her own way, of course – and we will hear nothing further from her on the subject."

~~*

Elizabeth spent a great amount of time with Mrs. Reynolds those first weeks she and Fitzwilliam returned to Pemberley. There was much she was required to learn, and Mrs. Reynolds was patient and an excellent teacher. It was apparent the housekeeper had been preparing to acquaint the new Mistress of Pemberley, whoever she would be, in the running of the household.

Elizabeth had the opportunity to meet with several of the young maids to see if any of them were suitable to be her lady's maid. Surprisingly, she found that she preferred Harriet over the others. Although the girl was young, she was friendly, accommodating, and had a sweet spirit that complemented

Elizabeth's personality. She also seemed to have a good knowledge of clothes and fashion, was adept at hair styling, and was always prompt and courteous.

Darcy had questioned the suitability of the young girl. "Elizabeth, do you truly think this is a sound decision? She is the one who began the rumours about us dancing together." He shook his head adamantly.

Elizabeth walked up to him and straightened his neckcloth, as they were dressing for church that morning. "I know, but I do not believe she meant harm. You said yourself the only person she told was her mother. While I understand her mother has always gossiped, the young girl was only doing what she most likely had been doing all her life – telling her mother about things she considers interesting." She sighed as she saw her husband looking at her and shaking his head. "Fitzwilliam, you were willing to give her another chance. I would like to give her a chance, as well."

"But she is so young."

"Yes, and because of that, she will be teachable. I believe what happened taught her a valuable lesson about integrity, respect, and loyalty. With her as my lady's maid, I hope to be able to instruct her in a great deal more."

Darcy sighed, reluctantly giving in to his wife, as he trusted her good sense, wisdom, and insight.

Georgiana and Mrs. Annesley returned home after spending a little less than two months in London. Their reunion in town had been sweet, as it had been several months since they had last seen each other. Mrs. Annesley was eager to meet Mrs. Darcy, as Georgiana had been speaking so highly of her.

Georgiana and her companion arrived at Pemberley a few days before the Kingstons were to join them. As they sat together that first evening, Georgiana expressed her surprise when her brother told her of the Kingstons' marriage.

"I am glad things worked out for her. I thought she was nice, but…"

Darcy laughed. "You were against her from the moment she arrived."

"It is only because I knew how much you loved Elizabeth." She looked sheepishly at Elizabeth and smiled. "As beautiful and kind as Miss West… as *Mrs. Kingston* is, I knew my brother's heart was not as engaged as it was with you." She turned again to her brother. "Have the rumours about the three of you ceased?"

Darcy let out a huff and looked about to make certain there were no servants in the room. "I have learned that it does not matter whether or not words are actually being spoken about you, because there still may be silent thoughts and opinions running rampant in their minds."

Elizabeth looked at Georgiana. "If you are surprised by their marriage, you are in for an even bigger surprise." She gave her a teasing smile.

"What is that?"

"She and Mr. Kingston are on their way here this very moment, as they journey to the Lake District."

Georgiana's eyes widened. "They are coming here?"

Elizabeth laughed. "They certainly are."

"Miss West…" Darcy laughed and shook his head. "It will take some getting used to calling her by her new name. Mrs. Kingston wrote to tell us of her upcoming marriage and their plans to make the trip up there. She asked if they could stop here."

"And you agreed?"

Darcy gave a nod to Elizabeth. "Your sister had the brilliant idea that inviting them to Pemberley would allow the servants to see how well the two ladies get along and will bring an end to anyone's continued speculations."

Georgiana smiled. "I think that is a wonderful idea!" A look of mischief crossed her face. "And I believe I will like her much better on this visit, now that she no longer has expectations of becoming my sister."

~~*

As they prepared for the Kingstons' arrival, Elizabeth realized this would be her first opportunity to act as Mistress of Pemberley while entertaining guests. She was amused that those guests included the lady whom she had feared would become the next Mistress of Pemberley. She hoped everything would go well, as she attempted to recollect all that Mrs. Reynolds taught her.

She spoke to the housekeeper the morning of their expected arrival to make certain everything was ready. Mrs. Reynolds assured her that they were and complimented her on her being so calm.

Elizabeth laughed. "I learned at an early age how to remain calm when everyone around me was frantic. And by that, I mean my mother. If I exhibited any agitation, it would have only made matters worse for her." She smiled. "It has served me well over the years."

"A very good trait to have, Mrs. Darcy. In this household, a calm outlook also makes things easier on the servants."

Elizabeth drew in a breath. "I appreciate all you have taught me, Mrs. Reynolds. I am extremely grateful to you."

The woman humbly bowed her head. "It has been my pleasure, Mrs. Darcy."

When the Kingstons' carriage pulled up to the front of the house, Darcy, Elizabeth and Georgiana stepped out to greet them. As they stood waiting for them to disembark, Darcy glanced up at the second floor. He looked at his wife and gave a nod, moving his eyes in the direction of the windows.

Elizabeth followed his eyes and saw several servants looking out. She shook her head. "So we are being watched. Does this always happen when guests arrive?"

"Not that I have ever noticed. It appears several have not settled it in their minds that there was nothing to the rumours." He let out a huff. "Shall we put on a good show for them?"

Elizabeth took her husband's hand and smiled. "It will not be a show, my dear. We, neither of us, shall perform for the servants." She waited for him to smile and then said, "What they see shall be genuine and not an act."

He gave her hand a squeeze. "I love you, my dearest, loveliest Elizabeth."

As Mrs. Kingston stepped from the carriage, Elizabeth thought she looked even more beautiful than she had when she saw her last. Marriage seemed to agree with her. If she was not mistaken, a look of pure contentment graced her features. She could not help but wonder if the anxiety of the unknown had played a part in her countenance when she had been at Pemberley months ago.

Elizabeth stretched out her arms and walked towards Angeline. "It is good to see you again, Mrs. Kingston. I am delighted you are here."

"Thank you, Mrs. Darcy."

"Please, you must call me Elizabeth."

"And you must call me Angeline." Her husband joined her. "Elizabeth, may I introduce my husband, Lloyd Kingston? My dear, this is Mrs. Elizabeth Darcy."

"He took her hand and bowed. "It is indeed a pleasure, Mrs. Darcy." He looked at Darcy. "It is good to see you again, sir."

"Yes, it is!" Darcy agreed. "And under much better circumstances!"

Elizabeth chuckled, wondering whether any of them were aware of the extent of the truth of that statement.

She could see that Mr. Kingston was very attentive to his wife and seemed to care for her deeply. She was genuinely happy for her.

Darcy introduced his sister to Kingston, and they walked inside. Elizabeth and Angeline locked arms and walked in as if they had always been the closest of friends.

Elizabeth quickly glanced up at the windows and saw that no one remained. She smiled, feeling confident that any niggling doubt about the two ladies had just been wiped from the servants' thoughts.

~~*

That night, as they dined together, Angeline asked whether they might have the musical soiree they had earlier planned but that had never taken place. She was delighted to let them know that, if they were agreeable to the idea, she would play the pianoforte and sing, and her husband would sing, as well.

"I think that is a wonderful idea!" Georgiana said. "I had been so looking forward to it."

Everyone looked at Elizabeth. "I would be happy to play and sing." She turned to her husband. "Now it is only left for my husband to decide if he will entertain us with his singing."

He scowled, but it was not taken seriously, as there was a

teasing glint in his eyes.

Georgiana laughed. "I think he would much prefer to enjoy the evening concert than entertain us at it."

"My sister knows me well," was his only comment.

Elizabeth sent her husband a playful glance. "Perhaps I shall have to work on him to sing." She turned to Georgiana. "Shall we draw up a little program with his name and assign him the song he is to sing? That way he cannot refuse, for once his name is on it, it is official."

Georgiana laughed. "That sounds like a splendid idea."

For the next two days, they all took their time to practice, save perhaps Darcy. He had come in several times when Elizabeth had been practicing to listen to her play and sing. He bore up graciously under her insistence that he perform. He never agreed or refused.

On the night of the soiree, there was much anticipation on everyone's part. The three ladies had worked together to print out lovely programs, with the names and titles of each performance. They had merely written *Fitzwilliam Darcy will perform a song* for his entry.

When the ladies presented the program to the men, Kingston looked at Darcy. "So what type of musical offering are you going to entertain us with?"

Darcy shrugged. "It does not say, so I have not yet made up my mind." He smiled and looked at Elizabeth. "I am considering, however, playing a song on crystal goblets filled with varying amounts of water."

"Fitzwilliam!" Elizabeth cried. "That kind of thing is only done on the streets of London! Do you also plan to have your hat in front of you to accept donations for your performance?"

He looked at his wife and nodded. "Now that is a splendid idea!"

Angeline laughed. "Fitzwilliam Darcy, I do not ever recall you having such a sense of humour."

Darcy looked at Elizabeth. "It is all due to my wife. She brings out things in me I never knew were there."

Elizabeth sent him a scolding look and shook her head. "Exaggeration must be one of those things!"

Georgiana chuckled. "That is very true! I never knew him to exaggerate!"

Later that evening at the musical soiree, the Kingstons sang several duets together. Elizabeth was astonished that their voices melded beautifully, and she could see their love as they gazed at each other. Georgiana played two songs, and sang a short portion in one, which pleased her brother immensely. Elizabeth sent him a pointed glance, silently admonishing him that if his sister could do what caused her nervousness, so could he. He only smiled back at her and gave a slight shrug.

When Georgiana finished, Elizabeth walked to the pianoforte. She addressed everyone. "As you can see, I will be playing two songs. The first will be an instrumental performed on the pianoforte, and the second I will play and sing." She smiled. "I hope you enjoy it."

Elizabeth played through the first song, concentrating on her fingering, for it was a fairly difficult piece. The second song she had chosen was one with fairly easy fingering so she could concentrate on her singing.

After finishing the first to some appreciative applause, she began to play her second piece. Just as the vocal part was drawing near, she felt someone behind her. She shivered as she realized her husband was standing behind her. She thought back to when he had done the same thing at Netherfield. It seemed so long ago, and so much had happened. Yet even after two months of marriage, his near presence still caused a thrilling tremor to course through her.

When she began to sing, there was an unexpected accompanying voice singing harmony along with her. It took everything in her power to not stop playing and singing and turn to just listen to her husband sing, but she knew he would have stopped, as well.

She struggled to keep her voice steady, for his was rich and mellow. It enveloped her not by just hearing the quality of his tone, but feeling it, as if he were drawing her near and whispering words of love in her ear. She shook her head, admonishing herself to remember there were others in the room and to concentrate on her piece!

When they had finished, they looked at each other, and Elizabeth felt tears threatening to spill. She was not certain whether he had felt the same way, but she knew that this gentleman, who was now her husband, loved her as much as anyone could love, and she returned the love as equally and forcefully.

~~*

Two Months Later

The Kingstons had taken their leave after spending four days at Pemberley, and after their departure, Darcy and Elizabeth were confident that the servants were left in no doubt that the rumours had been only that. There also had been no further accusations by Lady Catherine, and Darcy assured Elizabeth he expected to hear from her any day in an attempt to restore the breach in their familial ties – in her own way.

The two walked aimlessly about one afternoon, as they habitually did. They were silent for a while, and then Darcy stopped and looked at his wife. "I recently heard from Wickham's sister. He is being moved to a hospital in London because she cannot care for him any longer. He has become belligerent, likely due to his limited abilities, and she does not trust him to be around her children." He shook his head. "They should have done it months ago."

"It sounds like a wise decision."

Darcy nodded. "But there is something else, Elizabeth, and I hope you understand."

She looked up and could see the turmoil on his face. "You are helping to pay for it." It was not a question.

He nodded. "Not for Wickham, but for the memory of his father." His shoulders slumped. "It grieves me that this man will likely receive more money from me than he ever deserved, but I cannot look at it that way."

"You are a decent, generous man, Fitzwilliam Darcy. I would have it no other way."

They began walking again and soon came to the stone bridge.

They walked up to its centre and stood, looking out over the briskly moving stream.

"This is where I first saw you when you returned to Pemberley."

Darcy laughed. "This is where you first hid from me, you mean."

Elizabeth sighed. "Yes, I hid from you, but I am not certain whether it was you I was hiding from, but rather my own feelings for you."

"Why were you afraid of your feelings for me?"

"Oh, dear! Where do I even begin?" She laughed. "For one, I remember you telling me that your good opinion once lost was lost forever." She shook her head. "I could only surmise that any good opinion you once had of me had been lost that day in Kent."

He took her hands in his. "Ah, but you see, what you said to me, although difficult to hear, made me realize a few things about myself that I had never considered." He looked down at their hands. "My gravest error was coming to you expecting you to accept my offer, especially when I spoke in a manner that offended and insulted you. I should never have made such an assumption or spoken so disparagingly."

"As we have discussed before."

He brought her hands up to his lips and kissed each one. "Yes, but when I realized you were at Pemberley, before we had seen each other…" He laughed. "Well, you had seen me, but I had not seen you. I could only assume you felt the same way about me. I had no hope that your feelings for me had improved at all." He shook his head. "I had decided that when we finally saw each other, I would treat you with the utmost civility and respect. But still, there was no guarantee…"

Elizabeth smiled. "You decided to woo me all the while Angeline was expecting an offer from you."

His shoulders slumped. "I know it sounds very wrong of me, but at the least, I hoped you would come to think better of me. I could hardly allow myself to entertain the thought that you would ever return my love and devotion."

Elizabeth tilted her head. "There is something I have never told you, my dear."

"What is that?"

"I am to blame for my uncle's accident. It was my fault I ran into him, because I was... I had turned..." She swallowed hard and looked up into his face through her lashes. "I had turned back to look one last time at your portrait."

"Did you find it interesting? An excellent portrait painted by a talented artist?"

"I believe I found the subject more interesting that the painting itself. I was fascinated by your smile, how comfortable you looked in your surroundings, and how handsome you suddenly seemed. I found you almost... irresistible."

Darcy started. "Irresistible? I find this incredulous!"

"It is the truth."

They stared at each other silently, and he began to lower his head to kiss her. She lifted herself up on her toes and met his lips as she brought her arms about his neck.

When she shuddered, Darcy drew up. "Are you cold, my dear? With autumn making way for winter, the air is much cooler."

Elizabeth rested her head against his chest. "With you by my side, my dearest Fitzwilliam, I do not think I will ever be cold again."

He let out a breathy chuckle. "Do you know how much that pleases me?"

"I think I do."

He pulled away and touched his forehead to hers. "Do you want to walk further or shall we return to the house?"

"I am a little fatigued. Let us go back."

They were almost to the courtyard when Elizabeth suddenly stopped. She lifted her hand and pointed. "Look, Fitzwilliam. Do you see what I see?"

He followed her gaze and smiled. "Why, there are four magpies!"

Elizabeth leaned against him and looked up with a teasing glint in her eyes. "Do you know what that means?"

He counted on his fingers. "One is for sorrow, two is for mirth, three is a funeral, and four is a..." His jaw dropped. "Elizabeth?"

She wrapped his fingers with hers. "I had not planned to say anything just yet, for I am not fully certain, but yes, four is for a birth. I believe later next year we will be welcoming our first child into this world!"

"Elizabeth, I could not be happier! An heir! He shall be a magpie, just like you. He shall be intelligent and lively, just like his mother!"

"Oh, no!" Elizabeth squeezed his fingers. "Our little owlet will be strong and wise, and just a little reserved, just like *her* father!"

Darcy laughed and placed his hand, still held in hers, over her still trim stomach. "Perhaps we shall have a whole tiding of magpies!"

Elizabeth looked up at him with a smile. "Or perhaps a parliament of owls?"

"Whatever our baby will be, owlet or magpie, dove or eagle, boy or girl, we shall love him or her beyond measure." He drew her into his arms and rested his head on her shoulder. He whispered softly in her ear, "You have made me the happiest of men, Elizabeth Darcy. My heart soars – much like a bird – with the deepest love for you."

~ THE END ~

ABOUT THE AUTHOR

Kara Louise grew up in the San Fernando Valley in Southern California, but now lives in the suburbs of St. Louis, Missouri with her husband, and their ever-changing number of birds, dogs, and cats. Their son, his wife, and their two granddaughters live nearby.

Other books by Kara Louise:

Darcy's Voyage

Only Mr. Darcy Will Do

Assumed Engagement

Assumed Obligation

Drive and Determination

Master Under Good Regulation

Pemberley Celebrations: The First Year

Pirates and Prejudice

Mr. Darcy's Rival

A Peculiar Engagement

and

Chance and Circumstance

~~*

www.karalouise.net

Printed in Great Britain
by Amazon

52310322R00165